VALLEY OF
THE SHADOW

To Eric Amberge,
with great respect
and gratitude for your
work!

Nov 23, 2015
ANC

RALPH PETERS' NOVELS PUBLISHED BY FORGE

Cain at Gettysburg (Boyd Award)
Hell or Richmond (Boyd Award)
The Officers' Club
The War After Armageddon

RALPH PETERS' CIVIL WAR MYSTERIES PUBLISHED
UNDER THE PEN NAME "OWEN PARRY"

Faded Coat of Blue (Herodotus Award)
Shadows of Glory
Call Each River Jordan
Honor's Kingdom (Hammett Prize)
The Bold Sons of Erin
Rebels of Babylon

and

Our Simple Gifts: Civil War Christmas Tales

Ralph Peters is also the author of numerous books on strategy,
as well as additional novels.

VALLEY OF THE SHADOW

RALPH PETERS

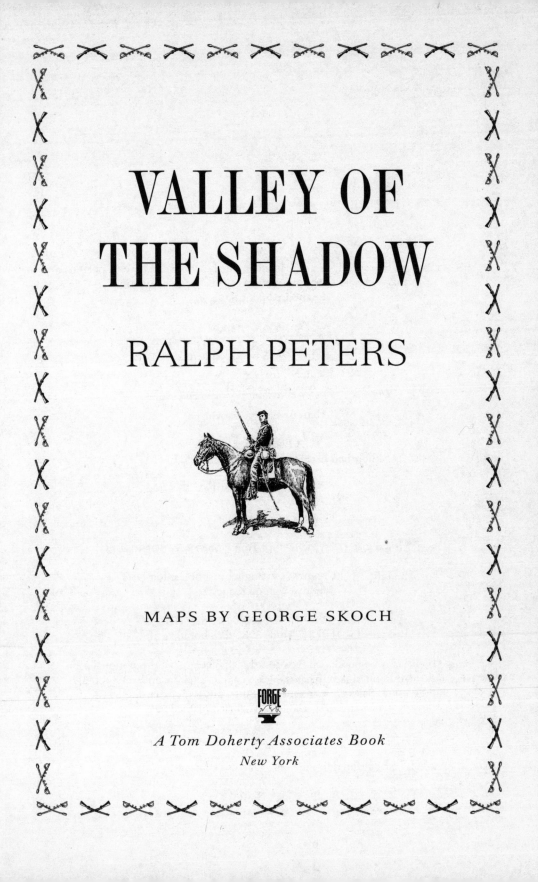

MAPS BY GEORGE SKOCH

FORGE®

A Tom Doherty Associates Book
New York

VALLEY OF THE SHADOW

Copyright © 2015 by Ralph Peters

Maps by George Skoch

A Forge Book
Published by Tom Doherty Associates, LLC
175 Fifth Avenue
New York, NY 10010

www.tor-forge.com

Forge® is a registered trademark of Tom Doherty Associates, LLC.

The Library of Congress Cataloging-in-Publication Data
is available upon request.

ISBN 978-0-7653-7403-5 (hardcover)
ISBN 978-1-4668-3981-6 (e-book)

Forge books may be purchased for educational, business, or promotional use.
For information on bulk purchases, please contact the Macmillan Corporate
and Premium Sales Department at 1-800-221-7945, extension 5442,
or write to specialmarkets@macmillan.com.

Printed in the United States of America

0 9 8 7 6 5 4 3 2

For Katherine
Of the vineyards and the glens

How They Organized for War

The terms used to describe Civil War units can be confusing. This note is meant to help those new to military affairs grasp unit sizes and how units fit together.

The basic organization was the *company*. This was the soldier's home, his wartime family. At the war's outset, a company may have had one hundred or more soldiers. By the end of the war, some companies consisted of a half dozen men or simply ceased to exist. A company was supposed to be led by a captain, with lieutenants to assist him, but leadership casualties might result in companies commanded by a lieutenant or even a sergeant.

The *regiment* was the soldier's extended family or clan. Asked to whom he belonged, a soldier would reply, "Sixty-first Georgia," or, "Eleventh Vermont." Regiments went to war with approximately eight hundred men. Some ended the war with fewer than a dozen survivors. A regiment was authorized a full colonel as its commander, but devastating casualties (especially late in the war) sometimes left a regiment under the command of a captain or even lieutenant.

The *brigade* united the regimental clans into a tribe. Strengths varied, but at the war's outset the standard was between twenty-five hundred and three thousand men in four regiments. Due to attrition, by mid-1864 it wasn't uncommon for a shrunken Federal brigade to contain five or six reduced-strength regiments, while some consolidated Confederate brigades included twice that number of severely battered regiments. Brigades were supposed to be commanded by brigadier generals (one star), but on the Federal side brigades frequently were commanded by colonels or even lieutenant colonels as field officers became casualties (promotions were more generous among the Confederates, and gray-clad officers from brigade through army levels generally held ranks one grade higher than their Northern counterparts).

Divisions consisted of two to three brigades (occasionally four or more in the Confederate States Army). A full-strength division fielded eight thousand to ten thousand soldiers, but by late 1864, divisions averaged between two thousand and five thousand men (Confederate divisions were fewer in number, but generally larger in size until the war's closing months). A division was supposed to be commanded by a major general (two stars) and usually was in Confederate armies, but Union divisions most often were led by brigadier generals or, by 1864, even colonels.

A *corps* at full strength might have two, three, or more divisions, with an authorized strength of twenty-five thousand or higher. In the summer and autumn of 1864, when this account takes place, it was rare for a corps on either side to approach that number of troops present for duty. In the Confederacy, a corps was commanded by a lieutenant general (three stars). Among the Federals, a major general usually commanded a corps.

An *army* was, by doctrine, a force of two or more corps, but occasionally an independent maneuver force of two or three divisions was designated as an army. North and South, armies were given names based upon geographic features. The North preferred river names—the Army of the Potomac or Army of the Shenandoah—while the South employed regional names, such as the Army of Northern Virginia or the Army of the Valley. In the Confederacy, lieutenant generals or full generals (four stars) commanded armies. In the North, they were commanded by major generals. When given a third star, Ulysses S. Grant became the Union's senior officer as a lieutenant general, while the South had a number of full generals. Armies varied widely in size, from well over a hundred thousand men to fewer than ten thousand, but the army remained the highest field organization on either side.

When the reader encounters the stand-alone term *Army*, thus capitalized, it refers to the Regular Army of the United States. By contrast, *army* is used when soldiers are referring to their own organizations.

Actual numbers of soldiers on any given battlefield can be infernally hard to determine, since records (especially among Confederates) could be spotty or were destroyed and because Yankees and Rebels counted men differently, with the Federals tallying each last cook, while the Confederates counted only those wielding weapons. Also, each side had different attitudes toward replenishing forces that had suffered casualties. Governors on both sides liked to create new regiments—allowing them to reward constituents with officers' commissions—but the South was better about supplying individual replacements to veteran units, while the North continued to generate new regiments until late in the war. An important result was that even in 1864, a Confederate brigade or division might outnumber the Union brigade or division it faced, but the Union would bring to bear a greater number of brigades and divisions on the battlefield.

The cavalry generally was organized along the same lines as the infantry up through division. The term *battalion* applied to infantry or cavalry meant a unit about half the size of a regiment (a "demi-regiment"), or a regimental element deployed for a special purpose or tactic. While the formal maneuver battalion is the building block of today's U.S. Army, it was an anomaly during our Civil War.

The artillery was organized into *batteries* of four guns in Confederate armies or six guns in Union formations. Batteries might be grouped into battalions, regiments, or even brigades, although the term *regiment* was most frequently used as a designator for "Regular Army" units in the North, so one might encounter Battery A of the 2nd U.S. Artillery.

Confused? Not as much as were the soldiers on those terrible battlefields.

(With special thanks to Brigadier General John W. Mountcastle, U.S. Army [Ret.], and Robert E. L. Krick for adjusting my fires.)

Therefore pride compasseth them about as a chain; violence covereth them as a garment.

PART
I

THE RIVER

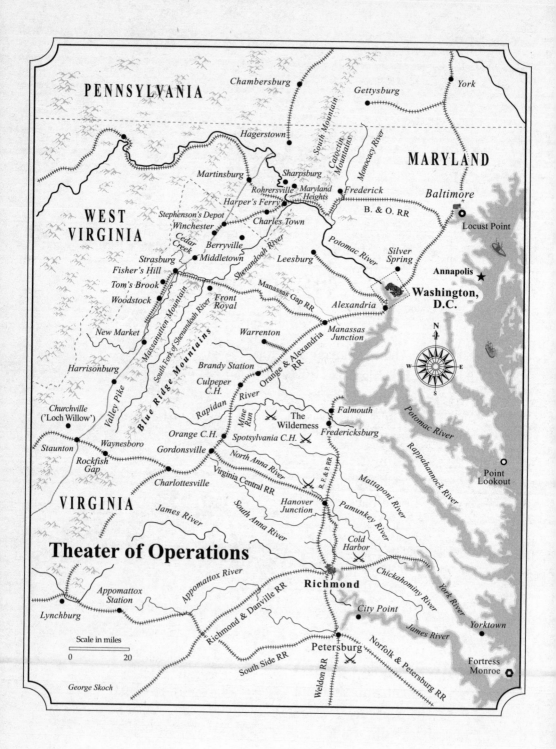

PENNSYLVANIA

Chambersburg

Gettysburg

York

South Mountain

Hagerstown

Catoctin Mountains

Monocacy River

MARYLAND

Martinsburg

Sharpsburg

Rohrersville

Maryland Heights

Frederick

Baltimore

Harper's Ferry

B. & O. RR

Locust Point

WEST VIRGINIA

Stephenson's Depot

Winchester

Charles Town

Potomac River

Silver Spring

Annapolis

Cedar Creek

Berryville

Middletown

Shenandoah River

Leesburg

Washington, D.C.

Strasburg

Alexandria

Fisher's Hill

Manassas Gap RR

Tom's Brook

Front Royal

Woodstock

Massanutten Mountain

South Fork of Shenandoah River

Warrenton

Manassas Junction

New Market

Orange & Alexandria RR

Harrisonburg

Blue Ridge Mountains

Brandy Station

Culpeper C.H.

Valley Pike

Rapidan River

Mine Run

Falmouth

Churchville ('Loch Willow')

The Wilderness

Fredericksburg

Orange C.H.

Spotsylvania C.H.

Staunton

Waynesboro

Gordonsville

North Anna River

Rockfish Gap

Virginia Central RR

R.F.&P. RR

Mattaponi River

Charlottesville

South Anna River

Hanover Junction

Pamunkey River

VIRGINIA

James River

Cold Harbor

Theater of Operations

Appomattox River

Chickahominy River

York River

Appomattox Station

Richmond

City Point

Yorktown

Lynchburg

Richmond & Danville RR

James River

Point Lookout

Potomac River

Rappahannock River

Norfolk & Petersburg RR

Petersburg

Fortress Monroe

Scale in miles

0   20

South Side RR

Weldon RR

George Skoch

ONE

July 6, 1864
Maryland Heights

Them shoes. Hard as skillet iron, as like to bust a man's foot as cozy it going. Sturdy, though. Say that, and tell the truth. Better than none, and welcome. Call them "good."

Nichols wished he could fix on that—he tried, he tried—the hard leather waiting to challenge flesh and bone, the side of fatback misery that attended every goodness in this life. But the frightful ache in his thigh had taken him captive, threatening him with unwanted, unmanly tears.

Which would not do none. Small he might be, but he would not be mocked by his fellow soldiers.

Around him, grease-faced men cleaned rifles.

He laid his hand gently atop the welt, as he might have soothed an ailing horse back on his father's farm. He knew he had been lucky, but knowing didn't ease the ache one mite. That pain was a brimstone torment, a tribulation. Still, he would not ride an ambulance wagon. Not that.

New shoes tucked beside him, he sat stripped bare but for a shirt that covered all such a meager garment might. Again, he touched the purple welt with its sickly yellow edges, swelling from his thigh, a thing unholy. He'd thought in that first instant that his leg must surely be shattered and torn right off, when whatever it was that hit him knocked him back, over, and down. Rolling in the summer wheat, he had grasped his wound with both hands to choke the pain. Only to find that his trouser leg—its wool worn thin as finery—had not even been rent. No blood smeared his hands, no poke of bone emerged. Helped to the rear, he had been further astonished to find he could almost walk.

But, oh, it hurt like Satan's own revenge.

And now he sat, petting the monstrous bump in half-dazed wonder, surrounded by ramrod clank and joshing men complaining gaily about their just-got shoes. Each man was pleased enough to get them, even those who had come to prefer going barefoot, but soldiers always complained. More than just a let-out of a man's feelings, it was a *duty*.

Sinful late, neglectful, ashamed, he thanked the Lord for his preservation. How could a man slight God at such a time?

Man, in his pride and selfishness, was a wicked beast. Ungrateful in the hour of his deliverance.

They'd harried the Yankees back into their trenches up on the Heights, work as hot as a midsummer harvest and this here batch of blue-bellies stubborn as mules put into a strange harness. But General Gordon, a righteous man in the eyes of the Lord God, was wise in the ways of war, in ways concealed to lesser men. And Gordon, or maybe even Old Jubilee himself—chaw of tobacco a cow's cud in his mouth and juice gleaming in his beard, General Early a spitting, crook-back man and harsh-mouthed as a heathen—such high men knew when it made no sense to chase after Yankees who weren't going to be no bother. Truth be told, the fighting had not raised half the ruckus, not a quarter, of the arrival of the supply wagons beforehand, bringing shoes that had been promised since Staunton.

As soon as he fitted his feet to the brute leather, Nichols had grasped that he'd have to cut the toes free or suffer the pains of a blasphemer gone over Jordan, and he'd left the shoes behind during the attack. It was as if he'd had the gift of the sight, since the shoes, at least one, must have been lost when that spent piece of shell or whatever it was knocked him down. And the shoes had been there waiting for him, faithfully, betrothed, when Lem Davis eased him to the ground in the shade they'd left to go fuss with the Yankees.

Sturdy shoes, they'd do. Nichols tried to look on the good side of things. Perfection was the dominion of the Lord, not Man the Fallen. And that was just how it was, always: a plump sergeant perched on a wagon, throwing something or other at you, hitting you smack in the chest, and your business was to be grateful. For shoes hard as the blades of a plow or for powder poorly stored, for provender lively with vermin—although he'd heard tell that a right wealth of Yankee rations had been captured at Charles Town and might be shared out soon.

The shoes would take softening and molding to the foot, the seasoning of sweat and the grumpy baptism of creek crossings— although a man had to be watchful of the foot rot marching wet. At least he had two feet attached to two legs still attached to his mortal flesh, a wondrous thing. Was that the sort of miracle of which the Good Book spoke?

He touched his curious wound again, unable to resist, and winced at its worsening.

"You just count your blessings, Georgie," Lem Davis said with a kindly twist of smile.

Nichols mumbled and nodded, pulling another tick off his calf, crushing it. Ticks seemed as bad in Maryland as in Virginia, and rolling around in the grass had not been helpful. But he was grateful for Lem's brotherly tone, for all of his fine brethren, the men of Company D and the rest of the 61st Georgia, no regiment in the whole great army none better, these hard-worn fellows grouped in the shade about him now, complaining not of the short, sharp fight behind them, but pleasurably of the shoes for which they had yearned on the withering marches down the Valley Pike.

Every man in the infantry hated that thoroughfare. Topped with rough Mack Adam and rendered not fit for foot of man or hoof of beast, a plain misery, it was a boon to the wagon wheel and artillery, whose cannoneers never had to march one step but rode about like princes. "Progress," that was the word the Pike called up, the rich man's delight in newfangledness. Such progress was just for the purse-proud man with the golden pocket watch, for the man

from the bank holding papers that made no sense. It was not the
wonderful sort in *Pilgrim's Progress,* his father's great, green book—
tattered, treasured—second only to the Good Book itself in its
worth to a man's soul. He wished he could read it now, that book,
right here in the shade that shielded a man from the sun's direct
attack, but not from the flanking movements of the heat in this
no-place place, here on the brim of Yankee-land, no cooler than
scorched Virginia, where it had not rained, he believed, since the
scrap on the North Anna, where Joe Cruce fell. And on their long,
unshod, hot, northerly marches, his warrior brethren, not unwilling but unable, had fallen before they heard a single shot, col-
lapsing, gone down into delirium, clammy and startlingly cold to
the touch, fish caught from a fast stream with bare hands. Dying
far from the battlefield. Or merely squatting distempered by the
roadside.

Skirmishers pecked the afternoon. Would they be ordered in
again? Against those fortified Heights? Was there anything up there
worth men's blood? General Gordon was a pondering man, erect
in body and spirit, but with General Early a fellow never quite knew.
Humped over and given to temper—every man in the army had
witnessed at least one memorable outburst—Old Jube had a touch
of the cottonmouth's meanness about him. And Nichols had heard
that General Breckinridge, a high politician fellow, had been stirred
into the batter, in between Gordon and Early. Some said Old Jube
was slapping Gordon's face, doing him down, although Nichols
preferred not to think that. There wasn't a man who didn't admire
John Gordon, commander of their brigade and now their division.
He seemed an honest Christian, which might not be the case with
General Early.

Nichols probed his thigh again and soon jerked back his hand,
as if he had grasped hot iron from a forge. Would he be able to
march, when the march resumed? He would not shirk, nor be eyed
as a malingerer. He had come too far and endured too much to be
mocked as a "hospital hero" once again.

He shut his eyes hard, not at the leg pain this time, nor at the face-pestering flies, but at the recollection of almost dying in the Danville hospital, in that filthy pesthouse of Damnation, the worst of those through which he had been passed like a thing unwanted, a boy not yet tested by battle and sickened unto death by the bloody trots. At one point, his weight had been shy of ninety pounds.

Compared with those hospital wards, war was a pleasure. And this hard jaunt into Maryland, perhaps even farther on into the North, was a downright joy compared to the soul-busting misery of the fighting from the Wilderness through Cold Harbor. He hoped never to see the like of the Mule Shoe's mud and savagery again. Then the plague had been of rain, not drought, and the queer thing was that two of his friends, Joe Cruce and Bill Kicklighter, had been killed not amid the horror of the Wilderness or the confusion of Spotsylvania, but along the North Anna, in the least of the fighting.

It had been a relief to march away from all that, to cross the high green mountains into the Valley. Even the dust through which they had marched seemed fresh compared to what they left behind. That man Grant. A murderer, surely. Moloch.

At Spotsylvania, the Seventh Seal had been opened. He had put a bayonet into another man's belly. Once, then—meanly—again. The bewildered look on the fellow's face, the amazement and disbelief, had made Nichols want to grin and vomit at once. The chaplain's words thereafter held no comfort.

He didn't want to burn in Hell for eternity. But he wasn't going to kneel to Yankees, either.

Skin hot and tight to bursting over his welt, he thought again of the Valley Pike, of its meanness to rag-wrapped feet, but beloved of the generals for its directness, an arrow pointed north. Where were they going this time? No one told them, ever. Not General Evans, Christian though he was. And not General Gordon, who could make the poorest soldier feel exalted. And surely not General Early, a profane man, spitting his sour tobacco juice and judging the world in words that befouled the air, a hard man he. They said Old Jube had not wished to leave the Union, but now hated

Yankees like farmers hated blight. Who knew the workings of another's heart? Jesus, only.

Squatting by a got-up coffee fire, Dan Frawley rasped, "If they done went to all this bother to bring shoes up from Virginny, all that way . . . tells me we're meant to do a sight more marching." He shook his head gravely. "Nothing but trouble ahead, boys, take your pleasures now."

In response: dry-throated acknowledgment that fell well short of laughter.

"Could use a tad more water in the pot," Frawley added, pushing clotted red hair behind an ear. "Starting to think Corporal Holloway skedaddled with those canteens."

Holloway, Tom Boyet, and the rest of the water detail were overdue, and every man sprawled in the shade was thirst-caught, beatdown, and still, dirty men with gleaming rifles, as always. *Would* they take another crack at those Yankees in their high trenches, waiting like rattlesnakes up there in fortifications they'd had years to prepare? Or would the generals decide to move along? Deeper into the rich realm of the Philistines? And let this particular nest of serpents be? The logic of generals passed all understanding.

"I do believe we're going to Pennsylvania," Lem Davis said, Lem of the Patriarch's beard and gentle heart, young wife dead of childbirth in his absence. "Dan, you cook up coffee slower than any man alive."

"Didn't see you rush to cook none. I figure on Pennsylvania myself. And that don't ever like to turn out well. I'd as soon stay southwards of the Potomac. Nothing good comes of crossing it, you ask me."

Sergeant Alderman had been listening. On his feet, arms folded, on the alert for officers, Alderman was a man who had earned his promotion. He took off his hat, wiped his forehead, and said, "My bet's we're headed to Washington, boys. I think we're out to give 'em a good scare. And let folks in the Valley get a harvest in."

"Heard something, Sergeant?" Lem asked.

Alderman shrugged. "Just front-porch talk. What I can't figure is why there aren't more Yankees getting themselves in our way. You'd think they'd be coming at us from every direction." He turned. "You going to be able to march on that leg, Georgie?"

"Like to see Old Abe's face, General Early showed up on his doorstep," Frawley put in before Nichols could answer.

"Have to wonder if Old Jube even *knows* where we're a-going," Ive Summerlin said, following the words with a yard cat's yawn. Ive's tone had taken on a harder edge since his brother disappeared along the march. "Might have the Yankees confused because he's confused himself." He spit dry. "Sometimes I think he's just looking for any old fight."

"Like Old Jack."

"That man ain't no Jackson."

"Well, thank God and Jesus Christ almighty for it. My back hooves are sore enough." Shifting the coffee can, Frawley turned to Nichols. "What do *you* think, Georgie? You're quiet as the preacher hid bare-ass under the bed when Farmer John come back early for dinner."

"You wouldn't talk rough if Elder Woodfin was here."

The others laughed, accustomed to Nichols' pleasant fear of the Lord and the regiment's chaplain. Their teasing had settled into a friendly routine and, nowadays, was more apt to remark on his struggling beard than on his love for Jesus.

"Might be something to Little Georgie's devotions," Frawley offered. More sweat had turned his red hair maroon. "Got through all that fighting back in Virginny, not a scratch on him."

"Must have skipped his prayers last night," Ive Summerlin noted. "Only man in the company hit today."

"Well now," Frawley told him, "I'd call that more lucky than not. Everybody has to get hit sometime. And Little Georgie's sitting there with nary a piece missing, praise the Lord." He smiled an older-brother smile and pulled the coffee off the fire before it cooked any sharper. Saved up, the grains had been boiled over too often. He glanced at Nichols. "Reckon it's a discomfort, though."

"Can you get your drawers back on?" Sergeant Alderman asked Nichols. He glanced back over his shoulder. "Something's doing."

Responding to authority as always, Nichols reached for his rags, but found his leg stiff as a cannon barrel. He meant to march, he was determined. *Just not yet, Lord,* he prayed. *Don't let them give us marching orders yet. Amen.*

In the wake of a pair of caissons, Corporal Holloway and his detail emerged from the dust. The men took their fine time coming on, laden with canteens, burdened with the good weight of fresh water.

Frawley turned to Nichols again. "Never did get me an answer. If *you* were a high general, where would *you* lead us, Georgie? New York City?"

"Home."

As soon as the word escaped his mouth, Nichols regretted it. He sounded weak, cowardly, girlish. As if he wanted to flee to his mother's embrace.

His mother, a woman as good as Ruth in the Bible. Her chore-strong arms had held him fast, unwilling to give him up to godless war.

His lone word silenced everybody, just locked them all right up. Nichols was about to insist that he didn't really mean it, that he thought going to Washington or maybe Baltimore or even Philadelphia would suit him fine, come what may. But Sergeant Alderman spoke first, laughing through his words:

"I swear to God . . . there's an honest man amongst us."

July 7, noon
Monocacy Junction

Rivers coursed through his life. First the Wabash, rich with fish and the promise of adventure, sun-dappled and seductive, had made of him a truant from the schoolhouse and its regimen of multiplication tables. Then the Rio Grande had shaped a man from a dreaming boy, as the men of his volunteer regiment perished on its sickness-ridden banks, going to graves in multiples day after day, until no wood remained for coffins and corpses were buried in undergarments, only to be uncovered again by the winds from the Gulf of Mexico. Not one of his Indiana comrades, left at a forlorn post by General Taylor, had heard a hostile shot before dying in vomit. Then, in another war, this war, he had saved Grant's freezing army on the Cumberland, only to be scapegoated for Grant's near disaster on the Tennessee. Now this river, slight and brown, had summoned him to a questionable destiny.

His staff, a meager collection, had gathered about him, all of them staring across the Monocacy, past fields gilt with wheat and Frederick's spires, northwest to the heat-softened mountains and the war that hastened toward them. There was nothing to be seen, not yet, only the sometimes thump of a distant cannon, but they all stared nonetheless, as if the Confederates might appear the moment they looked away, those lean men clad in gray and brown and patched-up rags of every harlequin color, who were bound soon enough to come pouring down the road from Frederick City toward this prize of bridges and main-traveled roads, where the Baltimore and Ohio Railroad, the highway to Baltimore, and the Pike to Washington converged.

Another invisible gun reported, a dull thud in heat as heavy as winter draperies, and Major General Lew Wallace felt the assorted lieutenant colonels and captains grouped around him tense. The first message from Clendenin, brought by a courier on a punished horse, had informed him that the cavalryman and his handful of troopers from the 8th Illinois had driven the enemy's advance guard back toward Middletown, only to be driven in turn as reinforcements bolstered the Confederates. Clendenin had been obliged to withdraw to Catoctin Pass, and Wallace knew it was but a matter of time before Reb numbers would tell again and Clendenin—a quick, earnest man—would be forced to abandon the pass and descend into the rich fields leading to Frederick. And Frederick was but three miles from this junction, which of a sudden had become the most important point in the entire Union.

The unconcern in Washington had beggared belief, even as ever more reports warned of Confederates in a host. Halleck, Wallace's nemesis since Shiloh—even before—had dismissed his initial concerns, agreeing with Grant's conclusion that Early and his corps remained in the defensive works at Petersburg and could not possibly be invading Maryland. It had only been thanks to Garrett, the railroad man, that Wallace himself was alerted to the crisis. The government had known nothing and cared less.

Only now, so very late, had the grand Mamelukes of Washington begun to believe in the deadly ghosts they'd all dismissed with scorn. But would there be time enough to hurry troops back from Virginia to save Washington, a city whose defenses Grant had stripped to make good his terrible losses? Wallace's mind was all too alive with images of the capital ablaze, the grand government buildings and the immense military stores, the Navy Yard and the Treasury's wealth of bonds, all consigned to the torch by vengeful traitors. It was all about time now, and Wallace intended to fight for every hour.

Another courier appeared on the road from Frederick, a dark speck chased by grand billows of dust. The weather was ripe and beautiful, but dry near unto drought and killing hot, and Wallace felt for the men who must march through it. Even if they were his enemies.

"What do you think's happening, sir?" Captain Woodhull, his junior aide-de-camp, asked. Woodhull's voice was eager and still pitched high with youth.

"Clendenin's giving them a fight," Wallace answered. "If he wasn't, there'd be more than one horseman chasing down that road."

But his spirits were not as confident as his voice. On his own initiative, he had gathered every soldier he could scavenge from his department, an administrative post meant to console him and his political friends, a return to the war in form, but not in fact. Until this day, the major achievement of his Baltimore headquarters had been to finesse the recent Maryland elections, ensuring that the right candidates were favored. His handling of the matter had pleased Stanton and Lincoln himself, but he still had not been offered a fighting command.

And he knew why: Halleck. Halleck, with his limitless vitriol, was a figure too high to dismiss without embarrassment, but too lacking in judgment to command in the field, so he sat enthroned in Washington, dispensing orders and venom with equal glee. "Old Brains" had maintained from the first that only his fellow West Pointers were fit for command and that amateurs such as Wallace would butcher their soldiers. He stopped just short of labeling volunteer officers as criminals. Yet at Donelson, Wallace had disobeyed orders shaped by West Point educations to save the Union right wing from collapse. And when, at Shiloh, he had obeyed his orders to the letter, only to arrive too late to join the first day's fight, he had been made the villain of the piece, although it was Grant and Sherman who had let down their guards and nearly lost an army. With all the spite of which the old vulture was capable, Halleck had stripped him of command and driven him into obscurity, letting him rot in Indiana while the war dragged on. Even when he saved Cincinnati, Ohio, from a Rebel incursion, it had made no difference. A man who held a grudge in perpetuity, Halleck had even argued against the Middle Department posting, determined to deny Wallace not only the battlefield, but even Baltimore.

So he had not informed Halleck at first when he left his headquarters for the railroad junction, which lay across the river from his department's western boundary. He was violating orders again, but Wallace saw no choice: Someone had to stand between these Confederates and Washington, even if the stand was doomed from the start.

Wallace could foresee his fate, whether he did good service or failed completely. Leading twenty-three hundred green volunteers, many of them mere hundred-day men, militia and convalescents wearing the grandiose designation "VIII Corps," he faced an approaching Rebel force reported to be between twenty thousand

and thirty thousand in battle strength. Allowing for the exaggerations of excited informants, that still meant fifteen thousand to twenty thousand Confederates on the march. And Wallace intended to fight them, well aware that he must be badly defeated. He meant to fight to delay them as long as he could. And Halleck would have a real defeat to pin on him.

The situation was so dire that he had been made happier by the chance to commandeer Clendenin's two hundred veteran horsemen than by anything since his wife accepted his marriage proposal. As for the rest of his scraped-up command, all he could do was to use the river and the good terrain along its southern bank to make a stand and count minutes earned with blood. Wallace had never favored mathematics in school, but twenty-three hundred raw recruits divided by a front greater than three miles provided a sorry answer.

He asked himself if he was merely playing with other men's lives, still a prisoner of *The Scottish Chiefs* and the other heroic romances of his childhood . . . yet he saw no choice but to do what little he could. To allow Early and his paladins to stroll into the nation's capital without making the least effort to delay them . . . better to fight and lose miserably, even if he robbed them of only an hour.

He didn't believe that Early and his army were headed for Baltimore, although he could not be certain and had to cover the upriver bridge as well. All logic told him the Rebels aimed at Washington, hoping to shock the North and unseat Lincoln in the autumn election, and to encourage English and French intercession on the part of the South, even at this late hour.

To prevent all that, he had one six-gun battery of three-inch rifles and an unwieldy twenty-four-pounder. Against the battalions of cannon that Early would bring to bear. Well, he thought with a bittersweet smile, his boyhood hero, William Wallace, would not have been daunted.

As a lad, he had dreamed of military glory, inspired by his father's brief army career and subsequent leadership of the local militia. And despite his disappointments and travails in Mexico, *this* war had seemed to grant it to him, only to steal it away again, as fickle as the Greek gods. It wasn't about glory now, though. There would be no glory here. Only time gripped like a miser's gold and the prospect of the Capitol in flames.

The far mouth of the covered bridge gobbled the courier. Invisible hooves slammed planks. Anxious of heart but strict of feature, Wallace watched as the rider reappeared and reined up, calling out to the nearby guards, doubtless asking where the devil that fool general was.

The man begged directions a second time before whipping his horse up the slope. The beast looked ready to drop. Celtic complexion further reddened by his exertions, the cavalryman saluted and fixed his eyes on Wallace, drawing a folded paper from his blouse and extending it without dismounting. Wallace stepped forward and took the missive. It was damp with the fellow's sweat.

Before unfolding the paper, Wallace asked, "How is it with Colonel Clendenin?"

Interrupted while reaching for his canteen, the man gasped, "Oh . . . he's giving them the right devil. That he is, sir. Cut from the proper mold, that boyo. But there's Rebs enough, a great and terrible lot of them."

"Does he still hold the pass?"

The soldier guzzled from his canteen. Water ran down through his whiskers.

"He did, sir, but he don't. We was all set to pull back, when I rode off. The Rebs, sir, they'd gone to flanking us every which way. They've infantry and guns up with their cavalry now, and they're terrible out of temper with the colonel, for he's giving them the loveliest bit of frustration."

Opening the scrawled report, Wallace thought: The poor bugger put it better than I could myself. We need to give them "the loveliest bit of frustration."

"Rest your horse, man," Wallace told the courier. "You're apt to need him over the next few days."

"Yes, sir, and that I will, sir. But if I may . . ."

"What?"

"Well, the good colonel up there, he's feeling a touch of the lonesome. If O'Malley's a judge of the weather."

"We all are," Wallace told him.

July 7, 3:00 p.m.
Sharpsburg, Maryland

Too damned hot for biscuits. The butter had separated on the plate, leaving pools for drowning flies, and the stink was downright grisly. Lemonade was fine, though.

Early waved Sandie Pendleton back up onto the porch, interrupting the boy's conversation with Ramseur's quartermaster.

Ascending in an aura of dust and spur clank, Pendleton called, "Yes, sir?" The boy had a narrow face and a wide writ. Twenty-three-year-old chief of staff. Damnedest thing. Inherited from Jackson and Ewell, no less. Tom Jackson must have lifted him out of the cradle.

"Here, now," Early said. "Eat up these biscuits. Before that woman comes back out on the porch. Be quick now."

Accustomed to Early's ways, the young lieutenant colonel made no protest, but tucked in with all the appetite of youth.

Between swallows, Pendleton asked, "Take one down for—"

"No. You eat 'em. Then you fetch me up that message from Bobby Lee again."

"About Point Lookout?" Pendleton brushed a crumb and a streak of butter from his chin.

"That's right. The one from Robert E. Lee's book of fairy tales for good Confederates. Have to read it a second time to believe it." Early drew a twist of tobacco from his pocket and tore off a chaw. "Take yourself some of that lemonade now. Not all of it. And get along."

He did appreciate that lemonade, had to admit. Woman of the house meant well. They always did. Most always. But the utility of womanhood was limited.

Sharpsburg. No good memories. That hateful hour in the corn-field, that bloody, wretched day. McClellan should have et them alive, but Little Mac's appetite failed him. Man afraid of his own shadow, of spooks and hants in gray. Jubal Early had never seen a battle waged with such determination at the front and such bliss-ful incompetence in the rear. Yankees had almost done it, though, almost wiped Lee's army off the map. Old Marse Robert letting himself get pinned against the river like that. And Hill off galli-vanting.

He figured he had seen worse since that day nearly two years before—at Spotsylvania, certainly—but nothing had marked him deeper than the slaughter amid those cornstalks. Remarkable busi-ness, what canister could do to men unprepared and utterly un-suspecting. One blunder after another. On both sides.

Ramseur himself now. At the end of the street, waving his troops on. Bully lad, that one. But there were times when gallantry had to give way to judgment. Ramseur needed to keep himself out of the sun, he was obviously still weak from his latest—third—wound. Tried to hide it, but Early could tell. Another man-child. Major general commanding a division, and just turned twenty-seven in the distinctly unmerry month of May 1864. That's what the army had come to now: scarecrows led by children barely got into long pants. And the cavalry . . . he didn't want to think about those sons-ofbitches and spoil the afternoon.

Ramseur would do. Fighting man, North Carolina boy. He'd do. If he didn't fall over with sunstroke.

Pendleton, Ramseur . . . it was enough to make a man in his prime, a seasoned forty-seven, feel old as Methuselah. He spit to-bacco juice from the high porch, careful to keep it short of the marching men.

Pendleton returned with the dispatch. It had been carried from Petersburg by Lee's youngest son, as if the kinship might lend the foolishness gravity. Sheer, damned foolishness. Here he was, up in Maryland, with fewer than eighteen thousand men and more peeling off each day, and no, it wasn't enough for Lee that he might get to Washington and turn Abe Lincoln out of house and home, making a great damned rumpus they might hear in London and Paris, no, that was not enough. Lee was still on the rocking horse of his cockamamie scheme for freeing the thousands of prisoners at Point Lookout. As if wishing would make it so.

Pendleton stood by, awaiting instructions.

"Well, sit down, son. You're not on dress parade. Take me a minute or two to digest all this here strategic wisdom." He spit again.

Rereading the message left him just as incredulous, if not more. He'd figured that Lee had been just flirting with the notion when the Old Man first raised it. But Lee was serious as a deacon, believing that Early could cross Maryland, march on Washington, and, just for a side bet, send part of his force to the farthest tip of Maryland, where those angels of deliverance would free twenty thousand Confederate prisoners, load a goodly portion into boats that would appear like spooks at a table-rapping, just blithely sailing through the Northern blockade, while the rest of the men newly freed would join Early's army armed with weapons taken from their guards, instantly organizing themselves into regiments and brigades. And since the guards were thought to be colored troops, there would be little resistance when a mob of Southern gentlemen reared right up before them.

One look at the map revealed the absolute madness of the scheme. Any force that reached the camp would be trapped on that peninsula. Even if the Yankees didn't seem to have figured out what he was up to yet, they'd surely know by the time he got to Washington. He'd be sending thousands of soldiers into a trap, sending them not to free those prisoners, but to become captives themselves. And not one boat was going to appear off the Maryland shore to rescue anybody. His men wouldn't have the prospects of a corncob in a shithouse.

It wasn't that Lee was mad, he understood. The old man was just desperate. He *needed* those men, any men. Never came up against a bastard like Grant before. Fought like a crazy drunk, too fool to go down. Just came back swinging again, crimson from crown to gizzard. The losses of May and June had been horrendous, on both sides. But the North could replace them, and the South could not.

He had not wanted this damned-fool war. But Jubal Early surely meant to finish it.

"What do you plan to do, sir?"

Early grunted.

"It's not specifically an order," Pendleton went on. "It says—"

"I can read, boy. Oh, hell. Send Johnson off, once we're past Frederick. He's a Marylander, he knows the lay of the land. See if he can do something. Cavalry's worthless, anyway. Bundles of rags on broken nags, and that's putting it sweet. Damned *banditti*, all of them. Can't be either trusted or relied upon." He snorted and took the last swig of lemonade. "Jackson and his damned lemons. I always think about that when confronted with this beverage. Old Jack knew what he was about, give him that. Put his faith in the infantry and artillery, arms you can count on." Early rose, straightening his back as best his arthritis permitted. Even standing was an effort in the sickening heat.

He took up his hat, pressing a thumb into the side he kept turned up toward the crown. "Draw up orders for Johnson. Give him some latitude, don't want him humbugging that we forced him to make mistakes he can make just fine on his own. And don't send them yet, let me read them first." About to descend from the porch, he turned again. "He still fussing with those Yanks on the Frederick road?"

"He was pushing them back through the pass. According to his last dispatch."

Early drew out his pocket watch and grimaced. The timepiece rarely gave him cause to smile. "Don't even report regularly. Scouting's all this cavalry's good for, and I can't count on Johnson or McCausland or any of them to do even that much proper."

Pendleton didn't offer a comment. Early knew that his chief of staff thought him too hard on the cavalry. But Early could not help himself. He hated the sight of a soldier on a horse—unless it was an officer leading his regiment or a battery commander keeping the saddle for the elevated view.

Jubal Early understood that he was not considered a fair man. But he differed with common opinion, preferring to view himself as merely honest. He did not exactly revel in making enemies, but found it an inevitable part of war, if a man put winning above parlor *politesse*. Goddamn South was too goddamned polite for its own goddamned good, that was the thing. Lose the war while stepping aside to let a petticoat pass. No, Jubal Early did not seek popularity, and he distrusted those who courted favor.

Take Gordon, now. Prancing damned prince, that one. Always so damned sure that he was right. Let Breckinridge enjoy the constant stream of wisdom from John Gordon for a while: Gordon always posing for his men, declaiming like a parson set to pass the plate. Early never could understand why the men did not see through it. Instead, they adored the high-flown sonofabitch and hung on his fancied-up talk.

The fact that Gordon had been right too often of late didn't help matters, either. Just puffed him up the more.

Early strode up the street, heat on his back like a nigger's bundle, aiming for Ramseur, who knew how to hold his tongue. But his mind was on Gordon now.

Gordon didn't understand that soldiers had limits. Push 'em, yes. But don't kill them for your highfalutin vanity. Gordon was just a damned know-it-all who'd had a streak of luck.

He rearranged his chaw with a thick forefinger. Near time to spit it on out.

Ramseur's last brigade plodded up the incline of the street at Early's side. The men were too worn down to cheer or jeer, their only noise the tin-cup clank of laden troops and the slap of footsteps. They looked as though they'd been rolled in dirty flour, carrying the dust of a dry month with them.

Ahead, an aide touched Ramseur on the arm, alerting him to his commander's approach. The young general saluted.

"Dod," Early said, touching his hat.

"Last of my regiments are closing, sir. Many a straggler, surely, but they'll be along."

Early nodded. "And you figure it helps somehow, you standing out in the sun, dumb as a coon?"

"I'm fine, sir. The men need to see their officers."

"Won't see much of you, once you're down with the heatstroke. God almighty, boy, show a lick of sense."

"I'm fine, sir. Truly." Ramseur's eyes lost their steadiness for a moment, as if he were searching his surroundings for reassuring words to speak to Early. He said, "No place on earth I'd rather be than right here."

"Not with that new bride of yours?" Early hacked out a single-syllable laugh. Women had spoiled many a fine officer. Poor, old Ewell. Even Pendleton had grown inclined to reveries.

"A man . . . may disassociate certain matters . . . ," Ramseur tried. "The public and the personal, I mean. They run on different tracks. My place is here."

"Maryland, maybe. Not in this damned street. One of your fac-totums can see to these here boys. You take yourself off now. I'll be calling for you soon enough." He looked past Ramseur, who was steady of eye again, to the division commander's bevy of aides and staff men. "Y'all get those soldiers fixed up proper, water 'em up. Like to be marching again in the early hours."

A chorus of yes-sirs. Early spit his done chaw in the dust.

There were times when he didn't know how his men did it, marching through such misery. Early didn't believe he could bear up under it himself, if he had to go afoot. Of course, he'd done his share of traveling hard when he was younger. War was for the young, Lee was right about that. Just needed a few old soldiers around to jerk the brakes on the limbers before the entire battery rolled off the cliff.

He stomped back up the stairs, single spur chinking, and pushed into the house he had taken as his temporary headquarters.

The stale heat and crowding in the parlor drove him back onto the porch. Through the opened door, he barked, "Hotchkiss! Captain Hotchkiss! Moore, you go find Jed."

Then he sat down in the shade to wait. In the few minutes he had been gone, a new layer of dust had settled over things. Nor had the lemonade glass been filled again. The heat just pinned a man down. Below, a wagon that still bore U.S. markings rattled up the street, driven by a teamster who—rare in this show-your-ribs army—had a belly on him. Only when the wagon passed could Early see it was filled with collapsed soldiers.

And Gordon wanted to march them harder still, afeared they wouldn't make it to Washington before the Yankees caught their scent and loosed the hounds. That primping Georgian, in all his shimmering vanity, would get himself to Washington, all right. With three men and a dog, not a goddamned army. And still the fool men loved him.

Early knew that few men and fewer women would love *him*. He consoled himself that he had accepted the bargain. But Gordon was a man he was born to resent. Not least after Gordon had been right that second dawn in the Wilderness. And after the Georgian made himself the hero of the Mule Shoe at Spotsylvania. Hero, my rump.

Bugger fought, though. Only reason Early saw for keeping Gordon on. He fought. And he could make other men fight.

That pestering wife of his, though. Following the army like a . . . like a . . .

He found he could not mouth the word that had risen to his tongue. The image of Fanny Gordon was so palpable that he blushed, as if he had spoken crudely in her presence. He despised and deplored the business of wives in the camps, but Mrs. Gordon commanded a certain respect even from him. A formidable woman, Early considered her. *Formidable*. How the Frenchies said it. And handsome enough to turn a younger man's head. At least Gordon had possessed the sense to leave her behind in Winchester this time.

Jed Hotchkiss came out on the porch, the army's wizard map-maker and a queer young man, splay-bearded, who never quite joined up and held no formal commission, but had been adjudged a captain by common consent, doing better work than a dozen colonels.

"Well?"

"Maps haven't changed, General."

"And?"

"Tell you the same thing I told you yesterday morning: If you want to take this army to Washington, the best way's through Frederick City and down across the Monocacy. Best room for maneuver to right or left, come what may. Keeps the Federals guessing, too. Until you tip your hand, you could be headed for Washington or Baltimore, either one." Hotchkiss stood clutching his treasures, awaiting an order to spread them out in the dust. The man guarded his maps the way a sultan guarded his harem.

No. Those maps were worth a damned sight more than a coop of Turkish harlots.

"Well, sit down, Hotchkiss. Tired of telling you. Never been one to stand on ceremony."

The mapmaker smiled. "You have your moments, General." He sat down. Dust puffed from the parlor chair that had been set on the porch.

"Do I?" Early asked. "Suppose I do, at that. What do you reckon? How many marches to get this army to Washington? Frederick way?"

"Three hard marches and a rush."

Early nodded. "Put us in sight of the Capitol July tenth." He snorted. "Shame we missed the Fourth." He calculated for a moment. "Cavalry could get there night of the ninth. For what those brigands are worth."

"If all goes well, sir."

Early leaned back, smiling. "Wonder how John Breckinridge will feel? Walking the halls of Congress? Not every former vice president returns a conqueror."

"No, sir. Sure enough not."

"Madcap world, Captain Hotchkiss, a madcap world. I do have

days when I believe I should have stayed home in Rocky Mount with a barrel of good whiskey." He turned his head toward the house, feeling the stiffness of age. He shouted: "Colonel Pendleton? Any damned body?"

In moments, Sandie Pendleton appeared. He, too, had recently married, despite Early's remonstrance. His bride was a woman of irksome vivacity, pregnant as a sow.

Early fished in his pocket for another chaw. "Orders for General Breckinridge. Get him started toward Frederick. His division and Gordon's, his whole wing. After dark, when it's cool."

"It's hardly cool even then, sir. But I take your point."

"Then get orders out to everybody else. This army converges on Frederick. Sweep away any damned militia, I've had enough of Johnson's pussyfooting. And let me read those orders for his ponyboys."

"Yes, sir. Anything else?"

Down in the street, a last, lone soldier limped along, more dust than man, rifle athwart his shoulders. He showed no interest in the occupants of the high porch, his only concern putting one foot down, then the other.

"Anything else, sir?" Pendleton repeated.

"See if there's any more of that lemonade."

July 7, 3:45 p.m.
Monocacy Junction

Lew Wallace watched as his men worked the ropes to lower the big brass gun into position. The twenty-four-pounder was the only powerful piece of artillery he had, and he'd ordered the construction of a demi-lunette, all done by the book, that would let it range the far fields across the river. Red-faced, with gritted teeth, the artillerymen did the work of a half dozen mules, yet beyond the normal condemnations of various deities, ancestors, and hypothetical females, the men seemed willing enough. He only hoped they would be as willing once the shooting began.

Watching his soldiers strain, Wallace felt a democratic, midwestern urge to strip off his blouse and help them. But generals had to remain aloof, he had learned, so the men would not realize how mortal and slight they were.

He listened for a renewal of the fighting west of Frederick, along the Hagerstown road. But the skirmishing and occasional clashes had calmed around noon and the fields remained still across the heavy hours. It had given him time to push support to Clendenin, whose men had fired up their carbine ammunition, and he had dispatched Ras Tyler to take overall command and to get what service he could out of his Potomac Home Brigade's Sunday-soldiers. It was a patchwork force, at best, but they might hold, if the Rebs didn't press too hard. Wallace purposed to keep the Confederates out of Frederick City through the night, then to read the situation again in the morning. Every delay was of inestimable value. But the real fight would be here, on the river line; that wouldn't change. Tomorrow or the next day would bring the bloodletting.

Below the grunting soldiers on the ropes—barked at by a sergeant with an impressive command of metaphor—the station telegrapher stumped his way up the side of the bluff. The fellow was as important as any colonel now, maintaining Wallace's lifeline to the world, a single wire. Odd for him to stray out in the heat, though. Corpulent, the telegrapher had not been subsisting on military rations. This had to be something important, Wallace realized.

One hoped it was not more bad news.

"Max," Wallace said to his aide, "see what that poor devil's got for us, before he collapses and we're all in the sink."

Captain Woodhull hastened down the slope, breaking into a trot, only to slow again where the bluff dropped off. Dry grass remained bowed where the captain passed.

The gun settled into place with a thud. The men sighed and loosed the ropes, although the sergeant's profanities continued.

Wallace turned back to the lesser spectacle of his aide and the heaving telegrapher. Woodhull was reading the message the man had carried.

Alerting like a bird dog, the aide looked up toward him. The captain began to run back up the slope, but Wallace gestured for him to approach calmly. Good or bad, news had to be handled with care. He didn't want to spook the men nearby: Rumors spread faster than cholera in an orphanage.

Woodhull continued running.

When he put the message into Wallace's hands, the general understood why. It was from the railroad's president, in Baltimore:

> *A large force of veterans arrived by water, and will be sent immediately. Our arrangements are made to forward them with the greatest possible dispatch.*
>
> *J. W. Garrett*

Across the fields, past Frederick, the cannon opened again.

June 7, 9:00 p.m.
Camden Station, Baltimore
Headquarters of the Baltimore and Ohio Railroad

John W. Garrett sat at his desk, scratching his nose. He did not keep liquors in his office, but would have been tempted to have a drink had a bottle put in an unexpected appearance. Having whipped off his subordinates to their myriad tasks, he still feared that some crucial matter had been overlooked, some vital word not passed. An immense amount of work had to be done, a daunting amount, but it *could* be brought off. *If* he kept his sanity. This night, and for as many nights to come as the purpose required, those trains would be loaded and moved, and he'd teach those military pups a lesson or two about getting things done.

Garrett prided himself on *commanding*—for that was the word he used to himself these days—the best-run railroad in the entire Union.

Surprising himself, he brought his fist down hard on the top of his desk, creating an earthquake among the pens and adornments.

It was as if he had observed a stranger doing the hammering. Master of himself again, he lowered the paw a second time, but gently. Self-control, in all things, marked the man.

Garrett abhorred inefficiency and could not imagine an organization worse run or more contentedly inept than the Federal Government. War had made a great, blind, lumbering beast of a creature clumsy enough before the first shot discharged. On the twenty-ninth of June, he personally had telegraphed the secretary of war, alerting Stanton—whom Garrett had regarded as rather a friend—to the reports from B&O station agents that Confederate forces were marching northward in dangerous numbers. Since then, he had not stopped forwarding the messages that started as a trickle and became a deluge. Yet Washington had done nothing at all for an entire week, dismissing his reports as impossibilities.

It was a damnable absurdity that the president of a railroad was better informed than the president of these United States. What was the purpose of taxation and fees? Merely to bloat the spoils system?

Stanton was normally a sensible man. But even the secretary of war had been confounded by the insistence of his generals that Early and his corps could not have reinforced the Rebels in the Valley and that any Confederate activity was no more than a raid or a diversion.

One hell of a raid, then, and one hot diversion, with Early rampaging through Maryland, tearing up tracks and burning bridges, and having a splendid time of it. Good God, he longed for just one sensible interlocutor in that foul-smelling city on the Potomac.

Oh, they were excited enough tonight, suddenly convinced that not only the Confederates but the Great Cham and Grand Turk were descending on Washington. Yet even now, with the crisis upon them, one department failed to speak with the other, and one command issued one set of orders, only to see contradictory orders issued by a rival.

This day had been exasperating above all others in Garrett's experience. He was used to getting things done—by blunt force, if necessary—but the tortured acrobatics he had needed to perform to get the fools in Washington to apply a single ounce of common sense had been infuriating. He had kept his temper with Stanton, of course, thanks not least to the orderly tick of the telegraph, but had been a tyrant otherwise. Refined manners had their place, and their place was in good society. Not in a railroad office during a war.

He sat back in his splendid chair, but found its embrace too tender for his mood. Planting his elbows on his desk, he let his fingers wrestle until the knuckles whitened. Good Christ, for a dash of old Peabody's aplomb! The English had that knack of remaining, or at least feigning, calm when faced with extremity.

A hand tapped his door. Not boldly.

"Come in." He almost added, "Dammit," but swallowed the words: A railway man had to be hard, but needn't be vulgar.

Moder stalled in the doorway. Afraid to proceed.

"Well, what is it?"

"They're disembarking from the ships, sir. I thought you'd want to know."

"Well, hallelujah! Somebody in Washington has an interest in saving the blasted Union. Secretary Stanton?"

"Yes, sir. We copied the message."

"Anything more?"

"Yes, sir. I mean . . . only that we have the extra repair crews and telegraph people ready."

"How many?"

"One hundred and twenty. Last count."

"Get more. Kidnap them from the Reading, if you have to."

"Yes, sir."

"And Moder . . . you make sure that every man in this company knows that trains carrying troops or military supplies—I don't care if they're hoop skirts and monkey jackets—will have absolute priority. And I'll not only dismiss the man who causes the least obstruction, but do my best to put the swine in jail."

"Yes, sir. Anything else for General Wallace, sir?"

"No."

Wallace. Poor devil. The only man in uniform who had taken his reports seriously. Initially, he'd thought Wallace a bag full of nothing, given the taint of failure and then his wife's all-too-loud whispers at Mrs. Hopkins' reception about her husband having written a novel. As if that might impress Baltimore society! A novel! About Spaniards in Mexico, or something of that ilk. Romantic, no doubt. Unpublished, of course.

Garrett could not imagine an endeavor less befitting a soldier or, for that matter, any man than scribbling out novels for women sprawled on daybeds. He had maintained cordial relations with the new department commander after learning of his literary bent, but had written Wallace off as better suited to the Baltimore Club than to battlefield gore.

Then the fellow had taken himself off to Monocacy Junction with a tatterdemalion collection of the lame and left-over in uniforms smelling of camphor, not blown powder, determined to fight the Rebels and damn the risk and sheer impossibility. A slender David with a Frenchman's beard and pomaded hair, Wallace had proven the only true man among the bloody, blue lot of them.

Which did not portend the defeat of the gray Goliath.

He had hesitated to send any further messages to Wallace after his excited report that veteran troops had arrived in transports off Locust Point. That message had been premature, to put it mildly. Oh, the veterans were there, all right, riding at anchor, regiments of the Third Division of the Sixth Corps, among the best in all the Union's armies. But they'd been sent with orders not to disembark until their division commander arrived and sniffed around. And when Garrett, frenzied, had gotten Stanton to intervene himself to bring them ashore, that horse's ass Halleck had ordered the troops to reinforce Maryland Heights—which would take them far from the impending battle.

Even now, Garrett was not certain which orders had prevailed or who truly was in charge of the wretched mess . . . but *he* was ready to take charge, if no one else would. He was going to get

those disembarking regiments packed into train cars and sent off to
Wallace, if he had to do it at gunpoint. Once the troops got to the
junction, Wallace could handle the Maryland Heights tomfoolery.

Good Christ, though . . .

When the war began, Garrett's personal sympathies had leaned
southward: He had viewed the B&O as a Southron line. But he had
not needed long to figure out who could pay and who couldn't—
and shortly thereafter the Rebels had taken to ripping up his track
and burning his rolling stock, stations, and warehouses. John W.
Garrett became the staunchest of staunch Union men.

And he had learned to profit amid war, despite the repeated
destruction, turning the B&O into the Union's backbone in the
East. If the government stationed its poorest troops and shabbiest
officers to protect the line, the protection still had worth—and cost
the line nothing. But there were limits to all things, and, as he had
told Wallace in clarion terms, he would not see the new iron bridge
over the Monocacy damaged or destroyed.

John W. Garrett hoped to save the nation's capital. But he was
damned well determined to save his bridge.

July 8, dawn
Rohrersville road, Maryland

Brigadier General Clem Evans rode back along his ranks, encouraging men where he could and wondering whether Joshua's
soldiers ever had been as weary as his brigade. John Brown Gordon was a splendid man and tolerably Christian, the finest leader
Evans had ever known. But Gordon did like to march men hard
and go at the enemy harder.

Times it paid, as it had that first afternoon in the Wilderness,
when Gordon had ordered the brigade to attack in two directions
while fighting in a third, defying military logic and whipping the
devil out of the bewildered Yankees.

But Evans also remembered the Mule Shoe slaughter, when
Gordon had been willing to sacrifice every man he led to hold the

line, even as Evans had tried to reason with him. Gordon had been right, of course. But it had gone down hard: the merciless orders and that imperious look on Gordon's face, the expression of an intelligent beast in ecstasy.

It wasn't that Gordon didn't care for the men. He surely did. But he cared for winning more than anything else this side of Paradise. Evans *liked* Gordon, liked him well enough . . . loved him, maybe . . . but, while he did not wish to blaspheme, there was something demonic about John Gordon, a devil revealed in his nakedness on the battlefield.

Even Gordon's younger brother, Eugene, a captain and Evans' aide, felt an awe of his older brother that was edged with fear. Love, yes. But fear, too.

Evans didn't want to make too much of things, though, or to be unjust to any man—least of all John Gordon. After Fredericksburg, in the wake of that horror, he had pledged himself to the Methodist ministry, if the Lord saw fit to let him survive this war. There would be no more lawyering and politics hereafter, a decision in which his beloved Allie concurred with all her heart. Nor would he preach the anger of the Prophets, only the perfect love of Jesus Christ.

"Just a little more walking now, soldier," Evans told a laggard shadow. "Rest those hind paws soon enough." He knew the names of almost all his men, took pains to know them, as a minister must know his congregants, but the lingering dark and the fog of dust blurred this fellow's features.

The soldier did not reply, but shuffled along.

Likely didn't even know I was talking to him, Evans figured.

The latest order he had received from Gordon called for a halt of two hours at Rohrersville, then for the march to resume. It wasn't enough time for the men to recover. And they'd be marching into the heat of the day. Evans understood the need to make haste, if they intended to reach the Yankee capital, that Gomorrah. But the soldiers had to be fit for a scrap when they got there.

Blame the devil, where *were* the Yankees, anyway? Nothing but

militia in the towns, running high-tail, and Sigel's fellows hud-
dled up back on the Heights. Didn't they have an inkling what
was passing?

Let the Lord be praised.

And God bless Allie and the children, the living and those who
had gone to eternal life straight from the cradle. He allowed himself to think of little Ida, the apple of his eye, and her trouble learning geography, then of tiny Lawton, a merry hellion, a year and a
half old. He thought, too, of the dreadful loss of Charlie, of other
losses . . . but at the end of all sorrows, Allie waited, her smile
as full of grace as Heaven must be. They had wed when he was
twenty and she fifteen—he could not wait longer, nor did she desire delay—and for eleven years she had been the finest wife to him
that any man could want, a woman of sweet ardor. He longed for
her every night.

At least their home was south of Sherman's path. He wondered
again if Allie had settled last winter's debts, incurred when he—a
cautious man with money—had upended the family's finances,
borrowing to come home and see his family on a month's leave.
The cost of all things, from railway travel to biscuit flour, had
soared, but pay had not kept pace as the currency withered. Last
month, he, a brigadier general, had strained to settle his commissary bill.

"When this cruel war is over," he muttered.

Too dry to sing anything, even a hymn, let alone a soldier song,
he tempered his stallion's pace to a meeker mildness, unwilling to
stir up dust to afflict his men.

Brilliant slants of light purpled the ridges. Evans tugged back
the reins.

"Who's that walking peg-a-leg there? George Nichols, that you,
boy?"

Nichols limped from the column, nodding a salute. Two of his
comrades moved to the roadside with him, one on each flank.

"What's the matter, son? New shoes a trial?"

The soldier seemed hardly more than a child between his broad-shouldered friends.

"No, sir. Nothing wrong a-tall."

Evans recognized Lem Davis as the man who spoke up next. "Spent shell casing got him back at the Heights, Genr'l. Fool won't take to a wagon, show some sense. That leg's swelled to busting."

Evans turned to his aide, performing as General Gordon might have done in similar circumstances, saying, pulpit-loud, "Hear that now, Captain Gordon? *That's* the kind of men we grow in Georgia." Then he bent from the saddle toward the boy. "You've shown a fine side, Nichols. But wait on the wagons now and take your ease. Hear?"

The lad stepped forward again. On that bad leg.

"If'n that's an order, sir, I'm set to obey it. But I'd as lief walk."

Evans told himself that, yes, it *was* an order. For the boy's own good. But he also knew that the ways of the heart were many and the needs of the soul were legion.

"Son . . . you do what you want," Evans told him. "Just remember that pride comes before a fall."

"I ain't going to fall none. Leg'll carry me."

In the shadows below a shimmering sky, Evans smiled.

"Well, then . . . y'all get along and catch up to your company."

The men saluted, each in his odd manner, just as none of their uniforms were uniform. Evans rode on.

Behind the last mob that passed for a march formation, he entered the domain of limping forms and quitters. That eager boy, Nichols, was made of rock-hard stuff, even if he looked barely fit for man-britches.

Turning his mount in the richer-each-moment light, Evans thought: Lord, isn't that just us, though? All of us? From that young private to General Robert E. Lee, we're so doggone stubborn we just don't know what's good for us.

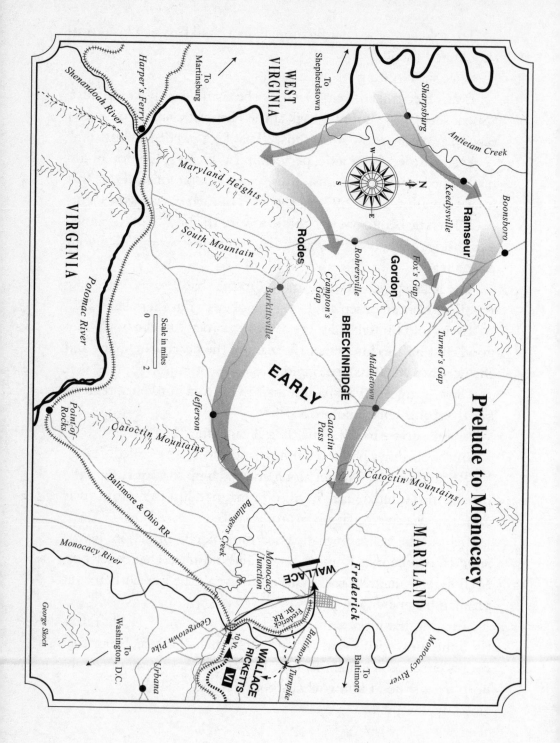

Prelude to Monocacy

VIRGINIA

WEST VIRGINIA

MARYLAND

Shenandoah River

Harper's Ferry

To Martinsburg

To Shepherdstown

Sharpsburg

Antietam Creek

Keedysville

Ramseur

Boonsboro

Maryland Heights

Rodes

Rohrersville

Gordon

Fox's Gap

South Mountain

Crampton's Gap

Burkittsville

BRECKINRIDGE

Turner's Gap

Middletown

Potomac River

EARLY

Catoctin Pass

Jefferson

Catoctin Mountains

Catoctin Mountains

Point of Rocks

Baltimore & Ohio RR

Ballenger's Creek

Frederick

Monocacy River

Monocacy River

Monocacy River

WALLACE

Monocacy Junction

Frederick Br. RR

Baltimore

To Baltimore

Baltimore Turnpike

Georgetown Pike

10 Vt.

WALLACE RICKETTS

VI

Urbana

To Washington, D.C.

Scale in miles

0

2

George Skoch

TWO

July 8, dawn
Monocacy Junction

S ir, sir!" The orderly shook Wallace, none too gently. "I hear a train. Coming from Baltimore way."

Wallace brushed off the man's hand and rose, stiff and groggy, from the floor. He heard the swelling throb of a locomotive. God grant it be the veterans.

He pulled on his boots and fumbled with his coat, forgoing sash and sword. Ross had orders to stop any train that approached the iron bridge, but Wallace feared that his own two stars might be needed to settle matters.

The noise of the great machine grew huge, then screamed to a hissing stop.

Righting his hat, Wallace hurried out of the shack. Sleep's claws pursued him: He'd known little rest for days. In the foreground, a locomotive steamed, impatient. Dark forms leaned from passenger car platforms and crowded the doors of freight wagons. Mist smoked off the river.

A figure alighted from one of the cars, moving with a haste that betokened anger: a big fellow, blacksmith brawny, followed by stumbling underlings.

Wallace strode toward the tall officer, who looked around as if anxious to land a punch. Sweat prickled Wallace's back.

"What's the meaning of this?" the new arrival bellowed at anyone who might hear. "Why has this train been stopped? What damned idiocy is it now?"

Wallace spotted Jim Ross, his senior aide and a newly promoted lieutenant colonel. Ross would be no match for the bull in blue.

Quickening his pace again, Wallace waved to Ross: *Let me handle this.*

"And who the hell are you?" the big man, a colonel, snapped. He marked Wallace's shoulder boards, but didn't recoil or salute. He merely lowered his voice to a muzzled growl. "You in command here?"

Wallace extended his hand. "Major General Wallace, Middle Department. To whom do I owe the honor?"

The scent of coffee rose from a cook-fire, teasing him. He wished he had been allowed a cup before this confrontation.

The big man paused, then accepted Wallace's paw, enclosing it. "Bill Henry, Tenth Vermont. Why have my men been stopped?" He freed Wallace's hand, which hurt. The colonel was short a finger, Wallace noted, and his uniform was hard used.

"You don't have orders to stop here, then?" Wallace asked. "At Monocacy Junction?"

"None."

Confined to the train, bleary soldiers eyed the two officers. One man emptied a slop bucket from a freight car.

"And your orders are?"

"Proceed to Point of Rocks. Either continue on the train, or march if the line's interrupted. Report to Harper's Ferry for duty at Maryland Heights."

Wallace tried to judge the man before him, what his temper really signified. "And the Tenth Vermont belongs to?"

"First Brigade, Truex commanding. Third Division, General Ricketts. Sixth Corps."

"Where's General Ricketts?"

The colonel shrugged, stretching a bit. His complexion had been burned as brown as a pig turned on a spit. "Doubt he'll be up before tonight. Hadn't arrived in port when we entrained. What's going on?"

A cup of coffee would have been a blessing. He would have liked to offer one to this still-seething colonel, too.

Hundreds of morning-blurred faces watched the exchange now, those on the train and more from the roused camp.

"Colonel Henry," Wallace began in a confidential tone, "if you proceed to Point of Rocks—and if the line has not been cut by now—you will take yourself and your men away from a battle coming to this place today or, at the latest, tomorrow. General Early is going to sweep over the ridges to our west with a reinforced corps, and his men are going to march as fast as their legs can go for our national capital."

Fending off sleep's last grip, Wallace straightened his back. "I have twenty-three hundred raw recruits, and two hundred good cavalry. The enemy's said to number between twenty and thirty thousand. That number may be exaggerated, but they're veterans all. Yesterday, we held off their advance guard just west of Frederick. But if you and those coming behind you continue to Point of Rocks, they will overwhelm us and be on their way to Washington. And your regiment will have done no good to anyone."

Wallace reached out a hand, but withdrew it before touching the other man's sleeve. "I *need* you, Colonel. I don't expect to beat Early. Just hold him long enough for Grant to reinforce Washington." He met the man's eyes in the seeping light. "I have no authority over your command. I leave the decision to stay or proceed to you."

The colonel stared down at him for a dreadful stretch of seconds. Off to the side, Ross held still. On the cars, the soldiers, too, were silent, all their routine foolery suspended. As if they sensed—knew—that their fate was in play.

"Let my boys cook up some breakfast," the Vermonter said at last. "And tell me where you want us."

July 8, 9:00 a.m.
Fox Gap, Maryland

They should've let us go, John," Breckinridge said. "They just should've let us go."

Erect in the saddle, as always, Gordon nodded. "Didn't, though. And here we are." He smiled. A gentleman always knew just when to smile. "Not a bad place at all, wasn't for this dust." He spread an arm toward the ripening fields that graced the valley. "All the bounty of Ceres."

Before and behind the two generals and their staffs, long gray columns moved through tunnels of dust. Above the dirty air, the sun attacked.

"All the more reason they should have let us go," Breckinridge told him. "Rich country, bountiful. The North has all it needs. Could've even spared us Maryland, way this Kentucky boy reckons." He coughed. "John, I put it down to New York greed, Boston pride, and damnable Yankee spite. That's what this war's about." He brushed dust from his long, slender mustaches.

Well, Gordon thought, pride and spite on our part, too, if love of a way of life in place of greed. None of them had expected this: the long years of blood and sorrow, of glory increasingly dimmed by lamentation. For months now, he had privately contemplated the possibility that the South might lose. He was in it to the end, all right, partly from pride and unabated anger, and partly in foreknowledge of what would fix a man's status after the war, win or lose. But the probable end looked different to him now than it had before the slaughter below the Rapidan: The South was bleeding to death.

The man who failed to look ahead fell behind.

He wished he had a confidant to whom he could unburden himself regarding the prospects of the ailing Confederacy. But no man dared utter heresy or hear it; all had to pretend to a flawless belief that by some astonishing run of the cards the game would turn in their favor, even now. Many, like dear Clem Evans, truly believed it, discovering hidden victories in every defeat. Clem believed in miracles, divine or earthly, and Gordon had no wish to weaken his enthusiasm: He needed men who would fight without hesitation.

Gordon *loved* to fight. His concerns about the war's outcome didn't alter that. On the contrary, he knew full well that he'd miss all this immeasurably: Nothing so enlivened a man as a battle. A side of Gordon dreaded the end, the demotion back to mundane life and petty concerns. But he meant to be prepared for it.

He thought a bit more on Clem Evans, who planned to become a Methodist preacher and practiced by delivering camp sermons. Immaculate belief was a powerful thing. It was a gift the war had taken from Gordon.

No, he could never talk to Clem, fond as he was of the man.

He even had to be circumspect with Fanny, who possessed blind faith that he, her champion, could not be defeated. Evidence meant nothing to such as her; her confidence shone like Persephone's in the Underworld. Nor would he deprive his wife of hope. When worse came to worst, her practical side would digest defeat and continue.

His splendid Fanny! She was as fine a woman as ever breathed, demure in the world and passionate in his arms, Penelope to his Ulysses. No, far better than Penelope, since Fanny had left their children in her family's care to follow him through the war, to nurse his wounds and sew on his latest rank. She would not sit at home working her loom amid the cowards. Fanny believed in a distant Christ, but wanted her husband near.

Beside him, Breckinridge alerted, canting his head like a hound dog figuring things.

"That cannon?"

"Didn't hear it."

"Listen now."

Gordon waited a fair time, then shook his head.

"Imagining things, I suppose," Breckinridge told him. He mused for a bit, then added, "Johnson's cavalry ran up against some militia yesterday. On the Frederick road. Gave him a fight, I hear."

"I doubt Johnson gave anybody much of a fight," Gordon commented. "I'm in accord with Early on that much. Johnson's brigands aren't worth a pail of oats. Cavalry's not what it was. Best men gone, horses ruined."

"McCausland, though, he'll fight. Full of pepper, that boy."

Gordon lifted a brow and sweat stung his eye. "Wouldn't stop for a few militia, I'll give him that."

"Assuming they're just militia."

Gordon smiled, but with no trace of pleasure. "I've been pondering that question myself, if truth be told." He pulled his horse away from the column. "Yankees have to figure this out, at some point. Sooner or later, it won't be farmers in soldier suits anymore. And we'll have a real fight on our hands."

"Well, we're ready for that, too," his temporary superior told him. "Let them come on out and get whipped, they'll find us ready."

Ever alert to the nuances of companionship, Gordon reassumed his genial tone. "I expect so, General, I expect so. And I *do* hope to host you in Georgia, after the war. . . ."

Ahead, a soldier staggered to the roadside and collapsed.

"Killing this army," Breckinridge sputtered. "Just killing it." He turned his well-formed face toward Gordon. The man's waxed mustaches were frosted with dust again. "You disagree, I know that, John. But I do believe we're pushing the men too hard. They're game enough, but the body's a sight weaker than the spirit."

Gordon knew it was fruitless to argue, or at least impolitic. Early brought out his combative nature, but Breckinridge was of a different breed, a gentleman. And like so many of his fellow gentlemen, Breckinridge was willing to push men to their deaths on the battlefield, but would not press them sufficiently hard to get them there before the foe was ready—and thus save far more lives.

No one since Jackson grasped the brute mathematics. Even if you lost one man in ten—or more—on the march, if you got to the fight before the Federals could double or triple their strength, you had the odds. It wasn't hard figuring. And it was a remarkable thing, how much men delivered if they were soundly led. Soldiers just wanted a little show, a handful of stirring words and a flash of courage from the man giving orders.

Beside the road, the fallen soldier raved as they rode past.

"Poor devil won't see Washington," Breckinridge said.

Gordon wanted to tell him, "None of us will see Washington, if we give the Yankees time to shift their beef. We should have been across the Monocacy yesterday, rather than fooling with Sigel and tearing up rails."

Instead, he said, "Hottest weather we've seen, I do believe. Prelude to Hades, and not even ten." He lifted his hat to the nearest soldiers and poured the Deep South into his sonorous voice. "Weather here'bouts leave you boys mindful of Georgia? Y'all settling thoughts on home, way I am myself? Peaches near to ripe on the branch, and the Lord smiling down on the cotton? Win this war, and we'll all go home a-grinning, that's a fact."

"Sure enough," a voice returned. "Home, *sweet* home!" called another. A third voice rhapsodized, "Get me some of that sweet well water'n drink it till I bust. . . ."

Breckinridge sneezed. "I swear, John Gordon, you start in to praising Georgia again . . ."

Amazing, Gordon thought, that a political man who had been vice president of the United States and had run for the highest office did not understand the value of praising Georgia in front of Georgian troops. Not least when a man intended to go back home and run for a seat, if the bullets veered off. Let the war be lost or won, the political future would belong to veterans, whether they sat in the governor's chair or stood behind it, out of sight of the Yankees.

Thinking on Washington again, Gordon pondered Early's likely intentions. Despite Black Davey Hunter's depredations before they whipped him back into western Virginia, Early kept a strict hand over the soldiers—of which Gordon approved. There had been no reprisals, at least not yet, for the burnings in Lexington and elsewhere, the wanton destruction and barbarism. He knew that Early intended to press the Yankee town fathers for ransoms, wherever he sensed full coffers and Union loyalties, but the soldiers were not to indulge themselves, a prohibition that occasionally demanded the wisdom of Solomon in its enforcement. Gordon approved of maintaining order and discipline—he would have no rampaging— but he also had sense enough to avert his eyes, nose, and salivary glands when his men cooked up fresh pork or a quarter of beef that appeared by magic.

Soldiers were like children, delighted to get away with small transgressions. One of the knacks of leadership was to know which mischief to ignore and when to descend upon a rogue like the Furies. The best leaders weren't the soft ones who meant to be kind, but those who firmly punished misdeeds the soldiers themselves despised.

If they *did* get to Washington—get inside the city—what did Early intend? Old Jube wouldn't say. Probably hadn't decided, Gordon figured. For all his barking and snorting, Early had trouble making big decisions; Gordon had realized that way back at Gettysburg. The revelation had come as a shock, since making decisions came naturally to him, the way what to do in battle just seemed obvious. It had bewildered Gordon to realize that all those fellows with West Point educations did not see things that were plain as Aunt Sally. On a battlefield, what struck others as audacity was only common sense, as far as John Brown Gordon was concerned. And if you did not know what to do, you attacked.

Gordon never found leading much of a challenge. Following was another matter, though.

Well, he hoped that Early was shaping up a plan, since they wouldn't be able to hold the city long, even if they took it. Have to destroy the military stores, of course, and put the right government buildings to the torch. The Navy Yard, certainly. That was part and parcel of war. Perhaps the Treasury, too. But the President's House? The Capitol? Gordon recoiled at the thought of such destruction.

Yes, he had seen the ruins of the Virginia Military Institute. And Governor Letcher's house had been burned to the foundation, his family prevented from rescuing heirlooms or even saving essentials. There would be no forgetting. But giving in to the impulse to retaliate was the opposite of strategy. And the South needed a strategy that weighed the possibility of defeat, with all its consequences. Vengeance was a very dangerous tincture, best administered in measured drops.

If they reached the streets of Washington, they would have to restrain the soldiers on pain of death. It was natural for the South to hate the North, given the years of Yankee depredations, but woe unto the South if the North learned hatred. Burn Washington, then lose the war, and only the nigger would profit.

The sun seemed hot enough to ignite fires. Still, Gordon felt they were lagging on the march. But he could do nothing, not with Breckinridge present.

He chafed, but smiled.

Adjusting his rump in the saddle, he asked, "Well now, Mr. Vice President . . . we do get to Washington, what would *you* like to do in that fair Thebes on the Potomac?"

"Take a bath," Breckinridge said.

July 8, 4:00 p.m.
The western approach to Frederick

Why didn't they come on? Wallace asked himself. They already had the numbers. What were they waiting for?

He steadied his sweat-glossed horse and scanned the horizon.

Days of little sleep had told on his nerves, and all morning it had seemed as though the Confederates were preparing to attack. Yet their probes had rarely risen above the skirmish level, and in the afternoon the Rebs had gone quiet. From moment to moment, he had waited for their guns to open, for gray ranks to swarm forward. But the attack never came, only odd encounters, as when a stray detachment of Reb cavalry somehow got into the streets of Frederick and collided with two squadrons of Clendenin's troopers. Back for a parley with the city's mayor, Wallace had nearly been caught up in the clash—which had kicked up so much dust the riders fought blind, lost souls in a maelstrom. In short order, the graybacks had found it politic to withdraw the way they'd come, disappearing after giving the town fathers a fright.

The mayor and his coterie had begged him not to give up the city to the Confederates, citing their loyalty to the Union and pleading that Frederick had already suffered, due to repeated Rebel visitations. Having witnessed the poverty of the South, Wallace barely refrained from chiding the men. If the war had harmed Frederick City, the wounds were invisible. Prosperity was evident on every side. Nor would he promise what he couldn't deliver.

"I'll do my best." Those were his only words, carefully chosen. He knew he could not protect the city much longer. The real fight would come on the river, three miles south.

Military stores were being evacuated from the yards, and what could not be rescued would be destroyed. As for the convalescent soldiers in Frederick's hospitals, not all could be removed . . . but the Confederates were not beasts.

He was proud of what he had managed to bring off. The little battle the day before had been splendid. Not only had Clendenin fought with art, but the Potomac Home Brigade had been unexpectedly stalwart, as had the strays and artillerymen he'd sent forward.

Now he had a veteran regiment in the line, those Vermonters, men with faces so darkened by campaigning that they might have been mistaken for U.S. Colored Troops. And regiments kept appearing down at the junction. Every hour that passed was an hour won.

Tomorrow would bring the reckoning, though. It could not be otherwise. Scouts had reported enormous clouds of dust just west of the ridges, clouds that betokened divisions on the march.

Nickering, his horse stepped back, then calmed again. Wallace patted the animal's neck, taking its smell on his hand. The heat was monstrous. The Vermonters had set the example by stripping to their shirts, and the recruits had aped them. Wallace didn't mind. But he felt that he had to remain in uniform himself, another of the pretensions rank required.

He remembered how, in his innocent years, he had written extravagant scenes of battle between Cortez and Montezuma The actions he had described seemed ludicrous now, impossible in their chivalry and glamour. He had captured neither the swift, brute shock of combat nor the grinding dullness that surrounded it. Even Mexico had taught him little, compared to this grim war that crimsoned a continent.

Captain Woodhull reappeared, returning from the Frederick telegraph station. He did not seem pleased with the world.

"Bad news, Max?"

"Yes, sir. I mean, yes and no." The young man's face was a Niagara of sweat. "Two more regiments arrived down at the junction. Makes five total, the whole brigade. With another brigade set to follow, maybe tonight, Mr. Garrett says. Colonel Ross wants to know if you'd like any more men sent up here."

"No. No more. If we can bluff the Rebs until dusk, I mean to pull everyone back across the river."

"The mayor—"

"The mayor's a fool. Good Lord, does he really believe we could hold an army at arm's length? Here? In the open? Does he want a fight in his streets?" Wallace shook his head. "If Early rides in quietly in the morning, the people of Frederick will fare a good deal better than they would under a bombardment." Bunching a sodden handkerchief, he wiped sweat from his eyes. "What's the bad news?"

"Telegraph operator ran away. The one in Frederick, not at the junction. I found the message from Colonel Ross on his desk."

Wallace hooked his lips. "Wise man, I suppose." He gestured back toward the townspeople with their carriages and parasols who, in defiance of his repeated orders, had clustered behind his lines to see a battle. "Wiser than those fools. Max, you try one more time to reason with them. If I go back there again, I'll lose my temper."

General Tyler steered his mount toward Wallace, but did not hurry the animal. Erastus Tyler had been put out to pasture, too, condemned to rot in Baltimore's defenses, but the man had handled his little force magnificently the past evening and had been ready to stand his ground today.

All of them had done handsomely: Tyler, Clendenin . . . and Captain Alexander, with his pop guns. The fellow looked like a college professor, but handled artillery like a young Napoleon. All these men whom Washington had cast aside or consigned to the rear . . .

Would anyone think well of *him* when this was over? There had been so many setbacks in his life. So many failures, in truth. His father had turned him from home while still half a boy—not out of cruelty, but to teach the prodigal son a needed lesson. Having left many a school and quarreled with many a master, he had found himself copying legal texts to survive, earning his soup by piece-work. Of course, the lawyer who took him in had been a family friend . . . but his father's firmness had been a required tonic. Still, he had failed in his first, halfhearted reading of the law and gone off to Mexico. That had been the dawn of his serious life. Upon returning home, he had passed the bar, wed, and even prospered. But the greatest humiliation had been yet to come: his scapegoating after Shiloh, the sort of shame a man never quite lived down.

Tyler reined in. His mouth gaped.

"What I wouldn't give for a good iced punch," he said. "Whole bowl of it." He lifted his hat, revealing a bald pate above his woolly beard. "Think they really mean to come this way, sir? They haven't been showing much spunk."

Wallace had begun to have his own doubts as the afternoon dragged on. Had the Rebs been laughing at him all the while, fixing him in place while they marched to Washington on a southerly route? Should he have let those veteran regiments continue to Point of Rocks? Had he failed again?

"They're coming," Wallace said, determined to be right. "They're coming right over that ridge."

Rather than look Tyler in the eye, he snapped open his telescope.

And there they were! Marching down three separate mountain roads, five miles away at most, endless columns surrounded by halos of dust.

"Look for yourselves," he told the men beside him.

July 8, 9:00 p.m.
Early's headquarters, Catoctin Pass

The tent did a fine job of trapping the day's heat. Kept the dust off a man somewhat, but there was little more to recommend it. Did serve for a hint of privacy, but Early much preferred to borrow a house, when a house could be had. His quartermaster had picked out a site on the mountainside, though, hoping to snare a breeze. Hope hadn't come to much.

By a lantern's light, Early stared at Brigadier General Bradley Johnson. "Understand what it says there?"

The cavalryman looked up from reading the order. "Yes, sir. I understand."

"Make all the noise you can. Burn bridges, army stores, anything touching the government. Make 'em believe the armies of Hell are headed their way and Baltimore's doomed as Sodom." He cackled, disdaining the sound of his own laugh, then sharpened his tone again. "Just leave the civilians alone, I'll have no wantonness. You know this country, these here are your own people. Don't go acting the fool."

"Point Lookout?"

Early grimaced. "You read the order. You get down there and free those boys . . . if practicable. No damned foolishness, though. South don't need any more dead heroes, category's filled."

Johnson nodded. Early had chastised the cavalryman for his dawdling before Frederick, only to have Johnson hurl back in his face Early's admonition not to become decisively engaged or to do anything to suggest that their goal was Washington. Early lost his temper, couldn't help himself. Few things enraged him as much as a cavalryman in the right.

Well, let Johnson and his band of thieves go roving. The sight of the mangy fellow was enough to set a man to missing Jeb Stuart, for all that fool's shenanigans. Early would never have backed the fellow's recent promotion to brigadier general, but Johnson had been a Breckinridge man in politics before the war, and the old ties remained.

Days were when Early feared politics alone would be enough to ruin the South, no need of Yankees. He'd had his fill of politics at that damned Richmond convention, but the filth of it all had followed him into the war. When peace came, he didn't intend to run for any damned office.

"Don't tarry, Johnson," Early said. "Go on, see to your men. I'll square things with Ransom."

Johnson saluted and went out. Immediately, Sandie Pendleton entered the tent.

"God almighty," Early said of Johnson. "Fool would sweet-talk a hoor he'd already paid for." He sighed at the world's inexhaustible frustrations. "Got 'em all rounded up, do you?"

"Yes, sir. General Gordon just rode in."

Early snorted. "Gordon."

Made him want a chaw. But there was too much talking to be done. Army full of lawyers, talk everything to death.

Pendleton held the tent's flap open and Early crabbed through. Outside, the skin-gripping air was mean, but cooler than in the tent. The quartering party had pitched it with the sides rolled up for ventilation, but Early had made them drop the canvas again. Didn't intend to sleep in the damned thing, just needed some privacy. Always said he didn't mind shitting in front of a thousand men, but preferred to think in private.

Well, there they were. Scattered about the near-dead fire that no man wished to approach in the lingering heat. The last, small flames gave an orange cast to men's faces, lighting them from below, creating devils. The air sparked with fireflies.

"All right, then," Early said. "Sandie's got your orders written down all nice and pretty, but I want you to hear the gist of things from me." He scanned the shadowed faces, pausing briefly, against his will, at Gordon's. Bugger always looked so damned superior, cock of the walk. The sight of Gordon made him gum a chaw that wasn't there.

"Ramseur's Division leads in the morning, stepping off at dawn." Early faced the young general, who had removed his hat. It was too dark to make out much, but Early sensed the prematurely receding hairline and earnest eyes. "Any damned militia lurking 'twixt here and Frederick, you clear them out fast, Dod. And don't stop, hear? Pass your lead brigade through town on the Baltimore road, as if that's where we're all headed. Make a demonstration, set them to quivering. But your following brigades will turn south for Monocacy Junction and seize the crossing. Fast."

"What if they put up a fight on the Baltimore road, sir?" Ramseur asked. "Shall I engage? How far out should I push?"

"They dig in their heels east of town, it'll be by the bridge. Only sensible place. No, don't engage. Not seriously. Just keep 'em occupied, amuse 'em. I want those peckerwoods thinking on Baltimore burning, but I'd as soon have them run off and sow panic as meet their Maker." Early grunted. "Make a little show of giving chase, they do run off. Mile beyond the river should be enough. But I don't want your boys drawn into a shit-flinging contest, no point in it. General Rodes will relieve your brigade on the Baltimore road, he's next in the order of march. He can take care of any proper fighting needs to be done, he'll have some time. Upon relief, the brigade will rejoin your division."

He turned to Rodes. "General, your division will cover this army's left tomorrow. Any Yankees still fussing after Ramseur's boys been relieved, you help 'em meet Jesus. Seize the Baltimore bridge, if it don't look to cost you. Yanks get spooked and pull off, you cross the river, demonstrate toward Baltimore with a few regiments, and turn your division south."

Early nodded at everybody and nobody, squinting to read their postures in the dark. These all were men who had seen the worst of war: There was no dread.

"Ramseur here will lead the march on Washington," Early stressed, "a city I expect to set eyes on in forty-eight hours." He glanced at Gordon, hoping to see disappointment, but Gordon's features—what he could read of them—remained superior, aloof. Pale scar on his cheek a badge of pride. Why men thought Gordon affable, Early never could figure.

Returning his attention to Ramseur, Early added, "Dod, you just make sure the telegraph wires are cut *before* you turn south. Then you move fast on that junction, hear? Grab the road bridge and railroad bridge, both of them, and keep right on going. Any resistance down that way, smash it quick. Your boys can brush away home guards and militia."

"*If* they're home guards and militia," Gordon put in.

Early turned on him, almost relieved to have the excuse. "Expecting the Army of the Potomac, General Gordon? Have I been inattentive? Did Useless Sumbitch Grant and Granny Meade sneak up on us? While I was at my Bible?" Exasperated despite himself, he turned to his chief of staff. "Sandie?"

Pendleton, a young man of pleasing manners, stepped forward and smiled at Gordon—with none of the malice Early knew his own smiles held in spades.

"General Gordon, we *have* had reports of veteran cavalry in the area. In limited numbers. That's to be expected, you'll agree. But a citizen of Frederick—whose sympathies lean in the proper direction—made his way to our headquarters to report there's no one in Frederick but home guards. Hundred-day men and the like."

"And when did this good citizen pay us a visit?" Gordon asked.

"Yesterday."

"Yesterday," Gordon repeated.

"Yesterday evening, to be precise. General Gordon, we have had no reports, no indications, of a significant Union force anywhere in our path. The Federals . . . do seem embarrassed."

"And even if they've rounded up a herd of goddamned Regulars, Ramseur can handle them." Early turned to Breckinridge, who seemed disinclined to enter the exchange. "Or does General Gordon have information he hasn't yet shared with us? Maybe Sherman evacuated Georgia? To hurry up north and catch us by the tail?"

Breckinridge said nothing, but looked toward Gordon.

"I have no information," Gordon said, "but sooner or later the Yankees—"

"Are going to burn in Hell," Early said. Pulling back on his temper's reins, he addressed Ramseur again, although he had meant to be finished with the business. "Whatever's down along that river, you finish 'em off quick, and then you get along down that Washington road. We wouldn't want to disappoint General Gordon." His voice had ranged higher in pitch than he wished it. It always did when someone got his goat. He knew it, could predict it, but never could do one goddamned thing about it.

Mastering himself as best he could, Early shifted toward Breckinridge. "*Your* divisions will halt this side of the river. Until the others have passed. You will position General Gordon's Division on the right side of the highway to Washington, where General Gordon can observe the army's progress across the Monocacy and resume the march when ordered."

Early knew he had just created more bad blood. He had not planned it that way, but Gordon had a genius for setting him off.

There was one last matter to which to attend.

"General McCausland? Where's McCausland?"

"Here, sir," the cavalryman said. "Just standing off from what's left of that fire."

"Yes, indeed," Early said. "I *have* observed that cavalrymen tend to withdraw when things get hot. McCausland, you and your mule-jockeys cover the right. Minus Johnson. He's setting off to cover himself in glory. Substantial amount of horseshit, anyway." Early grunted pleasurably at the latter thought. "Uncover any fords not on Jed's maps. Then get on down to Urbana, push right along. Clear the road for Ramseur's boys—I'll have no excuses—and screen the march. No reason you couldn't reach Silver Spring come nightfall."

The darkness had fallen heavily and the fire had faded to coals. His generals had become mere forms, highlighted by the occasional glint of a button or a belt buckle.

"Questions?"

Ramseur's voice crossed the darkness. "Where will I find you, sir? If I need to report?"

Early smiled. "I mean to take my breakfast in Frederick, gentlemen. I have weighty matters to discuss with the local authorities . . . who I am convinced desire to make a substantial contribution to the Confederate States of America." He cackled again. "Under threat of seeing their fair city put to the torch."

After Early retreated into his tent, Gordon sought out Pendleton.

"Sandie . . . for God's sake . . ."

"He doesn't mean it, sir. He has no mind to burn Frederick. But the moneybags in Frederick won't know that."

The fireflies blinked like skirmishers. Gordon believed he could actually smell the heat.

"And Washington?"

Pendleton hesitated. Gordon could just discern the chief of staff's features, not well enough to read them.

"He doesn't say," Pendleton confided. "But I hardly think—"

"Sandie, Jackson *made* you. And you helped make Jackson. You know we've been dawdling along. Oh, the marches themselves are hard enough, I'll admit that under duress. But they haven't been *direct,* they haven't *gone* anywhere. We've been fiddling around with no-account Yankee detachments and minor supply depots, splitting off in every direction and tearing up rails we could just as well rip up later. And now we're behind, by my reckoning. Sooner or later, even the dumbest Yankee in Washington is going to get some inkling of what we're up to."

Infinitely frustrated, weary, and crusted with sweat, Gordon continued: "And what on earth is he *thinking*, Sandie? He and I have our differences, but we're not enemies. We're both on the same side in this blasted war, last time I caught up on the Richmond papers."

Pendleton stood stock-still, a barely breathing outline in the darkness. Gordon knew that the young man was wise far beyond his years, an expert judge of his fellow man, and skilled at measuring just how much to say. But he and Gordon had been in agreement many a time over the months, even when the chief of staff declined to support Gordon's position publicly. Pendleton had not survived Jackson, Ewell, and now Early by offering strong opinions. The boy had physical courage, more than a surfeit. Uncanny judgment, too. But speaking up just wasn't in his blood.

Voice low as a regicide's, Pendleton said, "Lynchburg, the business in the Valley . . . now this . . . this raid or invasion, or whatever one may call it . . . it's his first independent command, his first truly independent command. And he's done pretty well, up until now. But with every success, the possibility of failure . . ." Pendleton shook his head, slowly, a dark shape in dark air. "Consider the responsibility, the weight he's feeling. We're all Lee could spare—and the truth is Lee really couldn't spare us, either. General Early loses this army, and he's the man who lost the Confederacy, that's how he looks on things. On top of all that, he's measuring himself against Jackson, he can't help it. He's just—"

"Jackson would've been in Washington by now."

"You don't see all the orders he receives from General Lee. Some . . . border on the fantastic."

"Sandie, every hour we waste we'll pay for in blood. Or failure." Gordon folded his arms. "Or both."

"He smells Washington now, he's got the scent. He wants to get on with things." Again, Pendleton hesitated before speaking further. "You really shouldn't badger him, sir. It doesn't help."

"We should've been across that river yesterday. If he only would've—" Gordon caught himself sounding like a spoiled child, if not a bully. There was much in what Pendleton had said, he'd known it all before the boy spoke one word. But so much went back to that lost day in the Wilderness, the missed opportunity . . .

Gordon softened his voice and his stance, serving up a portion of geniality, however thin the crust.

"I do ride on ahead of my horse sometimes," he said with a smile meant to be felt, if not quite seen. "Sandie . . . if there's any way I can help the man . . . genuinely help him . . ."

Weighing his words again, Pendleton said, "I'm sure you'll get your chance, sir."

July 9, 1:00 a.m.
Monocacy Junction

Weariness pinned him to the floor, but Wallace couldn't sleep. When tired, he slipped too readily into pessimism. And he was morbidly tired.

Two additional regiments had arrived from the Baltimore docks, with claims that the rest of their division was on the way from Virginia. Nonetheless, he felt less confident than he had before the first veterans appeared, asking himself yet again if he was being vainglorious, demanding that men die in a hopeless fight. *Was* this about redeeming his reputation, even as he lied to himself that the battle's outcome must ruin him? Was all this born of the romance of novels, a child's dream of a gallant forlorn hope? Played out at the expense of other men's lives? The visions that kept him from sleep conjured slaughter and panic, fleeing men and disaster. Nor did the vermin haunting the blanket that served as a mattress soothe him.

Was this what theologians meant by the dark night of the soul?

Or did he just need sleep?

The withdrawal from Frederick had gone smoothly, untroubled by the Rebs. The townspeople had been furious, though, cursing him and the troops they had recently cheered. Wallace consoled himself by recalling the cries of "Go ahead! Run for Baltimore!" That was precisely what he wanted people to tell the graybacks when they arrived, that he had withdrawn his small force toward Baltimore, his little ruse. And then he would be waiting for Early when the Rebs strolled down the Washington road.

Even that slight surprise might help, buying an extra hour.

He turned from one side to the other, feeling uneven planks through the blanket's nap. Another creature scurried along his calf, making him jerk and slap at himself. The heat's embrace was smothering.

As sleep teased Wallace, Ross stumbled in. He looked a sorry wreck, but had insisted on keeping his post.

"Sir?" His voice rasped. "General Ricketts is here, he's just behind me."

Wallace sat up and fumbled to a knee. "My coat."

Before he could dress, Ricketts entered. The division commander wasn't especially tall, but broad enough to give the door frame a fright. By candlelight, the man had an Irish look of the hardest sort.

Wallace held out his hand. The other man slapped his own hand against it, gripping firmly but quickly letting go.

"General Wallace? Jim Ricketts. I hear Early's on the loose."

"He'll be in Frederick by morning. Three miles from here." Wallace thought for a moment, rubbed an eye. "He could be there now."

"I suppose I'm in it, then. What's Early's strength?" There was absolutely no nonsense in the division commander's voice. "Railroad fellow made it sound like the Mongol Horde was upon us."

"Reports claim twenty to thirty thousand, so I figure fifteen to twenty."

Ricketts nodded. "Sounds right. What exactly do you intend to do?"

"Fight."

"Here?"

"Here."

"How many men do you have? Of your own?"

"Twenty-five hundred, a few hundred of them veterans. You?"

"Five thousand. Total. When my last regiments arrive. And that's counting every cook." Ricketts shook his head. "Don't care for the odds. Good position?"

"The best defensive line between Frederick and Washington. You'll see it, come first light. Meanwhile, Colonel Ross can guide any more troops who come in, he knows the ground."

"And your objective? In making a stand?"

Wallace fought a yawn and lost, but there was no point apologizing. "Three things: First, I want to know for sure whether Early's on his way to Washington, or if he's headed for Baltimore, after all. That drives every subsequent decision. Second, I want to push aside the curtain and find out how many men he's really got. I mean, good Lord, he's marched all the way from Lynchburg, and no one's certain what his force consists of." Wallace tried to shake off the weariness gripping him, to speak cogently, urgently. "Third, if his objective *is* Washington, I want to hold him up as long as possible, give Grant time to transfer a corps or two and save the city."

Ricketts stared straight into his eyes. The fellow was cold as an iron bar in January. He considered Wallace's words, then asked, "You have a plan? That includes my men?"

Wallace nodded, escaping his weariness in a burst of enthusiasm. "And excellent ground, truly splendid! Since your men began coming in, I've shifted my green troops to the right, to cover the fords to the north and the bridge on the Baltimore road. It's a great deal of ground, but the terrain's steep this side of the river, and there aren't many fords up there. I'm gambling that Early's *not* going up that way."

Struggling to keep his own eyes steady, he met Ricketts' gaze again. "*Your* men will concentrate here, as my left wing. There's a covered bridge on the Washington road—you could see it from the porch, if we had some moonlight—and an open-deck rail bridge off to its right. Early intends to cross right here, I'm convinced of it."

He raised his hands in excitement, as if about to grip Ricketts by the coat. "There's good ground to anchor the left of your position, I think you'll like it. Open fields, but higher than the north bank, you'll have the advantage." A nervous smile overtook his features and he realized his hands were shaking. "You'll see it all at first light, I'll show you everything. I believe we can give them a time of it, General Ricketts. We'll give them a time. . . ."

"I have no guns," Ricketts said with a first, faint hint of emotion. "I was ordered to leave my artillery at Petersburg. I'm a damned artilleryman, and I don't have a single battery." He shook his head, becoming human at last. "Don't have one ambulance, either. Or my field surgeries. I have to believe we were meant to fill up the Washington forts. Before things came undone." He glanced down at the planks and looked up again. "What kind of artillery do *you* have?"

"One battery, six three-inch rifles. And one good howitzer."

Under Ricketts' whiskers, his mouth formed an acid smile. "Early will hardly be able to claim you had an unfair advantage. Cavalry?"

"Five squadrons of the Eighth Illinois. They're well officered. And some mounted infantry."

"So . . . *if* my entire division closes . . . we'd have seventy-five hundred men, at most, a third of them green as shamrocks, with no artillery to speak of and not enough cavalry to picket a field latrine."

"I do have ammunition stacked. And a train waiting back of the hill to take off the wounded. And we have the river to our front, it's really a splendid position."

"And your position is how many miles long?"

"Three. Approximately. A bit more."

Ricketts sighed. "General Wallace . . . we haven't the chance of two mice facing a regiment of cats. You realize this is madness?"

"Yes. I do."

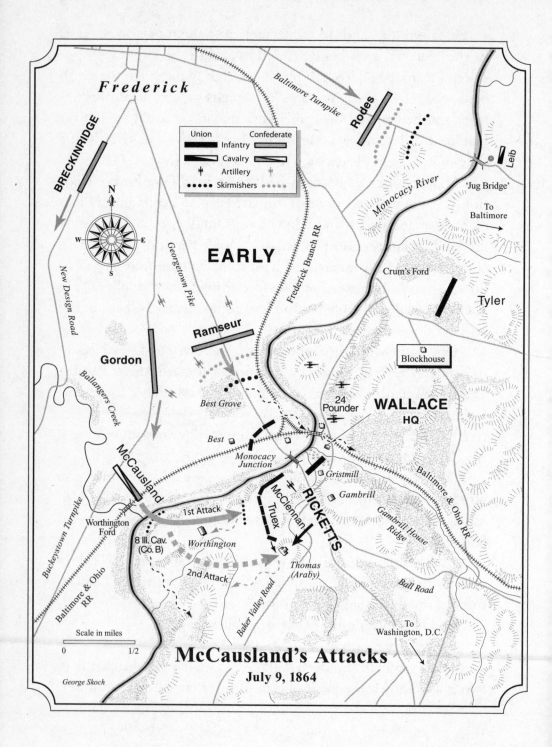

Frederick

Union
- Infantry
- Cavalry
- Artillery
- Skirmishers

Confederate
- Infantry
- Cavalry
- Artillery
- Skirmishers

Baltimore Turnpike

Rodes

Leib

'Jug Bridge'

To Baltimore

Monocacy River

BRECKINRIDGE

N
W E
S

New Design Road

EARLY

Georgetown Pike

Frederick Branch RR

Crum's Ford

Tyler

Ramseur

Blockhouse

Gordon

Ballangers Creek

Best Grove

24 Pounder

WALLACE
HQ

Best

Baltimore & Ohio RR

McCausland

Monocacy Junction

Gristmill

McClennan

Gambrill

Buckeystown Turnpike

Worthington Ford

1st Attack

Truex

RICKETTS

Gambrill House Ridge

8 Ill. Cav. (Co. B)

Worthington

Thomas (Araby)

Baltimore & Ohio RR

2nd Attack

Ball Road

Baker Valley Road

To Washington, D.C.

Scale in miles

0   1/2

McCausland's Attacks

July 9, 1864

George Skoch

THREE

Amid the scents of fresh hay and charred campfires, Ricketts surveyed the battlefield Wallace had chosen. No one could have selected a better position.

Ricketts' Second Brigade stretched across the Washington road and into the rising fields on the left flank, with the river a moat to its front. In a hollow off to the right, his First Brigade awaited orders while one last regiment, the 14th New Jersey, drew rations. Wallace's green troops had been placed in strong positions to the northeast, above the river's bends, giving them every advantage that could be culled from the terrain. A victory might be impossible, but Jubal Early would face a troublesome morning.

"That's how you play a low-card hand, son," Ricketts said to an aide. "Ride down and tell Colonel Truex I want to see him."

The lieutenant touched the brow of his cap and tugged his horse about.

Ricketts wished he had his division's complement of artillery, even half of it. There were excellent fields of fire to the northwest, where the Rebels appeared to be taking their merry time. Skirmishing had chipped the air for hours, but Early didn't seem in a rush to see Washington.

He'd come on, though, before the morning was out. And many a man would have supper with the Devil.

Guarded of speech, Ricketts had not told Wallace how bad things were. When he embarked at City Point, it had been unclear whether other troops would follow. The haste and confusion had been appalling, and he had limited himself to his own concerns, seeing his two brigades marched aboard their vessels. He could only hope that the rest of the corps was on its way to Washington.

The carelessness on every part had been so pronounced, it bordered on frivolity. How on earth could Early have arrived within forty or fifty miles of Washington, shooting his way north for two hundred miles, without anybody in the government or the whole damned Army noticing? Now here *he* was, James B. Ricketts, lately the proud and aging captain of Battery I, 1st U.S. Artillery, a brigadier general leading men whose spirits were as badly worn as their shoes, soldiers exhausted by two months of grisly fighting and faced with odds as close to hopeless as any in his experience.

Well, Ricketts thought, I've been on the edge of hopelessness before, and God bless Frances. He'd been shot four times and abandoned at Bull Run, and his wife had been told he was dead. On learning that he was alive, if barely, and a prisoner, she had bullied her way through the lines and past Jeb Stuart, a friend from their Rio Grande days, to find him in a blood-swabbed, fetid house where she had been greeted by a pile of limbs. His wife had fought the surgeons to save his leg, then traveled along on the prison train to Richmond, insisting on remaining by his side, first in the filthy, sickness-ridden poorhouse, then in Libby Prison, which was worse, begging food to nourish him and accepting bread from a woman of the streets . . . only to be told that he had been selected for execution in retaliation for the impending hanging of Southern privateers.

Frances had gone to war, threatening to shame the Confederacy before the great, wide world should it execute a badly wounded, honorable officer. Frances, not Jefferson Davis, had won that fight. On the cusp of 1862, he had been exchanged, with his wife threadbare, ill, and beaming by his side when they reached Fairfax.

His Frances, his Fanny, his champion. It saddened him immensely that this proud, determined woman, a distant cousin and far prettier than his own looks merited, tormented herself in the belief that he had never quite gotten over his first wife's death. And the worst of it was, she was right: Harriet pulsed through his dreams, if he willed it or not.

He had learned as a boy that fairness was foreign to humanity, and nothing in his past had proven otherwise. He had known joy, but never had met justice, not even in sleep. And this day, here in Maryland, promised to be unfair, unjust, and hopeless.

The thing was not to let on.

Anyway, hopelessness lay at the heart of soldiering, did it not? And the odds had been even worse for Wallace before his boys arrived, yet the fellow still had been willing to make a stand. Ricketts could hardly do less.

If Early's graybacks wanted a fight, he intended to give them one. He only hoped to be as stalwart as Frances.

Hoofbeats. Clattering over the road and pounding a cut field. Trailed by a rider bearing his brigade flag, Truex followed Ricketts' aide up the slope. Truex had spunk and thrived on hardship, a man who never drank too much or quit a fight too early.

For a last few moments, Ricketts looked away. He no longer thought of wives, alive or dead, but scanned past the low ground and a gristmill to the covered bridge on the left and the railroad bridge on the right, the day's great prizes. Blockhouses guarded the railroad bridge, one on each side of the river, and Wallace had reinforced them with rifle pits, digging still more defenses to shield the road bridge. Tough chewing for Early's boys, if the green troops stood their ground.

Truex reined in his horse. Despite the heat, he wore riding gloves.

"Orders, sir?"

"Men ready?"

"Fourteenth's still drawing. Won't be long."

Ricketts nodded. "Had yourself a good look at things?"

"Not bad ground, sir. If we had the entire corps . . ."

"We don't." Ricketts waved off a fly. "Just hope that our last regiments arrive."

"Rebs don't seem to be feeling an excess of vigor."

"Give them time." Ricketts considered the tiny figures in the fields—not quite a ridge—across the river. He put the range at just under a mile. "They'll bring up artillery soon, that's what they're waiting on. Try to blast us out and spare their men." He slapped a hand at the fly again, only to have another join the fray. "They don't want to make a frontal attack, not across that river. No matter the odds." He looked at Truex. The colonel had a gambler's face, with noncommittal features but quick eyes. "What would you do, Bill? If you were Early?"

"Flank us," Truex said without hesitation. "Press our front sufficiently to fix us, find a ford on our left, and turn our position."

And that will cost them time, Ricketts told himself. Wallace's vision was downright infectious: They were fighting the hands on a pocket watch, the patch of dirt was meaningless.

"And that's why I haven't placed you in the line," Ricketts told the colonel. "The real fight isn't going to be down at that bridge." He pointed leftward, past a fine brick house and into the high fields where his blue ranks ended. Rain-starved corn moved faintly in the breeze, while wheat shocks stood like pegs in neighboring fields. Another house, less grand, could be glimpsed not quite a mile past the mansion, masked by trees above the hidden river. "Those fields. They find a ford, they'll come across those fields, hollering like devils."

"I should deploy a skirmish line up there," Truex said.

Ricketts shook his head. "Not yet. Let General Wallace play his hand, he hasn't done badly. We'll call trumps, if we have to." He smiled, aware that his smiles were meager things. "Besides, we both could be wrong. Wouldn't be the first time two old Mexican pistols misfired."

The situation did remind him of Buena Vista, though. Holding Rinconada Pass with two guns, against impossible odds. He'd been infernally proud of himself, although he wasn't the glittering sort who gained brevets. But the carnage that had seemed immense in Mexico was almost quaint compared to the bloodletting now.

"If I may ask . . . ," Truex began in a careful tone, "what do you make of General Wallace, sir? Really?"

Ricketts took the question seriously, since it was one he had been asking himself.

"More guts than sense," he said abruptly, as if the words had escaped against his will. "More guts than common sense." He nodded. "And that may be precisely what we need."

Yet it was clear that Wallace had been out of the war for years, unaware of the viciousness that marked the fighting now, blind to the fact that the best men had been killed and the rest rubbed raw. Ricketts himself had only returned to field command in March, after another ugly convalescence climaxed by distasteful court-martial duty, and the division he had been handed was unreliable. He'd done his best to stiffen the men, but the Wilderness had not added to their laurels. Nor had Spotsylvania. Somehow, though, their performance at Cold Harbor, amid that slaughter, had been superb. He had learned through carnage that he led some splendid regiments—especially in Truex's brigade—but that others might not bear up under a hammering.

Amid the high fields across the river, explosive billows of dust rose over the Pike. The sudden clouds differed notably from the long, soft plumes that trailed infantry columns.

"There they are," Ricketts said.

Hand extending the brim of his hat, Truex squinted.

"Artillery," Ricketts explained. "Can't see them yet, but those are guns, you can bet your shoulder straps." He watched as the lead team appeared on a crest, tiny with distance, charging headlong down the Pike. Changing direction sharply, the horses swept rightward into a field, revealing the limber and gun they dragged. Ricketts could almost hear the crack of the whip and the driver's cries, the slap and jangle of harness—he all but smelled bronze and iron, powder and sweat. The remainder of the battery followed after, cannon bouncing over the furrows and caissons lifting their wheels one at a time, like dogs hoisting their hind legs.

"Twelve-pounders," Ricketts said. "You can tell by the way they handle." Then he added, "I damned well wish they were mine."

9:15 a.m.
Best farm

Stephen Dodson Ramseur handed the message to a sergeant. Possessed of an unerring sense of direction, the man had proven a more reliable courier than any officer.

"Get this to General McCausland. Tell him the need is pressing."

As soon as he spoke the last words, Ramseur regretted them. The written message conveyed all, and it wasn't the place of a sergeant to add emphasis.

McCausland had to find a ford, and soon. Attacking that covered bridge headlong would be criminal folly, unless the assault combined with a flanking attack. The whole cursed army would soon be brought to a standstill if McCausland's efforts failed, but Ramseur feared he'd bear the blame himself.

The sergeant rode off without a salute or fuss. His horse threw dust and pebbles toward the staff.

To Ramseur's left, a section of Napoleons opened fire. His horse quivered at the first blasts, then stilled again. Positioned in the high fields, the guns could just range the blue lines across the river. Militia those blue-bellies might well be, but someone had tucked them into a grand position—smack astride the Washington road and right above the river. Even the sorriest Yankees could exact a scoundrel's price, if a man was fool enough to rush them.

Nothing had gone right. Lilley's Brigade had started late and the passage through Frederick and southward had been slow, with Yankee cavalry needling the advance. Now this: Instead of a handful of Federals at the bridge, it looked to be as much as a brigade drawn up for a fight.

He had sent two reports back to Early, but had yet to receive a reply. Early had seemed to favor him of late, but the old man's caprices could alter in a blink. If the city fathers of Frederick had put him in a foul mood, Early might even relieve him on the spot.

He needed McCausland's horsemen to get across that river.

10:00 a.m.
Gambrill House Ridge

General Tyler isn't being pressed," Ross announced, dismounting. "Nothing but skirmishing on the right flank, sir. Lighter than down here." The aide pawed sweat from the tip of his nose. "General Tyler described the situation as 'a flirtation, not a courtship.'"

"Let's hope there isn't an unexpected seduction," Wallace said. He still worried over the steadiness of the Home Brigade men, should the Rebels attack in strength. He could not afford to lose the Baltimore road, his only realistic line of retreat. And a retreat was bound to be forced on him at some point, he had no illusions. "No trouble at the fords?"

"No, sir. I rode the entire line. Poison ivy and water snakes, not a whole lot else. The men are ready, though."

Wallace nodded. "Early has no interest in Baltimore. But General Tyler can't let down his guard."

A round of solid shot thumped onto the hillside, bounding past Wallace like a child's ball refined in Hell. Wary of seeming fearful to those around him, he did not gee-up his horse to move out of range.

An odd thought made him smile, though: If a shot injured the horse he rode, would he be liable, or would the Federal Government? Matters had been so upended that in his haste to reach the junction days before, he had taken the train, leaving his mount, and had rented a gelding from a Frederick stable. The animal wasn't bad as such beasts went, but it did seem queer to go to war on a rented horse.

A shell burst down in the marsh, making a splash but doing no damage. Soldiers cursed, as soldiers always did.

The initial Confederate gunnery had caused a number of casualties, but the men were under better cover now, in their rifle pits or shielded by the terrain. And Captain Alexander was putting up a fair duel with his little guns, while the howitzer was giving the Rebs a time of it.

Across the river, puffs of smoke marked the fields where men were doing their best to kill each other, a famine-thin blue line holding Rebel skirmishers at a distance.

By Wallace's reckoning, Early had squandered three hours.

A party of horsemen cantered across the road, coming toward him, their multi-hued banners teased out by their pace. The spectacle put Wallace in mind of the storybooks about knights that had brightened his childhood.

His mood had been much improved by three hours of sleep.

As Ricketts drew close, Wallace said, "Well, General, the Rebs don't seem too anxious to cross our river."

Ricketts bent his big torso toward him. "Would you be? They're not fools."

"What do you think they'll do?" Wallace asked.

Ricketts shrugged. "Come around a flank."

Wallace nodded. "Our left, I expect. Seems plain."

"I'm sure they're prowling around right now, figuring out where they can cross."

"There's a ford, a fairly good one," Ross put in. "Down behind the Worthington place. Clendenin has one of his companies guarding it."

"*Watching* it," Wallace corrected. He turned to Ricketts again. "Best we can do, given our numbers. Provide some warning, if they come that way."

Wallace felt anew how terribly few soldiers he had, even with Ricketts' division fallen from Heaven. He suspected that all those present were thinking the same thing.

Ricketts leaned toward him again. "Sir, I'd like to push out a skirmish line, a heavy one. Between that brick house and the far one. Can't quite see the one I mean from here."

"All right. Good. Just hold back a strong reserve, we're going to need it. Any word on your other regiments?"

Ricketts' face darkened, answering the question without speaking. Wallace realized again how weary he remained, despite those three magnificent hours of sleep, and how easily he might slip into foolishness. Of course, he would have been informed immediately had a telegraph message come in. And trains didn't slip past quietly. It had been a fool's question.

It promised to be a long day.

As Ricketts saluted and turned back to his duties, a rider galloped over the fields they'd discussed a moment before. He was coming from the direction of the ford.

10:30 a.m.
Worthington Ford

Tiger John" McCausland gave each of his regimental commanders a no-tomfoolery look.

"Here now," he said, settling his attention on Jimmy Cochran of the 14th Virginia Cavalry. "How many Yankees down there? And no tall tales." He gestured toward the contested ford, which lay behind a lip of land and below a fringe of trees. The firing was just intense enough to annoy him.

"Billy Vincent says a troop. Maybe two."

"Damn it, Jimmy. Handful of Yankees? Holding up your boys?"

"They're tucked into a runt forest. Maybe half dismounted. With those repeaters. Didn't want to squander—"

"You get on back down there. Dismount your regiment, every man. You open on them from left and right of the ford, but leave the main approach open. Put all the fire on 'em you can, you pin those blue-belly sumbitches to the ground." He turned to Henry Bowen of the 22nd Virginia. "Hen, you form up in column of fours again. We're going over this here bump of dirt and straight across that ford. With sabers."

Bowen started, an almost imperceptible contraction of the

muscles, but McCausland noted it. "And I'm going with you. I am sick and tired of all this dawdling. We are going across that ford, and those blue-bellies are going to run like fire in a cotton barn when we do. Then we are going to get up on that high ground and sweep on over those Sunday-best militia boys. And the infantry can lick our tails and call it molasses."

Finishing up with Ferguson and Tavenner, he said, "Milt, the Sixteenth will follow the Twenty-second. W.C., your Seventeenth follows after." He fixed his hard stare back on Cochran, who had disappointed him. "Soon as W.C. clears the ford, you come right on. I want everybody up atop that hill, fast as man and beast can cover the ground. Rally at that high house you saw back a ways. Get your men fixed, and meet me in the yard." He glanced around a last, fierce time. "Quick now. Go."

Down by the ford, the skirmishing had a determined sound. McCausland meant to finish it up. Right quick.

The colonels remounted and rode for their regiments. Still a thousand men in the brigade, McCausland figured. Plenty to deal with the uppity militia blocking the army's way.

Foot in the left stirrup and right leg swinging over his stallion's haunches, it struck him again that justice was about to be served up hot. Forever berating the cavalry, Early had become just about intolerable. Whether they performed splendidly or poorly made no difference. And McCausland, who had made his name as an infantryman, only to be thrust into cavalry command, was not about to be shunted aside like a poor relation. He'd had enough of playing second fiddle at the Virginia Military Institute, where he'd been junior to mad Tom Jackson on the mathematics faculty, both of them blackboard soldiers teaching the indifferent sons of the gentry. Today, he'd been meant to "support" Early's latest pet, Dod Ramseur, a pup in scarlet ribbons. Well, Early was going to see who could churn the butter.

He'd *earned* his nickname, Tiger John, and was not about to be mocked by any man living.

As quickened with excitement as their riders, the pawing horses of the 22nd Virginia hardly looked like thoroughbreds, but they'd do. And the faces of the men, brown as walnut oil, had been cut to planes of bone by long campaigning.

Positioning himself just beside the head of the column, McCausland looked at Bowen and drew his blade.

"Sabers!"

"Draw sabers," Bowen hollered. The command echoed down through the captains and lieutenants commanding the companies.

The rasp and clang of steel rang loud as a foundry. On the whole, McCausland preferred pistols for an attack. But he sensed in his gut that a regiment charging with sabers would panic the handful of Yankees across the ford. He didn't want a drawn-out fight, he just wanted them out of the way.

Pointing with his sword, he spurred his horse. Hen Bowen drew alongside. They let the front fours pass.

Right on time, Jimmy Cochran's dismounts opened up, hundreds of rifles dwarfing the sound of the previous skirmishing.

Screened by trees, the head of the column turned onto the wagon track that led, that could only lead, to the ford.

"Charge!" McCausland shouted.

The foremost men did not wait for the command's repetition, but kicked their horses to life and howled like Furies. Coming to mighty, thundering life, the entire regiment took up the cry.

McCausland and Bowen rode on the left, under trees and through wild grass, not quite keeping pace.

Cochran's dismounts poured fire on the Yankees.

With another explosive yell, the lead riders burst from shade into sunlight, spurring their horses into the water, splashing madly, wet sabers gleaming as fountains of water threw rainbows. McCausland pulled up short of the bank. Bowen imitated him. Didn't want to play the fool, miss the ford and go for a swim.

The crashing and thrashing in the river seemed nearly as loud as the gunfire. Another wave of Rebel yells swept forward.

McCausland did not see a single rider fall. In moments, the first rough-clad horsemen were slapping through the mud of the far bank.

The last Yankee cavalrymen took flight, running and leaping to horse, spurring away.

The fight for the ford was over.

"Yanks won't claim any battlefield brevets from that one," Bowen said.

11:00 a.m.

Boundary fence of the Thomas and Worthington farms

Ricketts rode the skirmish line he'd put in behind a rail fence. The sun would bake the men, but there was no shade to be had on the killing ground. Terrain was battle's tyrant.

"Everybody down. Lie down," he called, voice firm but not harsh. "All of you lie down. And just stay ready."

Approaching a pair of officers from the 151st New York, he told them, "Dismount. Both of you. *Now.* Send your horses to the rear."

Only one man would remain mounted along the skirmish line, and that would be him.

The soldiers tucked themselves in, a field of grain behind their line and a struggling cornfield, waist-high, beyond the fence. The breeze had died and the stalks stood ragged and still. Maddened insects leapt, their world disordered. His veterans sought comfort, however brief, but clutched their rifles closely. The earth smelled of crops and heat.

Ricketts rode on, calmly, inspecting the lines of fire his men would enjoy, scanning for trick ground that might betray the surprise he meant to spring on the Confederates. When the skirmishing snapped to life down at the ford, Wallace had given him free rein to emplace his forces, and Ricketts had advanced a skirmish line whose strength was a full third of his First Brigade. The remainder of Truex's units had taken a position between the river and the brick mansion that Wallace's man, Ross, called "Araby."

Whatever the house's name, it would see its share of bloodshed before the day was out.

The obtuse angle of his main line left the men exposed to en-filading fire from the guns across the river, but nothing could be done. Again, the terrain was their master. Only his Vermonters, tucked into a swale as a reserve, were fully protected.

His skirmishers were settled in, hidden, as close to the earth as men who were not under fire ever got. Their officers knelt be-hind them, heads held below the top fence rail. He had made any man who wore a high-crowned hat remove it.

The Rebs would see one man, and that would be him.

How he wished he had just a single battery of his own! His Regular cannoneers from the 1st Artillery would have wreaked merry mischief on the Rebs. Half-bedazzled by the perfect fields of fire beyond his line, he could not stop thinking as an old red-leg, dreaming of double canister and sudden, barked commands.

Wishes were useless things.

He had followed the clash down at the ford by the noise, first the brisk skirmishing, then the sharp eruption of rifle fire, climaxed by a ruckus and wild Reb cries. As the first fleeing horsemen found the high road and galloped back along it, he warned his men not to jeer, curt when he was briefly disobeyed. He could imagine only too well what that handful of cavalrymen had faced. They'd bought what time they could.

To his rear, down by the bridges, the firing picked up. He could read it well enough not to find it worrisome, but he did spare a thought for what might happen if Early brought the full weight of his forces to bear.

No sign of it yet, thanks be to Providence.

Reversing his course along the line, he let his horse slow. He could not afford to look anxious, either to his own men or to the Rebs, when they appeared. "Just keep yourselves quiet," he told his men. "And we'll give the Johnnies a welcome they'll remem-ber. Just rest and be quiet, I'll tell you when to stand."

Ricketts felt no fear—only the usual quickening, the tightening of the muscles, and, yes, the thrill of impending battle. It was a terrible business, and this time the stakes were incalculably high. But there was a part of any true soldier that, against all reason, longed for the game to begin.

He rode past officers down on one knee. "Keep your heads down, boys. And wait for my order."

All of the faces were earnest now, the jokesters and campfire bullies as taut as the silent sorts, some praying, Ricketts was certain, and others merely bothered by the flies. These were men who had seen not only the elephant, but every hideous beast in war's menagerie. They knew what they were about. But they could not know if they would live or die in the next half hour.

He preferred setting troops in motion. Activity worked its own charms, while waiting passively led the mind astray.

Even his own thoughts were not strictly disciplined, despite the weight of command upon his shoulders. Frances intruded. And Harriet. Should this day be his last, he would leave some practical matters in disorder, burdens unfair to his present wife. But nothing could be done. Not now.

A wry smile dented the set of his face. If he was killed . . . and if the priests and parsons were right about the great beyond, be it Purgatory first, or straight to Heaven or Hell, would he be reunited forever with Harriet? Or did a subsequent marriage take precedence before the Judgment Seat? Surely Heaven would not be some sort of Mormon confederacy or a Mussulman's harem? Would Harriet still be young and fair, while he appeared old and fat? And Frances, with her enormous heart and steadfast will, deserved her due. He had married good women, better than he deserved, his greatest good fortune.

He stopped himself, coming back to the glint of sun-heated steel, of blue cloth on brown earth, of eye-burning sweat. Here and now. This day, this hour. In this field, under this sun. All of his life had aimed him toward this.

"Don't drink that canteen dry," he told a youthful soldier. "You're going to want water long before you see another well."

He sought to balance his tone between authority and bantering, something he had never fully mastered. Artillerymen did not jabber like the infantry.

"Stay down, stay down now."

When the firing ceased down at the ford, he had known it was only a matter of minutes before the Rebs came at them. He was almost surprised at their slowness. Waving off another assault of black flies, he halted his horse. Facing the house beyond the cornfield.

And there they were: emerging from the trees, men who had become his mortal enemies because of pride and political skullduggery, darkies and busybodies. Most of the Rebs were on foot. Those who rode soon dismounted.

The officers were easy to spot: They were the only men who remained in the saddle.

Well, they wouldn't stay mounted for long.

His men could see nothing from their hides, nor could they hear much, if anything, but they tightened as one—he felt it like a sudden temperature change—sensing the approach of battle, as veterans did.

Ricketts had nothing more to say to them, not until it was time for the fateful order. He didn't want to move his lips, to appear to be giving commands, in case some Reb was eyeing him through a spyglass. Let them wonder why an old fool in a blue suit was sitting on a horse, alone in a dried-out grainfield in the heat. Just let them wonder.

And let them come on, straight through that corn, he begged of any higher power that could hear. James B. Ricketts was not much given to prayer, but he asked for help now: *Lord, let them come straight on.*

11:20 a.m.
The Worthington house yard

The men near McCausland hurried about, full of purpose but still a tad shocked at the order that there would be no horse-holders this time. Every mount was to be tied to a tree or fence, while every cavalryman in the brigade would go into battle as an infantryman. McCausland was certain that the illusion of infantry formations on their flank would be all it took to set the blue-bellies running for their mothers' teats.

He nodded at his reassembled colonels. "Brigade front. Two lines. Every flag held high—you tell your boys to wave 'em and wave 'em hard." He pointed across the cornfield. Just beyond it, a lone Yankee horseman sat watching them. Well, let him have a good look and warn his Sunday-soldiers what was coming.

Probably a few more Yankees about, he figured, vedettes out on the flank. Maybe the same turn-tails who'd run down at the ford.

"Midway through that cornfield, order your men to the double-quick. And I want them hooting and hollering. Those blue-bellies need to hear us long before they see us, let 'em think it's Doomsday and the legions of Hell are swarming." His expression turned as cold as the day was hot. "We're going to show Old Jubilee how Virginia Cavalry fight. Y'all get moving."

Three of four colonels saluted and strode toward their mounts. Only Tavenner hesitated.

"Shouldn't we send a few boys forward to scout things?" the colonel asked. "See what all might be out there?"

McCausland felt his expression turn downright cruel. "Worried about a few militia, W.C.?"

11:40 a.m.
Ricketts' skirmish line

Flags flying, God help them. Everything but a brass band. The Confederates had dressed their two ranks as if on parade, stepped their colors forward, and come straight on, every officer mounted. It was a glorious spectacle, and it was absolute folly.

Ricketts held his horse steady and kept his expression steadier. Every man along his line looked in his direction, the soldiers flat on the ground and wed to their rifles, the officers kneeling or crouching low—Ricketts was damned well going to court-martial any idiot who popped up for a look at what was coming.

And the Rebs . . . they hadn't even sent skirmishers ahead. They just prettied up those two long lines and advanced.

Their first rank marched into the corn, filling their little portion of the world with a thrashing, crashing noise that seemed to rival the artillery duel to Ricketts' rear. The flag-bearers waved their banners like frantic signalers.

One officer caught Ricketts' eye: He rode forward with one hand cocked on his hip, deigning to draw neither sword nor pistol, as disdainful as a schoolmarm catching out dunces.

The thrashing in the cornfield grew louder as the second rank entered the stalks.

Going to be an early harvest, Ricketts thought.

He knew he had them, but even so, the spectacle of their advance sent a quiver through him.

Then the dab of fear was gone again and there were only those brave, doomed lines, pushing through the crotch-covering corn, rifles held abreast now, their order disturbed by the resistance of the stalks.

He began to feel a child's impatience, yearning to order his men to their feet, to spring his surprise. He *ached* to do it. But he needed to wait until the very last moment.

And if a Reb sharpshooter dropped him first? There were plentiful reasons to shout the order immediately, with the Johnnies already in range.

Rabbits dashed under the fence and through his line, startling his waiting men. One of the creatures leapt over a sergeant's shoulders.

Just wait now, Ricketts told his men without speaking. Just wait a little longer.

The Reb officers pointed the way with lofted swords, riding before, beside, and among their men, between regiments, between ranks. Proud, such proud men. Pride had made this war, Ricketts told himself for perhaps the thousandth time. All of this death and destruction was just about pride.

One Southern voice called out and dozens of officers repeated the command. "Double-quick . . . march!"

The rustling in the cornfield swelled. The Rebs began yelling and howling. Smaller animals fled the approaching waves, field mice and distraught squirrels. A bewildered fox ran by.

He felt his soldiers clench tighter and tighter. The officers looked toward him, expressions demanding, "What the hell are you waiting for, you old fool?"

No, not demanding. Pleading.

Ricketts refused to move the smallest muscle.

He could see the names of battles embroidered on the advancing, shot-through flags, but couldn't quite read them. Faces grew distinct.

He waited, counting the seconds.

He could not see the whites of their eyes, only glittering darkness under hat brims.

He raised his hand sharply, pointing at the Rebs.

"On your feet! *Fire!*"

The officers sprang up, followed by their men. Even before his orders could be repeated, they were obeyed. The officers shouted:

"Fire! Fire! Fire! Fire! Fire!"

But these men, his men, had learned how to kill. Instead of shooting urgently and wildly, they rested their rifles on the top fence rail, taking an extra brace of seconds to aim.

When the volleys rippled out, the Confederate lines disappeared.

Riderless horses galloped in every direction. Flags drooped and fell, blanketing cornstalks. A few officers remained mounted, shouting orders. His men did their best to shoot them.

Here and there, a grayback rose and ran like hell for the farmhouse. A few stood and fired toward the fence, but too quickly, too shaken to aim. Out there, in that burnt green field, men were crawling in agony, others just skedaddling, low to the ground. Even at Cold Harbor . . . or at Spotsylvania . . . Ricketts had never seen so swift a repulse.

More Rebs were up and running now. Ricketts' men sent up a cheer, a roar. But they kept on firing, even as some hotheads leapt the fence to charge after the Rebels.

"Call those boys back!" Ricketts shouted. "Get them back here right now!"

Even as he issued the command, one of his soldiers, swift and sure, collared a staggering Rebel in midfield. Discipline left something to be desired, but enthusiasm counted, too.

Royal flush on the first hand, Ricketts told himself. More hands still to play.

11:50 a.m.
Worthington farm

Tiger John McCausland rode among his fleeing soldiers, screaming at them.

"Goddamn you, damn you, god*damn* you . . . stop your running . . . stop, goddamn you, or I'll shoot you myself."

He pointed his pistol at one man after another, but did not pull the trigger. Men fled into the grove behind the house or leapt yard fences. Some halted in the trees or sheltered behind outbuildings, but others, too many, raced back down the hill up which they'd come. A few soldiers hunted their horses, as if they expected to be allowed to ride off.

McCausland fired into the air. "I'll shoot the man who doesn't stand and fight."

The last escapees from the cornfield limped and staggered, hatless, weaponless, blood-drenched. Some of them looked at him insolently, as if to say, "Go ahead and shoot, you sonofabitch."

It only made McCausland that much angrier—regretting that he had not pulled the trigger on the unwounded men who'd behaved as craven cowards.

Hen Bowen rode up beside him. There was blood on the colonel's face, but he seemed able. Bowen's horse bled, too.

"General . . . *General McCausland* . . . they'll rally, they're just spooked . . . give them some time."

"We don't *have* any goddamned time."

"Just let me and Jimmy rally our boys, they'll be all right. W.C. and Milt are rounding up theirs."

"God*damn* it, Hen. If Early hears . . ."

"He's done a sight worse himself. Whupped by a pack of coons back of Spotsylvania." Bowen smiled grimly. "Think he'll live that down?"

McCausland was in no mood to be appeased. Yet he calmed sufficiently to lower his pistol, panting in the weariness left by fury. But when he considered the inevitable jokes about his nickname, "Old Tiger John turned out to be a house cat" and the like, rage boiled his complexion again.

"Then you damned well rally those yellow sonsofbitches. Damn them all to Hell, they're going back in."

"Just give us a little time, sir." The colonel wiped at his sweat, smearing the blood across his face. "The boys were just surprised, you know how that goes. Even the best troops lose all sense, you give them a good enough shock. They'll remember themselves and be shamed till they're mean as hornets."

"They'd damned well better be," McCausland told the regimental commander. "Because we're going to rip the living hearts out of those Yankee bastards."

Noon
Gordon's Division, south of Frederick

How's that leg getting on?" Sergeant Alderman asked Nichols.

"Tolerable, Sergeant. A sight better."

"I don't want to see you on canteen detail again. Unless I tell you to go myself. Hear?"

"Lookee there," Dan Frawley interrupted. "Jest you look. Yanks are holding on, all right. Smoke an't backed up one bit."

Lem Davis shrugged. It wasn't his fight, at least not yet. Fingering his thornbush beard, he renewed the earlier conversation. "I *still* say the finest goobers come from down in Sumter County. And I'll hear no man defy me."

"Eat some now, I had some," Tom Boyet put in.

"Think we feed 'em to the Yanks at Andersonville?" Nichols asked.

"Maybe the shells," Ive Summerlin said.

As if by mutual compact, the sprawled and sitting men looked across the river again, pleased to have the rare chance to sit out a battle and watch.

"I don't see any real fussing," Ive offered.

"That there was my point, what I said." Frawley took off his straw hat. The rim looked mule-et. His long red hair appeared cooked, like it had started out maybe brown and boiled up in the heat. He wiped his forehead with a big, scarred hand. "Nary a man seems hurried worth the mention, just picking and pecking. End up camping right here tonight, things don't soon start to going." He considered the prospect. "Tad far to fetch water." He placed his hat back atop his roasted skin.

Sergeant Alderman slapped at a fly bothering his neck. "Don't get too far ahead of yourselves, boys. I expect we'll be eating dust again, headed for Washington. Once they stop their fool play over there."

Down where the hidden river had to be, black smoke rose, a contrast to the paler smoke of rifle fire.

"Something's burning," Tom Boyet said.

"Yanks are smart," Lem Davis said, "they'll burn themselves any bridges fit to light."

"Might be that," Boyet agreed. He was the smallest of them, but for Nichols. Made tight, though.

"Time to boil up another pot?" Frawley asked Alderman.

The sergeant smiled, which was ever something of an occasion. "How many pots you done cooked up with that dirt you pretend is grounds?"

The sergeant's easy tone reassured them all. This time, they might just watch other men die.

Nichols had found the talk an oddity as his brethren observed the battle, calculating its course from rising smoke, the noise of the firing, and the occasional glimpse of troops. There had been a good fuss on the right, when a burst of gray smoke had risen above a fringe of trees on the high ground, with plenty of shooting to go along as fixings, but that hadn't lasted five minutes. The rest of the doings just sounded like more skirmishing, the rifle noise going up and down, without a muchness of guns to give things a shake. His comrades had commented on the fighting as calmly as if sizing up hogs at an auction, almost uncaring about who had the advantage. It was as if they felt duty-bound to be fair, like a prize-fight judge come in on the train from Atlanta. They didn't cheer on their own kind particularly, or damn the Yankees like revival preachers. Lem and Dan, Ive and Tom, they just took it all in, appreciating the finer points of the scrap, like a town man savoring a fat store-bought cigar.

Nichols had prayed another selfish prayer, the kind you weren't supposed to send to the Lord. He asked that they truly be allowed to rest this day, that just this once other men might bear the burden. His leg remained swollen and discolored, black, purple, and jaundice yellow, although the skin was a little less tight and the lump seemed smaller, if hardened. He had asked Elder Woodfin, the regiment's chaplain, to look it over the night before, since surgeons weren't to be trusted. They had prayed together, and Elder Woodfin had assured him that his leg would be fine.

Still hurt, though. And his new shoes had not been a perfect blessing, not even after he cut his toes free from their prisons.

But he'd marched all the way and meant to keep on going. No man would call him a skulker, now or ever.

"Yes, sir," Lem Davis said, slow-voiced and pawing his beard.

"Those Yankee boys are burning themselves a bridge. That's old wood smoking."

"Could be a field caught fire," Tom Boyet said. But he was a town man.

"Ain't no field. That's wood smoke," Ive Summerlin seconded. Ive's voice remained sharp at the edges. There had been no word of his brother.

As the firing lulled again, Lem Davis took up a scrape of dirt and let it sift through his fingers. "Grant 'em the drought, and it still ain't the soil back home." His eyes left them. Thinking on that farm that was no good to him now, Nichols figured. And on that young wife dead.

Just to be contrary, Dan Frawley told him, "Seems right fine to me. Even better, back on that farm yesterday."

The heat pressed down on their words as heavily as it weighed upon their bodies. Dan tended to the coffee. Nichols didn't want himself a cup, but looked forward to it anyway. Drinking coffee together kept things right.

Lieutenant Mincy wandered over. The man had a nose for coffee sharp as a patteroller's hound.

"Why, if'n it isn't Lieutenant Mincy!" Frawley called. "Any sign of those famous Yankee rations we heard been captured? Officers eat 'em all up?"

A decent-natured man most all the time, Dan was tetchy about the way officers grabbed up captured vittles. Officers had to pay for their food from the commissary, so they didn't miss an opportunity to eat for free at Abe Lincoln's expense. Sometimes there was a plenty to go around, other times there wasn't.

That was a plain fact. But it was another fact, and every man knew it, that General Evans, a perfect Christian or nigh unto one, never took more than his share, and rarely that much.

"That coffee boiling?" Mincy asked.

"No, Lieutenant," Lem teased, "that's possum stew. Just a little thinned out."

Dan was bewitched by the thought of those captured rations,

though. He was a big man, plow-horse big, with an appetite near
sinful. "Wouldn't do a man any harm, get a powerful meal in his
belly," he told them all, closing his eyes and tucking back a strand
of that clotted red hair. His voice took on the reverence due only
to thoughts of salvation, not this earth. "Tin or two of Yank sardines, some cheese. And biscuits, place of crackers. With real drip-
pings. And meat hasn't yet been salted down and don't war agin'
a man's jaw. Wouldn't mind none where I found it, neither."

"We'll be marching long before a good feed comes along," Alderman said sharply, spoiling the tone. There was a rusty nail be-
twixt him and Mincy, who had been lifted up from third sergeant.
No one really begrudged him the promotion, not even Alderman,
really. A brave man, if a thirsty one, Mincy had been wounded
twice—right bad at Gettysburg—but came on back for more. But
every man needed a bone to gnaw, and Alderman's bone was Mincy.

Food, real food, had savored up in every mind, thanks to Dan's
dreaming. Lord, though, Nichols thought, wouldn't it be fine to
share out a big, fat ham among my brethren? Wouldn't that be a
blessing?

Someday . . . if the Lord spared him . . . he was going to go
home, marry a good Christian woman, and know a hot dinner
waited for him every single day for the rest of his life.

General Gordon rode across a near field, with General Evans
at his side and their aides keeping their distance. Usually, each man
greeted the troops he passed, Gordon erect and nodding slightly,
a kingly man, a Joshua, and Evans smiling and waving, an expression on his face just short of shyness. Today, though, they just rode
on by, Gordon stern as a Patriarch confronted by Sin Incarnate, as
Elder Woodfin put it, and General Evans looking troubled as Job.

Job had three daughters, Nichols remembered. That always
stuck in his mind. Jemima, Kezia, and . . . Nichols found he could
not recall the third name, which troubled him greatly, for he prided
himself on his knowledge of the Good Book. It dogged him wicked,
that missing name. But he did recall the next verse, which began,

"And in all the land were no women found *so* fair as the daughters of Job." Nichols always wondered what Jew girls looked like.

Such pondering was meant for another day, though. He'd observed General Gordon enough times now to recognize that impatient-of-the-fool-world look he took on. It meant that Shadrach, Meshach, and Abednego were headed back into that Fiery Furnace soon enough, and a man had better pray that the Lord felt merciful.

FOUR

July 9, 12:30 p.m.
Gambrill House Ridge

From his vantage point on the high ground, Wallace stared at the burning bridge. He had not wanted it put to the torch so soon, merely readied. His order either had been misunderstood or had been flawed—a possibility he could not discount, given his weariness.

No matter the fault, it was his responsibility, and he accepted it. He long had believed that the lowest thing an officer could do was to blame his subordinates for his mistakes and failures. He had seen enough of that out west, under Halleck.

The worst of it was that more than two hundred infantrymen, a mix of raw Home Brigade men and a detachment of Ricketts' Vermonters, were all but cut off on the other side, their only path to safety the open deck of the rail bridge.

Nor did he want them to panic and quit the fight. They were buying time cheaply, measured against the great scale of the war. He understood, full well, that it didn't seem much of a bargain to the men in combat along that rail embankment or defending the blockhouse, but they were doing heroic work in a hard hour. He hoped the veterans would prop up the morale of the Home Brigade soldiers sufficiently to keep them potting Confederates.

They had done surprisingly well thus far, repelling every probe, as well as an attack that came sneaking along the river. But he needed them to buy a bit more time. For him, for Washington.

The bridge was an inferno now, flames peaking and timbers

crashing. The men who set the wheat shocks to fire the bridge had done a proper job.

One more problem for Early.

Not that Wallace lacked problems of his own. It had been a terrible hour. Even before some enthusiast set the bridge alight, bad news had tumbled over him. First, the telegrapher fled, cutting his communications. Then, when the first wounded men were carried back to the evacuation train, the locomotive was nowhere to be found. The engineer had driven off at the first cannonade. Next, the howitzer, his only heavy artillery piece, had been fouled by a nervous cannoneer dropping in the shot before loading the powder. Despite every effort, the gun remained useless and likely to stay that way. And the Johnnies continued to deploy additional batteries, keeping up a relentless bombardment.

Ricketts had done splendidly, though, repelling the first significant attack. But Early was just getting started, and those high fields would allow Reb numbers to tell.

Grateful for Ricketts—immensely so—he applied himself to shifting his meager reserves, dispatching staff men to trouble spots, and disbursing ammunition with largesse—it wasn't the time to be thinking like a bookkeeper.

He stilled his horse and drew out his pocket watch. It ran a bit fast, but Wallace was pleased to see the hands marking twelve forty. He had stolen six precious hours from his enemy. If he could hold three hours more, Early would have lost the best of the day.

Why wasn't Early pressing harder? Why?

1:15 p.m.
Best farm

Ramseur knew he was about to taste some bitter medicine. He only wondered how large the dose would be.

Early looked hot as a Tredegar furnace. Chawing, spitting, and glaring. Usually, the army commander unleashed a barrage of profanity the instant he faced a man who had disappointed him. But Early only spit and stared hot lead, interrupting himself with glances across the river, working his cud of tobacco as though grinding a living thing to a painful death.

Quiet as Presbyterians on Sunday, the staff officers about kept a wary distance.

Desultory skirmishing continued in the low fields, by the rail embankment and river, and the guns kept up their bombardment of the Yankees, but it all seemed weak-loined and feeble to Ramseur now. And the devilish thing was that an aide had just delivered a letter from his wife that he ached to read: With a child on the way, her frailty had become worrisome.

At last, Early spit out his entire chaw, a monstrous clump, and said, "God almighty, Ramseur, why the hell aren't we over that little creek?"

"General Early, the Yankee position is—"

"I didn't ask you about the damned Yankee position. I read your messages. And I've got eyes in my head. I asked you why we're not across the river. *And* you let them burn that goddamned bridge. . . ." He turned to General Breckinridge, who had ridden over with him. "Ever feel you been pissed on by your own dog?"

Ramseur tried again. "Sir, General McCausland sent a message not ten minutes ago. He's preparing to attack again. He's certain he can sweep the Federals away."

"Ha!" Early said. The pitch of his voice went higher, near to a screech: "McCausland couldn't take a shit without being led to the outhouse."

Twisting his bent spine, Early demanded his field glasses from an aide. But he had not looked through the lenses for a full minute before he handed—almost threw—the binoculars back to the captain.

"Can't see worth a damn from up here." He bobbed his head toward Ramseur. "That's your damned problem. You're not close enough to see a goddamned thing." And to Pendleton: "Sandie, stay here with this gussied-up flock of geese passes for a staff." He pointed to the aide who bore his binoculars, a new addition whose name he could not recall. "You ride on with me." Turning again, he said, "And you, General Breckinridge. You come along. And you, Ramseur."

"Where are you going, sir?" Pendleton asked. "In case I need to find you?"

Early snorted. "Not so damned far." He pointed. "Just to that cracked-open barn down there. See if we can't find the battle."

Ramseur reached for Early's bridle. "Sir, that barn's within range of Yankee sharpshooters. Their artillery shot our men out of it."

Early glared at him. "Hell with Yankee artillery. I can't see, I can't command. I can't command, I might as well go home to Rocky Mount and drink my fill of Brother Cantwell's whiskey." He kicked his horse into motion. Then he yelled back, "Flags stay here. Just get in my goddamned way, all you're good for."

For all his age and deformities, Early could ride. He galloped down through the fields at a pace Ramseur found hard to match. Breckinridge lagged behind and seemed content to catch up when he could.

They weren't in front of the barn more than a few seconds before bullets started hunting them. Early pretended he didn't notice. Determined to show his own mettle, Ramseur played along. But his thoughts strayed to his wife and the child she carried.

"Them glasses," Early said.

His aide handed him the binoculars.

As he scanned the enemy position across the river, Early let his horse nose trampled hay. The army commander grunted now and again, stopping once to claw at his tobacco-juice-stained beard before raising the glasses again.

"Smart," he said. "Give 'em that."

He moved the glasses along to the right. Then he stopped, straightening his humped back so abruptly that Ramseur expected to hear a mighty crack.

"God almighty," Early said. "Those are Sixth Corps flags." He lowered the glasses and fixed his attention on Ramseur. "And you didn't even know. Did you?"

Ramseur said nothing.

Early took on his most sarcastic look and spoke, loudly, to Breckinridge: "Didn't even know he's facing Sixth Corps boys, when all he had to do was goddamned look."

For an ugly stretch, silence gripped the generals. Despite the shot and shell, each man held still.

Ever the politician, Breckinridge tried out his make-peace voice on Early: "Doesn't look like more than a brigade."

"Wherever there's a brigade, there's a damned division."

Early plunged into activity. Tossing the field glasses back to the aide, he told him, "Ride like merry hell back to Colonel Pendleton. Tell him General Rodes needs to give them a push on the Baltimore road, take him some prisoners. I want to know if we've got Sixth Corps boys there, too. You understand me?"

The aide dug his spurs into his horse's flanks.

"Ramseur, you get back to that clapped-up multitude of yours and start pressing hard on those buggers this side of the river, just clear 'em out. Get your paws on that railroad bridge, at least."

Ramseur nodded.

"General Breckinridge," Early continued, "I want *you* to get a division across whatever ford McCausland stumbled on by whatever God-given miracle occurred and finish up with those bluebelly sonsofbitches. Before McCausland loses the whole damned Confederacy while we're here tugging on our willies."

"Yes, sir," the former vice president said.

"Which division of yours is closest?" Early demanded, just as an artillery shell smashed into the barn, showering the generals with hay.

"Gordon's," Breckinridge said, coughing.

1:45 p.m.
Worthington farm

After letting each of his colonels take their turn, Tiger John Mc-Causland peered through the upstairs window a last time. He was furious at himself for his earlier haste—had he only had the wits to climb the farmhouse stairs before ordering his attack, he would have seen the Yankees lying in wait, plain as could be.

"Look at that," he said, although his shoulders blocked the view, "just you look. I don't care if they're Sixth Corps troops, they barely have enough men to reach that brick house. Line's as skinny as a starving cat, and the flank's in thin air."

"Boys are ready to go back in," Hen Bowen offered. "Hopping mad. Way I told you, sir." He tut-tutted himself. "Almost pity those blue-bellies."

"Don't."

McCausland took a last hard look, then turned from the panorama to the colonels. "We're going to work around them. Keep the men hidden, behind that bump of a hill off to the right. Hen, you lead the way, pick us a jump-off point. Same order of regiments for the attack. Hit 'em like a hammer, turn their left, and keep going. No parading, come over the crest at the double-quick. Get on 'em fast as we can. And skirt that damned cornfield." He looked around at the sweat-faced men. Bowen had washed off the blood he'd worn with well water. They all looked ready, if sobered.

Early would *not* scorn the cavalry today.

"Have your men head straight for that big brick house, both sides of it. Go!"

2:00 p.m.
Thomas farm

Ricketts ached to hear a train or to see his last two and a half regiments come marching along the road. He needed every man, but remained shy a good fifteen hundred of those he'd promised

Wallace. Even five hundred . . . three hundred . . . would have been as welcome as Christmas to a child.

Another Confederate battery opened across the river, thickening the air with its shot and shell. The impacts seemed almost constant now, with Reb cannon firing on them from various angles. He had ordered his men to lie down, but there was nothing else that he could do for them. The line Truex's brigade had been forced to occupy, from the yard of the brick house down to the river bluff, was exposed to the enemy guns for most of its length. And the only consolation—a grim one—was the thought that if he were commanding the Rebel artillery, there'd be a great deal more damage.

Truex met him by the gates of the lane that led up to the mansion.

"Sir . . . I need more men. At least a few hundred. My left's dangling."

"For God's sakes, Bill, I don't *have* more men." He almost added, "And you know it." But fewer words were always better than more.

Ricketts had already stripped his Second Brigade of all the companies he thought safe to remove from the river line . . . although he suspected he'd call up the rest before long. There simply were not enough soldiers. Too much ground, not enough men: the defender's eternal complaint.

"You'll just have to do what you can," he told the colonel.

Truex nodded, touched two fingers to his hat brim, and spurred his mount back up the shaded lane. Explosive shells bracketed the mansion's outbuildings as soldiers hauled laden stretchers down the slope.

The fragrance of early harvests had been smothered by the stink of powder and men.

Ricketts led his staff party up the lane before Truex's dust had settled. Obliged to see things himself. That was yet another constant dilemma, the need to balance control of his entire division with the need to be close enough to the point of decision.

There was much to be said for being a grizzled captain in charge of a single battery.

He reached the yard of the house just in time to see the Rebs swarm over a low hill off to the left, long lines driving for his flank at a perfect, fatal angle.

He rode for Truex, but the colonel was already acting, calling in his skirmishers from the fence that had served them so well, then riding for his flank to refuse the line.

The Rebs came on fast, no nonsense about them now.

"Hold as long as you can," Ricketts shouted as Truex galloped past.

He *needed* those missing regiments.

"Sir," an aide called out, "you're too far forward."

"*I'm* not too far forward," Ricketts snapped. "The damned Rebs are."

On they came, yelling and hooting, pausing to fire, then trotting forward again.

They caught Ricketts' flank regiments just as they were realigning themselves. Men went at each other with clubbed rifles, some even with bayonets, a rarity. And fists. Fighting engulfed the mansion and the thrust was clear: The Johnnies had momentum, his own men had been caught on the wrong foot.

The racket was so extreme, there was no point in shouting. He signaled his intentions to his aide and standard-bearer by pointing—quickly—down to his Second Brigade.

Robbing Peter to pay Paul, he thought. And not enough coin to satisfy either one.

"Tell your colonel to re-form on the Pike," Ricketts shouted to a major from Truex's staff. "I'll shift the Second Brigade to support your right."

Stopping now and again to fire, his veterans withdrew down the slope that led from the house toward the junction of the Pike and a farm road. Soldiers fell, but not too many. The Rebs didn't seem to be pursuing with serious intent, whether under orders to halt or unsure of what might await them down below.

He glanced back and saw Truex rushing about, ablaze with urgency, imposing order where there, briefly, had been none.

Amid the roar and chaos, Ricketts sensed that the tide had begun to turn again.

2:20 p.m.
Gambrill House Ridge

From the hillside, Wallace watched the Confederate flank break into pieces. It wasn't even under fire, or not under much. Yet the body of men disintegrated, dispersing about the sprawling yards of the mansion, among the outbuildings, and even into the adjoining fields. As if uncertain where they were or why they had come to this place, the men who had rushed forth in impressive lines had become a mob.

He bent toward Ross to be heard. "Find Truex or Ricketts. Quick as you can. Tell them I suggest a counterattack . . . an *immediate* counterattack, with whatever troops are at hand. Aim left of the house. They're disordered, they won't hold up. But we need to hit them *now*."

The instant he realized that Wallace would say no more, Ross kicked his horse hard and galloped down into the semi-chaos of troops re-forming after their short retreat, of stragglers and wounded men, ambulatory and not, of shouted orders and ammunition boxes thrown from the backs of wagons and broken open with rifle butts, of shrieking horses and shell bursts.

Wallace longed to ride down there himself, to take direct command. He burned to do it. But he knew his place was here, where he could see most of the field and issue orders, where he could be found.

The hardest part of battle wasn't fighting.

Georgetown Pike (the Washington road)

Captain William Lanius, aide to Colonel Truex, had separated from his commander in the confusion. He was helping to re-form the 14th New Jersey when Lieutenant Colonel Ross, whom he recognized as Wallace's aide-de-camp, rode up and gasped a question.

"Where's Colonel Truex?"

"Don't know," Lanius admitted.

"You've got to find him. *I've* got to find him. Or Ricketts. Somebody. General Wallace thinks the Rebs are all in a mess. Up by that house. He recommends that Colonel Truex counterattack. Immediately."

"Yes, sir. I'll see to it."

Well, Lanius figured as Ross rode off again, better to be broken for doing too much than for doing too little. He steered his horse through the press of men to Lieutenant Colonel Hall, who was bleeding from the neck and ignoring the wound.

"Sir, General Wallace orders you to charge that house. The Rebs have nothing to them, they're played out."

Hall snorted. "Didn't have nothing to them a few minutes back." But he began shouting orders.

Lanius pushed on to the 87th Pennsylvania. Lieutenant Colonel Stahle already had his men formed up, awaiting orders.

"Colonel Stahle!" Lanius shouted. "General Wallace says take that house back now!"

2:30 p.m.
Thomas farm

They were cavalrymen, after all, that was the cursed thing. They had every bit as much spunk and fight in them as any infantry soldier, McCausland believed, but they had been trained to form up, maneuver, fight, and regroup on horseback. They could skirmish well enough dismounted, but this . . .

He rode across the fields, bellowing at stray soldiers to re-form on their colors. When he passed the skeletal semblance of a regiment, he gave them the orders he would have given infantrymen, but their understanding fell short.

They had done well, had done just fine, sweeping right over the Yankees, driving them. And then the attack had simply petered out, as if the lot of them had decided as one that it was just too risky to press on and finish the kill. And McCausland did have to admit that there was a sight more Yankees down in the swales and hollows he hadn't spied out.

But he'd had his fill of mathematics in Lexington. It was a matter of spirit now, of not giving up, of facing down the Yankees, of bluffing them right off this field.

As he neared the brick house again, he heard cheers. The wrong sort.

Yankees came swarming up the lane and through the grounds. Some of his boys were inside the mansion, sharpshooting, but as the blue-bellies closed the distance the rifles retracted from the windows and did not reappear.

Tavenner found him. "Gave them a right licking, sir."

"And now they're set to give us one. See to your men, W.C."

The realization that it would be his fault if they were beaten back just increased his fury. Determined to overwhelm the Yankees, he had put all his men on the line, had kept no reserve. And now he needed one.

He rode toward the melee around the great brick house, ready to apply his knuckles to a Federal mouth should the opportunity present itself.

"Kill them, damn you!" he shouted. "They're nothing but worthless coward Yankee bastards, kill every one of them."

2:40 p.m.
Thomas farm

Ricketts personally guided his Second Brigade's regiments—barely half of those who should have been present—into place on their new line, freeing up the First Brigade's right to advance again and complete the repulse of the Johnnies. Someone, bless him, had led a splendid countercharge, and the Rebs were going high-tail and white-tail from the brick house back across the fields, with his men cheering and shooting through the smoke drifts.

He told the brigade commander exactly how he wanted the line established, then rode up past two guns Wallace had sent and onto the high fields surrounding the brick house.

Dead men from both sides lay intermingled, the routine leavings of advance and retreat. Corpses presented a sameness, despite their odd contortions or surprised expressions. But the wounded came in a nearly endless variety, from the moaning boys he passed and the terrified pleaders, through the men who cursed the universe and their bloodied, broken limbs, to the leg-shot, spade-bearded, black-eyed Johnny who looked up as he rode by and called, "They'll come back, you nigger-loving bastard, our boys are coming back."

And they did come back, twice more, in attacks that were brave, determined, frail, and hopeless. They were dismounted cavalrymen, all of them, not infantry brigades, and Ricketts realized that all his command had just endured was little more than teasing.

His men seemed to understand that, too, and took it meanly. The last time the Rebs tried to cross those fields, they concentrated on the foolish mounted officers and shot down five.

3:00 p.m.
Worthington Ford

Nichols caught the voice of Elder Woodfin before he could make out a word the chaplain spoke. For all the thrashing and splashing up ahead, the artillery banging away on the left and the oaths of cannoneers gun-stuck in the ford, there was no mistaking the chaplain's mighty call, a bull voice that commanded the Lord's attention.

Lieutenant Colonel Valkenburg stood on the near bank, shouting to be heard. "No time to take off your shoes, men, hurry on. Bottom's rocky, anyway. Keep on moving."

Nichols had a fair admiration for most officers, but a special liking for Valkenburg, who had been kind to him once and who had done fine service in the Wilderness. Handsome fellow, too, the kind the girls liked, bad girls and the good.

Nichols hoped a girl might take to him. After this fuss was done. A good girl, in clean gingham. Who wouldn't play jokes and laugh at him, but like him rightly and truly. A fair-haired girl, if he had his druthers, who could cook and who read her Bible. The kind of girl his mother wouldn't mind and his pa would take to.

"Get along now, men. We're needed up top," Valkenburg encouraged them.

Nichols and his mess mates splashed on in, sinking knee-deep, thigh-deep, waist-deep, holding their rifles high, with cartridge pouches looped over them. The water was shock-cold, but warmed up fast, running muddy and fast enough to carry off a child, but not a man.

He felt the waters wash him. Like the Jordan.

Elder Woodfin stood atop a rock on the far bank, as if the Lord himself had planted him there, a steady hand raised to Heaven. His words rang clear now, the shouts and busy batteries no more than a frame for his pulpit voice: *"Jephthah passed over unto the children of Ammon to fight against them; and the Lord delivered them into his hands. And he smote them . . ."*

Foot tricked by a rock, Nichols stumbled. Saved by the grip of Ive Summerlin, he righted himself just before the water washed over his cartridge box. That bad leg again.

Colonel Lamar himself came back to hurry the men along.

"Come on, boys, get on up that bank, come on. The old Sixty-first's going to settle things right fast, come on now, Georgia!"

". . . *even twenty cities, and unto the plain of the vineyards, with a very great slaughter,*" the chaplain recited, disdaining mortality.

Judges 11:33, Nichols recollected. But bad things happened in the following verses.

" 'Very great slaughter' all right," Ive said, nearly losing his own balance. "Reckon on that."

3:00 p.m.
Worthington farm

Gordon rode the fields and folds with his brigade commanders. He had restricted each man to a single aide to keep the party small, with flags and banners held back in the trees. The terrain posed an ugly problem with no good solution: There was no alternative to crossing broad fields lined by at least two fences that would need to be climbed over or knocked down. Worse, great shocks of hay studded the fields to be traversed, obstacles that would break up advancing lines. Beyond those impediments—bad enough—he saw two well-placed Federal lines, the second two hundred yards behind the first. If more Yankees lurked in the low ground to their rear, he had no way of knowing.

Didn't see any batteries lined up. That was queer. Yankee artillery was a monstrous thing, devastating, plentiful. Yet, here . . . he could spot only two guns for certain and what might or might not have been a third set back.

What if the Yankees had kept their batteries hidden? To spring a surprise?

He said nothing of his fears to his subordinates. He never did. And far too much of the day had burned away to spend time on debate and deliberation.

Drawing up on a mild rise, he waited for his brigadiers to settle around him and soothe their horses. Every equine mouth was green with foam: Their march had been hurried, their scouting fevered.

"Well, gentlemen . . . your eyes see as well as mine. There is no good way to do this." He considered his three brigadiers: Evans, the man he trusted most, with his parson's smile and fervent heart, commanding Gordon's old brigade of Georgians. Zeb York, with the remains of ten Louisiana regiments combined under his command, their rolls not amounting to half of a full brigade. Reared in Maine, but seduced by Louisiana, York had been one of the few truly wealthy men to go to war and stick it out. It was said he owned—or had owned, given present conditions in Louisiana—nigh on two thousand slaves. This day, the men he led numbered barely a third of that. But York would fight like a bull, charging ahead. And Bill Terry, newly made a brigadier general, somehow combined intelligence and gallantry, two qualities the war had taught Gordon were generally exclusive of one another. Terry's Virginia Brigade gathered in the survivors of fourteen regiments shattered in the Wilderness or bled out at Spotsylvania. Especially Spotsylvania.

Clem Evans would fight with heart, York with his knuckles, and Terry with his brain. Gordon had a purpose for each man.

"We're going to advance *en echelon,* from the right. Overlap their left, spook them into weakening their center along that crest."

"Looks like that could require some serious spooking," Zeb York told him. York retained the wealthy man's sense of a God-given right to speak up. Gordon knew it, expected it, and tolerated it. York followed orders, that was the thing that mattered.

"Well, that's where you'll play your part, Zeb. But you're running on ahead of me." Gordon fixed his eyes on Evans. "Clem, you'll be on the right, you'll go out first." He saw the flicker of doubt in Evans' eyes, but it was only a flicker, soon snuffed out. "The Georgia Brigade's going to face the worst of it, I understand that. But I need you to keep the pressure on their left. Zeb here will be in trail, on *your* left. He won't dally now, just give the Yankees time enough to issue the wrong orders." Looking from one man to the other, he said, "I expect you to break both of those Yankee lines. Between the two of you."

Arching his back, Gordon stretched before resuming the perfect posture he kept in the saddle. "Bill, you're my reserve. But I want your Virginians positioned to move *en echelon*, too, should the need arise. You'll be on Zeb's left, toward the river. Just keep your eyes wide open and be ready."

"Virginia's *always* ready, sir."

Gordon almost snapped, "Not on the twelfth of May, you weren't," but restrained himself. Holding his tongue was often a trial, but only a fool made an enemy of a man who might one day prove a useful friend.

"Indeed," Gordon told him, "indeed. I count myself the child of unsullied fortune in the privilege of commanding these three brigades. I hold none more valiant in all the armies of the Confederacy." He smiled slyly, though not meanly. The slyness was meant to be seen and appreciated. "Of course, we'll see who shines brightest today. Questions, gentlemen?"

"Thought you were going to get rid of that old red shirt?" Zeb York asked. "You stick out like the Queen of Sheba herself, get yourself killed. Then where'd we be?"

Gordon smiled the perfect smile again. "Why, I expect some grateful brigadier would get a promotion." He twisted the smile from easy to wry. "Need y'all to be able to find me, when you seek my counsel."

"Yankees don't seek you first."

"That's your job, Zeb. To keep those blue-bellies off me." He put the smile back in the smile chest. "All right, gentlemen . . . you will form your brigades behind that hill. Bill, you won't stretch that far up, so keep your men back of the barn a ways. Flags down. Until you advance."

Terry nodded.

As he surveyed the faces before him—none jovial now, each earnest—he paused, for a hair-split, at his brother's eyes. Gene was to be a major, if spared this day. Gordon wanted the younger man to live for that promotion and long thereafter. But Eugene would have to do his duty at Clem Evans' side.

He had noted his brother's worried look when York raised the matter of the flannel shirt. Fact was, Gordon didn't care for the garment. Even washed thin, it was too hot for the day, and turning back the sleeves hardly made a difference. But the men loved to see him in it. And they certainly saw him.

It continued to amuse, if not amaze, him how much his fellow officers and even his own kin failed to understand: Even a fearful man would die for a general in a red shirt. A. P. Hill understood that, but few others did. Early certainly didn't.

Damn Early, though. The army should have been a dozen miles down the road by now. They'd lost a day, thanks to that shabby money-raking in Frederick and Ramseur's knack for tying himself in knots. And damn that fool McCausland, for waking the Federals up to their open flank. And damn the sorry Maryland dirt underfoot, the whole fastidious, interfering, Negro-worshipping Union.

It was going to be a bloody, bloody day.

Gordon had saved his warmest smile for the last, a smile that promised intimate friendship with every man it fell upon. He believed that his hero, that other Ulysses—so unlike the beast in Union blue—would have donned just such a smile to win over Achilles, Agamemnon, or Menelaus.

"Not a man here has ever let me down," Gordon announced. "And I know you never will." He tugged on the reins just enough to make his beloved black horse prance. "Let's kill us some Yankees."

3:15 p.m.
Intersection of the Georgetown Pike
and Baker Valley Road

Ricketts turned to face Wallace, who had just dismounted beside him. He realized that his temporary commander had come down to the road, rather than summon him, to shorten the interrup-

tion of his work re-forming his lines. Wallace seemed a consider-
ate sort, gentlemanly, stuffed with brains, a dreamer. They were
different types, almost opposites, but Ricketts *liked* this man who
was about to destroy his division.

Moving clumsily, obviously exhausted, Wallace stepped close.
"Let us walk for a moment, General Ricketts. Apart from the men.
I shan't take much of your time."

There wasn't much "apart" to be had, between the dressing
ranks and sergeants all but hurling ammunition. Litter bearers
moved back and forth like a two-way column of ants, depositing
their cargoes and fetching more. Inevitably, a wagon had overturned, narrowing the road. Clutching his shoulder, the driver
cursed magnificently.

The two generals stepped along, gesturing to the men to remain at ease. The shade, what little there was, had magnetic force,
but by unspoken agreement, Ricketts and his companion left it to
the powder-smeared, sweat-gripped soldiers.

"Your troops have done splendidly," Wallace told him.

"Except for those two blasted regiments. God knows where the
devil they are right now." He had sensed, with finality, that those
precious regiments and strayed companies would not arrive in time
to affect the outcome.

Of course, the outcome would not have been changed, anyway. Only the fight's duration was in dispute.

"I'm sorry," Wallace said. "The railroad seems to have let us
down today."

Ricketts shrugged. "Fortunes of war." Mind back on business,
he said, "I've stripped the riverfront. Your boys will have to hold
it. I've pushed out a heavy skirmish line again. Changed its orien-
tation, of course. I learned that lesson. Main line's still by the house,
best ground. Flank's refused by one regiment, all I can spare from
the firing line." He gestured at the men filling the hollow that cradled the Pike. "Reserve's down here, two regiments. The Rebs will
have to pound their way through, and they'll pay the devil's wages."

He knew what Wallace was thinking. It would be the very

thought he harbored himself: *If* they come the way we think they'll come.

"There was a mounted party on a scout," Ricketts added. "All officers, judged by the gait of their horses. Postures, too, that high-and-mighty way most of them have. Rode the length of the hill ten minutes ago."

"I saw them," Wallace said. "Infantry commanders would be my guess. Weighing courses of action."

"They'll come that way, all right. No real choice."

Wallace nodded. "It'll be soon. They're pressing harder across the river, like they mean it this time. Not sure how much longer our boys can hold, they're in a bind."

"Those Vermont boys are stubborn."

"I made a mistake. The bridge, the fire."

For the first time in hours, perhaps aeons, Ricketts smiled. "Generals don't *make* mistakes, sir. Didn't anyone let you in on the secret? First thing a fellow learns when he gets to West Point." Voice almost jovial—he recognized the hilarity that sprang from desperation—he added, "Never made a single mistake myself."

Wallace smiled, too. But Ricketts thought, for a flashing moment, of the wretched court-martial of Fitz John Porter, of his own shabby part in it. Mistakes? What was a man's life but a trail of mistakes?

Letting his smile fall away, Wallace said, "We've cost them a day. That's something."

"Cost them a good bit more, before we're done."

"If . . . I ordered you to withdraw now . . . you could save your division. There's still time for an orderly withdrawal. I doubt the Rebs would contest it. They just want us out of the way."

It was a tempting thought. A wonderful thought.

"We haven't been beaten yet," Ricketts said.

"We will be," Wallace said, almost whispered.

"Yes. But we haven't been. Not yet."

"You'll lose half your division. At least."

"You told me yourself that every hour counts."

Wallace appeared taut with nerves, half-starved, dark eyes sunken, and shoulders caved like an old woman's under a shawl. Not the way the illustrated papers portrayed heroes. But Ricketts understood, thoroughly and clearly, that Wallace meant to stay and fight it out. With or without the men Ricketts commanded. He was trying to be just, but war mocked justice. The man was far too decent to be a general.

"It does," Wallace said. "Every hour counts."

"Then it's my duty to contest the field."

"God bless you," Wallace said, faintly, enunciating each word.

Ricketts was tempted to say far more than was his habit, to lash out and damn the idiocy in Washington, the stubbornness of every general officer not present where they stood, the pigheadedness of government and the creatures who fed off its carcass like monstrous insects. Above all, he wanted to say, "I just hope to Christ in Heaven all this is worth it, that somebody in Washington has decided by now to step away from the bar of Willard's Hotel and do their duty."

But Wallace doubtless harbored the same thoughts; there was no point in speaking aloud. The men might hear.

"Best see to my lines," Ricketts said brusquely. "Rebs will be coming along."

"General Ricketts? In case we . . . should become separated. I want to thank you." Wallace held out his hand.

Ricketts accepted the paw, but the time for genteel communion had passed them by. He nodded toward his begrimed men in their shabby uniforms.

"Thank them."

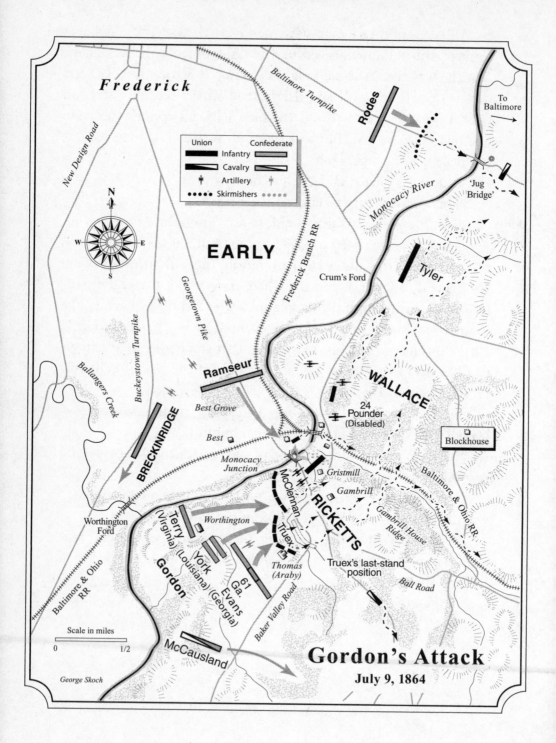

Frederick

Baltimore Turnpike

Rodes

To Baltimore

New Design Road

Monocacy River

'Jug Bridge'

Union   Confederate
          Infantry
          Cavalry
····· Skirmishers ·····
          Artillery

EARLY

N
W   E
S

Georgetown Pike

Frederick Branch RR

Crum's Ford

Tyler

Buckeystown Turnpike

Ballangers Creek

Ramseur

WALLACE

24 Pounder (Disabled)

Blockhouse

BRECKINRIDGE

Best Grove

Best

Monocacy Junction

Gristmill

Gambrill

Baltimore & Ohio RR

McClennan

RICKETTS

Gambrill House Ridge

Worthington Ford

Terry (Virginia)

Worthington

Truex

Baltimore & Ohio RR

York (Louisiana)

Gordon

61 Ga. Evans (Georgia)

Thomas (Araby)

Truex's last-stand position

Ball Road

Baker Valley Road

Scale in miles

0   1/2

McCausland

George Skoch

Gordon's Attack
July 9, 1864

FIVE

K eep your alignment, men," Lieutenant Colonel Valkenburg called as he rode between their lines. "Keep up your alignment."

The sound of nigh on a thousand men advancing seemed to hush all else in the world. Even the thump of the guns on the far bank faded. Nichols believed he could hear his heart, fearful and no denying it.

The first field they crossed had been stripped bare of crops, leaving a man with his own feeling of nakedness. They were still out of range of the Yankee rifles, but exposed for all to see, and each step brought them closer to whatever the Lord had in mind. Horn-hard feet and rough shoes slapped baked earth, raising pale dust to bother throats consigned to the second rank. Sweating untowardly, like a fat man, Nichols felt shrunken.

In the next field, yet uncut, the *shish-shish-shish* of feet and calves pushed through ripe wheat with the sound of a thousand scythes.

The day was hot, bright blue, gold, green-rimmed, marred here and there by smoke. Despite his wash of sweat, Nichols felt light, with his blanket roll and haversack left behind in the trees, every man going forward with just his fighting tools. Still, he sensed a ghost where the blanket had gripped, the wet cloth cooling now, despite the sun. He'd learned so much he hoped he lived to tell it, how a man could be hot and chilled at once, sick with fear and ready to kill with fury.

"Keep your alignment, men."

Up ahead, nothing good. Across a dreadful stretch of fields, flat enough for volleys to sweep them clean, the Yankees waited, hunkered down, no doubt licking their lips. In between, fences challenged the advance, with haystacks scattered about, as if the blue-bellies had set out a steeplechase course.

In dead air, flags hung limp. Along the lines the 61st Georgia's officers called out encouragement. Excepting Colonel Lamar and Lieutenant Colonel Valkenburg, every one of the officers walked, not because they'd dismounted to spare themselves, but because there were no horses to be had, at least not for the money printed in Richmond. It was a poor time, a hard time, for rich and poor alike among his people, with gentry afoot who had ridden all their lives. Determined they all were, though, every one of them. Nichols felt that sure as Revelation.

So far still to go, a small eternity. Fresh sweat popped. Insects rose, clouds of them. He had turned up the front brim of his hat, the way he always did, the better to look along the sights when the time came, and blackflies teased his eyes. He blinked and blinked again but kept both hands on his rifle. Wasn't no right-shoulder-shift this day, just rifles held at port, the way General Gordon liked things.

Just seemed a mean, long way across those fields. He couldn't figure why the Yankees hadn't let loose with artillery. Unless their guns were already primed with canister, a terrible thing, wrathful.

He fixed his eyes on that first fence. Didn't want to look beyond it.

The day was hot in the nose, hot in the mouth. Field dust, hay dust, peppered his nostrils, so different from the chalk-cake dust of roads. Breathing almost required an act of will. But his leg had stopped hurting, he barely felt it. He wondered why that was?

A man was a riddle, but the Lord God was a mystery.

Officers pointed the way with their swords and it almost seemed the blades tugged them along. Nichols was glad to bear a rifle, to feel its weight and solidity. Above all, he was glad to feel the smell-close press of his fellow soldiers around him, the presence of others that braved a man up and kept him from shaming himself; glad, too, to see familiar backs in the first line up ahead, to know men not just by their faces, but by their shoulders and signifying movements. Beside him, on his left, marched hard Ive Summerlin, who took every fight personal. To the right, Lem Davis panted, beard alone enough to fright the Yankees, the beard of a Methuselah, though Lem was not so old.

His friends, his kind, his war-kin.

Step forward, step again. Brittle soil crumbled underfoot. A butterfly, confused, fluttered about. His mother said that butterflies brought good luck.

He wanted to be brave inside and out. But he knew that he only could go forward like this, across these endless fields, with his brethren close. He felt himself quiver like a fevered child, the way he was ever inclined to in the moments before he could lose himself in doing.

Men killed hogs kinder than they killed each other.

That fence. A soldier learned to hate fences. Unless they were there for burning when things were quiet.

Them Yanks all tucked in. Waiting. Bits of blue speckled the distance, signs enough for a man to imagine their line, how it would explode.

At that fence. That's where it would start. They'd wait till then.

A part of him wanted to run, a shameful part. His heart raged to burst right out of his chest, to escape his flesh and run off by its own self. Sweat sheathed him.

"Get over that fence!" Colonel Lamar roared. "Company C, open a gap!"

Men rushed from the forward line, ripping at the boards and clubbing the planks with their rifle butts. One fool fellow had cocked his rifle and it shot into the air, a stunning sound that tore right through the day.

As soon as the first rank mounted the fence, the Yankees opened fire. Men splayed their arms and fell—backward, forward—dropping their weapons, casting them off, hats flying, bodies crumpling, some caught halfway, folded over the top rail, rumps in the air, as if awaiting a spanking.

Other men climbed the slats or leapt over. Some paused to help their friends. More and more of the fence simply gave way.

"Come on, boys, come on! Re-form. Re-form and keep moving."

It was hard doings. The first line had become a ragged thing, blundering amid haystacks. It still went forward, though.

"Hold your fire, don't fire. Our time's a-coming. Re-form, and hold your fire!"

Yanks weren't holding theirs. Men dropped.

Nichols crowded through a gap in the broke-down fence, brushing past witch-finger splinters.

Lieutenant Colonel Valkenburg rode through another gap and cantered along the line, calling, "Fill up the first ranks. Sergeants, do your duty!"

"I don't need no sergeant pushing me," Ive Summerlin declared. He trotted forward, toward a hole the Yankees had made in the gray line.

Nichols followed after. Hadn't wanted to, hadn't decided to. Just did. As if Ive pulled him along on a hidden rope.

Lem Davis came after. Big and breathing like a run-out steer.

The Yankees fired as fast as they reloaded.

A few men, very few, paused behind the haystacks, malingering, gripped by fear. Most just stepped along, though, like they couldn't do anything else, and that was that. Both lines were jumbled now.

"Keep going, keep on going!"

Some of the junior officers and sergeants continued to holler about re-forming, but it was as if they did it just to feel better, to keep themselves occupied.

Everyone moved quickly now. Not running, not quite. Forming back up in their accustomed, imperfect way, anxious to get out of the shocks and stacks, craving order as much as they craved safety, needing their comrades stink-close again and ranked up, so a man's chances evened out.

Just as Nichols spotted him again, rounding a haystack, Lieutenant Colonel Valkenburg fell sideward from his horse. As if shoved hard.

"Just keep moving, Georgie," Lem said. "You just look straight ahead."

Wasn't right. It wasn't right. Of all people.

Nichols felt himself tempted by awful words, Satan just a-begging him to utter them.

Men fell on every side.

That second fence. Men couldn't wait, could not just march toward it. One dashed forward, then another. All of them. Amid the wild racket of Yankee volleys.

"Georgia! Georgia!"

Again, men tumbled as they topped the fence, splendid targets for the Yankees now. Nichols spotted Zib Collins, who was supposed to be on stretcher duty and safe, bearing a rifle and fumbling over the obstacle. Then Zib held stone still. For one queer instant. As if at the behest of a man with a camera.

Zib's head just burst, brains splashing everywhere. As if his skull had been struck with a railroad hammer.

"Georgia! Forward!"

Yanks had easy shooting now. But as soon as the bulk of the men were past the fence, Colonel Lamar halted them, cursing those who failed to obey promptly, employing lusty profanity, although the colonel, once a noteworthy sinner, had found his way to Jesus the past winter.

"Form up! Form up, Lord God almighty! Hurry up, boys, hurry!" Nichols shut his ears to the other words blazing by.

They formed back up, right fast. But Lem was on his left now, Ive a few spaces distant on the right.

Eyes hunting the flanks, Lem said, "Seems like we're aiming to take on the Yankees just us'n."

But they were back in solid ranks, instilled again—only the Lord knew how—with order and a refreshed, deepened confidence, going forward as one.

Yanks were little more than a hundred yards off now, not so thick a line, after all.

"At the double-quick . . . forward!"

"Georgia! Georgia!"

"Charge!"

The blue-bellies didn't wait. It was only a bullied-up skirmish line. They fled. Yet, all the dead, the wounded this much had cost . . .

One man shrieked like a woman, a rare thing.

Colonel Lamar steered his horse ahead of the colors. The flags were carried by different soldiers now. The colonel paused just beyond the dip where the skirmish line had lurked.

"Halt and re-form. Halt, boys. Re-form."

"Sure now. Jest let them Yankees have another free shot," Ive said bitterly, for the hearing of those around him.

But these were dutiful men, ferocious and resigned, and they formed yet again after their brief charge, and they went forward again, and the second Yankee line exploded, so many rifles in play that after two volleys you couldn't see the blue-bellies, just the smoke.

"Forward! Georgia!"

The colors tumbled, the battle flag. New hands reached out. The torn cloth lofted again.

Suddenly, unreasonably, they all began to howl, Nichols and his brethren. It felt wonderful to be a part of this sudden burst of power, to lunge forward again, hallooing, as if their war cry itself must slay the Yankees.

Hundreds of points of light blinked through the smoke. There were bodies underfoot now, from earlier struggles, their own kind, in cavalry jackets and rags.

Another man he knew from home, James Hendrix, clutched his belly and dropped to his knees.

"Onward! Georgia!"

The firing grew so fierce, it felt like walking into a storm wind. Men crouched as they went forward, as if assaulted by a driving rain.

They were close, so close. The racket of the Yankee volleys was ear-busting.

Another man groaned and dropped but paces from Nichols. It was a bewildering thing how any man could stand without being hit.

"Realign. Align on the colors!" Colonel Lamar bellowed. But even as he spoke, the colors fell again. Only to rise a fourth time or a fifth.

The colonel's voice broke off. Men fell. Blood spattered. Nichols found his own face wet without knowing whose blood he wore. His hat was gone.

Another voice called, "Halt. Volley fire. By company. Company officers—"

Then that voice, too, fell away. But the men halted and did as ordered, standing at the edge of the expanding cloud, firing into it on command, then independently, as the smoke engulfed them, too.

A voice reported that Colonel Lamar was dead.

The regiment, the entire brigade, hardly seemed to exist. Nichols was faintly aware that he was shaking. But he dutifully reloaded, fired, and reloaded again, blasting into the smoke, aiming in the direction of those muzzle flames, unwilling to go back one inch.

They crowded together, toward the regimental colors. Before he knew it, Nichols was but a plank length from the single flag remaining. He fought madly, jamming home his ramrod, barely getting the stock back against his shoulder before pulling the trigger again, hating. Nobody was going to take those colors, nobody.

The flag toppled. This time, Lieutenant Mincy dashed forward to raise the staff, only to buckle and drop flat on his face.

The Yankees had been killing all the officers, concentrating on the officers, purposeful and cruel. The revelation made perfect sense to Nichols, but still came as a shock.

He filled up with a hatred less than Christian.

The Yankees didn't come forward, and the remains of the Georgia Brigade would not move back.

The smoke became choking thick.

"Kerenhappuch!" Nichols said. Then he shouted, *"Kerenhap-puch!"*

Lem turned. "What the—"

"Job's third daughter! Kerenhappuch!" Nichols began to laugh as he felt for a cartridge.

"Best fix on matters to hand," Lem advised.

They fired into the man-made fog, spotting rough forms now, Yankees no more than thirty yards away. Closer.

"Stand your ground, Georgia!" a grand voice called. "Georgia, hold fast, you're licking them!"

"Well, that's a damned lie," someone said.

"Georgia, stand your ground!"

"That's General Gordon!" The sound of the man's voice, the sense it evoked, the image of the general remembered, filled Nichols with a determination he had not known he could muster. He wanted to rush forward, to go at the Yankees bare-handed. But he stood and fired, obeying the last order he had received, regular as a machine.

Moments later, word passed along the shrinking line that Gordon had been shot.

4:00 p.m.
Thomas farm

Gordon sat up, chasing breath, head hammering and puke dizzy. It had happened fast, the way it always did. Two rounds, maybe three, had struck his horse in a brace of seconds. The animal had reared, throwing him clean, but he'd landed hard.

He tested himself anxiously, checking bones. His vision wouldn't settle and the noise was terrible, terrible. Hands gripped him. He slapped them away.

"I'm all right, damn it," he said. "Give a man his space."

He remembered, looked about. Faces. An aide. "Is York up?"

"Yes, sir. Louisiana's in the fight."

"Tigers," Gordon muttered, meaning to speak firmly.

"Yes, sir. They're right tigers."

"I've got to . . . help me up."

Hands, too many hands, assisted him. "General Evans. I need a report from Evans."

"General Evans has been shot, sir. Your brother has taken temporary command. Until—"

"Colonel Lamar is to command it."

"He's dead, sir."

Gordon bellowed. One wordless howl. Johnny Lamar. Old friend.

The moment of rage cleared his head.

"A horse . . ."

My kingdom for a horse . . . my brigade, my kingdom. Clem Evans, Johnny Lamar . . .

"Take my horse, sir. I'll ride Sergeant Cook's."

"Just give me Cook's horse." He tried to smile toward the sergeant, unsure if he managed it. Then he told all of them: "Georgia must hold its ground. Can't retreat." He looked at the aide. His vision was sharp again. "You said General Evans has been shot. Wounded?"

"Yes, sir. In the side."

"How bad?"

The captain shook his head. "Can't say, sir. Heard he was conscious, though."

"Find my brother. As soon as he can locate a ranking officer, he's to relinquish command. Then find General York. Tell him to keep pressing them, not a step back. Only forward." He tried to find the stirrup with his left boot, but failed twice. Still dizzy, after all.

"Help me."

A sergeant fit the stirrup to Gordon's toe. Gordon gathered the strength to haul his bones up into the saddle.

"Y'all go on now," he told the little crowd. "See to your business."

He rode back through the smoke, sure of his direction, the way he always had been, in the deep forests of north Georgia or on battlefields. His body seemed sound, if aching. And his head was clear enough now. He spurred the strange mount toward the river, where Terry's Brigade had been ordered to halt. He'd sent them forward just far enough to clear out any threat of a flanking maneuver.

The smoke thinned. Noise still clapped his ears, though, a sharp pain. As Gordon emerged from the gray fog into the sunlight, the blaze hit his eyes, his skull, with the force of a mallet. He realized that his hat was gone. But he looked better—fiercer—without it, he fancied.

Alone, he galloped across fields strewn with bodies, most of them in gray or shades of brown. His men, McCausland's. A few Yankees by a fence. The cries of the wounded knew not North or South, only abrupt, unmanageable suffering. But pity was not his dominion. His purpose was to win battles.

Over a rolling crest. Down the far slope, Terry sat his horse, flanked by his staff.

As Gordon reined in, Terry looked him up and down, almost regal, as if condescending to breathe the same air. Yet the fellow was pleasant for all that, as Virginian as fine tobacco and proud women.

"New horse, I do believe," the brigade commander remarked.

The black, dying or dead, had been his favored mount.

"I was inconvenienced," Gordon told him.

"Seems you tired of your hat, as well."

"Never was a proper fit."

"May my brigade be of service, sir? In this heady hour?"

"Yes. You may be of service, Bill. No more time for foolery." He turned in the saddle and pointed to a crest back up the slope and to the left. "Move your men up there. Quick as you can, without disordering them. You're going to roll up the Yankees and put an end to this."

"Bad up top?" Terry asked, serious now.

"Spotsylvania. Smaller, but as bad."

Terry took a moment to swallow that. "And when I get to the top, I'm to—"

"I'll meet you there."

Terry had become faintly unsettled. "But if something should happen? I hear—"

"I'll meet you there," Gordon repeated. "If I don't, you'll see what needs doing, where to attack."

Prepared to ride off, facing myriad tasks, he nonetheless paused before digging in his spurs. Struggling to think like Ulysses, who understood the ways of men like no other: their yearnings, their pride.

"Now we'll see what Virginians are made of," he announced to all who might hear.

4:15 p.m.
Georgetown Pike (Washington road)

Wallace had sent an aide to warn him that his detachment of Vermonters was in retreat, leaping across the girders of the rail bridge, chased by what looked like a full Rebel division. Ricketts pictured men shot in the back and plunging into the river. Who had been in command? Young Davis, was it? Few officers left his senior, far too few. The Wilderness, Spotsylvania, Cold Harbor. Well, Davis had done yeoman's work, holding out with his pitiful handful. But the fact that mattered now was that the Rebs would soon be in his division's rear.

Ricketts felt he was playing poker with disappearing cards.

Wallace had claimed he could hold another half hour, but that had been almost fifteen minutes back. Ricketts imagined the Home Brigade men—who had not done badly at all—losing their courage in one fateful instant and starting to run. He knew how that contagion went. This was the hour for veterans, with all hell bubbling up. But even veterans would hold only so long before they broke.

He was tired. Growing too old for this. But he remained determined to stay at the table to play this final hand. Wallace had authorized him to retreat whenever he deemed it necessary, but Ricketts disliked quitting. Stubborn, all his life. Far more than was politic. One of the reasons he had remained a lieutenant for epochs, then a captain for ages.

And the one time he had softened his principles, at that damnable court-martial, he had marked himself with an odor that wouldn't wash off. Better to be stubborn and pay the price.

He could no longer see the brick house, although it stood but a few hundred yards away. A cloud had grown around it, spreading along the crest, dense as a nightmare. The noise told him his men were holding, though. A few skedaddlers wandered back, and a multitude of wounded men had withdrawn, but the fight was not yet over, not just yet.

And the dead? The lives he was betting in a hopeless game?

He would not order a retreat while Truex held that ridge. He just would not do it. But he had directed his Second Brigade to swing back, now that the river was lost and their flank turned. He intended to firm up a third, last line on the Pike.

Perhaps he could bring off an orderly withdrawal? Even now? With the First Brigade falling back upon the Second, and the Second withdrawing again. Things would need to go smoothly, more smoothly than battle generally allowed, but there was a chance: Hold the Rebs while the Home Brigade men cleared off and Wallace saved the guns, then withdraw in stages, making any Rebel pursuit pay a premium.

He had been taught, many years before, that a fighting withdrawal was the most difficult military feat, and he doubted things would go nicely. But if you held a poor hand, you had to play boldly.

"Over there," he greeted a Second Brigade officer he recognized. "Put your men over there, when they come up. Build a firing line this side of the road."

Black with smoke and powder, the major stared in bewilderment. "Sir . . . I have no men . . . I don't know where . . ."

Before Ricketts could shape a useful question, Truex's aide, Captain Lanius, emerged out of the smoke, galloping down from the shrouded battle line and nearly riding over a wounded man. One of the many, many wounded men.

Before Ricketts could admonish him, Lanius called from the saddle, "Colonel Truex's compliments, he needs help. Right now, sir. They're breaking our center, Louisiana Brigade. We're holding up on the left, it's a bloody mess, but we're holding. It's the center that's cracking."

Ricketts made an instant decision that changed his plans again.

"Tell Colonel Truex I'm sending him my reserve. No. Wait. You can guide them up yourself."

His "reserve." Two bloodied, played-out regiments, with several companies already stripped away. His best hope of a last defense of the Pike.

After he had spoken, Ricketts felt a rush of doubt. But it was too late. He had promised help for Truex.

Ricketts played the last card in his hand.

4:25 p.m.
Thomas farm

Brigadier General Terry hurried his troops along, all but giving each man a boot in the haunches. Getting them up to that crest in good order, if a tad breathless.

No sign of Gordon. As Terry approached the high ground, all he could see was bald dirt and a world of smoke beyond it, set to the noise of all the devils in Hell banging pots and pans.

Spotsylvania? Bad as that? My, oh my. Terry believed he had glimpsed a spot of alarm in Gordon's eyes. And Gordon was the most confident creature, man or beast, that Terry had ever met. Oh, surely Gordon had known doubts, the man was human. But Terry had never seen a sign until that afternoon.

If he *had* seen it. With Gordon, a man could be certain without being sure.

Surprising him, the leading men in his brigade began to growl as they neared the ridgetop. Climbing blindly, with the fighting still hidden from view, marching up toward the smoke and sky, they just started in to snarling, like animals that had put up with all they meant to stand. It was an uncanny sound, one Terry did not recall from previous battles.

Had to wonder what men sensed, how they came to that wordless knowing that enthralled them all at once, melting them into one big pot of mischief.

Terry heard cheering, Southern cheering, from down along the river, off toward those bridges, loud enough to compete with the roar of battle. Sounded like Ramseur might have got up from his daybed.

Growling and snarling, rabid, his men were ready to savage all in their way. It filled him with pride.

Terry reached the true crest, horse high-stepping again, and there was Gordon. Sitting upright on that borrowed nag, cool as branch water, as if he had nothing more to do than wait on old Virginia.

It was Gordon restored. In that red shirt, and still without a hat.

When the first rank spotted Gordon, the soldiers sent up a cheer.

"Hurry on, now. Hurry on," Gordon called. His regular voice of command was back upon him, ordering men to their deaths in a tone that was downright affable.

Riding up to that "inexplicable paragon of mystifying, exasperating manliness"—as Zeb York once had put it—Terry said, "Virginia is at your service, sir."

A fence ahead. Then a field. Another fence lower down, broken. Beyond it, the battle, with all the sparks and smoke of Vulcan's forge.

As the two generals watched, a pair of Yankee regiments marched up from the low ground, oblivious to their presence, headed into the maelstrom and exposing meager flanks.

Terry's men surged forward on their own. Growling again. The sound seemed to take even Gordon aback.

"Hold on now, hold on!" Gordon called, princely even on that borrowed nag. "You'll get your chance, boys, your time's going to come. Just get through that fence and form back up."

"Something's got into them," Terry said. "Not sure they'll be bridled again, once we turn 'em loose."

The men rushed the fence, funneling through a gap, breaking down more gaps, or climbing over the rails in their impatience.

Hurrying to assuage some terrible need, the Yankees marching into the fight still showed no awareness that they were about to be gobbled. The bluecoats were formed up smartly, advancing at right-shoulder-shift, as if on parade.

"So much for all those reports of militia and mules," Gordon said. "Let those Federals clear the slope, then advance, once you're formed up."

But the time for orders had passed. A pack of hungry dogs smelling fresh meat, Terry's men began to run down the slope toward the Yankees. Somebody yelled "Charge!"

"What the devil?" Terry demanded.

Hundreds of men poured over and through the fence, joining the attack. It was the wildest thing that Terry had ever seen. But he had his orders, his sense of how things should go, and he rode forward to halt them, to beat them back into their proper formation.

Gordon caught up with him.

"Not going to stop them now," he said. "You were right, they won't be bridled."

Terry's Virginians raised a Rebel yell.

4:40 p.m.
Thomas farm

Yanks are running," Ive Summerlin hollered.

Nichols saw it, too, the sudden breaking up of the line of shadows, the individual flights.

He felt relief, immense relief, as if he had just stopped running after ten miles. Exhausted. He wanted to sit down. His leg decided to hurt again.

"Let's go. Get them sumbitches!" somebody shouted. And they all plunged forward, into the torn smoke, howling. Nichols screamed, too, running along with the others.

It was all so sudden, so reasonless. They had stood there killing each other, as though they would just keep shooting until all but a last one was dead and maybe him, too. Then the Yanks broke.

Some tried to resist even now, but were clubbed down, shot down, run through. Others raised their hands where they stood, faces fearful—faces that surely had worn murderous looks spare minutes before. Ive Summerlin shot a Yank in the belly before the man could get his hands high enough. And they kept running, stumbling over the wounded and dead, even kicking them out of the way, charging down the slope through drifts of smoke. Ahead: a confusion of Yankees, shrieking horses, stray commands.

"Git 'em, git 'em!"

The Yanks weren't done, not quite. Nichols ran past herded prisoners, men made sheep, past individual combats like wrestling matches at the fair, only without rules, and he came up short just as a Federal line, ragged but still standing, fired from the far side of a road.

The volley felled Rebs and their prisoners alike.

The blue-bellies yelled, "Pennsylvania! Pennsylvania!"

A nearby voice, Louisiana-toned, said, "I'll give them shit-eating bastards Pennsylvania. . . ."

Nichols' own kind formed up again, with amazing rapidity, even though no officers were near. He joined a line of strangers and near strangers, faces he knew but couldn't quite slap a name on. In seconds, men had reloaded, raised their rifles, and fired into the blue line, just as the Yankees unleashed a volley of their own.

Men fell. The smoke thickened again.

A Yankee officer rode right between the two lines, galloping up the road, crazed, or perhaps carried along by a runaway horse. Men fired at him, but he eluded the bullets. Then he was gone, a wisp, and the men on foot went back to slaying one another.

Nichols loaded and fired, reached down into his cartridge box again—and found it empty. He knelt to snatch cartridges from a Federal lying open-eyed and still, but had no sooner bent than a fresh volley felled the soldiers who had stood to either side of him.

Nichols looked from one fallen man to the other, a broom-bearded sergeant pawing the air and a fair boy writhing. It made him want to stand up and shout at the Yankees, "You're *whipped*. We whipped you, fair and square. Why don't you quit?"

As if his outrage had willed it, the last Yankee line began to dissolve. Brave men ran. Men in gray seemed to be everywhere now, rushing up from the left, even appearing behind the last clots of resisting Yankees.

Men threw down their rifles and raised their hands. Wherever a Yankee officer tried to bring off his men, he was quickly shot. Still, the killing dragged on down in the hollows.

It was over, though. Some men just didn't have the sense to see it. Or the Christian strength to bear defeat. But for all the shooting and shouting that continued, a fellow just knew that things had finished up, the way you knew the blood was all drained out of a strung-up hog.

Nichols stood. Dumbly. Out of worldly ambition of any kind.

There were Yankee prisoners in numbers enough to work all the fields in Georgia. Powder-blackened men with sour expressions, some weeping, though not from fright or weakness, a man could tell that. Their fear of death had passed, replaced by lesser dreads.

A broken-toothed fellow in brown homespun came smiling up to Nichols, long, greased hair gone thin and hanging below a black hat a witch might have worn in a picture book.

"Who're you with, there, sonny?"

"Sixty-first Georgia," Nichols said proudly, defiantly. "Evans' Brigade, General Gordon's Division."

The ugly mouth cackled and formed new words: "Bet y'all glad Ramseur come to save you, ain't you now?"

Nichols knocked the man down.

Early dismounted on the crest, amid the dead and dying.

"Stay in the saddle, Sandie," he said. His voice carried no hint of sorrow or remorse, only cold determination. "You ride off yourself, send out couriers. Tell all of them—Gordon, Ramseur, Rodes–I said not to get carried away. No more prisoners, I can't herd any more. Let them run off, I don't choose to be encumbered. This army already favors a band of gypsies."

"Yes, sir. Anything else?"

"Tell McCausland he may find the road to Washington open now, if he cares to look. And if he doesn't mind too awfully much, I'd appreciate him doing what I goddamned well ordered that fool to do this morning. He's to get on down that road and keep on going."

"I believe he's already dispatched most of his command, sir."

"Tell him to send off the rest."

"They're caring for their wounded."

"Let somebody else do it. God almighty, I'm going to get some use out of his clapped-up jockeys yet." He chewed a cud that wasn't there, a ghost of old tobacco. "Any word from Johnson?"

"No, sir. But he should be a good ways along now, putting a scare in folks."

Early tested a fallen Yankee with the tip of his boot. "He won't get within fifty miles of Point Lookout." He pondered for a moment. "Crazy idea. No sense being too hard on Johnson on that count, fool though he may be. You go on now."

Early squatted. The way common soldiers did when they were about to loot a corpse. But he didn't touch the body, only looked at it—the hole in the temple nearly the size of a dollar, the blood darkened almost brown, the lazy flies, gorged, feasted, surfeited.

"Damned Sixth Corps. Looks like someone in Washington done woke up." He lifted his eyes to the staff men gathered around. "Going to have to get an early start tomorrow morning."

5:30 p.m.
Baltimore road, east of the Stone Bridge

Wallace could not speak at first, but needed to calm himself and catch his breath from the pounding ride. He had been relieved to find General Tyler and his men exactly where they were supposed to be, but the level of firing just across the river, toward Frederick, suggested that few were apt to be there much longer.

Wearing a harried look, Erastus Tyler waited for his superior to speak first.

"Well, we've lost," Wallace said.

Tyler nodded.

"We've lost, but we cost them a day. A full day."

"Yes, sir."

"Ras, you *must* hold the bridge, keep the Rebels from crossing. This road's all we have left. Ricketts put up a remarkable fight, we can't let his survivors be cut off."

Tyler, too, appeared wearied. Stained. Not just with the salt that collected from a man's sweat, but by life. They all were.

"Do my best, sir. Men held fine all day. Only a few ran off. But they're tired now. Unsteady."

"We're all tired."

"Just telling you the truth, sir. They will not hold against a determined attack. Some will fight, but not enough. And not long enough. Not with everybody else running. Panic's catching, you know that."

And running his men were, Wallace had to face it. He had waited too long to withdraw, zealous for each additional minute, tallying the hours as a child might, selfish, blinded. When he left the battlefield, with Ross tugging his mount's bridle to make him go, he had fled a debacle, with his own men disappearing and Ricketts' remaining soldiers all but surrounded.

Ricketts. The Republic owed that man a debt.

And Alexander had brought off his guns. Even that howitzer.

Not everyone had quit, there had been heroes. Many of them.

And officers were still out there, along the line of retreat, attempting to lead the remnants of companies and regiments amid the confusion and the Rebel pursuit, to save what could be saved.

Wallace knew that he needed to move on himself, to rally as many men as he could, to gather numbers sufficient to block the road to Baltimore at whatever point presented itself, to fight again. In case he had been wrong about that, too, and Early planned on burning the docks and warehouses, the rail yards and the arsenal.

He had to see to countless tasks, but he only slumped in the saddle, allowing himself a stolen moment of rest, overtaken by the day, overwhelmed at last. He just wanted to sleep. Between clean sheets.

How many men had his obstinacy killed? And how many of those deaths had been unnecessary, offerings made too late to affect the result, men left to die when he should have begun to clear the field and spare what lives he could?

Selfishness. Pride. Vainglory. So many sins were disguised by the fine word *duty*.

Waking himself, Wallace told Tyler, "I'm depending on you, Ras. Hold the bridge. As long as you can. Do your best. Give me two hours. One hour."

And Wallace turned back toward his shattered army.

7:00 p.m.
The Baltimore and Ohio Railroad,
east of Monocacy Junction

Ricketts and his staff followed the rail line. The Reb pursuit appeared to have slackened and the men let their winded horses slow to a walk for a stretch.

He had waited too long, making the wrong guesses toward the end. The Rebs had overwhelmed them, that was true. But Ricketts already saw the things he might have done differently. *Would* do differently. Another time.

Would he be allowed another time? With his wrecked division?

He hoped that Wallace had escaped the Rebs. The damned fool. A damned fool, and a good man. For any blunders he might have made, Wallace had done a dozen and more things right. He had seen what needed doing and had done it, where a timid man, one thinking of his career, would have found excuses so convincing they were sure to get him promoted. Together, they had bought a day for Washington. *And* bloodied Early's army.

His own losses were terrible, though. He would not know the true numbers for days, as soldiers left to save themselves filtered back in to their commands, as they always did. But the numbers would be grim, not least those taken prisoner. He barely had escaped himself, refusing his staff's entreaties to ride off until the Rebels had almost boxed them in. He believed that Truex had gotten off the field, too. But the toll of regimental officers looked to be crippling.

They passed a slump-shouldered group of soldiers—his men, judging by their hard-worn uniforms. Most had brought off their rifles, but not all of them.

"You men gave them the devil today," Ricketts told them. "And we'll give them the devil again, when we have the chance."

"Strikes me the Devil got his own both ways," a wag called out. "Any of you officers got a spare beefsteak?"

That was all right. When men could joke, it meant they were not broken. The division had been shattered, but not destroyed. The men would come in. And those two missing regiments would be found, with hell to pay when he found the man responsible for their absence from the field.

He worried a bit about his future, but not overly much. He had been the subordinate, and his division had fought handsomely. He was unlikely to bear any blame. But it had been, after all, a defeat—no matter its contribution—and the entire effort might be portrayed as foolhardy by those safe behind mahogany desks in Washington.

He was unlikely to suffer any consequences. But Wallace? No breed of man was more vindictive than those who shied from battle in the rear. If Wallace had enemies, this would be their hour.

Off to the right, ahead of them, firing erupted.

"Best pick up the pace, sir," an aide counseled.

9:30 p.m.
Thomas farm

Nichols sat. It was all he could do, all he wanted to do, to the extent he felt any least desire to do anything. He had eaten, Yankee food, of which there was plenty. Brined pork, beans, and crackers without weevils. He had eaten like a machine, spooning up the food steadily, not tasting much, filling the empty space in his belly as if that might fill the other emptiness.

After he had knocked down Ramseur's man, the 61st Georgia and the 12th Georgia Battalion were ordered to stop where they were and leave chasing Yankees to others. Wandering back a stretch over the field, he had come upon Tom Nichols of Company A, a namesake but no kin. Tom's brains were hanging out of his temple, and the wounded man pawed one-handed at the slops, either trying to shove them back in or brush them away from his skull. Nichols knelt down to see if there was anything he could do, trying not to show the horror he felt, and helped Tom to a drink from his canteen. It was almost as if Tom had already turned hant, for he seemed to feel no pain. He still had a scrap of his wits, though.

"If I can get back to Virginia," the dying man declared, "just get back to Virginia . . . get me a horse . . ." His eyes met Nichols', but it was beyond knowing what Tom really saw. "Never going to cross the Potomac again, never going to cross the Potomac again, never." He went back to smearing his brains across his temple.

Nichols sat with him until a pair of litter bearers appeared to take him to a field surgery. It was clear from their looks, from any expertise they had acquired, that Tom was a goner. But Nichols had already known that.

". . . a horse . . . ," Tom said, the last words Nichols heard from him.

He meant to pray thereafter, to thank the Lord for delivering him this day, but he kept putting it off. After trying to banter with him, to cheer him, Lem Davis and Dan Frawley had let him alone, just keeping watch on his doings from a distance. He didn't resent that, didn't feel anything about it. When Tom Boyet fetched his blanket roll and haversack for him, setting both down by his side, he had lacked the means, the courtesy, to thank him.

Nichols wanted to see his mother again. He wanted to live that long. Tom would not live that long.

He knew he should be thankful that so many of his brethren, his close brethren, had survived. But he felt the death of Lieutenant Colonel Valkenburg unreasonably, deeply, seeing him fall from his saddle again and again, until it was maddening. And Colonel Lamar, too, it didn't seem fair. He hoped the colonel had died in grace, forgiven his last profanities. Lieutenant Mincy stuck in his thoughts as well, although it was told he might live to drink coffee again, surviving his third wound, a blessing. Nichols meant to pray for Mincy, too. And for General Evans, who also promised to live. But it was just too hard to move, to part his lips.

He sat in the gloaming, shirking his duty to help out with the wounded, his own kind and the Yankees.

"It's a terrible thing," he said suddenly, speaking out loud. "It's a terrible thing."

But had a man asked, he could not have told him what that terrible thing was.

When the roll was called, in the virgin dark, the 61st Georgia, which had gone into battle with one hundred and fifty men, answered with fifty-two voices.

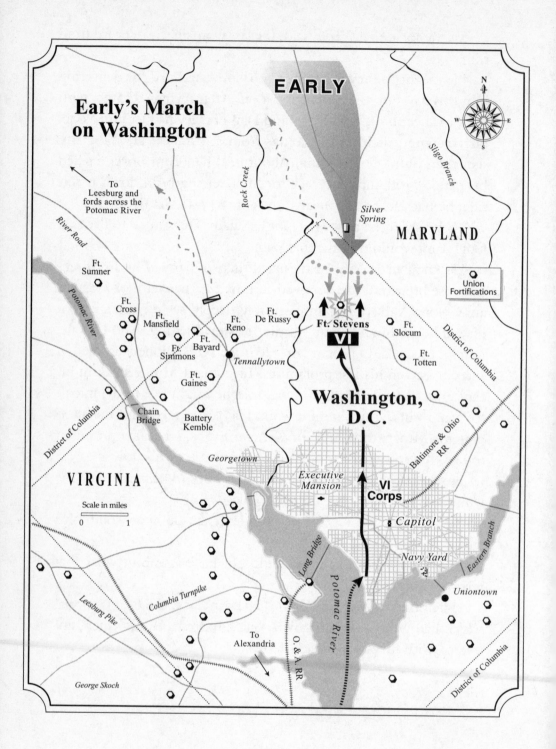

Early's March
on Washington

EARLY

To
Leesburg and
fords across the
Potomac River

Rock Creek

Sligo Branch

Silver Spring

MARYLAND

River Road

Ft.
Sumner

Potomac River

Ft.
Cross

Ft.
Mansfield

Ft.
Simmons

Ft. Reno

Ft. De Russy

Ft. Stevens

VI

Ft.
Slocum

Union
Fortifications

District of Columbia

Ft.
Bayard

Tennallytown

Ft.
Totten

Ft.
Gaines

Chain
Bridge

Battery
Kemble

**Washington,
D.C.**

District of Columbia

Georgetown

Executive
Mansion

**VI
Corps**

Baltimore & Ohio
RR

VIRGINIA

Scale in miles

0   1

Capitol

Long Bridge

Navy Yard

Eastern Branch

Leesburg Pike

Columbia Turnpike

Potomac River

Uniontown

To
Alexandria

O. & A RR

District of Columbia

George Skoch

SIX

July 11, 4:00 p.m.
Northern outskirts of Washington

Gordon stared at the Capitol's dome in the distance. Gilded by the afternoon sun, the great bell rose above the city and its girdle of forts, a fabulous dare. Gordon's longing to seize it, to violate those precincts, was as palpable as the desire he'd felt toward unruly women in his bachelorhood.

The plank-slap sound of skirmishing troubled the nearby fields and apple orchards. Artillery shells, ill-aimed, thrilled overhead, exploding randomly in the army's rear.

"We should attack now," he said. "With every man we've got."

Astride his sweat-slicked horse, Early snorted. "And just how many men do you think we've got?"

"Enough. If we go in now." Gordon's voice burned.

"This army's stretched back twenty miles, heat-sick and dropped by the roadside."

"My men *cheered*, when they caught sight of that dome."

"Ha! Three men and a dog?" Early spit amber juice. "I saw your boys stagger up. Half-dead of thirst."

Gordon gazed across the fields to the earthen fort and its entrenched wings, the last barrier between his troops and the Capitol. "The Federals are thin. They haven't got enough men up. There's a stretch on the right that's all but undefended, I rode out there myself." He turned to his fellow division commanders, Ramseur and Rodes, somber men covered in dust, their uniforms traced with sweat-salt.

Neither man offered encouragement. Ramseur looked away.

"Get everybody up, let 'em rest a spell," Early said, voice milder, tired. "Hit 'em hard in the morning, go right through 'em."

"We should go in now," Gordon said stubbornly. "Men who can skirmish can fight. Well enough to break those lines. There's nothing to those Yankees. And their gunnery's abysmal, those troops are dregs."

"Like the ones on the Monocacy?" Early paused to spit. The tobacco juice might have been a stream of venom. "God almighty, even if we went right over the walls of that there fort, what then? We haven't got the men present to make good any gains." He shook his head with finality. "It can wait for morning, morning's time enough." The commanding general called up one of his small, trust-no-man smiles. "Glory enough for everybody. Even you."

As a last resort, Gordon looked toward Sandie Pendleton, who sat his horse some yards off. But the chief of staff's face remained studiedly blank. And Breckinridge, who might have seen sense, was off rounding up the strays from his own division.

"The men would do it," Gordon said, but resignation had already entered his voice. "If we ordered an attack, they'd take that city."

"And hold it? With what?" Early's voice grew anger-tinged again. "Take these worn-out sonsofbitches into that damned flesh-pot, and I'll be damned if we ever round 'em up again." His face, his voice, mixed spite and exasperation. "Tomorrow morning, we're going to march down those streets like a proper army. A *proud* army." Of a sudden, he softened and nudged his horse toward Gordon. "Lord, John Gordon . . . we've come all this way now. Did any man here really think we'd get this far?" Early straightened his back as best he could, sweeping his paw toward the dome that shone but a few miles distant. "Look at that. Just *look* at that."

Rodes spoke up at last. With a tentative smile. "Does appear we took them by surprise. Hard to believe, I swear."

Sandie Pendleton, alert and watchful as ever, said, "What's that?" The chief of staff pointed toward the city, down the road behind the fort and the rifle pits.

Clouds of brown dust rose from the city's thoroughfares, swelling and approaching as the exhausted generals watched.

"Sonofabitch," Early said.

July II, 5:00 p.m.
The War Department, Washington, D.C.

Sitting behind his perfectly ordered desk, Major General Henry Halleck was not displeased by developments. It appeared that disaster had been averted, with two Sixth Corps divisions disembarking at the docks, their rush to fill out the city's defenses hindered only by Lincoln's childlike foolery as the president stood stoop-shouldered on the wharf, delaying the troops to repeat his bumpkin's joke, "You have to be quick, if you want to catch Early."

Lincoln was just one more of Halleck's burdens.

No blame could be attached to Henry Halleck, that was the thing. Even if the veterans forced-marching up to Fort Stevens failed to block the Confederate advance, *he* could not be blamed. All of the mistakes had been made by others; he had issued no orders that might leave him culpable. No, only the others were at fault. Grant, of course. Halleck sometimes feared that the greatest mistake of his life had been allowing the man to continue serving in uniform after Shiloh. Now that ungrateful nobody had gotten far too big for his unwashed britches. Grant had assured them all that Early's corps had not left the Petersburg lines. Halleck could hardly have been expected to know what the general in chief had mistaken.

And when Secretary of War Stanton had approached him with the warning dispatches from the railroad man Garrett—another self-important creature meddling in the war—Grant had assured them again that the danger was a chimera. If any blame there was, it lay at Grant's feet.

Outside of his office, officers and clerks hastened about, packing documents for an evacuation. Halleck believed that the danger had already passed, that the city would *not* fall, but he let the men continue their frantic efforts. He meant to be prepared, no matter what happened. And it wouldn't hurt those do-nothings to sweat a bit.

Yes, matters appeared to be in hand. And if they weren't, it would not be his fault. Should the Rebels surprise them all a final time and enter the city, the fault would lie with the absurd local command arrangements Stanton had permitted. Augur, McCook, and Meigs would be the generals to cashier. And Wright, commanding the Sixth Corps . . . obviously, it would be his fault now, if Early and his rabble torched the Capitol. Any court-martial-convening authority would grasp immediately that Henry Halleck's hands had been tied by the willful mistakes and incompetence of others.

He heard cannon in the distance, but the fires were desultory. Really, nothing to worry about, he shouldn't think. Not now. Grant had gotten reinforcements into the city, their arrival timed to the hour, if not the minute. All would be well.

If Lincoln did not interfere, of course. The man was a marauding donkey.

Halleck often had felt himself slighted, despite his august position as the Army's chief of staff. He had been called from the battlefield to oversee the infernally muddled bureaucracy, but knew himself to be the man who should command the armies in the field—rather than see authority dropped in the laps of men who didn't even begin to know their Jomini, to say nothing of de Saxe. And a bit more Vauban would not have harmed the likes of Monty Meigs, when it came down to it.

Could Meigs read French? Halleck doubted it. Probably forgot every word after leaving West Point. The truth was that there wasn't a single first-rate mind in the entire Army, other than his own, and he'd come to wear his nickname, "Old Brains," with pride—even if mediocrities spoke the words in malice, just as they made fun of his protuberant eyes. All of his life he'd been mocked by jealous inferiors.

Beyond the walls, the city had grown raucous as the reinforcements arrived. The evening before, grim dread had possessed the mob. Now it noised its beery, squalid pleasure at its rescue. The people were unworthy of their government.

In time, Halleck had come to see how vital his purpose was here, in this treacherous city. The orders Grant issued to far-flung commands had to be put right before they were passed along, and Stanton's enthusiasms needed tempering by someone else's good sense—to say nothing of the president's madcap notions. No, his place was here, after all. If he would not find battlefield glory, he would know, nonetheless, that *he* had done more to save the Union than any vainglorious popinjay with a pistol.

And there were consolations. The crisis had afforded him the overdue chance to kill Lew Wallace's military career, once and for all. Wallace had suffered a catastrophic defeat—viewed by objective military standards—throwing away the few troops interposed between Early and the Washington defenses. Properly interpreted, the reports of the battle made it clear that Wallace had committed an unbroken series of follies, compiling a spotless record of incompetence. Now his force was scattered throughout creation, Baltimore was exposed, and a veteran Sixth Corps division had been savaged, thanks to his nonsense. Nor did Henry Halleck subscribe to the view raised by that ass Dana that Wallace had delayed Early for a critical span. Defeat was defeat, and Wallace had been defeated.

Yes, Wallace. Halleck could almost smack his lips in his pleasure at the man's downfall. He had been unable to prevent Wallace's appointment to the Middle Department post, but now his every objection had been vindicated.

Wallace would have his lesson ground into his face. Two years before, the upstart had possessed the temerity to criticize *him*, Henry Halleck, before a huddle of officers awaiting a Tennessee riverboat. Of course, the remarks had been reported back to him, resulting in Wallace's first dismissal from active service: Shiloh might have been forgiven, but not such disrespect.

It had filled Halleck with delight when, the afternoon before, he had convinced Stanton to sign the order replacing Wallace with

Ord in command of the Middle Department—while leaving Wallace in place, powerless, at Ord's beck and call. Prolonged public humiliation was better than an outright dismissal from service—although that, too, would come.

Judged by his telegram sent in response, Wallace had been stunned—wonderfully so.

Let the man burn in shame. Let him rue each breath.

Those slanders uttered on the Tennessee could go on Wallace's gravestone.

The assistant adjutant general rapped on Halleck's open door. Permitted to enter, he reported that an additional corps of reinforcements had been confirmed as on its way to Washington.

"Shall I tell the men to stop packing up the records?" Townsend asked.

"Not yet," Halleck responded, smiling coldly.

July 11, 9:00 p.m.
Silver Spring Mansion

Sandie Pendleton sat on a wine-red couch whose intricate woodwork spoke of the China trade. It was a rich man's possession, firm but welcoming, and Pendleton felt a tremor of guilt at gracing it with the rump of his filthy uniform. Certainly, his beloved would not have approved: Her outward gaiety masked great care in household matters.

He did not join the others in draining the choice bottles from the cellar, but sat at a carefully judged remove from the table where the generals laughed in a fog of tobacco smoke, illumined by painted oil lamps and silver candelabra. He knew he was but a higher form of servant to these men, but he did not resent it. The role had dignity, meaning. He wrote the orders and saw them copied, sent them off, and waited for the results. He could speak with Early's authority to officers his senior—but did so carefully, in a gentleman's tone, of course. When others slept, he worked. When others drank, as on this torrid night, he remained alert, declining even the offer of a Havana. And he watched.

Holding out his unaccustomed smoke, Early told the gathering, "I can tolerate a fine cigar, but damn me if I don't start thinking of Grant every time I put a match to one. I hear the bugger smokes a box a day."

"Blair always had a nose for good tobacco," Breckinridge reminisced. "A nose for Havanas, and a palate for wine." He held up his glass. "Many a fine evening, many a time, I was a guest between these walls, you know."

"And now you're a guest again," Early said, chasing the words with his high-pitched chuckle. "Pick yourself out a feather bed. Hah." He rubbed his belly like a child. "Mighty fine ham, too. Old Blair keeps a proper smokehouse." He turned to an orderly. "We clean his pantry out of them sardines?"

Pendleton had observed Gordon pocketing two tins. Presents for his wife, he suspected—so many goods had grown rare in the South. Gordon did not offer them up, but smiled like a big cat.

Breckinridge smiled, too, staring into the shadows. Pendleton assumed that the man's thoughts had wandered to those last years of peace, to his troubled years as vice president of the now sundered nation, to friends torn away.

Nor was Pendleton the only one present thinking along such a path. General Rodes cocked a lopsided smile, long mustaches bristling. "My suggestion, gentlemen, is that we make up a fine imperial litter from one of these chairs . . . and have the men carry General Breckinridge into the Capitol in the morning. Right up to the vice president's seat. And justice be done!"

"Here, here!" Ramseur seconded.

Even Early managed a smile. "Have to ask for volunteers, though. I won't order any man to carry a politician on his shoulders. No, sir. We're already carrying enough of those bastards on our backs." He grinned at Breckinridge. "Present company excluded, of course."

Breckinridge's smile remained small and wistful. "It's an odd thing, you know . . . seeing that dome today, completed. . . ." He lifted an eyebrow, pondering, and turned his head gravely from one side to the other. "Think of that, gentlemen . . . to finish such a project in the midst of a war, to have such resources at hand . . . we didn't think of such things in '61. Did we?"

"I've got half a mind to *un*finish it," Early declared. He took a graceless slug of wine and grimaced. "You fine gents can purr over this Frenchified concoction, but I'll take Virginia whiskey, given my druthers."

Gordon, who had spoken little, held his glass before a candela-bra, admiring the ruby and purple shades of the wine. "I'd say old Blair has a taste for the *finest* things." He glanced around at his comrades. "*And* the money to pay for them, evidently." He turned to the serving orderly. "Any more of this down there? The Lafite?"

"Cases of it," Breckinridge answered for the man. "It's the el-der Blair's favorite." His lips parted gently. "He always said it was Thomas Jefferson's favorite, and that Jefferson knew his wines." He turned toward Gordon, who was caught in mid-drink. "I re-call one splendid evening—absolutely splendid—when Francis dis-missed the servants and poured our wine himself. I remember it vividly, vividly. He'd brought up a special vintage—1818, I think it was—and told us it was the finest year Lafite had ever bottled. The man was almost in poetical raptures." He grinned, but his mood seemed fragile. "I couldn't tell the difference myself, I lacked an education in such matters. But we all had a splendid time, ab-solutely splendid. Good, old Francis . . ."

The former vice president lost his smile and turned back to-ward Early. Pendleton noticed the man's fingers twining around the long stem of his glass, as nervous as a recruit before his first battle. "General Early . . . I would take it as a personal kindness, were we to spare this house. The burning of Governor Letcher's home was unfor—"

"Already told you I would, didn't I? Made 'em put the furni-ture back myself, worthless camp followers. Shoot 'em for low thieves, if we didn't need help with the wounded." Early grinned. His teeth had been fouled forever by tobacco. "Don't intend to spare his cellar, though. Spoils of war, fair game. But no more speechifyng about Jean Lafitte or whoever brewed this up. Or I'll strike the match myself."

Breckinridge attempted to smile along. "I don't believe Mr. Blair would begrudge us this calming beverage. On such a night. He's a gentleman of infinite hospitality."

Early leaned in over the table, almost toppling a wine bottle. "I'll tell you this, though. I will *not* take any pains with that other house, his son's. What will be, shall be. The man's the damned postmaster general of the scoundrel government making war on all of us." He smiled grimly. "Francis Preston Blair can provide hospitality for the generals. Let his son's four walls provide for the infantry."

Breckinridge nodded, but the gesture had no meaning. It was as if he had not heard a word of Early's tirade. "Really, the dinners here were magnificent. White-shouldered women in Worth gowns . . . bejeweled . . . so fine, so very fine. . . ."

"Tompkins," Early said, "you go on down and bring us up another armful of bottles of this slop. It does drink easy, I'll credit the Frenchies with that much."

Pendleton missed a stretch of conversation after that. Breckinridge's vision of women . . . of white shoulders . . . had summoned his wife to mind, the frustrated joys and the startling disappointments. He had expected prompt bliss from his marriage, in those rare days and nights stolen from the war, assuming that satisfaction was ordained, inevitable. Even Jackson, prickly as a hedgehog, had taken ease in his beloved's company. Or look at Gordon: When Gordon and his wife appeared together, they fairly shone. It was as if they completed each other, growing radiant in one another's company, their happiness a paradise, a refuge. Even the public affection they displayed barely remained within the bounds of decorum, one caress short of scandal. John and Fanny Gordon were . . . happy.

Pendleton told himself patience was in order. Events had trans-
pired too swiftly, due to the war. His wife was young and his rare
visits after their broken honeymoon all had been too brief, hardly
permitting simple familiarity. Yet he could not reason away his
wife's revulsion at marriage's private aspects, her frozen horror. Her
ignorance and dread had been bewildering, leaving him uncertain
of what to do. And when he did what men did, hoping the deed
would change her, it left Kate weeping and him feeling like a brute.

Still, there would be a child in the coming months. Perhaps she
might warm to him afterward?

In the mornings, dressed, she would smile and kiss him, calling him pet names, treating him as she might a favored doll. But
midnight made her shudder and withdraw.

He sometimes imagined asking advice of Gordon, who exuded
mastery. But Sandie Pendleton knew that he would never discuss
his wife with another man.

How it shamed him that his thoughts often strayed to harlots
as he embraced his wife.

"Sandie?"

He woke. Glad of the interruption. "Sir?"

"Order go out to Johnson?" Early's voice had slowed to a faint
slur.

"Yes, sir. Over an hour ago."

Early turned back to the gathering of generals. "Fool Point
Lookout business. Called it off. Let Johnson and his men come
on back and make themselves useful."

"Horses are going to be blown," Rodes said. "Lot of hard riding."

"Better now than later. I need this army all gathered up. Here."
He turned his bent torso from one side to the other. "You enlisted
men, all of you. Clear on out. We need to have us a parley 'twixt
the generals."

None of the orderlies waited for a second command.

"All right," Early began, "I want your views. What to do,
whether to attack. I'll give you my opinion once I've heard every-

body out. Y'all talk now." He smirked. "Gordon, you're not shy. You start things off."

A man of flawless posture, whether on horseback or at table, Gordon still managed to straighten another degree. "I fear . . . our hour has passed, sir. You saw the reinforcements pouring in."

Early's smirk tightened. "Go on."

"In my view, we were just too late. A half day, a day, it hardly matters now."

"I suppose I should've marched the men harder, that your point?"

"No," Gordon said. "Looking back, I believe that every man here did his best." He held up empty palms. "Fortunes of war."

"I thought you'd want to climb the walls of that fort yourself, come morning."

"The heart goes one way, the rational mind another."

Early shook his head. "Rodes?"

"I'm with John. The men we saw come up, the way they filled in the lines . . . those were veterans, that easy way they had . . . no wasted effort." Rodes smiled, eyes aglow in the candlelight. "I don't know if anything we might accomplish now would be worth the risk. After all, we've pulled Grant's plan for the summer up right short and raised merry hell. Whipped the Yankees, from Lynchburg to the Monocacy. Campaign's served its purpose."

"I'm not sure the whipping was all on one side day before yesterday," Early told him. His eyes flared and subsided again. "How are you minded, Ramseur?"

"Dogs have had a good run, sir. Every hunt has an end."

"Mr. Vice President?"

"If those *were* veterans we saw . . . Army of the Potomac men . . . I don't think the fortifications can be taken. Not without a cost so high it would destroy this army. Leave it weakened to helplessness, anyway. Burning a few—"

Early rose from his chair. A glass broke on the Turkey carpet. "I *disagree*, gentlemen. We've come this far . . . and I do *not* intend to just throw up my hands. Not when we've come this far."

He patted himself down, as if feeling for his tobacco pouch. "We attack at first light. That's my decision." He grunted and turned. "Sandie, call in the orderlies again. I feel the need for another bottle of this captured treasure."

For the first time since Early had taken command, Pendleton spoke up.

"Sir . . . perhaps . . . given the possibility of further Union reinforcements overnight . . . perhaps the attack might be delayed? Until you've had the opportunity to inspect the—"

"Hell and damnation," Early said, taken aback. "Even Sandie thinks I'm a damned fool now." He snorted, but with a surprising lack of meanness. "God almighty, you're right, son, right as a fair wind. Wine just has me going. Only makes sense to have a look in the morning, not play the fool." He considered the solemn faces of his generals. "But all of you better be set to attack the minute I give the word."

Every man murmured his assent, the inevitable loyalty.

"Now somebody get me another bottle of this Frenchy swill."

July 12, 5:30 a.m.
Fort Stevens, Washington, D.C.

Major General Horatio G. Wright prayed for the Johnnies to be damned fools and attack. He had two divisions of his corps ready to fight, as well as the local agglomeration of glorified militia, impressed clerks, and invalid veterans—the latter garbed in embarrassing pale blue uniforms. And there were guns. Plenty of guns. If the unblooded artillerymen in Fort Stevens and elsewhere along the line could not employ their batteries effectively, his infantrymen would do it for them. And the fort itself was formidable, even if he would have made a number of improvements, had he been in charge of the city's defenses.

The damnable problem was that no one really seemed to be accountable, no one possessed clear authority. He'd received a plethora of orders and countermanding instructions the previous afternoon, a mad confusion of conflicting objectives and contradictory purposes. At last, he had just followed the orders that made the most sense, riding into the right fort at a gallop, just in time to see the Confederates filing into the fields beyond a streambed.

The Johnnies had looked exhausted, and their skirmishers had lacked their usual spunk. He had wanted to go at them, as soon as Frank Wheaton came up, but the idiot who ranked him sent out his own sorry troops instead, and a poor lot they were. Permission to do too little had been granted a great deal too late— but this morning offered another chance at vengeance.

Let them come on. Just let them try it now. He meant to give Early and his tribe of ragamuffins Cold Harbor in reverse. Let them come down that long, easy slope with all the batteries hammering them. Let them ford that stream and try to come up the last half mile of open ground, let them struggle toward the earthen walls, howling all they wanted. Horatio Gouverneur Wright intended to slaughter them.

And when they were bloody and broken, his best brigades would advance to finish the business. Let bloody Upton at them, and they'd never presume to cross the Potomac again.

He stood on the walls of the fort in the blooming light, scanning the orchards opposite, counting Early's batteries, and marking the picket lines. There would be no more blind assaults, no more Cold Harbors. He had no taste for charging madly and squandering his men. He just wanted Early to come on and swallow his medicine.

The imperfections in the fortifications, the evident lack of upkeep, annoyed him, though. He could not help noting every minor flaw. Oh, the bastion and redans were strong enough, they'd do the trick, but in the steadier days before the war he would have cashiered a young engineer who took so little care.

Well, better to be a corps commander here than a captain of engineers in the Dry Tortugas. He doubted there was any spot on earth so forlorn and grim. And Florida had not been a great deal better, a territory of impossible denizens, man and beast. War had brought some advantages, that was true enough.

Still, Wright was a builder at heart, not a destroyer by nature. And when peace came, he'd return to the engineers—with sufficient seniority not to draw the wretched assignments that tortured junior officers.

He raised his field glasses. Yes, let them come on. And we'll thank them properly for killing Uncle John Sedgwick, for all the blood spilled between the Rapidan and the James, then the mess at Petersburg in June.

When Sedgwick fell at Spotsylvania, Wright had been unsure of his own ability to lead a corps in battle. Now, but two months later, he felt as if he had been in command for years, it seemed as natural as sitting in a saddle.

A man was flesh and blood, though, general or private, and his kidneys prodded him to climb down from the parapet. When he turned to go, he saw Emory Upton crossing the yard in evident pursuit, clearly in need of another tongue-lashing about jumping the chain of command. Upton was insufferable, a bothersome Christian of the sort that must have driven the Romans to persecution, and a brilliant soldier with a thirst for blood. A newly anointed brigadier, Upton doubtless had another one of his schemes to offer up. And truth be told, the little Bible-pounder had shocked them all at Spotsylvania, breaking the Rebel lines, then doing it again in the early fighting at Cold Harbor, a saint with a murderer's soul.

Wright only wished he could have another cup of coffee before dealing with the man.

"Clarke," he told an aide, "fend off General Upton until I've at least had time to piss. I don't need him trying to help me with that, too."

Down in the yard, Upton realized that he had Wright's attention. The fox-faced bugger saluted with a grin.

If Early does come on, Wright decided, he was definitely going to turn young Upton loose on him.

Moments later, as the corps commander stood over the piss trough, footsteps marched up behind him. Without turning his head, he said, "Oh, Christ, Upton!"

"Ahem."

It wasn't Upton, but Charles Dana, the assistant secretary of war.

Wright secured himself. "My apologies, Mr. Dana."

"Bad form of me to intrude. Under the circumstances. But I thought it might be my only opportunity to catch you alone." He rumpled his features. "I suppose we might move a few steps away from this ammoniac perfume, though."

They walked together, climbing the ramp to a side parapet. Upton either was under physical restraint or, for once, was displaying sound judgment and keeping his distance.

Up on the wall, they paused by an unmanned howitzer.

"The president may come up. To have a look at things," Dana said. "He's a man of infinite curiosity."

Oh, Christ, Wright thought.

"Anyway," Dana continued, "we wouldn't want any embarrassments. If Early does attack, we'll spirit the president off. But he does have a penchant for lingering." Dana looked away for an instant, as if checking for spies, and met Wright's eyes again. "Frankly, the man can get in the way at times. Means well, though."

"And if Early doesn't attack?"

"Oh, fire some guns, send out some skirmishers. Make a little show. You understand. And for God's sake, laugh at his jokes. Nothing makes him happier."

"Anything else, sir?"

Dana shook his head. "I shouldn't think so. You'll manage." The assistant secretary sighed. It had the studied quality of a performance. "You realize that I'm speaking to you in confidence, Wright. Frankly, the secretary and I have little faith in some of your nominal superiors here in the city, the command situation appears to have been lacking. We expect *you* to do what's required." Dana straightened his frock coat, as if about to meet men of greater importance. "But err on the side of caution. Another setback now would be inconvenient. Do I make myself clear?"

"Yes."

Dana joined his hands together, a gesture poised between prayer and strangulation. "Then here's to a glorious day! The 'Salvation of Washington,' in the nick of time! Rather dramatic, I must say." He turned to go. But after a few paces, he confronted Wright again. "Look here . . . do you believe that Early's going to attack? A serious attack, I mean?"

Dear God, if only he would, Wright thought. And do it immediately. I'd give them all a show.

"No."

July 12, 6:30 a.m.
Silver Spring, Maryland

Gordon found Early and Pendleton standing at the edge of an apple orchard, peering across the open ground between them and the city's fortifications. Early held a pair of field glasses at his waist, but seemed transfixed. The army commander looked bruised and battered by life.

Gordon had drunk little the night before, had left the conclave of generals as soon as courtesy permitted, and had doused himself with cold well water upon waking. He felt alert and ready. Wary, though.

Old Jube could hold his liquor, but it never helped his mood the morning after. No orders had reached Gordon, either to attack or to prepare for a withdrawal, and at last he'd run out of patience. He believed more strongly than ever that an attack would end in defeat, if not disaster. He hoped to reason with Early, fearing that an assault was now a question of honor for the old soldier.

The situation wanted extreme delicacy. The last thing Gordon intended was to prod Early to attack on a point of pride. Be as Ulysses, he told himself, employ the guile of the ultimate survivor. Never injure the pride of Agamemnon.

"Goddamned Sixth Corps," Early said by way of greeting. "I knew it, I goddamned well knew it. Look at the goddamned flags."

The commanding general did not sound in good spirits.

"Yes, sir," Gordon said. "Rode out for a look myself. Lines are just plain bristling."

"Goddamned French wine," Early said. "Not fit for man or beast." He looked at Gordon. "Change your mind again? Want to attack those sonsofbitches, after all?"

Choosing his words with care, Gordon said, "Reckon I had enough of the Sixth Corps on the Monocacy. I'd be honored to pass along the privilege, sir."

"Hah! Taught them a lesson, though."

"That we did. We did, indeed." Gordon smiled his best Ulysses smile, perfected in the looking glass of life. "I doubt they'll denude this fair city of troops again. And those are troops that will never be free to join Meade and Grant. They might as well be our prisoners. Or dead." Again, Gordon selected his words with precision. "Sir, if we've had our differences . . . my hat's off to you for bringing the army this far. Such a small force, really, it's—"

"It's a goddamned shame, that's what it is. Come so close. Those Sixth Corps sonsofbitches . . ." Early offered Gordon a cockeyed look and let his high-pitched voice climb even higher. "What do you think would happen if we went at 'em? Right now? Bust right through and march into the city?"

"We'd get in, but never get out."

A succession of looks, none promising, crossed Early's features. Then he appeared to slump, inside and out. "Going to be another man-killing scorcher," he muttered. "Damnable weather, damnable."

He met Gordon's gaze, and despite any lasting effects of the flood of wine he'd drunk, Early's eyes showed that brilliant spark that redeemed many a sin and drew good value from each tribulation. Inside that bent frame, Early was *alive*. Gordon, of all men, could recognize it.

"Goddamn it, Gordon," Early told him, "you'd be an easier man to like if you'd just be wrong now and then." He shook his head. "Grand fight on the Monocacy. If I haven't told you that."

"You haven't." Gordon smiled. But when Early grinned in return, Gordon sobered again. "It cost me."

Early nodded, looked away. "I know. You and Johnny Lamar. Friendship. Hah. Always found it easier not to have too many friends. Plays hell with a fellow's way of thinking." He raised the field glasses to his chest, then lowered them again. "Any more word on Clem Evans?"

"He'll live to fight another day. If there's no infection. Going to be hurting, though." It was Gordon's turn to shake his head. "Fool had a packet of straight pins in his pocket. Bullet hit the pins, shattered them. He'll be drawing out bits for years, I don't envy Clem the discomfort."

"What the devil was he toting pins for? Like a damned washerwoman. . . ."

Gordon shrugged. "Fanny tells me good steel pins have gotten hard to come by. Been looking out for a pack or two myself."

Early curled his lips, seeking his old, safe irascibility. The effort failed. "Have we come to that?" he asked Gordon earnestly. "Generals scavenging pins?"

It dawned on Gordon that there would be no attack. Early had already made his decision, but couldn't yet speak the words.

A Yankee gun opened from one of the redans. A cannonade followed, with the shells falling short or otherwise straying, noisy, spendthrift, and impotent.

"Guess the Sixth Corps didn't bring their artillery. Schoolboys with ramrods, goddamned waste of powder," Early said.

"Wouldn't necessarily want to get much closer, though," Gordon remarked. "Lot of guns on that line."

"Blue-belly sonsofbitches have a lot of everything, that's the problem. I'll bet that bastard Grant don't have any pins in his pocket."

For the last time that day, but not for the last in his life, Gordon thought what a shame it was that they hadn't attacked the moment they arrived the past afternoon. Even if it had only been with "three men and a dog."

He wondered if, at that very moment, he was standing at the Confederacy's last high tide.

"Oh, hell," Early said. He turned in the saddle. "Sandie? Sandie Pendleton. You come up here, boy."

Pendleton trotted up the few steps to Early. The chief of staff had kept a discreet distance from the generals' conversation—yet close enough to overhear, Gordon was certain.

"Sir?"

"Orders."

"Yes, sir."

"All divisions are to remain in their present positions, postured for defense. Pickets will advance in strength to keep the Yankees occupied . . . but there will be no general attack. All subordinate commanders will prepare for a withdrawal after sunset."

"Where to, sir?" Pendleton asked.

"Virginia, you damned fool."

PART
II

THE VALLEY

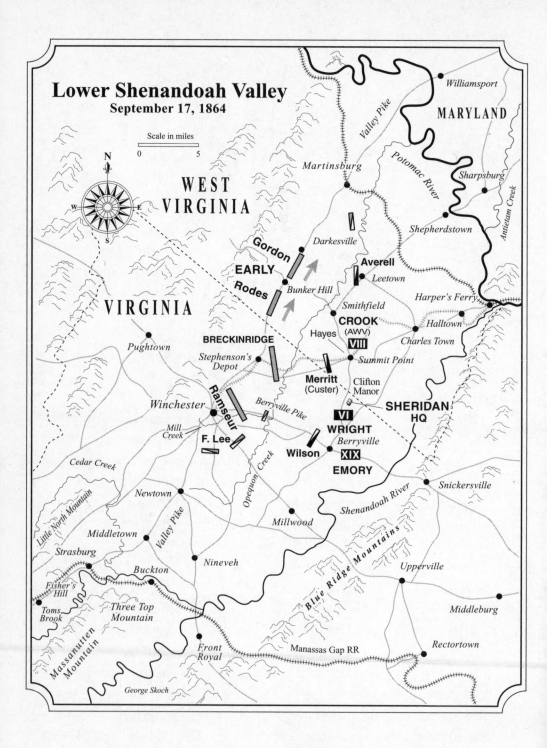

Lower Shenandoah Valley
September 17, 1864

Scale in miles
0   5

WEST
VIRGINIA

MARYLAND

Williamsport

Potomac River

Martinsburg

Sharpsburg

Antietam Creek

Darkesville

Shepherdstown

VIRGINIA

Gordon

EARLY

Rodes

Bunker Hill

Averell

Leetown

Smithfield

Harper's Ferry

CROOK
(AWV)
VIII

Halltown

Pughtown

BRECKINRIDGE

Hayes

Charles Town

Stephenson's
Depot

Merritt
(Custer)

Summit Point

Clifton
Manor

SHERIDAN
HQ

Winchester

Ramseur

Berryville Pike

VI

WRIGHT

Mill
Creek

F. Lee

Wilson

Berryville

XIX

EMORY

Cedar Creek

Opequon Creek

Snickersville

Newtown

Shenandoah River

Little North Mountain

Middletown

Valley Pike

Millwood

Blue Ridge Mountains

Upperville

Strasburg

Nineveh

Middleburg

Fisher's
Hill

Buckton

Three Top
Mountain

Toms
Brook

Front
Royal

Manassas Gap RR

Rectortown

Massanutten
Mountain

George Skoch

SEVEN

September 17, 1864
Rutherford house, Charles Town, West Virginia

He thought of apples. The day promised to be warm, but autumn's chill was scouting in the forenoon, preparing for the invasion of cold to come. The cool air called apples to mind, the hard, mouth-puckering treasures of his childhood, attacked with strong teeth and a carefree heart. He liked his apples softer now, best when ladled up as pulp from a pot. Julia made fine applesauce. Her mother had let her learn that much from the kitchen slaves.

Well, if his wife wasn't one for fancy cooking, that was all right. He wasn't much for fancy eating. And Julia had made all else in his life bearable. He hoped, in the years ahead, to pay her back.

If Sheridan proved to have matters in hand, he intended to visit New Jersey for a night before returning to City Point and the war's enormity. Look at the for-rent house his wife had picked and talk out the children's schooling. Simple chores that war had transformed into pleasures.

Seated in a rocker, he lit another cigar and tossed the lucifer match down from the porch. Even a strong Havana could not defeat the sensations of memory. Those crisp, chill apples had been little glories, each bite sharp, and regret pierced him: He could no longer risk the cherished treats. His years alone in the Northwest had been hard, not least on his choppers. Nor had the years that followed been much kinder. Privilege had come to him too late for some things: He commanded mighty armies, but feared biting into the first apples of fall.

A rare mood of self-indulgence, almost a swoon, seized him that morning. He wanted Sheridan to appear so they might settle the campaign's course, get the business moving. But sitting alone, unbothered, was a reprieve, reminding him of how strained life had become and of the pains he took not to reveal it.

Amid the clutter and clatter of yet another occupied town in another army's rear and the dust of streets churned by laden wagons and caissons, he found himself gripped again by the force of memory, banishing for a little while the gore of the past five months and the stink of war, in favor of the scents of buried decades, the sweetly pungent autumn rot—so unlike the reek of rotting flesh— and the clean, cold winds that scoured the Ohio Valley. The master killer of his age, he had learned in a bloody school to value innocence.

A teamster passing the house cursed his beasts and found himself swiftly hushed. The man glanced back toward the porch in terror.

Yes, Grant thought, I am a terrible man. But I will make an end of this.

The two aides he had brought along guarded the front fence, shooing off gawkers and well-wishers. Around the captain and major, the provost marshal's guards bristled with nerves. Such men, made small by war, saw dangers everywhere: partisans, raiders, assassins.

Grant didn't worry. The tide had turned; he felt it. It was now a matter of finishing what was under way.

He didn't know whether to admire the Rebs' tenacity or to condemn their hopeless waste of lives.

Maybe both.

Bill, his manservant, eased around the side of the house and paused below the porch, smiling. Bill had magnificent teeth, although he was the older of the two of them.

Grant took the cigar from his mouth. "Come to stare now, too?"

"Nawsuh, nawsuh. Not till I sees some cause be worth the staring."

Grant smiled, almost laughed. "Well, what is it, then?"

"Folks round here claims these Rutherfords be strong Secesh. Darkies 'fraid you going to burn this here house down."

Canting his head an inch, Grant asked, "You saying they *want* me to burn it down? Talk straight."

"Nawsuh, old Bill don't have him one toe in that creek. Don't think they'd mind, though. Say these here people Cunfeddrit as Genr'l Lee hisself, and then a mite. Black folk thought you be re-memberin' Chambersburg, what them Rebels done."

"I don't believe our hosts had a hand in that."

"Secesh, all the same. That's all I'm saying." Bill shrugged. "Feeling desirous of a nice, hot dinner, Genr'l? Kind Miss Julia trouble you to eat? Share it with that heathen man you come to see?"

Grant laughed. "I don't think General Sheridan will be staying." Tapping his cigar, he added, "Neither will we."

Pained to relinquish his vision of how the day should unfold, Bill shook his head, stamped once, and pawed the banister. "Mighty fine chickens hereabouts, say that. Yassuh. Spite all them soldiers a-lurking and a-looking, wonder a single hen be left alive." He sighed. "But your mind made up once, it made up good. Learned that much, yassuh."

"I'll give General Sheridan your regards. You get along now, see everything's packed and ready."

"Should've let me shine up them boots. Miss Julia don't like you looking like no field hand."

"We go to Washington, you can shine 'em up." With his cigar, Grant gestured toward the soldiers gathered in small groups along the street, all of them sneaking glances in his direction while pretending to be immersed in doubtful duties. "Last thing those boys need is another general with a high shine on his leathers."

His manservant went off, muttering. Bill was nigh on the only man left who would always tell him the truth. Even if the truth came roundabout from the darkey's mouth.

Bill and John Rawlins. Rawlins, too. With his weak lungs and worrisome cough. And Cump Sherman.

Grant flicked the butt into the yard. And there was Sheridan, already dismounted and striding up the street on his tiny legs, long arms dangling and chest thrust out like a pigeon's breast, with a flat-crowned hat slapped down on his bullet-shaped head. Had the man not been such a priceless killer, he might have done for Paddy the Mug in a traveling comedy show.

Well, neither of us will win any prizes for beauty, Grant thought.

Grinning, Sheridan met Grant's eyes and offered a gesture midway between a salute and a friendly wave. He came on fast, Little Phil, the way he always did, a man of profane energy, small and explosive. Still, he managed to cajole the loitering soldiers, threatening them gaily with duty in the line and an end to their easy living in the rear. And the soldiers loved him for it, it was the queerest thing. Sheridan excited soldiers so easily it was uncanny, and he made them discover reserves of courage and daring they had never dreamed they might possess. He'd killed Stuart and made the eastern cavalry.

Now Sheridan faced a greater task and had shown a hesitation that was unlike him. It was high time for a reckoning in the Valley: Cump had delivered Atlanta, shifting the political odds in the North, but Phil had to score a decisive victory here, before the election.

There could be no more raids on Washington, no more northern towns reduced to cinders. No more Chambersburgs.

What had Early been thinking? Was it mere spite? Hadn't he seen that retribution must come?

Sheridan swung through the gate, greeting Grant's aides by name. He tipped his hat, smoothed his mustaches, and let Grant feel the flash and force of eyes that looked faintly Chinese—eyes that could veer from merry to murderous quicker than a man could pull a trigger.

Spanking dust from his uniform, an instinctive courtesy, Sheridan leapt up the porch steps and said, "Sam, ain't it fine to see you?"

Grant rose. "Where's that big black nag of yours?"

"Getting a new shoe. Right foreleg. Month's been hard." Sheridan smiled. "You should ride him sometime. You're the horseman."

"Might not give him back." Grant dropped the playfulness. "You're smart enough to figure why I came up here." He resisted drawing out the campaign plan buttoned in his pocket. Willing to give Sheridan first say.

The smaller man smiled again, but it seemed an effort now. "Presumably, not for the sake of my Irish charm. Sam, it's all right. I've got him, I'm ready to move." Sheridan made to unbuckle his dispatch bag. "My plan—"

"Come inside," Grant told him.

He led Sheridan into a parlor and pointed to a beautifully polished table. "Over there." It was a handsome room, with a pink-and-white Belgian carpet dirtied by boots. A finer place it was than Grant had ever provided for his wife.

Glancing about, Sheridan asked, "We alone?"

"Provost marshal suggested that the residents have the courtesy to go visiting. Secesh to the core, I'm told."

Sheridan smoothed a map over the tabletop. Then he stopped and straightened, looking up into Grant's eyes. There was no shyness, no timidity, in the man.

"Sam, I read the papers, goddamn them. I know what they're saying. 'Sheridan won't fight. Time for a new general.' Calling me 'Harper's Weekly' because of all the damned jockeying back and forth around Harper's Ferry. But, Christ, I've had Halleck and Stanton—even Lincoln—telling me they'd like me to whip Early, please, but to take no risks, whatsoever. They'd like a victory before the vote, but they positively do not want a defeat. 'Be careful, be cautious.' And I'm supposed to protect Washington as my first priority, they make that clear. I know they fought you over giving me this command, but bugger me to Sunday . . ." A little bull, he grunted. "They want me to perform magic tricks while squatting on the Potomac."

"Best way to protect Washington is to smash Early," Grant said.

He looked aside just for a moment, thinking of his own problems with Washington, with Halleck's meddling and Stanton's imperiousness. After much persuading, Lincoln had been the deciding vote in trusting Sheridan with the newly organized Army of the Shenandoah, but the president still worried that Sheridan, at thirty-three, was too young. None of them grasped that at thirty-three a man was as good as ancient in this war. The problem wasn't the young generals, but the old ones.

"I'm sick of people who always take the frights," Grant added. He bored in. "Phil, I didn't give you this command so you could 'cover Washington.'"

"I know that. But Halleck—"

"Don't worry about Halleck."

"Stanton?"

"From now on, you answer only to me. Directly. The president's agreed."

Sheridan slapped the table so hard, the crystal baubles chimed on the oil lamps. "By God, Sam, by God! That's better than all the redheaded sluts in Mayo." Heels rising off the carpet, he added, "I've just been waiting for my opportunity. And I've finally got Early where I want him. Anderson's gone back to rejoin Lee, he just marched off. Took Kershaw's entire division and a battalion of guns. Early clearly doesn't expect a fight."

"That's news." It told Grant Lee was feeling the pinch at Petersburg.

"I had it from a Quaker girl in Winchester. Anderson and Early weren't—"

"'Quaker girl'?"

"Braver than any ten men you'll find in these parts. A darkey carries the messages, he's got a pass from the Rebs to cart in vegetables."

Grant couldn't help smiling, but his smile did not equal confidence. "A Quaker girl and a darkey potato man . . ."

"It's confirmed, though, I've had the cavalry out. Kershaw

cleared Front Royal yesterday." Sheridan was almost pleading. "Sam, this is our chance. Early's strongest division's gone, with a quarter of his guns. And he spreads out his force, the risks he takes are madcap. He thinks I'm cowed." Sheridan grinned. "I'm going to eat that bastard raw, one bite at a time."

"Show me," Grant said.

They leaned over the map. Up close, Sheridan smelled more of horse than of man, but that never bothered Grant. Engrossed, the Irishman traced converging roads, describing how he would bring his entire army to bear on Early's extreme right, cutting the Valley Pike at Newtown south of Winchester, which would force Early to attack in turn, at a disadvantage. Then his cavalry divisions would outflank the Confederates and envelop them.

Grant took out a fresh cigar and offered one to Sheridan, who declined.

"Sam, the past month hasn't gone to waste, believe me. We've been skirmishing every day, with a few real fights thrown in. Gave me time to study the ground and get to know this army. Feel out my three corps, get a sense of the strengths and weaknesses." He cocked an eyebrow. "Wright's fine. Good, old Sixth Corps. Have to wait and see about Emory. But Crook's boys are much better than I expected, I must say. George just got himself in a pickle at Kernstown, plain outnumbered. And my cavalry . . . damn me to blazes, they're going to give Early's bunch a royal time."

Glad to listen, Grant said nothing.

With zeal in his Chinaman's eyes, Sheridan charged on. "Sam, our cavalry's been wasted for years, outpost duty, guard the trains . . . they're a *fighting* force, for Christ's sake. And with Spencer repeaters—remember that first morning at Cold Harbor? Dismounted, they can stop infantry, bloody 'em up."

"Yes," Grant said with a passing chill in his voice. He preferred not to think of Cold Harbor in any respect.

"But there's more to it, much more. Cavalry can *attack* and beat infantry, too. At least mine can. I believe it with every inch of my soul that I don't owe the devil."

The little man had a way of filling every room he occupied, a charisma that made Grant marvel. Sheridan could have sold plain syrup to a medicine show, with a promise to raise the dead.

Now he was ablaze with his ideas: "It's a matter of getting the combinations right—artillery, infantry, horse—and the timing, the coordination. The different arms have never worked as a team, not really. Not the way they should. This is *modern* war, the future. Speed, range, surprise. And the mounted divisions are well officered now, the dead wood's fallen away."

"Generals?"

"Torbert's doing fine, he was the right pick to head the Cavalry Corps. Averell may have to go. At his best, he gives the Rebs a nasty time. But he's not always at his best."

"Relieve him."

"Might. Not yet. But the young bucks," Sheridan pushed on, "Merritt, Custer . . . Wilson, too. Sam, they'd fight the Rebs barehanded, I swear to God."

"Shouldn't come to that."

"And the Reb cavalry, they're little more than rags and reputation. We beat them every time the numbers are even. Haven't kept up, they're still a muddle of Walter Scott and the county-fair steeplechase race. They're poorly mounted, unsteady . . ."

"Never underestimate an enemy," Grant said. He thought: The way I did Robert E. Lee. It was a mistake he would always rue, although he had refused to let it stop him.

"Well, I damned well won't go in fear of Early, either. I plan to move fast now, he won't know what's happening until it's too late. I've sent the cavalry raiding across the Opequon every day. He'll assume any movement of mine's just more of the same. But this time my whole army will be on the march." Sheridan placed his fists on the table and leaned in toward Grant. "I can break him, Sam, I'll whip him and break him."

This was the Sheridan Grant valued, the slashing, can't-be-stopped officer he'd brought east from Tennessee. The plan didn't matter half so much as the man.

Grant chose to keep his own plan in his pocket.

"Phil, you'll have to move soon. It's politics now. Can you go by Tuesday?"

Sheridan smiled. "*Not* Tuesday. I mean to attack on Monday. Before dawn."

"That's less than two days out."

"My army's ready."

"All right," Grant said. "Go in."

Accompanying Sheridan to the blacksmith's shop, Grant paused by an oak tree.

"Don't hesitate," he said. "Ignore any orders from Halleck. Whip Early and move south. Far as it makes sense. Then pull back down the Valley, burning every barn, granary, storehouse, and depot behind you."

Grant paused to choose his next words with precision. The morning cool had been vanquished by summer's rear guard. Sheridan waited silently, all his joviality tucked away.

"We're going to put an end to threats from the Valley," Grant said. "Make sure the Rebs can't feed off it anymore, can't even move through it. Leave it so barren a crow flying over will need to carry his own provisions along."

Sheridan nodded. "Burn a town? Or two? Retribution for Chambersburg? Teach them a lesson?"

Grant shook his head. "Don't burn their houses. Going hungry will be enough for the worst of them."

"The bastards need to feel the war. Every man, woman, and child."

"We need to *end* the war. And think about what comes after." Grant considered the first fallen leaves, their mottled yellow. "Bad enough, Rebs blaming Sherman for every struck match down South. When Hood fired those warehouses himself." He made a barely perceptible sound, cold laughter. "Not that Cump would mind burning out every last plantation in Georgia. But blaming him for Hood's doings isn't fair." Grant reached out, as if to touch the trunk of the tree, but only pawed the air and dropped his hand again. "Only make him meaner, he's sensitive to the newspapers. Cump gets going again, he'll make Georgia howl."

"Speaking of fairness," Sheridan said, "Wallace still begging you for a division?"

Grant rubbed his beard. "Believe he's given up. Poor devil. Saved Washington, and Halleck does his best to drum him out. Old Brains does hold a grudge." He looked at Sheridan with renewed curiosity. "You're about the only officer who ever got on with Halleck."

"As long as I filled out the requisitions correctly and all the supplies were accounted for, he didn't harp."

Grant nodded. "And you'd still be a glorified clerk. If Halleck had his way."

Sheridan grinned. "A man has to take matters into his own hands. But about Wallace?"

"Did what I could for him. Gave him back his Baltimore command. For what that's worth."

"You know, I'm apt to lose a division commander at some point . . ."

"No," Grant said. "It's not just Halleck. Washburne won't hear of it. Wallace has political enemies back in Indiana. And Lincoln needs the Indiana men."

Sheridan's black eyes glowed with scorn. "And it doesn't matter what a man does on the battlefield? If he's on the wrong side of some crooks in a gimcrack statehouse?"

"No," Grant said. "It doesn't."

Bill enjoyed the adoring eyes as he ate the skillet of chicken. With colored folk crowding the kitchen shanty, half of them field hands new run off to town, he hurried to finish before Grant returned and called for him. Fool man lived on sliced cucumbers slopped with vinegar and cooked-black meat a hound dog wouldn't eat. Bill preferred a fried-up hen himself. With hot biscuits dipped in grease to burn your mouth.

"Hmmm-mmm. He eat like him a genr'l hisself."

"Cap'n," Bill corrected. "Cap'n, that's all. Man shouldn't go exaggerating himself."

"That's sho'."

"Why he ain't got no soldier suit? Him a cap'n?"

"Scare all these white folk round here," Bill explained. "Genr'l don't want no trouble, he got enough. I'm traveling in disguise."

He had gone round the side of the house to show them how he could walk right up on the general, while all the coming-by white men got shooed away. The chicken had been only one of his rewards.

The black folk that hadn't run off farther north were an embarrassment, though, afraid to do much of anything for themselves, living day to day, as though they were convinced they'd be slaves forever and didn't much mind. And yet, they had ideas downright fantastical about what might be heading their way in glory and jubilation: fried chicken every single day and a feather bed at night. Made no sense, but what did, anymore?

He knew the other black folk, too. The sort who wore uniforms now, who bowed and scraped around their fine white officers, but longed to stick them a bayonet deep in a white man's belly. And the truth was that most any white man would do, although a Reb was their preference.

Hadn't turned out very well at Petersburg. When they blew up that big hole in the ground. Rebs had gutted the Colored Troops like caught fish. And the white Yankee prisoners standing by hadn't complained, if the telling was right. Even gave the Johnny Rebs encouragement, so they said.

Fool thing, how white folk could have spent going on four years butchering each other worse than hogs and still not understand what hatred meant, real hatred. It was as if they hadn't read their own Bibles. Some of them were learning it now, though, at long last. Especially the Johnnies, the poor ones who held no slaves. That carried no sense, either, but life was made that way.

Their hearts were grown bitter as wormwood, as bitter as gall, the way the Good Book told.

And walking the streets of the Southron towns the Yankees had took over was near as bad. He had lived long enough to know a thing or two about men of any color, so he recognized the mark of Cain on the white faces in Virginny and he heard their sullen quiet louder than a bobcat's screech. Wasn't no kindness left, no Christian feeling, in the set of those faces and those eyes when they saw a black skin come along.

Wasn't even hatred, tell the truth. Didn't have the dignity of hatred. It was just the sort of meanness a man might feel toward a dog that had displeased him, that bit him after being given a feed. And that was the thing, the all-wrong part about it: Southron folk looked at a black man as if *he* bore the blame for all their suffering, as if the colored race had been a visitation, unwanted, unsought, just like the cholera. Bill feared for what the future might hold, once white folks stopped killing each other and started looking around for somebody else to truss up and gut.

Wasn't no trouble about his personal future, that was a blessing. The general was fond of familiar things and was like to bring him along where his doings took him. Old 'Liss Grant was a good man, not particular. Poor as a nigger himself back in Missouri, before the war took him up like the hand of Jehovah. Even when this war tired itself out, Bill calculated that the general would be all right. Powerful folks had gathered him in, like angels in a chariot swooping down.

"Him eat all that up. . . ."

They watched him, those kindred-eyed faces of differing darkness, faces of his kind, at once expectant and docile. Reverent, they studied him as he finished a last wing, impressed by the thrall he held over Grant and downright worshipful after they learned that he had seen President Lincoln in the flesh . . . which was a true-enough thing, although he had fattened the tale a bit, allowing the president to ask his advice about the Negro's future.

Wiping his chin, Bill smiled and said, "Now wasn't that fine? Run out of compliments, talking about that chicken." He produced two cigars, one for himself and one for the man who had been introduced as the pastor of this flock, though he bore no outward sign of it beyond a shabby frock coat and collarless shirt.

"General Ulysses S. Grant's private stock," he explained. "Finest cigars in this here country, North or South. 'An excellent mix of tobaccos.'" Among his own people, he did not affect the toadying minstrel-show talk that even Grant preferred.

The preacher accepted the cigar, but as Bill produced a match to light his own smoke, the old man said, "Shouldn't we pray first, Cap'n Bill? For the peace of the Lord to descend upon this land, upon this blighted Babylon of our exile, this bleeding Egypt?"

"Don't you pray for peace to come too soon," Bill told him.

September 18, 3:30 p.m.
Martinsburg, West Virginia

You men are drunk," Early said. He spit tobacco juice at Gordon's feet.

Beyond the storefront awning, rain slopped the street. Wet uniforms clung.

"Some of them are," Gordon said. "I'm seeing to it."

"No goddamned discipline," Early muttered. "I didn't march them up here for some Roman orgy."

"No," Gordon said. "Not for a Roman orgy."

Sandie Pendleton and Hennie Douglas, an aide of Early's, watched from a corner of the boarded walkway, earnestly silent. Gordon stood alone. He had already sent off his entire staff to gather up his men and prepare them to march.

"Damn you, John Gordon. Don't you get superior with me, up on your goddamned high horse. You were ordered to rip up the B and O, not turn your rabble loose."

"Work's done. That railroad won't be running again for some time."

Early looked at him with a narrow-of-eye intensity that approximated hatred. The army commander's beard was particularly filthy with tobacco slop, despite the rain that had soaked them all for hours. Gordon had once overheard a soldier describe that beard as looking like somebody with the trots had shit all over it.

"Well, you just do what I told you," Early snarled. "God almighty, I never want to see another spectacle like the one I saw this day. Soldiers drunk before noon. I should shoot half of them." He spit again, into the rain. "You march it off 'em, Gordon. Get 'em on down to Bunker Hill, rest 'em just enough, then you make Stephenson's Depot by first light. Or you may not *have* a damned division, hear?"

Gordon held his tongue, drew himself up formally and saluted. The two men glowered at each other, on the outs again. Gordon wondered if the formula for their discord could be found in Newton's laws. It just seemed that inevitable.

Early turned and stomped off through the street mud, leaving problems great and small behind him. Yes, discipline had broken down. Especially in Gordon's old Georgia Brigade, his dependables, the men he had once called his "Myrmidons." The fighting on the Monocacy had ravaged them, snapping some thin twig deep in the men, something hidden. The casualty list bore most of the blame, of course. And the matter of leadership, with so many officers dead or gone to hospital. Clem Evans was on his way back, maybe even in Richmond by now, and Clem was sorely needed. He counted on Clem to take the brigade in hand once he resumed command.

The Louisiana men were a problem, too. No doubt the Virginia Brigade would take its turn. The campaign season, long and uninterrupted, had worn everyone down, from the slaughter in the Wilderness to this forlorn street.

Yes, the drunkenness was inexcusable. It had infuriated Gordon, too, although it wasn't so stark a blight as the plague described by Early. Someone had gotten into a reserve of whiskey early that morning, even before the columns reached the goal of their raid. As for Martinsburg, it was one of the few Lower Valley towns known for Union sentiment. The men had not been inclined to show restraint.

As Douglas and Pendleton moved to follow their master, Gordon said, "Hold on there, Sandie. Wait a minute, son."

Reluctantly, Pendleton halted. Douglas continued, striding off as quickly as a boy escaping a spanking.

"What's going on?" Gordon demanded.

"He just learned about Grant. Meeting Sheridan yesterday."

"Rumor's been making the rounds of this town all day."

"Well, he didn't hear any rumor. He got it from a Yankee telegraph message."

Gordon hooked the corner of his mouth. "And now he's worried."

"That's about it. He's ordered General Rodes to hurry back toward Winchester. He expects you to make haste, too."

"And make haste we shall," Gordon said, crossing his arms. "Didn't need two full divisions to tear up some railroad tracks in the first place." He curled his mouth again. "General Early still convinced that Sheridan's got no fight in him?"

Pendleton paused. "He feels Sheridan may be deficient . . . in certain aspects of leadership. But Grant showing up . . ."

Gordon shook his head. The rain remained steady, unlike a number of his soldiers this day. "With Anderson and Kershaw gone, Sheridan has us two or better to one. At least, that's my reckoning. Doesn't take an excess of courage to strike with that kind of odds."

"No, sir."

"And you realize we're all that stands between those Yankees and many a thousand hearth and home. After Chambersburg."

"Chambersburg was almost two months ago. The Yankees haven't done—"

"Sandie, why do you think they slapped together a new army just for the Valley? Biggest force they've ever sent out this way? And why do you think Grant picked his own pup to command it?" Gordon sighed. "They haven't forgotten, Sandie."

"I don't think General Early really expected McCausland to

burn the town. I really don't. He expected them to pay up, the way every other town has. McCausland exceeded his—"

"No. He carried out his orders to the letter. I was in the tent."

"But the general didn't really mean—"

"Then he shouldn't have said it. Don't make excuses for him, Sandie. Not about this. Loyalty has its limits." Gordon lifted his sodden hat and sleeked back his hair. "Burn down a fat Dutch town in Pennsylvania, and, Lord help us, Atlanta's only the start." He reset his hat. "We didn't give them a cause. We gave them an excuse."

"Well, they'll have to fight their way through us."

"If they don't start chomping on us, bits and pieces."

"General Early didn't expect Grant to come scratching around."

"Expect the unexpected. As for Sheridan, he may not have been a lion since he took command, but he hasn't done badly, either. He's been feeling us, getting his bearings. Hasn't made one significant mistake, he's no Sigel or Hunter. And their cavalry scares the hell out of me. Wouldn't want to be looking the wrong way. Just because I had a bee in my bonnet. Understand?"

Pendleton nodded.

"All right, I've had my say. Let's hope Sheridan's taking a day of rest this splendid Sunday. Any word on Clem Evans?"

"No, sir."

Profoundly disheveled, a soldier stumbled down the street, dragging his rifle. He sang with bursts of power, but the melody and words were unknown to man.

"Don't worry," Gordon said. As if to himself. "They'll fight. They'll fight well enough."

"Anything else, sir?"

Gordon smiled. One of his Ulysses smiles. "General Early still grumbling about Mrs. Gordon's presence in Winchester?"

Made uncomfortable, Pendleton said, "Not so much, sir. But you know how moods take him. It's just that . . ."

"What?"

"Well, he knows that you and I—"

"Enjoy splendid relations," Gordon helped him along. "A shared sense of honor. Between gentlemen. What did General Early have to say? Regarding Mrs. Gordon?"

Pendleton looked into the rain, as if counting the drops. "He . . . did hope I might persuade you . . . to send Mrs. Gordon back to Richmond. You know how he feels about women around the army."

Summoning a practiced grin, Gordon took the young man by the shoulder. "Well now, son . . . if *you* can persuade Mrs. Gordon to retreat, God bless you. I can't."

The soldier braying his nonsense song paused across the street to serenade them. And Gordon lost his temper, appalling himself even as he snapped at Pendleton, who surely would be classed among the innocents.

"Damn Early to blazes! *Damn* the man! *You* know about his . . . his trollop? For want of a harsher word? Surely, you do. Everybody knows about his bitch. Man keeps a poor-white woman in a shack up the hill from the town he calls his home, fathers three or four brats on her, then rants and raves like old King Lear, 'beneath is all the fiends.' Looking down on honest women as if they're tavern whores." He grunted. "At least, *we* had the decency to marry."

In a simmering voice, Gordon added, "Men have needs, and women have theirs, too, don't think they don't. No sense pretending otherwise. Wedlock's all about filling a woman's belly, not filling up teacups. But those vows keep things decent in society, they keep us *all* safe." He shook his head. "Take life's pleasures, surely, and thank the Lord. But don't be a damned hypocrite." Folding his arms, he concluded, "I never have cared for furtiveness in a man."

The singing soldier flopped on his rear in the mud, and quiet prevailed. The rain eased sharply and the gray sky brightened.

After a moment, Pendleton whispered, "Yes, sir." The boy had gone pale—deathly pale—which mystified Gordon.

"Oh, you go on now, get along," Gordon told him. "I'll get this noble division of mine on the march."

Sliding lower into the mud of the street, the soldier attempted another musical foray.

"And I'm going to start by lifting that bastard up by his unwashed ears," Gordon declared.

He plunged into the fading drizzle, straight of back and hard
of mien, but thinking, helplessly, of his wife, excited by his own
words about desire. At that moment, he would have walked into
whatever parlor full of clucking hens he found her in, pulled her
out into the hallway, pushed up her skirt, and taken her right there
against the wall. And Fanny would've wanted it just as badly.

A rainbow graced the sky above the town. Gordon didn't
trust it.

September 18, 6:00 p.m.
Clifton Manor, Berryville, Virginia

Sheridan stood in the plantation's muddy garden, talking to Crook
and avoiding the mansion's interior. His quartermaster had selected the place for the army's headquarters, citing its central loca-
tion between the corps, but comfort doubtless had been the man's
concern. Comfort, and a not-yet-depleted cellar.

Some of the bottles had been put to good use on the newspapermen who haunted the army's rear, and Sheridan saw that as no
small advantage: The general who failed to flatter and court the
scribblers was a fool. But nothing else about Clifton Manor pleased
him. Southern grandeur, even tattered, repelled him. Too much
for his mick blood, he told himself. All the pretensions of the Anglo-
Irish, but without the frankness of their greed and bigotry. Here,
filth and iniquity dressed in frills.

The South was in need of a lesson, and now the South would
learn.

As for that Irish blood of his, he talked it up when it suited
him but was not convinced it mattered. His immigrant parents
insisted—swore—that he had been born in Albany on their long
plod to Ohio, but a hard remark he'd overheard during one of his
parents' all-too-frequent squabbles implied that he had arrived mid-
passage, somewhere upon the Atlantic. His father had cried that

the blighted brat should have been drowned at once, instead of becoming an anchor around a man's neck, worse than a wife. Complicating his nativity, his mother once spoke carelessly of a County Cavan birth. The uncertainty annoyed Sheridan, but left him free to choose his own allegiance. And he chose not only the United States, but their Northern half and Ohio, a land of industrious men and sturdy women, the West, the future.

Built on crown grants and nigger blood, the fine houses of Virginia were sordid, proclaiming the pride of dissolute, violent men who never did a day of honest work, the men who'd made this bitter, brutal war. The mansion behind him brought out the peasant vandal in his soul—his people were not of the better breed of Sheridans—and he would as soon have put a torch to its walls as sleep within them.

But the man who meant to master an army had first to master himself. And all else had gone right on this sainted Sunday, with one stroke of luck falling hard upon the other. He swam back up to a surface of good cheer.

"Buck up, George," Sheridan told his old friend from the Indian frontier. "If you don't get into the fight tomorrow, we'll still have to finish the remnants of Early's army. I'll let your boys lead the infantry pursuit, right behind the cavalry." He grinned and lit a fresh cigar. "Glory enough for all, and some to spare."

Hands clasped behind his back and shoulders a trifle bent, Brevet Major General George Crook said, "It's not about glory, Phil. You know me better than that."

Exhaling, Sheridan asked, "Then why the mope?"

Crook looked down the plantation's lane to the country road beyond. His fellow corps commanders were still visible, though barely, trailed by staff men and aides as they rode back to town. "I didn't want to fuss in front of the others . . . but I'm troubled by the plan, the changes. You're putting a cavalry division and two full corps on a narrow road through a mile-long ravine." He smiled, not happily. "Local people even call it a 'canyon.'"

"They don't know canyons."

"Maybe not. But even if my corps never crosses the Opequon, even without my boys, you're still putting a cavalry division and five infantry divisions on a single road. That's a lot of camels through the eye of a pretty small needle." He straightened his back. "You'd brace the staff man who suggested that."

Sheridan tapped his cigar. Beyond the fields and tented camps, a brilliant sunset promised a perfect morning. Rays gilded puddles left by the afternoon's showers. The rain clouds had swarmed northwest, where Early, unsuspecting, had marched his men.

"I've thought that over," Sheridan said. "Any soldier would. I expect little resistance, that's the crux of it. Scout reports are encouraging, the risk's worth taking. Go straight for the enemy's heart while he's got himself unbuttoned, don't waste time. It's a covered approach, as well, that's half the beauty. Cavalry screen along the front for a good ten miles, while the infantry moves in a single column of fours. Surprise the hell out of them."

"Phil, you're counting on everything going right."

"And it *will* go right." He tasted the cigar again and winked. "When I saw Grant, the old plan was well enough. But to come back and learn that Early's marched not one, but two, divisions away from Winchester . . . with another scattered and only Ramseur left . . . it's almost enough to make this sinner believe in Providence." He grinned. "If I can't swallow Ramseur whole by nine a.m., tie me up and offer me to the Comanches."

"Well, I'll be cheering you on. From the rear of the army."

Sheridan renewed his grin. "Somebody's sour, after all. Come on, George. I'm keeping you as my reserve because I can count on you. Let Wright and Emory feast on Ramseur—if Emory's even needed—and we'll eat up Early's other divisions piecemeal. Turn the cavalry loose in a great envelopment, it's a solid plan." He reached out and clapped the taller man on the shoulder. "Might send you in for the *coup de grâce*, we'll see."

"Speaking of the cavalry . . . ," Crook said. Along the lane that had taken the other commanders back to their corps, another troop of horsemen approached the plantation, a gay and glittering bunch, with one golden-locked officer waving a floppy hat and trailing a red scarf. Crook muttered, "When you explain the new plan to *them,* you'd best speak slowly."

Sheridan laughed.

In their last moments alone, Crook said, "Just keep that road clear, Phil. Through the 'canyon.' Even if the provost marshal has to resort to bayonets."

Sheridan cast off the stub of the cigar. "I'd say you sound like my mother, but the truth is she never worried about me much. A hard lot they were, my people." He reinforced his grin a final time. "We'll be all right, George. All wagons and impedimenta have been forbidden the road. Until the last of the infantry has passed."

"Well, may the Devil be with you. I'm off to tend to my boys." Crook paused. "Has Grant or Halleck—or anybody—decided on my command's designation yet? Do I still command the Army of West Virginia, or are we the Eighth Corps now?"

Sheridan tut-tutted. "Still the old-Army stickler. . . . George, I don't give a damn what you call your outfit. As long as those mountain-creepers of yours can fight."

The cavalry generals and a bevy of colonels jingled and clanked into the carriage circle before the mansion, laughing and preening, as if they'd intercepted the Champagne wine Sheridan had sent to Berryville for the newspapermen. He'd dispatched a keg of the season's first oysters, too, along with deft, dishonest hints about the army's activities. The trick to dealing with newspaper fellows, Phil Sheridan had learned, was to treat them like kings, but keep them in the dark.

Tomorrow, he'd delight them with a victory.

EIGHT

September 19, 2:30 a.m.
Summit Point, east of Opequon Creek

No," Rud Hayes told his adjutant, "let them sleep." With the handle wrapped in his handkerchief, he took up the coffee-pot. "I won't have my men standing in formation, waiting for orders I know won't come for hours. We're bringing up the rear, it'll be a wait." Yawning, he extended the pot. "Slurp of this fine mud, Russ?"

Dappled by the firelight, young Hastings waved off the coffee. "Just had some of Sergeant Bannister's brew-up. Open a man's eyes, I'll give it that, sir." He saluted and faded away between the tents, a man in search of a purpose, striving to fill Will McKinley's shoes.

He'll do, Hayes thought. Just needs a bit more tempering.

Squatting by the fire, Doc Joe spoke in the bantering tone he reserved for their moments alone. "Never going to make general, going easy on your men, Rud." He grinned and showed a broken tooth that made him look more a ruffian than a surgeon. "You intend to pass that coffee over here?"

Hayes stepped around the fire and poured, savoring scent and steam. The day had been damp and the night was chill, a fore-boding of October.

"Told you a hundred times now, Joe. If I never see a star, that's fine with me." He smiled back at his brother-in-law, who had followed him through the war and sewn him up more than once. "Not that I'd mind. But I'm content to be one of the good colonels." He settled the pot beside the fire and took up his own cup, letting the fragrance complete the work of waking him.

" 'General' would sound better at election time," Joe said.

Hayes lifted an eyebrow. "Sure about that? The men have some colorful words for generals nowadays."

Joe drank and grimaced. "Soldiers are always complaining— you should hear them waiting in line for sick call. Oh, sure enough, they curse the generals now. But after the war, they'll adore them like pagan idols, wait and see."

"After the war . . . ," Hayes mused. Heated by the coffee, the tin cup stung his lips.

"After the war, Grant's going to be president, mark my words. Now . . ." Joe paused, drawing up his shoulders as if for a public speech, and Hayes knew what was coming. "You might want to show a little more gratitude to the folks back home. Win the election next month, there'd be no disgrace in resigning your commission, none whatsoever. Take your seat in Congress. Will of the people."

Too quick a swallow scalded Hayes' tongue and throat. But even pain reminded a man that he was still alive. After the worst of his wounds, suffered at South Mountain, he had learned to value each day.

Despite the half hour's reprieve Hayes had meant to grant them, his men stirred in the darkness. His adjutant was trying to look out for him, to ensure he was not caught drawers-down, but the boy couldn't feel the rhythm of command. Russ was a fine young man, loyal and brave, but he lacked McKinley's finesse, the ability to read a commander's mind and get a step ahead of things, the right things. Hayes missed Will. Nonetheless, it had only been right to send him to Crook's staff, where he would have a greater chance of advancement. Lucy regarded Will, a hopeless mooncalf around the ladies, almost as another son. She had been pleased when Hayes wrote to tell her of McKinley's new position.

He had almost killed Will at Kernstown, dispatching him to guide a stranded regiment back to safety. He had not expected to see him alive again. But after a suicidal gallop cheered on by the men, the boy had returned to his side, blackened by smoke and flashing his fine, white teeth. Will McKinley had earned his chance at promotion.

Well, Will was gone and Russ Hastings would come along. Meanwhile, Hayes wasn't having any more of his brother-in-law's ambitions for the family.

"Joe, I told the party boys back home that, if nominated, I would not go home to campaign. And that, if elected, I would not take my seat until the war ends. I mean to stand by that."

"You'd do more good in Congress than here. No great shortage of colonels, Rud. You'd think the Army calved them."

"Any man who resigns his commission for politics should be scalped." The fire had failed, but embers glowed. Hayes gestured at the surrounding camp. "*They* can't resign. Never seemed quite fair to me."

Joe splashed the dregs of his coffee on the ground. "Rud, you've paid off any obligation you ever had. Wounded twice, seen your share of fighting."

"Took me a while to learn how to do things right," Hayes said. He still felt a rawness of tongue and throat from his hasty swallowing. "Figure I ought to put what I've learned to use."

Joe dismissed that. "No one's going to be grateful, Rud. Not even the soldiers, not really. All this talk of duty's a disease of the mouth that's infected men who know better. And don't ever use the word *honor* around me, I've heard that one enough. *You* try being a surgeon amid this carnage. Trade places with me, and I'll show you honor's results and duty's end." He stabbed the fire's remains with a stick. "I might as well have been a proper butcher and saved my pap the cost of an education. This Army's a scheming, scrambling sack of scoundrels, angling for promotion at any cost. The only thing honor gets a man is killed."

"Stranger might mistake you for a cynic, Joe."

"Better you hear the truth from me, than read more of Emerson's nonsense—was *he* ever in a war? Not that I know of. The men who write the books always stay at home." He discarded the stick he'd used to torment the embers. "You're a *western* man, Rud, you don't need New England 'wisdom,' anyway. More coffee in there?"

Hayes poured the last of it for his brother-in-law. "I may be an Ohio man—and proud of it—but my family's roots go deep in New England dirt. They're not all fools up thataway."

"Devil they aren't. Or Harvard Law School would've taught you how to argue a better case with yourself. I'm not letting go of it. You're going to win that election, you know you are, and you need to go to Congress. Damn them all, you should've gotten a general's star after Kernstown."

"They don't give out promotions for defeats."

"Or for fighting a rearguard action for nineteen miles? And whipping the Johnnies at the end of it all? You saved Crook's whole damned army."

"Lucy wouldn't care for your language, Joe."

They smiled at each other, knowingly and warmly.

"My sister's a Methodist," Joe noted. "I'm merely methodical."

"Lucy . . . ," Hayes said, looking away. He set his tin cup on the ground and absently scratched the last of his summer boils. It had been a painful season in the saddle. And he'd had a bad round of poison ivy, too. First time in his life he'd been impatient for the cold to overtake him. "I do wish I could . . ."

"Don't you worry," Joe told him. "It's hardly her first child."

"No."

"She'll be fine."

"She wants a daughter, you know," Hayes mused. "After all the boys. . . ."

"Rud, for Christ's sake, she's forgotten."

"Neither of us will."

"And what would your hero Emerson say? One infant's death, amid this unholy slaughter?"

"Emerson would recognize the value—the validity—of each life."

"Balderdash. For God's sake, Rud, you couldn't have prevented it. Typhoid doesn't play favorites."

"I never should have let her bring him to camp."

"She wanted to be with you. It was her decision."

"Eighteen months old," Hayes said. He sighed, but put the iron back in his spine. "You're right, I know that. As a matter of intellect. But I'm starting to think that intellect is the lesser part of a man." He scratched himself again and added, "Lucy believes he's in some celestial paradise, waiting for her up on a fluffy white cloud."

"You don't, of course."

"My reason stands against it."

"Well, she's got other, healthy sons to be thankful for. And a husband who's still alive. Despite his own best efforts to get blown to pieces."

Abruptly, Hayes said, "I never wanted this war."

Irascible again, Joe said, "But you wanted to end slavery, don't say you didn't. You always wanted that, 'long as I've known you."

"I thought it might wear away, that we could chip at it, bit by bit." Smoothing his beard, he spoke to his brother-in-law's ears but to his own heart. "All those Negroes I defended in court . . . I believed I was doing the right thing, the moral thing. It seemed so clear. Now I see that I helped ignite all this. We all did, the self-righteous, the idealists . . . Emerson, too." He jerked his head as if struck. "Good God, I want it to end, to bring an end to it."

"Then go to Congress."

"No." He attempted another smile, but failed. "Anyway, brother-in-law of mine, I haven't been elected yet."

"You will be. No Copperhead Democrat's going to beat our twice wounded, well-beloved colonel."

Around them, the camp roused with curses and struggling cook-fires, with grumpy men laboring over damp wood or stepping off for privacy. Hayes did not need daylight to follow their ways. They had become his ways, too.

It was the oddest thing. For all the slaughter and even his wounds, he had never been in better health in his life. A sickly boy and a young man who flirted with tuberculosis, he had found hard muscles and refreshed lungs in the air of army encampments, even as camp life killed men by the scores and hundreds with measles, dysentery, typhoid, and the smallpox. And the years scrambling over the mountains of western Virginia chasing Rebs had left him with legs thick as tree trunks. Nearing forty-two, he was, despite those saddle boils, truly in life's prime.

Emerson was right, so right, about life's ineffability, its inexhaustible richness, and the divinity that resided within each man, rather than in a cold and distant God. Emerson saw the beauty behind the veil and the soul's inherent greatness here on earth. The only thing his idol lacked, Rud Hayes had come to see, was a sense of humor. His soldiers had taught him the necessity of laughter.

Out in the fire-specked darkness, Lieutenant Henry demanded a count of the staff's enlisted men, striving for authority and sounding like the boy he had recently been. Another eager soul, Henry had been brought in to fill Hastings' position when Russ moved up to take Will McKinley's place on what Doc Joe liked to call "the Army carousel."

Hayes smelled biscuits, frying meat, and a hundred pots of coffee.

"You know what the damnable thing is, Joe? The thing I hate, that always sickens me afterward?"

"Rancid bacon?"

Hayes ignored the attempt at wit and said, "The way I feel in battle, right in the thick of it."

"Fear?" Joe asked, surprised. "Every man feels that."

A bugle sounded, followed by another.

"No," Hayes said. "Alive."

4:00 a.m.
The Valley Pike, north of Stephenson's Depot

Men weren't puking themselves belly-white anymore, and that was a kindness. The march the past evening had been the Devil's own

foot-burner, and many a man had staggered to the roadside, emptying himself from the wrong end, maybe even falling to his knees
in a pagan mockery of prayer. "The wages of sin!" Elder Woodfin
had cried, striding past those sickened by whiskey. "Hell's going
to stink a thousand times worse than your vomit. . . ."

Nichols had been proud, though, that of the men who'd in-
dulged, only a handful had been from the 61st Georgia. And those
men had paid a terrible price on the march, with the chaplain
preaching that hellfire itself was rushing up their throats.

Nor had they been given time to sleep off their misery, for the
brigade had stopped but three hours at Bunker Hill before the sergeants came hollering again and all but dragged weary men back
onto the road, drunkards and those who had taken the Pledge alike.
Now, with the pace yet another trial to foot and mortal spirit,
empty-gutted men cursed themselves to damnation, but kept on
going.

And a voice, solemn and terrible, had come out of the darkness after one of the chaplain's sallies, the voice of good Lem Davis, who had not touched whiskey since the death of his wife and
a child stillborn; Lem, who had not drunk one drop in Martinsburg; Lem, who had borne himself like a brawny Job, enduring:
Lem had declared, "I have no fear of hellfire," just that and not a
word more. And nary a man had answered, for Lem's tone had
not asked, but Nichols had been glad that the chaplain had moved
along to inspire some other company and had not heard Lem blaspheme, for he dreaded what else Lem might say, should he be admonished.

Who knew, from day to day, which man would pray and who
would sink to outrage? So many things had grown changeable, and
men had become as tetchy as wild beasts. It almost felt like a family
nigh onto breaking up, threatening to go different ways for reasons that would not quite fit to words, maybe just the hand of the
Lord at work, the Lord who commanded love but passed understanding. The men would fight, let no low wretch claim otherwise,
but the days between the skirmishing had grown baneful, with

flaring pride fading overnight into doubt. Maybe it was just that every last man was tired as a beast worked to its end.

Surely, they were weary men this night, hurrying through the darkness and the dust, hastening southward yet again, alert to every rumor coursing through the ranks, reading omens into each courier's passing and yearning to see the expressions on the faces of Generals Gordon and Rodes as they trotted forward to cries of "Make way, you men, make way!" But there was no least light from above, nor burning bush nearby, only the hack of men clearing unsound lungs and the jostle and jangle of infantry, Georgia infantry, rushing it knew not where. Surely, word would come quickly, though, on a tide of shouted orders, for generals riding together at night's bottom was a sign, even if they were famous friends, as Generals Gordon and Rodes were known to be.

Out there somewhere, waiting, lurked the Midianites.

In Martinsburg, Gordon had been as wrathful as Moses confronted with the Golden Calf, ready to smite, unlike himself in the fury and dread of his language, cursing the drunkards—his own men—who had shamed themselves, their officers, and the Confederacy. Not Sodom, not Gomorrah, had been so chastised. The general's vocabulary would have made Lucifer blush, and no man, not one among them, had ever heard Gordon, a Christian man, speak thus. Elder Woodfin himself had been left speechless, as shocked as any soul, before Gordon marched them off at a murderous pace. And John Brown Gordon rode before them, a Joshua, hot and brooding, aflame with silence.

In the wake of a nothing-much scrap the week before, Nichols had gotten himself a new pair of shoes, assured by Elder Woodfin it was not theft to remove them from the dead Yankee, but good husbandry of which the Lord would approve, as he surely would lift the South up from its trials. Yet on this march neither shoes nor prayer saved a man's feet from aching sorely. The brigade had rushed to Martinsburg and now was rushing back, but the rushing northward had been done in good-enough spirits, while this sour-bellied return boded no good.

"Going to be a fight," Dan Frawley said. "A man can smell it."

Sergeant Alderman told them all, "Only thing I smell is the unwashed manhood of Georgia. Y'all keep marching."

6:00 a.m.
Locke's Ford, five miles north of Sheridan's main attack

Burnished by the early morning light, his favorite scout reported: "Won't be no surprising them, General. They're up wide-eyed and looking. Got them some sharpshooters this side of the creek, up by that old cabin, on the ridge there. They're on the look-out."

"Far bank?" Custer asked.

"Far bank's higher."

"I can see that."

"Got rifle pits low down, near on the creek, but most of them's up top, hid in the trees. Fence rails piled up. And you've got to cross you a down-running field before you reach the creek, all open shooting. Ground favors the Johnnies."

"How far? In the open?"

"Sixty, seventy yards. Varies a bit."

"How many of them?"

"Maybe a bled-out regiment."

We'll have the sun at our backs, Custer thought. And in their eyes.

"Good work, Sergeant Willoughby." Custer turned back to the line of trees concealing his brigade and made straight for the 6th Michigan. The regiment's colonel was yellow as a Chinaman with jaundice, but Kidd had refused to leave his command today.

They all sensed something momentous.

"Colonel Kidd!" the young brigadier called out. "Hot work!"

Kidd saluted. By the look of him, the colonel might well collapse, but Custer wasn't going to order any man out of a battle who wanted to fight.

"Forward to the next tree line. Dismount there. You'll see a shack and some sheds up across a field, place stinks of Rebs. Have your scalawags rush them and drive them out."

"Right, sir." Kidd drew off his riding gauntlets and tucked them into his blouse. His hand came to rest on his holster. "With your permission?"

Custer nodded. "I want you dismounted, too, Jim."

Kidd waved his command forward, one of the Michigan Brigade's bloodied, brilliant regiments. Custer joined them.

In a mere brace of minutes, the 6th was on foot and snapping their Spencer carbines to life.

Leaning down from the saddle, Custer asked, "See the cabin?"

"Yes, sir."

"Then let's go."

The colonel looked up at him.

Custer grinned. "Wouldn't miss this for all the tea in China, Jimmy." Keeping to his saddle, he drew his saber with a practiced, gorgeous motion. "Don't mind company, do you?"

"I don't imagine I really have a choice," Kidd answered fondly. Turning to his men, the colonel shouted, "Wolverines! Open order! Forward!"

The men moved out, piercing the last fringe of trees and trotting up across a fallow field in bands of skirmishers, trained for independent action and no drill-book infantry nonsense.

The Rebs opened fire, sharpshooters up by the cabin and a few outbuildings. From across the creek, a greater number of rifles added support. Men in cavalry jackets dropped, and for a dangerous instant, the advancing troopers wavered.

Kidd ran ahead, shouting, "Come on, boys, and damn them!"

Custer pranced out in front of them all, long hair flapping and red scarf trailing over his velvet collar, seemingly amused by the hiss of bullets. "Another stripe for the man who takes their coffeepot! I'm thirsty, you Wolverines!"

Led by their colonel, the men surged across the field, howling the brigade's own battle yell. Custer rode with them, leaping his horse across a stone wall and making straight for the cabin.

A few Rebs stayed too long and fell. The rest ran.

Custer pulled his horse around and located Kidd. "Well done, Jimmy, well done! Now you put those Spencers to work, keep the devils over there occupied."

He was about to ride back to his waiting brigade, to organize the next phase of his attack, when a rust-whiskered sergeant marched up, shoving a prisoner.

"Your pardon, sir, but coffee there weren't. Only this dirty dog and a lovely rifle." He pronounced the last word "roy-fool," Irish as a shamrock on St. Paddy's Day.

Custer nodded his thanks, but quickly turned his attention to the prisoner. The fellow looked as wild and filthy as some desert prophet, with dark eyes that stabbed and ragged trousers that ended at midcalf, revealing starved legs. Custer could smell him from six feet away.

The remains of the fellow's tunic were so discolored that Custer had almost missed the rank on one sleeve.

"Well, Corporal, hard luck," Custer said. "Who do you march with?"

The fellow was not above a wry smile. He wanted a few more teeth. "Reckon I'll be marching under some back-of-the-army Yankee soon enough."

"I'd reckon that, too. Who *did* you march with?"

"General Breckinridge. Darn proud of it."

A lively duel had sprung up above the creek.

"Fine officer, General Breckinridge," Custer said. "I believe he means me some ill this morning, though, so with your permission . . ." He touched his hat in a friendly salute.

But if he was done with the prisoner, the Reb wasn't done with him.

"You Custer?" the Johnny called out.

"Sure, and that's *General* Custer," the sergeant admonished him.

Custer grandly swept off his hat and made his stallion rear.

"Ain't he sumpin?" the prisoner said.

*   *   *

Custer called forward his 7th Michigan and the 25th New York, a regiment newly assigned to his brigade to rebuild its strength.

Lieutenant Colonel Brewer of the 7th and the eager Major Seymour of the New Yorkers rode up and awaited orders. Custer noted that Seymour's men had adopted the red scarves of his Michiganders.

"Mel," he told Brewer, "your regiment leads. Column of fours until you pass the hill where Jimmy's boys are potting away, then wheel them into formation for a quick charge across that creek. May have to dismount some men, once you make the other bank. Get on their flanks, root the devils out, if they won't run. You might want—"

"Sir, if I may?" the New Yorkers' commander interrupted.

"You'll follow Mel's outfit," Custer said. "I was getting around to you."

Seymour squared his shoulders. "Sir . . . given that this is our first proper engagement since my regiment was privileged to join your brigade . . ."

Oh, here it comes, Custer thought. But better too much spirit than too little.

"I request the honor of leading this attack. My men wish to show their mettle."

Custer looked at Mel Brewer, who shrugged. Mel had led his share of attacks and more.

"Splendid, then!" Custer told his newest subordinate. "Don't fuss. Move fast and get across that creek. Then dismount and get up the hillside on their flanks."

Beaming, Seymour saluted and yanked his horse about, too excited to wait for his dismissal.

Custer met Brewer's eyes. Each man lifted an eyebrow.

"Prop him up, if he needs it," Custer said. "If he lives through the day, I don't doubt he'll do fine."

"Aye, sir. We'll do what's to be done."

"Off you go, then."

"Sir? Don't you think we should be hearing cannon? If Sheridan's going at them? It's five miles distance, and not a mile more."

Brewer was right, Custer realized. But he refused to be daunted. Brightening, he said, "Well, bully for the cavalry, if we get to Winchester first! Go on now, Mel."

Brewer saluted and returned to his men. Seymour's New Yorkers came forward in column, uniforms unweathered and Spencers braced on their thighs.

Abreast of Custer, Seymour shouted, "At a canter . . . for*ward*!"

After waving his newest troopers along, Custer turned to ride back to Jim Kidd's perch to watch the fight. The morning's ration of drollery had been fully consumed, and it was time for him to oversee his brigade and behave himself.

But he would have preferred to be the first across Opequon Creek. Nothing like a mounted charge in the morning.

He dispatched a rider to fetch Pete Stagg, commander of the 1st Michigan, his favorite regiment and his reserve this day. If any problems developed now, he didn't want to waste time explaining things. Pete could take things in with his own eyes.

Meanwhile, Custer rode on alone, recrossing the field that had seen the first attack. Old, crushed furrows were straddled by a body or two, and wounded men who could walk trudged toward the rear. Gaining the crest near the cabin, he remained mounted, the better to see. And the better to be seen.

Custer watched the New Yorkers swing around the hill and leave cover, followed by the 7th Michigan. Bugles sounded the charge too soon, before the New Yorkers had wheeled from their column into lines by battalion. Their order broke as they tried to execute the close maneuver at a gallop. Ragged clusters of horses and riders plunged down the slope toward the drop to the creekbed.

Pete Stagg rode up, accompanied by his two field officers, George Maxwell and Tom Howrigan. If that sergeant had been as Irish as poteen, Howrigan had still more of the green about him, a lovely, raw man.

"Jesus, Mary, and Joseph," Howrigan said, "what are those buggers about?"

The men watched as Seymour's New Yorkers splashed into the creek, only to be met by a nasty volley that made them pause when they should have dashed ahead.

The Rebel firing was a serious business and a deadly one, and the riders milling about in the creek, popping away with their Spencers from the saddle, merely offered themselves as targets. Then somebody sounded "Recall," and instead of rushing the far bank, the forward-most troopers spurred their mounts to the rear.

The sun caught their wet brass and steel amid clots of mud thrown upward from the bank.

Worsening matters, the retreating New Yorkers galloped into the 7th Michigan, throwing Mel Brewer's own attack into chaos.

Custer yanked off his wide-brimmed hat and slapped it against his leg, not once but over and over. "Damn me, damn me to Christmas, that mule-pimping jackass . . ."

His horse shied, bringing him back to his senses. As he mastered the beast, Custer looked around at the officers who had joined him. "Not one of you will repeat what I just said," he told them in a no-nonsense voice that suggested courts-martial and hangings. "The New Yorkers just have to learn our way of doing things."

But he was hot.

"Pete," he said to Colonel Stagg, "bring up the First and fix this."

Stagg saluted and rode back toward his men, followed closely by Maxwell and Howrigan. On impulse, Custer spurred after them, but veered off toward the copse where his mounted band waited.

By the time he reached the bandsmen, the First, a crack outfit, was already on the move.

"Time to earn your hardtack, boys," Custer called out. "Follow the First, stay with them. And keep one eye on me. When I wave my sword, you give 'em a rousing tune."

Then he was off again, galloping across the fields and leaping hedges with all the delight of a boy let loose on the world.

When Custer regained the cabin's grounds, he recognized Maxwell below, leading two squadrons toward the creek to feel the Rebels while Pete Stagg formed his attack. The Johnnies were putting up a fair resistance, as if they had read the portents of the day.

A number of Maxwell's men fell from the saddle, but he kept his squadrons in hand.

Howrigan, though, galloped hell-for-leather back toward the cabin. Custer could see from a distance that the major's temper was up. On the crest, he whipped his horse toward Kidd, not Custer.

"Damn it, your firing's slack as Methuselah's pecker. You call that support, James Kidd? They're shooting our men off their horses."

As Custer watched, more amused than troubled, the Irishman's saddlebag jerked, tore open, and spattered. The major's stallion backstepped.

Bewildered for a moment, Howrigan looked around himself, wide-eyed. Reassured that he had not been hit, he pawed open the satchel and extracted the dripping neck of a broken bottle.

"God damn their black souls, the buggers," he cried. " 'Twas my last bottle of Saint Brendan's piss."

Despite the deadly goings-on, the men about him laughed.

Down below, on the approach to the creek, the bandsmen had gotten ahead of half of the 1st Michigan's squadrons. Custer permitted no cowards among his brass-blowers, but it took him aback to see them near the front of the looming attack.

In for a penny, in for a pound, he decided.

He drew his sword, lifted it high, and waved it.

The band struck up "Yankee Doodle," his favorite tune for a charge. Stagg's bugler called the men forward.

The 1st surged down the slope and into the creek to face the same rough handling as the others, but Stagg's lads didn't falter. Splashing and crashing through the water, the lead men reached the far bank and spurred their horses up the steep incline, digging steel into flanks, cursing and lashing, until the beasts found their footing.

They next faced a tangle of undergrowth and Rebs hidden in the trees, but these were bully boys. After slipping from their saddles, Spencers in hand, they pushed up through the brambles, emptying magazines toward any movement.

Still, it promised to be an ugly scrap.

Atop the commanding ridge across the creek, forms in gray and butternut started running. It didn't make sense to Custer for them to break like that. The Rebs rarely fled while they still held the least advantage, then they slipped away, covered by sharpshooters.

Soon, too soon, he heard other bugles from the far high fields and spotted blue-uniformed troopers advancing along an open stretch up on the high ground.

He turned to yellow-mugged Jimmy Kidd, who'd been watching events through his field glasses.

"Lowell?" Custer asked.

"That's his flag. Reserve Brigade."

Custer snorted. "And Merritt with him, no doubt." He felt the first real warmth of the day and suddenly found himself conscious of the time. "We should've finished this. Without any help." But then he shrugged. "Well, first blood, not the last." He grinned and threw back his locks. "Plenty of opportunity ahead."

He rode down through the creek, trailed by his brigade flag, with staff men spurring their horses to catch up. Topping the far ridge, he saluted Merritt and nodded at Lowell. "Delighted to provide entertainment, gentlemen. But you interrupted the play."

"Oh, shut up, George," Merritt said.

7:30 a.m.
Ramseur's headquarters, Dinkle farm

Don't send any more of your boys forward," Fitz Lee cautioned Ramseur. "Wait a bit."

"Blue-bellies need a lesson," the division commander snapped back. "Yank cavalry's getting altogether too fond of themselves."

"Lord's own truth," Lee agreed. He cleared his raw throat. "But let's wait a while. See what's what."

Both men listened to the crack of rifles and bugle calls a mile to the east, where Ramseur's forward elements and Johnson's cavalry were sparring with the Federals.

"It's just another of their damned raids," Ramseur said. "I need to send out Pegram, give them just what they're asking for." He canted his head to look up at Lee. "How's the 'fluenza?"

Swallowing a cough, Lee said, "I'm licking it." The truth was that he felt sick as a gut-shot dog. And his old Comanche wound had come calling again, to add to his pleasures.

Lee had been awakened by a courier from Brad Johnson, warning that the Federals were advancing in strength up the Berryville Pike toward Winchester. Before he could hack and spit his way up from his sickbed, another rider had brought in a message from Lomax, reporting Union cavalry probes to the north, not far from Brucetown. Lee had dressed as swiftly as he could, but merely pulling on boots was an ordeal. And riding into Ramseur's lines, he had not liked the way things felt at all. Sick man's notions and gloom aside, the danger seemed real enough to talk reason to Ramseur, who was ready to further divide his small division and send a brigade out into the unknown.

Of course, there was more than fighting spirit behind Ramseur's impulse to rush forward willy-nilly. Brought in to bolster Early's struggling cavalry, Major General Fitzhugh Lee understood Ramseur's emotions. Hardly an envious man himself, he'd felt an untoward jealousy of Wade Hampton, vying for Stuart's favor: Limited doses of envy, even spite, were common enough in the military, persisting right alongside the jovial comradeship Lee preferred. But the rivalry among Early's infantry division commanders had gone beyond competition to verge on unwholesomeness. Rodes, an old hand at division command, and Gordon, who just seemed to have a knack for the business, kept things friendly enough, at least on the surface of that deep pond. And Breckinridge, their elder and a recipient of dignities aplenty, seemed above the pettiness, as much as a man could be. But Ramseur was smarting from a number of errors and his rashness at Stephenson's Depot, just as Lee felt a lingering sting over losing to coons in blue suits at Fort Pocahontas. The problem was that the younger man's remedy for rashness was more rashness.

Younger man? Ramseur was but the younger by two or three years, Lee cautioned himself, and his own frontier service, his status as a veteran, of which he had been so proud when the war began, had become no more than the guff of campfire tales, of joshing and reminiscence against a ruckus of fiddles and banjos. Apart from friendships sundered by secession, his years in the 2nd Cavalry meant nothing now. The scale of this war had forged a whole new world.

The firing spiked. Ramseur moved to issue orders.

"I'm sending Pegram out."

It was clear to Lee—painfully, tragically clear—that Ramseur wanted to score a pretty win before Early got back.

As for Early, Lee had sent him a signal, following up with a courier. He needed Early to hurry on down, to judge how things were forming up and, if need be, concentrate the outnumbered army. Before Ramseur threw away what slight advantage of terrain he had and the blue-bellies poured into Winchester.

The cavalryman caught Ramseur by the upper arm.

Stepping close so that no man but Ramseur would hear, Lee said, "Dod . . . I have never begged another man for anything in my life. But I am *begging* you not to advance Pegram's Brigade. Something's just plain wrong out there. Stay put."

He released his grip on the division commander. Ramseur's expression had passed, quickly, from anger through resentment to a hint of doubt. He stared at Lee as if he hated him.

"I'll give it another fifteen minutes," Ramseur said. "That suit you, Fitz?"

Unsettled soldiers had been watching them, but Ramseur, absorbed, seemed oblivious. Calling up a grin from his deepest reserve of strength, Lee announced in his hear-me-now voice, "Splendid,

General Ramseur. They'd never get by these men of yours. You could hold this position all day."

Ramseur flashed hellfire eyes. But he said nothing.

Lee could no longer restrain his cough and gave in to a fit.

He just wanted to be back in his borrowed bed. He had awakened not only to the news of the Yankees, but to sodden undergarments and soaked sheets, along with a fever that seemed to hollow him out. He could smell drool in his beard, smell his big body. But the purest lesson he had taken from his uncle was that sickness, even agony, did not excuse a man from doing his duty.

And he feared there would be a surfeit of duty this day.

Raising the stakes, a battery whumped in the distance. Lee caught the startled look on Ramseur's face.

It didn't require fifteen minutes for the division commander to change his mind about the wisdom of leaving his entrenchments. A courier arrived from one of Ramseur's outposts.

Wide-eyed and sweating like a sick man himself, the rider failed to salute, crying out, "Sheridan's whole army's out there."

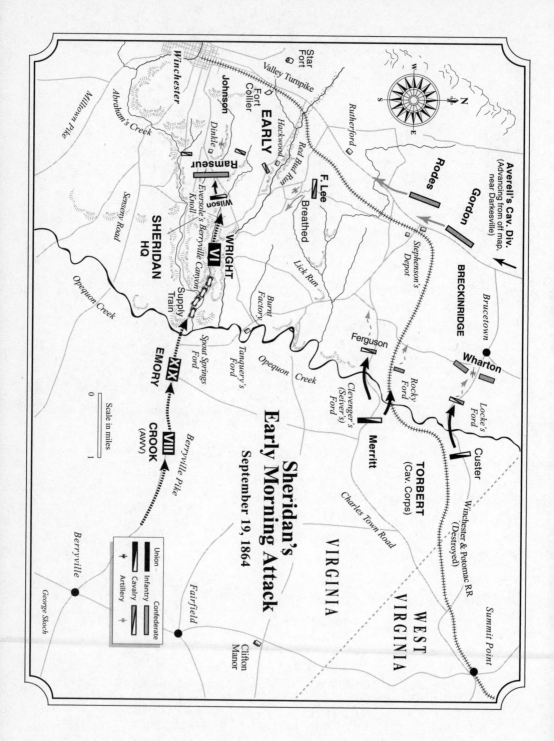

Sheridan's Early Morning Attack
September 19, 1864

George Skoch

Scale in miles
0 — 1

Union
— Infantry
— Cavalry
— Artillery

Confederate
— Infantry
— Cavalry
— Artillery

Averell's Cav. Div.
(Advancing from off map,
near Darkesville)

Winchester
Star Fort
Valley Turnpike
Fort Collier
Johnson
EARLY
Hackwood
Rutherford
Red Bud Run
Dinkle
Ramseur
Wilson
Eversole's Berryville Canyon
Knoll
SHERIDAN HQ
WRIGHT
VI
Abraham's Creek
Senseny Road
Milltown Pike
Opequon Creek
Supply Train
Spout Springs Ford
Tanquery's Ford
EMORY
XIX
CROOK
(AWV)
VIII
Berryville Pike
Berryville
Fairfield
Clifton Manor

F. Lee
Breathed
Lick Run
Burnt Factory
Opequon Creek
Ferguson
Clevenger's (Setver's) Ford
Rocky Ford
Merritt
TORBERT
(Cav. Corps)
Charles Town Road
VIRGINIA
WEST VIRGINIA
Summit Point
Custer
Winchester & Potomac RR
(Destroyed)
Locke's Ford
Wharton
Brucetown
BRECKINRIDGE
Rodes
Gordon
Stephenson's Depot

NINE

Sheridan struggled to keep his temper. The last of the Sixth Corps divisions—Davey Russell's lot—had just emerged from the gorge, well behind schedule. It was a good thing, Sheridan told himself, that Wright had gone forward to guide Ricketts into position, or the corps commander might have gotten a tongue-lashing that cut bone.

Damned muddle. All of it.

Sheridan's approach to leadership was crisp: You never showed fear or doubt; drove subordinates hard, but praised them generously; cut down threatening peers; and gave your superiors victories, damn the cost. But many a day he was tempted to strip the skin off a general or colonel serving under him. Today, Horatio Wright wanted a flaying. To say nothing of Emory, whose Nineteenth Corps seemed to have disappeared.

Quick-marching along the Pike, the regiment leading one of Russell's brigades soon spotted Sheridan. The men cheered, and Sheridan waved, offering his troops a practiced smile. He made out Upton, a brutal babe in arms, chiding the soldiers forward. Sheridan valued Upton. Despite the lad's dreary fondness for Bible verses, the young brigadier was a killer, Old Testament, not New. Astride his roan he looked savage as a Comanche.

But the rest of the day's business crawled, as if his army were a mule of a mind to test its master. Wilson's cavalry had done its work, securing the mouth of the gorge and knocking back Ramseur's boys from their forward positions, but even those early attacks had gone in at much too slow a pace. Now the situation demanded infantry to finish off Ramseur before Early reinforced him.

As the army slogged up through the "Berryville Canyon," Sheridan's plan had begun to come apart. It made him burn. The war had taught too damned many officers caution. Audacity and ferocity won battles, the Rebels saw that much.

He had realized, too late, that inspiriting an entire army was an altogether different matter from instilling dash in a few divisions of cavalry. For the first time, the scope of his new command seemed daunting: What if, after so many triumphs, he failed?

George Crook had been right about trusting a single road, and that galled Sheridan, too. He liked Crook and respected him, but remained alert to hints of Crook's old seniority. Before the war, Crook had been not only his superior officer, but something of a friend. And outward friendship still prevailed, with Crook behaving impeccably. Somehow, that made things worse.

In an instant of weakness, almost of panic, he imagined himself relieved and Crook replacing him.

Sheridan stiffened his spine: That would *not* happen.

He had passed so many officers on his climb, though. Even Davey Russell, his captain early on, was stuck leading a division under Wright. For all the good cheer his old comrades displayed toward him, Sheridan could not help feeling that more than a few would have liked to see him fail.

Unjust suspicions? Perhaps. But an officer didn't win stars through Quaker forbearance. Life was a constant battle. Every man born short of stature—and every Irishman—learned that out of the cradle: A man got what he had the grip to seize.

In the fields and gullies off to the west toward Winchester, skirmishers pricked the morning. Wright's lines filled out at last, their dark blue almost black against the greenery, and batteries unhitched between the groves. Well and good, but time was pressing hard.

And Wilson's horsemen had gained this ground at a cost. John McIntosh had been shot in a clumsy attack. Sheridan had ridden up to the wounded man's litter to tell him, volubly, that he had done nobly, but the cavalry action had been a piecemeal donny-brook, victorious only because of initial surprise and swelling numbers. A sound brigadier, McIntosh would lose a leg. Sheridan had pressed Wilson's troopers forward for as long as it made sense, but now it was the infantry's turn at work. And, veterans or not, Wright's soldiers had the slows.

Below Sheridan's hillock, a break developed in the flow of troops. Unwanted wagons creaked out of the gorge and paused, waiting for orders, blocking the road. Sheridan had expected Emory and the Nineteenth Corps to appear, ready to outflank the Rebs on the right.

If Emory didn't emerge from the maw of that gorge at the double-quick . . .

And what the devil were all those wagons doing, clogging up the egress from the gorge? He'd ordered the trains to bring up the army's rear, he'd made it clear.

Sheridan's staff men kept well off him: They'd learned to read his moods. And when still more wagons—whose damned wagons?—appeared in place of regiments and brigades, a livid Sheridan turned to order an aide with rank to ride back and attend to the problem.

Then he decided to gallop down there himself.

"Flags stay here," he snapped. "Forsyth, Moneghan, ride with me. Bring two couriers."

He spurred Rienzi toward the Pike, waving his hat to troops who cheered to acknowledge him. His smile was as forced as an old man's shit.

The soldiers had to believe that he was confident, that he had the day in hand. A bold smile at the proper time could be worth a full brigade.

Where the hell *was* Emory? Even Old Bricktop could not have strayed from the single road assigned him. . . .

Galloping through a fog of wagon dust, Sheridan pointed his mount toward the gorge, cursing Heaven and earth in anticipation. He promptly became entangled in the worst confusion he'd seen on the verge of a battle. Avoiding a crowd of purposeless men, his horse nearly collided with an ambulance. A less skilled rider would have been hurled to the ground.

The declining road was Hell under green leaves, cluttered with every encumbrance that burdens an army. Supply wagons and spare caissons swarmed the narrow Pike, wheels interlocking. Drivers raged and whipped each other's teams to clear the way, making things worse. Put-upon men fought bare-knuckled, while others loitered, content to avoid the fray pending in the high fields. There wasn't space for a rat between the flank of the hill and the drop into the ravine. Still worse, some idiot surgeon had set up shop at the one spot where wagons might have skirted each other.

A pile of arms and legs stood near the road, souvenirs of the cavalry attack and hardly the welcome Sheridan wanted for troops headed into battle.

The wagons belonged to Wright's Sixth Corps, their presence a flagrant violation of orders.

"Satan's whore of a mother," Sheridan muttered. "Buggering Christ."

He bullied his way down the narrow Pike, ordering idle men to clear the way, although they had nowhere to go. At last, he spotted Emory forcing his way up the track with faint success. Emory had lost his hat. His red hair spiked.

As he closed on the general commanding the Nineteenth Corps, Sheridan exploded.

"You shit-licking bastard. You're supposed to be up and ready to attack."

Emory was having none of it. He leaned out of the saddle as if about to punch Sheridan in the face. "*I'm* not going to be your whipping boy, Sheridan. If you want to know where my soldiers are, just look up that damned hillside. I've had to set my men scrambling through the brush to get past this mess."

"These wagons aren't supposed to be on this road."

"Well, they're not *my* goddamned wagons."

"I know whose wagons they are."

Sheridan wanted to smash somebody, something, anything.

Wright, who had it coming, wasn't there, and Sheridan couldn't restrain himself.

"This is *your* goddamned shambles, Emory. As the senior officer on the spot, you should've damned well taken charge and cleared the lot of them off."

Emory gave him another hard-boy glare. "I told Wright to his face, back across the creek, that his trains were to wait while my men went forward. Care to know what General Wright replied?"

"Don't you dare lecture me, Emory."

"He reminded me that you'd placed *him* in command of the field this morning. And he ordered me to damned well wait my turn while *his* trains went forward." Emory's eyes belonged to a wolf. "In fact, I'm violating my orders by trying my damnedest to get past all this." He jerked a thumb toward the army's rear. "I'm supposed to be back *there*, sitting on my saddle sores."

Sheridan found it unbearable to be caught in the wrong. He turned and called to Major Moneghan. "Find the provost marshal. Any of his men. Tell them to clear this road. If a wagon's stuck, push it into the ravine. Hell, push them all over. Just clear this road."

He turned back to Emory. "Get your men up that hill and into position."

9:00 a.m.
Brucetown

After a ride much lengthened by poor information, Sandie Pendleton finally found the generals. Breckinridge and Wharton stood talking on the porch of a ruined store.

"Compliments," Pendleton gasped, saluting briskly. "General Breckinridge, you're to withdraw your infantry from this position and move to Winchester with all possible speed. Yanks are pressing Ramseur. It appears to be a significant attack."

"Plenty of damned blue-bellies up here, too," Wharton objected. He was leading Breckinridge's Division while the former vice president commanded the army's wing. "At least two divisions of cavalry. With those damned repeaters. Our cavalry can't hold 'em, can't begin to."

"You have General Early's orders," Pendleton told him, a tad too curtly. He was as short of patience as of breath.

Squinting against the sun, Wharton looked up at him. Evidently seething, but restraining himself. "Tell General Early I've been hotly engaged since dawn . . . in an effort to prevent a large body of cavalry from crossing the Opequon. To no avail. We're now attempting to hold them close to the creek. There. Now you have it in prettied-up language, fit for a staff report. But I'm telling *you* plain as calico, Pendleton, if I withdraw my infantry, their cavalry's going to run all over us, once we're in open country. I can fight a time where I am now, but if I pull out too soon, we'll have a disaster. And not just for this division."

Pendleton never had cared for Wharton, who was given to unkind remarks about staff men. "Doesn't sound like much of a fuss to me, General."

Breckinridge tried to smooth things over. "Sandie, it's been plenty hot up here. You rode in during a lull. They've been coming at us hard, on multiple approaches. Plenty of them. They'll surely come again, any minute now. We need to hold them east of the Valley Pike. Or this entire army will be outflanked."

Pendleton could see it. All too clearly. But the situation at Winchester was desperate and worsening. The decision was General Early's to make, no one else's.

With a dust-scathed voice, Pendleton said, "I've given you General Early's orders. He expects you to obey them."

He pulled his horse around before the generals could renew the argument.

Wharton turned to Breckinridge. "It's plumb insanity."

Breckinridge shook his head, dismayed. "If Early were here, he'd see it."

A few fields away, Yankee bugles sounded the charge again.

"Not sure how long we'll hold, as it is," Wharton noted.

" 'Long as we can, Gabe," the former vice president told him.
" 'Long as we can."

10:30 a.m.
The Winchester battlefield

Fitz Lee didn't want any man to know how ill he remained, but
he half believed he should bind himself to the saddle. The dizziness wasn't constant, that was a mercy, but his head felt the size of
a pumpkin and as delicate as an egg. The day was mild—perfect
fighting weather—but he remained greased with sweat. Wiping his
forehead to spare his eyes, he rode as hard as he could bear to ride.
Determined to do his duty.

He rode well enough to leave Breathed's horse-artillery battery
hundreds of yards behind, along with the mounted detachment
guarding the guns. Only Breathed himself kept pace with Lee. The
artillery major had a flair for horsemanship and war that belied
his prewar training as a doctor.

Lee could have used the young man's medical skills, but gunnery took priority this morning. The boy-faced major had left his
Maryland home to establish a medical practice in Missouri, only
to hasten back as secession spread, coincidentally sharing a railcar
with Jeb Stuart and thus deciding his fate. The joke current in the
cavalry was that Dr. Breathed dissected Yankees with shrapnel, but
the young man's taste for war went even further: He relished defending his guns with pistol and saber.

Lee often marveled at what war revealed in men, but the rev-
elations could also be unsettling. He wondered how one such as
Breathed could ever again find contentment in smearing ointments
on children or giving ear to a woman's vague complaints.

Every surge of Lee's horse seemed a ruffian's blow, pounding
his spine. But he would not relax his pace. Desperate to seize the
terrain he'd scouted earlier, he galloped headlong toward the fine,
high field. Longing to lie down and to shut his eyes.

The Yankees, however, had chosen to be inconsiderate.

The queer thing was that they'd been massing all morning, a multitude, but Sheridan had yet to advance his body of infantry. It made no sense, since the Yankees had the numbers, plain as Hazel. Ramseur was stretched to the point of opening gaps of twenty, even forty, yards between regiments, with no reserves, just praying that Rodes or Gordon or Breckinridge and Wharton would appear. The Yankees overlapped his front, they had the weight to crush him. Yet they didn't come on.

Hadn't studied the terrain, either. Or if they had, they'd drawn some poor conclusions. That was one dispensation from the Lord. The Federals appeared set to rest their flank in the fields south of Red Bud Run, a creek down in a chasm, with no attempt to secure the heights to the north. And that ground had been wrought by the Lord for artillery.

"Over there," Lee shouted, hoarse and breathless, barely able. "Major, put your guns in battery over there and aim due south." He drew up and Jim Breathed reined in beside him. "Attend to this personally. Plenty of Yankees will make their appearance shortly."

Breathed snapped open his field-glass case, intent on a better look.

"Oh, they're over there," Lee assured him. He coughed.

"And fool enough to cross *those* fields?" Breathed asked, pointing. "I'd have them in perfect enfilade."

"Knock 'em down in rows."

With Breathed leading this time, they trotted to the lip of the field above the creek. Behind them, arriving cavalrymen eased their pace, husbanding hard-used nags, with four guns and extra caissons rattling behind them.

Lee intended to linger just long enough to see the battery positioned, but not a moment more. He had to ride north, see how Lomax was faring. The din of action, including the thump of artillery, rolled down from Stephenson's Depot and the countryside beyond. According to reports he'd received, two Yankee mounted divisions were in action to the north. Lee foresaw an attempt at a grand envelopment, imagining advancing waves of blue. He commanded less than half their number, shamefully mounted. And the Yanks had their infernal repeating rifles.

Well, if a man couldn't *be* strong, he'd best *look* strong.

If only the blasted dizziness would quit ambushing him. . . .

He just had to stay in the saddle, only that. His uniform clung, sodden, drenched by a private rainstorm. He prayed to stay upright through this fearsome day.

"That's right," he called to a sergeant. "Set her in just so." Breathed's cannoneers looked like filthy workmen, not the proud soldiers Lee knew them to be.

He felt himself wobbling again, the whole world tilting.

"You all right, sir?" Major Breathed asked.

Lee tried to smile, unsure if he succeeded. "Just pondering the lot of Man the Fallen, Major. And the frightful justice of the Lord."

"Put a few rounds in those trees? See what they've got in there?"

Lee stared across the ravine, focusing by strength of will. The Yankees were out there all right, deep in that grove. He'd seen them marching up from another vantage point. But the terrain was broken, rolling and plunging, with patches of trees interrupting lines of sight. Entire brigades could play peekaboo like children. It was a landscape that favored the artful defender. And Breathed's guns held the only perfect artillery position Lee had found all morning.

Why didn't the Yankees come on, though? What were they waiting for? Did their delay serve a purpose? If so, what could it be? Was Early doing exactly what they wanted, hurrying down to Winchester? The blue-bellies could've crushed Ramseur hours before, with the strength they'd already had up.

Well, their delay was going to cost them dearly.

Lee closed a palm over his eyes, trying to force the world back into good order.

"Sir? Shall I give them a few rounds?" Breathed asked again.

"No. Don't warn them. Surprise them." His empty stomach

burned, but he doubted that he could keep down as much as a biscuit.

"Sir . . . if I may speak as a doctor . . ."

"A minor indisposition, Major, all but behind me now." Lee considered the dismounted cavalrymen deploying in skirmish order to shield the guns, weighing the meager force he had provided. There just were not enough men to go around. Not enough of anything, really. Except spirit. And even that, were the truth to be told, was not all it had been. "Can't spare any more cavalrymen," he told Breathed. "You'll just have to make do."

"Yanks try coming up out of that ravine, I'll prescribe a dose of canister."

To the north, miles off, the sound of fighting intensified. Lee imagined sabers clashing with sabers. He needed to be *there*, not here any longer.

About to ride off, he wiped his beard and addressed the horse-artillery major a last time.

"Hold this position, son," Fitz Lee told Breathed. "You hold this position."

11:00 a.m.
The rear of Sheridan's army

Rud Hayes rode at the head of his brigade, confounded by the beauty of the day. Beyond the dust of an army on the march, a mild sun flirted with autumn. Dreaming of colors to come, the green groves slept. Fields gleamed and cornstalks faded. The earth, the air, emanated a grace past understanding, the transcendence philosophers struggled to explain. Swedenborg, Emerson, it mattered not: The language of men could not confine such wonder, this brilliance of life.

It often struck Hayes how nature remained unmoved by human folly. Up ahead, cannon grumped—not yet with the full growl of battle—but these fields would meet soldiers or lovers impartially. It put Man in his place.

Men were such small things, really, measured against the stars, and yet each life was the center of a universe. In West Virginia, they had clashed in a war of ants atop mountains as grand as Eden. Men had perished miserably amid splendor, and those who gave them orders could only hope their deaths had a greater meaning, that this hard war made sense.

Riding by his side, Russ Hastings asked, "Think we'll go in, sir?"

Hayes judged the distant smoke. "Only if things go badly."

The young man longed to prove his worth, to show that he could rival Will McKinley's skills as an adjutant, but Hayes felt no craving to see his men bloodied again. If they remained out of the fight this day, it would bring no shame upon them. They had done their duty before and doubtless would do it again. But killing had to be confined to duty, never a matter of personal advantage. This murder condoned must not become a passion.

In the early days of the war, it had alarmed him that men killed so readily, then gloated. Sometimes he felt that the true purpose of discipline was not to get men to fire when ordered to do so, but to ensure they ceased firing when that command was given.

Hayes had never caught the contagion of common religion, but there had been times in this war when he feared for his soul.

He could not deny that battle thrilled the senses—disturbingly so—but he never lusted for it between-times. Content to follow orders, he did his best when required, and that was enough. He knew too many of the men he led, not only by sight and name, but in the deeper ways rooted in shared hardships and winter encampments. No glory gained at their expense appealed to him.

Nor could he feel hatred toward those across the lines. He would fight them and kill them because it was a necessity, because his cause was true, however scarred. But he could not, would not, hate them. Instead, he worried over Southern friends. He hoped, when peace returned, to renew acquaintances from his Harvard days and others forged of convivial evenings back in Cincinnati. How could he hate Guy Bryan, all but a brother?

He longed to see Guy again, whether in Ohio or Texas, and he hoped that Guy could put his own rancor behind him. Surely this war would long haunt its survivors, but Hayes did not mean to let it master his span, should he be spared. War might take his life, but it would not blunt his affection for his friends.

A pair of birds winged through the dust. Hayes wiped cracked lips with a rag. His boils bit.

At times, it seemed that the greatest challenge was not to defeat those who wore a different uniform, but to avoid becoming a man of demeaned worth. If he could not share Lucy's Methodism, he certainly shared her faith in goodness and honesty, in the value of dealing justly with all men. If a fellow could not be great, he could be good.

War made that hard.

Hard, but not impossible, and Hayes refused to give in. Even in politics, he had proved that a man need not be craven. If politics asked compromise, it need not feed dishonesty. In this brief life, all a man possessed of value was his character. That and the love of those who adorned his life.

Lucy, above all, Lucy! He dreaded disappointing her as other men dread Hell.

A courier hastened toward him, raising dust within dust.

His brigade had not received its marching orders until well into the morning, hours after even he had expected to go forward. All matters had run late, which meant that blistering urgency lay ahead.

To live amidst war was akin to enduring a plague year: The man who rose hale and merry at dawn could not know if he would live until the evening. Dafoe would have understood.

The courier could not stop his horse and pounded past Hayes and his staff before managing to halt his mount and turn it.

"Begging your pardon, sir," the lieutenant cried, "General Crook and Colonel Duval request your presence up yonder at the crossing."

"How do things look?" Hayes asked.

Gleaming with sweat, the young man answered, "Confused."

11:15 a.m.
The Union line at Winchester

Despite the presence of the man's brigade commander, Ricketts felt compelled to speak directly to the major leading the 14th New Jersey now:

"You'll be the man at the heart of it, Vredenburgh. This division's at the center of the advance, the flanking divisions guide on us. That makes your regiment the unit of direction. Do not veer from the line of that damned road." He pointed at the Berryville Pike. It led out past the skirmish line, where trees and smoke obscured it. "Follow it, if it leads to the Pit of Damnation. And maintain contact with Getty on your left. You understand?"

The major nodded. Vredenburgh had performed heroically at Monocacy, but this was another day. It irked Ricketts that despite his efforts to rebuild his division, he still had majors and even captains leading regiments. While no end of colonels prowled the army's rear.

Bill Emerson, the man Ricketts had moved up to replace Truex as his First Brigade commander, felt obliged to put down a few cards:

"Just hug that road, Pete," Emerson told Vredenburgh. "Put your color guard on it and tell them to stay on it, or you'll blow their brains out yourself."

That was hardly the tone to take when speaking of good men. Ricketts nearly fired off a remark, but restrained himself: Too late now to propound a theory of leadership.

Ricketts' mood had turned surly enough as his watch ticked round the hours. A day that had started off well enough, with ham biscuits and fair weather, was turning as ugly as a squaw with smallpox. The entire Sixth Corps, in position for hours, had waited all this while for a single division of the Nineteenth Corps to appear, at last, on its right. Ricketts did not doubt that the delay would prove worth more than a division to the enemy.

Had Sheridan possessed the manliness to attack with the Sixth

Corps alone, Ricketts was certain they could have crushed the meager Reb defense. With Getty on his left and Russell in reserve—without Russell, for that matter—they could have struck the Johnnies like an avalanche. But Sheridan, despite his swagger, moved with a spinster's caution. Limited to prodding the Johnnies with skirmishers, Ricketts had watched as Reb artillery rolled into position, battery upon battery. And the guns, no doubt, would soon be followed by infantry. If Reb reinforcements had not already arrived. With the broken terrain, the swaybacked fields, odd groves, and overripe cornfields, the ground over which he had to advance was a division commander's nightmare.

Couldn't Sheridan see it? Why hadn't he struck the Johnnies early and hard? Their line had been thin as rice paper.

"All right, Major," Ricketts told Vredenburgh. "When you hear the advance sounded, move immediately. We've lost too much time already."

"Yes, sir. New Jersey will do its duty."

Profoundly ill-tempered, Ricketts almost said something completely unfair. Again he controlled himself: You never took out your spleen on your subordinates. The 14th New Jersey had fought magnificently at Monocacy, and the regiment had paid for it. It would not do to scorn decent men because he was mad at Sheridan.

Monocacy. Truex had led the brigade then. And the fellow had led it well. Then, in August, Truex had lied to him over a matter of horses. It had been a small enough thing in the midst of a war, but Ricketts was old Army. The subordinate who lied to his commander and went unpunished would one day do worse. Despite the man's battlefield record, Ricketts relieved him.

He hoped he would not regret the action this day.

Monocacy, Monocacy. Poor Wallace, the man of the hour, had gone unrewarded, barely allowed to cling to his Baltimore post, while Ricketts had come in for praise beyond all deserving, in his own opinion. He had tried to speak up for Wallace, to do the man justice, only to find that the politics of the Army, once the arbiters turned against a man, remained unforgiving.

His old wounds ached, both of the flesh and of the spirit.

Ricketts turned his horse from the New Jersey line just as another surge of artillery fire probed his position. Oh, yes, the damned Rebs were waiting for them now.

Bill Emerson trotted beside him, yapping about the effectiveness of the breechloaders his old regiment, the 151st New York, had been issued. They were out on the skirmish line now, popping away.

"Arm the whole brigade like that, and you'd see something," Emerson assured him.

"Well, it won't happen today. Christ. There's Wright again." Ricketts spurred his horse.

His corps commander rode at a canter behind Ricketts' second line. With a full complement of aides and all flags flying.

What now?

"Shall I come along, sir?" Emerson asked.

"Stay with your brigade," Ricketts called over his shoulder. "Get your boys moving the instant you hear that bugle."

He knew his men would go forward, but Ricketts was unsure of how much grit they'd show in a crisis. They'd behaved well enough in the minor scraps over the past month, but something had bled out of them on the Monocacy, a spirit that went beyond the casualty count. The officers would need to stay near the front of today's assault.

As Ricketts closed on Wright and his coterie, Warren Keifer, his other brigade commander, rode toward the corps commander, too. As ambitious as he was brave, Keifer had a fondness for the company of his superiors. An Ohioan with political connections, Keifer had defied the doctors to return to the war after his serious wounding in the Wilderness. Now the colonel rode with one arm in a sling and a star on his mind.

Well, let him win his promotion, Ricketts told himself. If he can hold his half-wrecked brigade together.

Amid a flurry of salutes, Horatio Wright asked, "Everything ready, Jim?"

"We've *been* ready," Ricketts replied. Demonstratively, he drew out his pocket watch. "Going on three hours."

Wright nodded. "Order's bound to come down any time now. Where will my courier find you?"

"Up by those guns."

"Good."

"We ought to be in Winchester by now."

"Well, we're not," Wright said.

"Any word on Early's movements?"

Wright shrugged. "I expect they'll be reinforcing. Nothing to be done."

For the third time in a matter of minutes, Ricketts held his tongue. Nothing to be done, indeed. Was Wright as blind as Sheridan?

No. But Wright had not risen to corps command through incautious speech or public displays of temper.

Ever so briefly, after praise spread for his stand on the Monocacy, Ricketts had flirted with the notion that he might be granted a corps command himself. His disillusionment had required no more than a look in the mirror as he shaved one morning. Every corps commander he knew had a pleasing appearance that he, drab and growing paunchy, would never possess.

He still marveled that he had somehow married not one, but two, true beauties. And both of them as good-hearted as Saint Clare.

In quick succession, two Reb shells exploded just to the rear of the party on horseback. Close enough to make every officer flinch.

"I suppose we've made ourselves a bit conspicuous," Wright declared.

Yes, Ricketts thought, and thanks for calling further attention to my division's position. He only hoped his soldiers wouldn't break. He didn't want to face the shame of that. Oh, they'd fight, they'd fight. But for how long?

It would come down to the dwindling number of veterans. They had to carry the new men and the shirkers, to drag them toward the Confederates. If the veterans quit . . .

He had to hit the Johnnies hard and fast, to avoid any faltering.

"All right, then," Wright added. "I'll leave you to your task. Give them the devil, Jim."

"What about Russell's division? Can I count on him behind me?"

Reining in his mount at another shell burst, Wright said, "I can't move Russell without Sheridan's consent." He offered a smile in lieu of soldiers' flesh. "Your boys can do this, Jim. Russell won't be needed." The corps commander's horse would not be steadied, but Wright managed a nod toward Keifer's sling. "Don't show yourself too openly, Colonel Keifer. Johnnies see that sling, they'll think we're scraping the bottom of the barrel."

And Wright, with his flags and paladins, went off, bracketed by shells. As Union batteries replied, smoke drifted down the lines of waiting men.

The waiting was terrible for them, Ricketts knew. Long delays made cowards of good men.

"This makes no sense," Keifer told him.

"Damn it, Warren . . . I know that much." Despite the mildness of the day, Ricketts found himself sweating. "Go back to your men. Stay ready."

"I've been ready since nine o'clock," Keifer said. "Longer, for that matter."

For a fourth time, Ricketts held his tongue. He simply rode away, back to an eminence affording what passed for a view of this wretched terrain. The battery occupying the ridge kept up a perfunctory fire. The old artilleryman in him wanted to dismount and give the crews a lesson in gunnery.

He let his own staff and colors catch up, then got down to empty his bladder. Before he could get to the business, though, a courier burst from the trees, lashing his horse.

Without waiting for his mount to still, the rider shouted, "General Ricketts, you're to advance at once!"

Removing his fingers from his trouser buttons, Ricketts re-mounted, loins complaining. It was turning into one thoroughly wretched day.

"On whose authority?" It was important, even now, to do things properly.

"General Wright's, sir. By order of General Sheridan."

Satisfied, Ricketts called, "Bugler, to me!" He drew out his watch to mark the time: It was precisely eleven forty.

Horn shining on his hip, the bugler brought his horse abreast of Ricketts.

"Sound the advance."

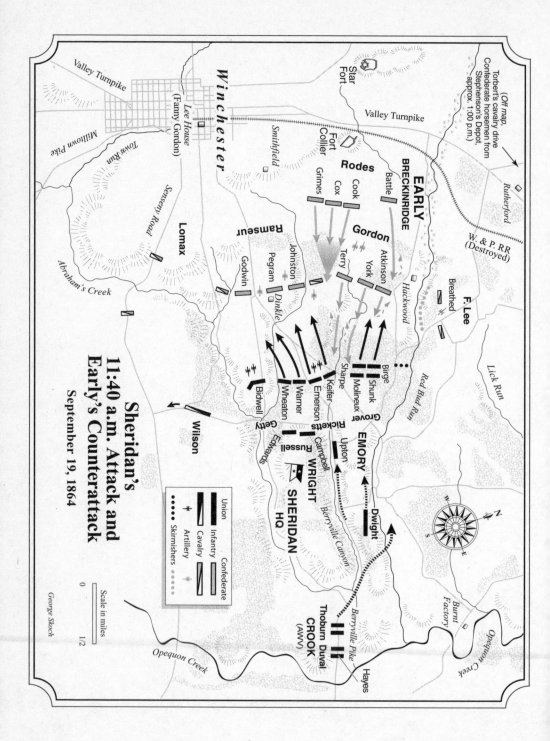

Valley Turnpike

Winchester

Lee House
(Fanny Gordon)

Millwon Pike

Town Run

Senseny Road

Abraham's Creek

Lomax

Smithfield

Fort
Collier

Fort
Cook

Grimes

Cox

Cook

Battle

Rodes

Star
Fort

Valley Turnpike

EARLY

BRECKINRIDGE

Rutherford

W. & P. RR
(Destroyed)

(Off map.
Torbert's cavalry drive
Confederate horsemen from
Stephenson's Depot,
approx. 1:00 p.m.)

Ramseur

Godwin

Pegram

Dinkle

Johnston

Terry

York

Atkinson

Gordon

Hackwood

Breathed

F. Lee

Lick Run

Red Bud Run

Sharpe

Shunk

Birge

Molineux

Grover

Bidwell

Wheaton

Warner

Emerson

Keifer

Rickets

Getty

Edwards

Russell

Campbell

Upton

EMORY

WRIGHT

SHERIDAN

HQ

Dwight

Berryville Canyon

Wilson

**Sheridan's
11:40 a.m. Attack and
Early's Counterattack**

September 19, 1864

Scale in miles

0   1/2

Union

Confederate

Infantry

Cavalry

Artillery

Skirmishers

CROOK
(AWV)

Thoburn

Duval

Berryville Pike

Hayes

*Burnt
Factory*

Opequon Creek

Opequon Creek

George Skoch

TEN

Nichols was wearied to a fright, so whupped down he nigh on lost his fear of the Good Lord. As the Georgia men marched out of the darkness into eye-cutting light, making haste just to halt and halt again, with every man sensing—just plain knowing—a fight lay up ahead, even that mortal excitement of the spirit had not been enough to master quitting flesh and punished souls. Men stumbled along, with equally tired officers coaxing them, pulling them, all but lashing them forward, and even the stalwart fell to sleeping upright at each sudden, tempting, unreasonable halt, leaning on their rifles as female leaned on male, snoring pillars of flesh, waiting to be roused, rumple-hearted, to hurry on down toward Winchester again.

The only blessed man in the entire regiment who retained his manly vigor was Elder Woodfin. The chaplain had begun the night march ranting like a prophet against drunkenness as the hardest fellows puked out the last of their rotgut, then he preached in the pauses, warming up to Deuteronomy and howling chapter 20 over and over again, challenging Georgia's manhood to rally itself to smite Israel's foes, who surely lurked:

"When thou goest out to battle against thine enemies, and seest horses and chariots, and a people more than thou, be not afraid of them: for the Lord thy God is with thee . . ."

That was heartening somewhat, although no man was pleased at the thought of "a people more than thou," which seemed all too frequent a situation these days. As night's black fur grayed and slant-light stung strained eyes, the chaplain proved as relentless as Jehovah, pounding the morning with iron words: *"Let not your hearts faint, fear not, and do not tremble, neither be ye terrified . . . ,"* and Ive Summerlin had muttered, "I'm too dogged tired to be terrified of much."

Instead of quickening against Ive's near-enough blasphemy, Nichols had found himself in sour agreement.

The daylight had taken on weight, yet another burden, and the dust was a smothering curtain a man had to gasp through. In the distance, rifles crackled, still far off, the concern of other men, and only as the sun climbed Heaven's flagpole did the cough of artillery call for broad attention.

Men griped and grumbled, heavy of eye, but their backs began to stiffen.

Couriers spurred their horses along the line of march, discourteous. As one lieutenant pounded by, brush-your-sleeve close and freely distributing horse-stink, Lem Davis, that good Christian of soft temper, remarked, "Bet that rich boy never sprouted one blister." To which Dan Frawley, nurtured with the milk of human kindness, added kill-voiced, "Feet probably never touched the ground in his life, even shits in his stirrups."

"And has a nigger to reach up and wipe his ass," Tom Boyet, who never had a nigger, said.

Of greater force than any Yankee artillery, Elder Woodfin bellowed, *"What man* is there that is *fearful and fainthearted?"*

"Passel of such, I reckon," Ive Summerlin grumped.

They were ordered off the road to clear it for guns and supply wagons, exiled like the people of Israel, into the fields and groves, the thickets and creek-cuts, hundreds of yards to the left to shield the trains against a surprise attack by the Yankees. Just made things worse, that did, with fall-down-right-here-and-go-to-sleep men required to push through briars and clumsy-climb fences, hurrying surly through foot-wetting streams that would have been dry in September, but for the mocking rain the day before, as if, unthinkable thought, the Good Lord had switched sides and joined the Yankees, a thing impossible.

"*. . . thou shalt smite every male thereof with the edge of the sword . . .*"

"Suppose a bayonet will have to do," Sergeant Alderman put in, his tired voice longing to be one of them again, to be among equals as he had been before his elevation to striped sleeves.

"Or a Barlow knife," Ive Summerlin proposed. Untangling himself from a scourge of thorns, he added, "Lord does work in mysterious ways."

They did fierce labor, marching cross-country while struggling to remain a proper regiment, a brigade, and not a mob, all the while keeping up with the horses and vehicles rolling along the Pike, at least a quarter mile to their right now, and every man afoot hating those who rode.

The battle sounds edged closer, yet remained without form, as the earth had been in the early time of Creation, so that a veteran soldier could not tell if either side felt serious about fighting, or even where.

With a marked limp, Captain Kennedy worked back along their ranks, or what passed for ranks, and surveyed the beat-down faces before calling, "Private Nichols to flanking duty. With them four yonder. Yanks are out there somewheres, don't get us surprised."

The captain, a brave man, yawned.

"Yes, sir," Nichols said, made instantly miserable by this separation from close comrades, condemned to join men from another company, good men, surely, but still . . .

Ive Summerlin laughed, not harshly. "That there's what you get, Georgie-boy, for being famed as the soberest man in the regiment."

"Here now, give over your blanket and haversack," Lem Davis told Nichols. "You won't want to be laden." And Nichols, after a moment's doubt, passed the treasures over his shoulder, relieved to be less encumbered for this duty.

Off he went across a stubble field, over earth clotted by yesterday's rain, thrusting heavy-limbed into the near-noon, catching

up to the four men moving abreast, them advancing almost lan-
guidly, weary as the ages and wary, too.

Louder and louder. Those guns. But the war was not yet upon
them, nor were they in the war. On this late and lovely forenoon,
when any man of sense wished to be elsewhere.

The flankers bickered about just how far out they ought to go,
cutting a path diagonal from the long gray caterpillar crawling
many-thousand-footed over the ups and downs of earth eternal,
five carved from the multitude, just five, headed off to skunk out
the Yankee army, that ungodly agglomeration of Amorites and Jebusites.

"Keep them eyes of your'n open," the corporal in charge warned.

Words to summon demons. No sooner had the corporal spoken
than a skirmish line of Yankees rose from thick, high clover and
coon brush, the closest of them not ten paces off, rifles leveled.

A burly sergeant thumbed rearward and said, in a used-to-things
voice, "You Johnnies just get along now, walk back thataway. And
count yourselves damned lucky."

Nichols opened his mouth to shout a warning to his kind, but
a less amiable Yankee pointed his rifle at Nichols' belly, stepping
so close that his bayonet almost touched the spot where a button
had gone missing.

"Shut your pie-trap, boy."

It was all wrong, overwhelming. This wasn't only a skirmish
party of Yankees. Long blue lines emerged from a yellowing grove.
More Yankees than Nichols had ever seen this close. With a grand
hurrah, the Federals rushed forward, thousands of them, hounds
let off the leash. Following his four fellow captives to the rear, to
Yankee Hell, Nichols paused to look back, with all the confused
longing of Lot's wife, only to stand stiffened, as if some backwoods
wisewoman cast a spell on him. He witnessed a thing he had never
seen, had never wanted to see, as the sweeping blue tide neared
his surprised brigade. He watched his gray-clad officers struggling
to bring the march formation, disordered by traitor trees, into battle order. The Yankees halted midfield and gave them a volley, dis-

integrating the gray ranks, then rushing at the remnants like hungry dogs. Barking, too.

Mortified, Nichols watched his own brigade break and run, a thing it had never done on any field. All of them—all of those Georgians who remained upright—just ran back into the trees, pursued by Yankees.

Nichols jumped at the tap on his shoulder. Whipping about, more nerves than man, he found a bewhiskered Yankee captain, no taller than himself, staring at him in wonder, hardly a pipe-stem off and smelling, indeed, of bad tobacco. On both the captain's flanks, a second battle line of Yankees advanced, but the captain and those soldiers nearest him paused.

The captain gestured at Nichols.

"Chonnie, your gun. Gif it me now, or be shot."

The captain wrenched the rifle from Nichols' grip. Bewildered, Nichols only then realized that he had held on to his weapon, at insane peril.

For all that, he rued its loss: He had fired many hundreds of balls, perhaps a thousand, from its barrel. Toward such men in blue. It was a fine piece, cared for like the prize horse of a stable.

The captain saw its quality. Turning to a soldier, he held out the rifle and said, *"Jacob, hier gibt's eine feine Waffe, schau mal. Leave yours und nimm this one."*

Turning to Nichols again, inspecting him as if weighing a purchase, the captain said, *"Du armer Kerl, du stinkst zum Himmel hoch. You go back there." He pointed eastward, toward humiliation. "No one is hurting you. Maybe you can eat."

But as Nichols shifted to step off, the captain caught his wrist.

"To which brigade are you belonging?"

"General Gordon's. I mean, it *was* his'n."

The captain straightened as if on parade. Delighted, he cried, *"Komm mal, los geht's! Der* Gordon retreats! *Los geht's, los geht's!"*

Nichols believed he had never felt a hurt as cruel as that inflicted by those words in English.

As the foreigner-Yankees rejoined the advance—hurrying

overjoyed—Nichols shambled into the trees, a crushed thing, scorched with tears. The shame of being captured, taken without even putting up a fight, was a terrible wrong. But the prospect of marching off to a Yankee jail seemed worse by a measure. He felt he would rather die than rot in a prison camp.

Surely the brigade would re-form. And the other brigades were back there waiting, closer to the Pike. When the Yankees ran into all of them, those sorry blue-bellies had to come reeling back. Gordon's old brigade could not be whipped, it could not happen. Even if General Evans had not returned to lead it this day, Colonel Atkinson was a Christian man. The men of Georgia could not falter long, they *had* to counterattack. . . .

Instead of passing meekly to their rear, he followed the Yankees.

11:55 a.m.
Union center

Ricketts dared the Confederates to kill him. Galloping past knots of men left leaderless and others clutching the earth—waiting for someone, even a corporal, to take charge—he spotted Keifer near the front of his brigade, bellowing orders as round shot roared past, each projectile a miniature hurricane, accompanied by a hail of Minie balls. Behind Keifer's mount, a crazed soldier flailed his arms as if trying to fly, splashing blood from the stumps of his wrists and keening. Keifer's words were unintelligible, but clearly he hoped to restore his failing attack.

The brigade commander spotted Ricketts and turned his horse to meet him.

The attack in the center had faltered almost from the start. And poor Getty, on the left, was trying to advance his division over even worse ground. Only the Nineteenth Corps, on the right, seemed to have made easy progress—although Ricketts didn't trust it. The Rebs didn't just quit.

Keifer's bad arm flopped in its dirtied sling. Before the colonel could speak, Ricketts said:

"I don't give a goddamn how you do it, but get your men moving again."

"Yes, sir. It's that damned artillery. And there's a gap on my right."

"Plug it. Then take those guns."

"Yes, sir. I'm trying."

"Don't *try. Do* it, man."

"Yes, sir. How's Emerson coming?"

"I'll see to Bill Emerson. Look to your own front."

A round shot howled by, so close they could feel its tug, almost an abrasion.

"I heard that—"

"Vredenburgh's dead, Dillingham's good as dead, and I need *you* to get the Rebs off Emerson's boys till I get *them* moving again. Plain enough?"

Keifer nodded.

"Well, get on with it," Ricketts told him.

Keifer would be all right, Ricketts decided. Just needed to be encouraged. And whipped a little.

He plunged back into the smoke, trusting to Providence that his own men wouldn't shoot him by mistake.

With half of Vredenburgh's neck and a shoulder torn off, Captain Janeway had taken command of the 14th New Jersey and sent a runner back for further orders—an unnerved officer's time-honored method of skirting a decision. Ricketts rode south until he struck the Pike, then turned directly into the Rebel fires until he found the inert lines of the New Jersey men, all lying flat, as if bedded down for the night.

Janeway ran toward him. Ricketts bent from the saddle.

Unwilling to destroy the captain's meager authority, Ricketts hissed, "Janeway, get these men moving. *Now.*" The junior man's face, boyish and gilded with sweat, showed earnestness, good intent, self-doubt, and naked fear—not of dying, but of making a fateful error at his sudden assumption of command.

"Captain," Ricketts tried again, "get your men up and continue the attack. Everyone else is making progress," he lied. "Keifer's almost at the Rebel guns. I need New Jersey to pull its weight today, don't shame your state. Now . . . you see to your work, and I'll get those Vermonters back there moving up on your flank."

Janeway saluted, foolish and formal, but rushed back to his men, calling, "Colors to me! Come on, New Jersey, we're being left behind!"

Poker was honest work compared to a battle, Ricketts decided.

He made a point of riding calmly forward, into the midst of the rising New Jersey troops, demonstrating a disdain for bullets no sane man could feel. "Come on, lads," he shouted, forcing up a smile. "I know I can always count on the old Fourteenth."

Given purpose and an example, men cheered him, a rare enough thing.

Ricketts made for the 10th Vermont, lied to their officers, too, and got the men going by shaming them as well. Then he praised and embarrassed the 106th New York back into action. As soon as the New Yorkers stepped off again, the Reb artillery showed it had their range, blasting great holes in their ranks, tearing men apart in a squall of blood. But the chemistry had changed and the survivors leaned into their work, quick-stepping forward, almost running, to regain their place beside their sister regiments.

His dead and wounded already crowded the fields and bands of trees, but Ricketts had his division moving again.

11:55 a.m.
Confederate center

Early screeched as he rode by Nelson's battery.

"Pour it into 'em, give 'em hell," the army's commander cried. "God *damn* their blue-bellied souls. Just pour it into 'em."

Ramseur's Division was holding, desperately, but Gordon, who had promised a prompt arrival, seemed to have blundered into a scrap of his own on the far left flank. Early needed Rodes' Division to come up—he needed it this minute—to plug the gap between Ramseur and Gordon.

It enraged him that he could not draw his army together purely by strength of will. He regretted the excursion to Martinsburg. Hell, he regretted half the things done and undone since '61. And yes, he regretted the folly of burning Chambersburg, which he had ordered in a fit of pique, an order that fool McCausland had carried out all too well, doing his spelled-out duty for once in his life, his duty and more. Early regretted poorly chosen whores and ill-made whiskey, feuds unresolved and decent men estranged. But regret, he knew, wasn't worth one busted rifle. Battle was of the moment, and a man in its midst did as well to celebrate past sins as to rue their doing. Conscience was a toy for men at peace.

He *needed* Bob Rodes. *Now.* And he needed Gordon to straighten out his fracas and steady the left. He needed that lazy-bones Fitz Lee, who had cowered too long on a sickbed, and his hardly better than worthless cavalry to do their part for once. But for the moment all he could do himself was give vent to his spite as the blue ranks rallied and pressed forward again.

"Pour it into those sonsofbitches," he shouted in that high voice he had learned to hate himself, a voice just short of cronelike, a squeak that failed to match his splendid rage. "Kill every goddamned one of 'em. . . ."

12:05 p.m.
Ramseur's Division

Stephen Dodson Ramseur watched in horror as his line broke and collapsed. Soldiers who had fought fiercely the minute before, coolly taking aim at the oncoming Yankees, began to turn from their barricades and trenches, ignoring the imprecations of their officers and fleeing, alone, then in little groups, and finally as a herd.

Delivered late and at close range, a Yankee volley scoured the line of piled-up fence rails shielding the last brave souls. Ramseur's stoutest men turned their backs and tried to outrun an avalanche.

The Yankees cheered and surged forward.

Caught afoot, Ramseur plunged into the mob of men turned wild-eyed and frantic, men stricken by an epidemic of fear and rendered numb to the blows their officers struck with the flat of their sabers.

"For God's sake, men! Stand and fight, stay and *fight*! Don't run like women, *stand*!" Ramseur bullied and begged. He might have been a mockingbird, for all the good he did.

Where was that priss Gordon, where was Rodes? Dallying over breakfasts? While he held Sheridan's army by himself?

"Stop, men! Make a stand! We're not whipped yet. . . ."

"Hell we ain't," an insolent private snarled.

"I *order* every man to halt. On pain of death," Ramseur shouted.

Not one man paused.

Ramseur picked up a discarded rifle, called, "Halt!" a last time, then started swinging the weapon by the barrel, clubbing his own men with the stock, sweeping it toward their heads as they scurried by. He hurt a few, left some bloody on the ground. All of them took it meekly, unresisting. That only made him madder.

Whether it was due to his bashing of skulls or divine intervention, a miracle gleamed: The last of his men, those who had been reluctant to withdraw, began to congeal, not quite in a line of battle, but in pockets of humanity crowding together, as if for warmth in winter. They turned their rifles on the Yankees again.

The blue advance was inexorable, though. It rolled toward them like a storm-driven tide.

But every moment, every slice off a moment, mattered terribly. The only hope of saving the rest of the army was to make the Yankees bleed for every yard.

So many of them, though. So many. Too many regimental flags to count.

His division was dissolving, from the left flank to the right. It *had* dissolved. And the Yankees seemed to be everywhere, with only random clots of gray-clad men and stubborn-to-the-death batteries resisting them.

A single aide remained to him, all others either slain or swept away.

Ramseur gripped the lieutenant by the forearm. "Find General Early. Tell him I can't hold them any longer."

12:05 p.m.
Gordon's Division

Georgia!" Gordon declaimed from the saddle, in a voice resonant and grand, a studied voice. "*Georgia* may have been *surprised*. Georgia may have been *tricked* by her low enemies. But Georgia has *not* been defeated. Georgia . . . dear Georgia . . . is not even dismayed. No, no! Not dismayed and barely incommoded. Georgia will *rally* and take her revenge on those tricksters garbed in blue." He glowered at the disordered, panting men. "Put plain, we're going to go back there and whip those bastards."

The cheers from his shattered brigade were halfhearted at best, but at least they were cheers. He needed these men, his old men, needed every man. And he needed them soon. The battle growled like a monstrous bestiary as gun crews served their pieces in a fever and his other brigades, Zeb York's Louisianans and Bill Terry's Virginians, swung out against the snout of the Union attack, matching in ferocity, if briefly, the Federal advantage in numbers.

Gordon turned to Ed Atkinson, leading his old brigade in the absence—much lamented—of Clem Evans.

"Ed, I know these boys need time. But time is one commodity we don't have. I need you to get them up and organized and back into the line. Won't be long before the Yankees realize we're snapping and snarling without a tail to wag." He stared at the good, earnest, brave, unready man commanding his Georgians, the best choice of those available to him after the crippling bloodletting on the Monocacy. "I'm off to confer with General Rodes, see if we can't cooperate, instead of just plugging up holes and crossing our fingers."

Bob Rodes, bless him, had rushed up and gone straight into the line, just in time to prevent a rout, filling the gap between Gordon's men and Ramseur's thinned-out ranks, unleashing his leading brigade like an iron bar slammed down on a china teapot. And still it wasn't enough. They were holding, and York and Terry had rolled back the foremost Yankees a few hundred yards—helped not a little by a battery some angel had dropped in the fields just north of a creek-cut, guns that swept the Yankees from the flank and did good business. But his gains and those of his comrades were as frail as a maiden's wrists.

Trailed by a much-reduced staff, Gordon threaded his way between knots of stragglers and wounded men withdrawing as best they could. There seemed little danger to his person back here, with the Yankee artillery occupied in supporting their advance, but stray shots did have a way of mocking men. He rode gingerly.

He found Rodes conferring with Early, Bob nodding in his priceless way and stroking his mustaches, while Early carried on like a shopkeeper robbed and upbraiding the constable.

As Gordon approached, he heard Early say, "Close-run thing, close-run, but we can hold now. Just shore things up, we'll hold them now, all right."

Rodes told him, "It won't be enough, they'll only pound us down. Sheridan won't quit. Grant saw to that, I reckon."

"And you propose?" Early snapped. "What? A charge? Like damned-fool Lee at Gettysburg?" He turned, sour-faced, to Gordon. "How about you, Gordon? What do *you* suggest? Figure I'd better ask, since you're bound to tell me anyway. Now that you're done dawdling down the road." He looked bitterly from Gordon back to Rodes and at Gordon again, shaking his head. "Jackson would have stripped both of you of your commands."

Gordon resisted noting that Early wasn't Jackson.

"I believe," Gordon said in a voice artificially calm, "that General Rodes is right. If we just defend, they're going to grind us down. Our only hope—a slim one, I grant—is to hit them right now, hard. We can do it, Bob here can do it. There's a gap opening up, just about in the center of their attack. My bet's on a corps boundary. Division, at least. The wing facing me's drifting north, while the other's hooking south. Bob's fresh boys can run right down the middle." He turned toward Rodes and smiled. "Or turn Cull Battle loose when he comes up."

"I haven't seen any gap," Early said.

"It's there."

Rodes jumped in, lying his teeth off: "John's right. I've seen it myself. They've split themselves apart, smack dab in the middle of their attack. I can ram right through."

For all his surliness, it was clear that Early was pondering matters, giving their recommendations a fair hearing in his peculiar way. And Early, Gordon knew, was an attacker at heart, not one content to surrender the initiative.

"Damn me to bloody, blue blazes, all right, then," Early declared. "Rodes, you see a chance, you go on in. Rip the guts out of those sonsofbitches." He grinned, surprising both men, displaying bad teeth above his clotted beard. He canted his head northward. "My huntin' ears tell me you've got yourself into another difficulty, Gordon. I'm hearing Yankee hurrahs. Best go see to it."

And Early rode away.

The Yankee artillery fire intensified.

"Christ," Gordon said. "Sheridan's not playing jacks, give the little mick that. By the way, there really is a gap, Bob."

The generals smiled at each other. "Well, if there wasn't a gap, I suppose we'd have to make one," Rodes allowed. "I can't see waiting politely while Sheridan leads the dance. Shock 'em, John, it's the only hope we've got."

"Bless you, Bobby. Give those boys the devil." He lifted his hat. "I'd better get back up there. Does sound unpleasant."

A round of solid shot struck the earth close enough to spatter both men with dirt and bits of stone. Rodes, who wore a new-looking uniform, seemed more bothered at that than at the prospect of battle.

"Close, that one," Gordon said.

Rodes smiled broadly, spreading his mustaches. "Close don't count."

No more time. Gordon pulled his horse around and teased it with the reins, no spurring required. One with its master, the great beast gathered speed.

Guns raged and the battle roared, deafening, newly alarming. Explosive rounds impacted and men screamed.

He neared a section of rifled pieces firing from a knoll, hardly a hundred yards along his way, and he realized that something was wrong. As if he smelled it well before he saw it.

The cannoneers, first of one gun, then of the next, ceased their labors and peered in his direction, openmouthed in shock. At first, Gordon thought they were startled by his appearance.

But that wasn't it, he sensed as much in a moment. He turned to look back at whatever had caught their attention.

Through curls of smoke, he saw a dreadful thing. It was Rodes. Unmistakably. It was Bob Rodes, no longer in the saddle, but flat on the ground, as soldiers tried to control his maddened horse. The animal sprayed everyone with blood. Aides and others rushed to the fallen general. All nearby activity came to a halt.

Gordon galloped back down the slope and leapt from the saddle before his horse had stopped. Running to keep his balance, he pushed men aside then dropped to his knees beside his friend and rival.

Rodes stared heavenward, unblinking. One side of his head was a slop of jagged bone, blood, and slime. Blood drenched his chest as well.

Gordon stood up, glaring.

"All of you. Back to your business." He firmed his spine and stiffened his jaw to master his own emotions. When he was certain

that he could continue to speak without flaw or weakness, he told them, "General Rodes wouldn't want you crying like women, he'd want you *fighting*. Killing goddamned Yankees. Now get to it!"

He grabbed a captain he knew to be reliable. "Ride back and find General Battle. Bring him here. I don't care what he's doing, you bring him here. On my order. And don't go blathering to everybody you meet."

"Yes, sir."

But Rodes, before his death, had himself summoned Battle to report. Drenched with sweat and horse foaming, the brigade commander appeared barely a minute after the aide had ridden off.

"Jesus Christ," he said when he got a look at Rodes.

Gordon turned to the dead man's befuddled staff. "Well, don't just let him lie there. Fetch an ambulance. Get him out of sight, take him back to Winchester." He turned to Cullen Battle, who was a hard man. "Damned shame and worse, but there's no time now to fuss. You're senior brigadier, I do believe?"

Battle, still appalled, could only nod.

"Well, take command, man. By General Early's order and on my word, you're to take this division . . ." Gordon realized that he was getting ahead of himself, that he needed to explain about the gap the Yankee advance had opened. But there was no time left, every sound around them had grown ominous.

Battle rescued the situation. "And take it into that gap out there, out front of us. Yes, sir. General Early overtook me, caught me up on what's doing. Damn Yankee fools."

"Thrash the devil out of them, Cull. Take Sheridan's scalp, if you can."

"Wouldn't say that around my Alabama boys. Might take you serious."

They looked down at Rodes a last time as two officers and a sergeant lifted him onto a litter. Battle saluted, followed by Gordon.

John Brown Gordon took off his hat and wiped an eye.

"Sweating like a Dalton hog," he explained. "Go kill some Yankees, Cull."

12:05 p.m.
The fields north of Red Bud Run

Major James Breathed deemed it absurd to stand on the "dignity of an officer." Needing to be in on the sport, he dismounted for a time and helped serve a piece, relishing the roar and recoil, the long trail of shot through the blue sky and the rising smoke, the abrupt devastation visited upon the Yankees. Fitz Lee had been right, damned right, that the high fields were a perfect artillery position. As the Yankees advanced, their right flank lay as open as a belly exposed by a clumsy surgeon's knife. His guns had never done a better day's service.

The Yankees appeared as foolish as they were craven, just blundering forward, one rank after another, and not one blue-belly officer in authority stopping to think, Why, my, oh my, those Rebs have *guns* over there, we'd best look into it. No, they just stumped forward, stalwart and stupid, and Breathed's guns swept them away like ants.

Fitz Lee had added more horsemen from Wickham's Brigade to defend the guns, but it seemed a waste of man-flesh and horsemeat now. The Yankees didn't even take an interest, just let themselves be slaughtered. The ladies of Winchester might have laid out a luncheon between the caissons, for all the danger posed by Sheridan's army. The blue-bellies didn't even respond with artillery, let alone an infantry assault.

They deserved to lose, deserved to be killed. This wasn't murder, just culling inferior beasts from the human herd.

Across the creek and to the right of his blue-clad, mindless targets, Breathed saw gray ranks advancing at last.

12:05 p.m.
Gordon's front

Nichols felt caught up in one of those dreams in which things made sense and didn't make sense at all, one of those troubling dead-of-night journeys during sleep when you watched yourself doing peculiar things, thinking all the while, That can't be right, that can't be right at all. He'd trailed the Yankee ranks over low hills and into swales, across shot-ripped fields and through groves sheltering skulkers, Yankees who took no interest in his wanderings, since each man's sole concern was his own hide in his own britches.

There were wounded men, too, and dead men, some from his brigade, but none he marked from his regiment, though he didn't look too hard, didn't want to blunder. Most of the fallen were Yankees, though, swept by artillery fire from fields off to the north, the guns spitting flame and puffing balls of smoke, bewilderingly unmolested by the blue-bellies. Errant shells from his own kind posed more danger to him than Yankees now.

Yankee wounded drifted past him, careless of all matters beyond their pain or bewilderment. Not one bothered him or spoke a word.

Trailing the last line of Yankees at a cautious fifty yards, he crossed a stream still clear of blood, flowing quick from some spring off in a grove. He could not remember crossing the stream before, although he knew that he had been too tired to note much all the ages ago that had been that morning.

He wasn't tired now, only gone strange, a kind of ghost, a ghost with a thumping heart. Not tired, though. Keyed up like a thoroughbred racer with peppered loins.

He stopped. Because the rear rank of Yankees stopped, just below the crest of a low hill. When they dropped to the ground, he dropped to the ground.

More shooting. Volleys. Closer. Not too close, but closer. And he heard again, at last, that kickering wail he knew, the Rebel yell.

They were coming, he'd known they'd come.

Nichols eased forward, crawling, to what he took to be a safer position, less exposed, maybe twenty yards behind the Yankees. Close enough to hear their officers shouting. It was odd to hear those words, the same words used by his officers, spoken in different accents.

A few Yankees ran past him. Nichols sprawled, playing dead. He knew that even frightened men preferred to sidestep a corpse.

More Yankees hurried rearward. Slowly, uniquely awkward, the wounded followed. Wasn't a stampede, though. 'Least not yet. He wondered if he should have remained in that streambed a little ways back. Might pay to crawl on back there, wasn't so far.

"They're flanking us!" a Yankee cried. "On the left."

And then they were off to the races, with their officers ordering their soldiers to withdraw and trying unsuccessfully to keep order.

Nichols contorted himself, throwing out an arm and a leg, imitating the dead, of which he'd seen plenty.

His heart drummed. So close. He could hear distinct cries, individual voices, wonderfully Southern. The two sides traded volleys. But the Yankees didn't intend to hold their ground, not this ground. While Nichols prayed in silence to the Lord, repenting his sins and promising flawless behavior, he felt the approach of the retreating Yankees, telegraphed through the earth. He pressed his eyelids tight, face turned toward the earth, struggling to keep his breathing shallow, afraid a Yankee would step on his flung-out hand, or stumble over him, and cause him to reveal that he was alive.

A Yankee line paused only yards away, close enough for him to smell them and hear their leathers creak, to hear their excited gasping, as if they had to gulp all the air and leave none for their enemies.

They fired a volley. He hoped he had not flinched.

And then they were gone, withdrawing far more quickly than they had come. He waited, expecting his own kind to arrive, but more Yankees came by, last strays and skirmishers, cursing in every language in the world. They ran like rabbits, most of them.

When the footfalls stopped and only the distant cannon shook the earth, he braved a quick look around. Just as gray ranks crested the top of the little hill where the Yankees had lain and waited.

His people halted.

Glancing back toward the retreating Yankees, he saw that a few regiments withdrew slowly, in good order, defiant still, while others had all but dissolved. Just beyond the little stream, one Yankee color-bearer, admirably brave, walked calmly backward, supporting his flag with one hand and emptying his pistol with the other.

Nichols heard fateful, angry commands in Southern accents. He dropped back flat on the earth. His own side loosed a volley over his head.

Some Yankees replied, but their strength had lessened greatly. After another volley, his people advanced at a walk. Wary of nervous men, Nichols allowed the gray lines to pass over him, just as the Yankees had done.

When they had gone, he finally stood up. His impulse was to run for his own rear, to find his comrades, to be safe again, safe, if not from Yankee bullets, at least from the awful fate of a man abandoned on a battlefield, alone. But first he needed a rifle worth the carrying.

He followed the advancing ranks in gray, glancing about for a weapon that had been carried with pride, cleaned and oiled, but he didn't get far before voices called from clots of wounded Yankees down in the swale.

"Johnny Reb, for God's sake, give me water." "Water, Johnny, on your mother's love." "Please, Johnny, water . . . water . . ."

There were so many voices, it spooked him. But no man here meant him harm.

"Tell my mother," one voice cried, "someone tell my mother." "Water . . ."

He tugged a canteen loose from a dead Federal, rolling the man over and revealing a black hole and clotted blood where once a nose had been. Brains slipped from the Yankee's head.

Nichols ran down to the creek. Blessedly, it was not yet tainted with blood. He filled the canteen and followed the trail of voices, returning again and again to the stream, until the water turned pink and began to redden. The men who retained some alertness beyond their pain were grateful to him. Some jabbered madly. Others wept or just stared. One gut-shot man, bubbling blood and reeking of bowel stench, drank until sated, then cried out to God.

Noble feelings had nothing to do with giving these wounded men water. Nor was it the conscious act of a Christian. Nichols had no high thoughts, none at all. He acted by rote, the way a man loaded his rifle in a battle, without thinking. The summons to action was crude, deep, and physical. He did not even pity the men to whose lips he brought a canteen. He just did a thing that needed doing, the way a man fed the chickens when it was time.

"I love you, Isabelle," a lieutenant told him.

ELEVEN

12:35 p.m.
Union center

With splendid discipline, the 5th Maine Battery's guns fired in sequence.

"Ignore the order, Stevens," Colonel Charles Tompkins told his subordinate. "Keep up your fires."

"But General Wright—"

"General Wright can remove me, should he find my performance wanting. Back to your labors, Captain, mind on the enemy."

Tompkins, commanding the Sixth Corps artillery, found alarm distasteful. If Wright had lost his stomach—which it appeared he had, ordering off these guns—a stoic posture was the proper tonic. In the best spirit of Rhode Island, his home state. He drew his pistol, though, as he steered between the caissons: not in fear of Confederates, but ready to shoot any cannoneer who ran.

The situation did have a nasty look. The field of battle was as confused as any Tompkins had known, and these guns were all that stood between the oncoming Confederates and a stolen victory. But a cool eye and steady hand calmed many a storm. Even if, in the end, he could not stop the Johnnies, he might at least give the infantry time to reorganize and leave things a bit less bad.

"Steady, steady," he whispered, as much to himself as to his mount.

Sheridan's attack had gone in late, stumbled, and resumed. The graybacks had counterattacked. Old Ricketts and Getty hit back in turn. On the right, the Nineteenth Corps swirled about in a maelstrom all its own. Now the Johnnies called the tune again, gamboling down the middle of the field, their tactics and timing impeccable.

Fleeing with vigor, a blond-bearded soldier nearly ran into Tompkins and his staff. Catching himself just short of a collision, he stared mad-eyed at the colonel, as if he had happened upon General Lee and Satan devouring children, rather than a redleg from Rhode Island.

Tompkins didn't threaten the fellow. The infantry was not his charge. His concern was his guns, and his guns were sound.

He suspected that the weakening in the chain of command had started with Sheridan and proven contagious to Wright. Tompkins had seen the phenomenon before. Generals, a peculiar breed, had to be given time to come around when nettled by doubts, and it was the work of subordinates to sustain things in the meantime. In battle, spirits altered in a blink, capricious as the April weather in Newport.

Tompkins nudged his horse forward and let the beast paw the ground behind the gun line while he peered through the smoke and shot-stripped trees. The cannoneers about him behaved splendidly. If the Johnnies wanted to pass, they'd pay a toll.

He rode up to Captain Stevens, who had heart, for all his misgivings. The lad was not the sort to defy orders—especially those from the corps commander himself. On the whole, that recommended the fellow. But obedience had to be clear-eyed, rather than blind.

"Canister soon, I think," the colonel said.

"Plenty of Rebs, sir."

Indeed, the Johnnies were many. Howling like all the monkeys in Panama. But hurling lead, not coconuts.

"Abundant targets ease an artilleryman's labors," Tompkins said. "Your number three gun's shooting long, you'd best see to it."

Tompkins waved up his adjutant.

"Bring up Adams' battery and McCartney's lot." He pointed. "I want them just there, on the left, to sweep the Pike."

"Sir, that's our last reserve, you—"

"I'd rather not debate the matter, Peabody."

The aide bustled off.

No, he had never seen that trollop War change lovers so often in a single hour. But the way to lose the day was to lose your head. *Steady, steady.*

Tompkins rode the gun line, alert to hints of weakness, but the Maine lads loaded and fired with all the snap of an exhibition drill. The colonel did not think it sensible for any man to live in Maine by choice, but the unimaginative sort who did quite lent themselves to bravery.

Gore burst from the belly of a cannoneer wielding a ramrod. Without a fuss, his sergeant drove the charge home.

"Number two gun there, mind your elevation," Tompkins called. His voice was firm as granite, but not too loud.

Powder-blackened, the cannoneers leapt to it.

Where was Russell, though? His division should have come up, it formed the reserve. And if ever the reserve was needed, now was the blasted time. Tompkins was glad that the men he led could not tell how thoroughly drenched he was by sweat.

The great gray wedge, a howling mob, had gotten unsettlingly near.

"Double-canister, Stevens, double-canister. Don't husband the inventory."

Along the Pike, a battery raced forward. Tompkins noted the guidon of Battery G, 1st Rhode Island Lights, under whose colors he'd begun this war. Adams, the present commander, was a cool one. He'd stand firm.

Before the Rhode Islanders finished unlimbering, the 1st Massachusetts Battery rattled up.

Quietly, Tompkins addressed his foe: "If you want that Pike, you'll have to take it from me."

The Johnnies were nearly close enough to hurl rocks. Afoot now, Stevens strode up to Tompkins' horse.

"Sir . . . we'll lose these guns. General Wright said—"

"Shoulders back, chest out, man. Better to lose the guns than lose the battle."

That was heresy, Tompkins knew, an assault on the dogma of gunnery's episcopate. You were supposed to save your guns at all costs, even if it meant you lost the battle. Well, heresy was an old Rhode Island specialty, beginning with Roger Williams and his pack, for whom even the Puritans were too orthodox.

Tompkins wasn't minded to budge an inch.

"Canister, Stevens, canister! That's the way!"

12:45 p.m.
Union center

Delighted to be unleashed at last, Brigadier General David Russell rode proudly through the chaos of the day, guiding his division into battle. Russell had feared his corps commander intended to withdraw. The notion had shocked him, since Wright was known as a steady man in a fight. But the best men had bad days, and that was the truth of it.

It would be all right now. Sheridan had appeared mesmerized himself, but had snapped out of his trance in time, recovering his spunk and telling Wright, in Russell's presence, to "send Russell in right now, put this in order."

And Russell meant to stop the bloody crumbling. He had been chafing, anxious to help Jim Ricketts and George Getty. The way Russell read the field, Early was desperate, throwing in all he had. If the Nineteenth Corps just held out on the right, Russell believed he could not only blunt the Rebel assault—which seemed to him to be thinning—but reverse the tide again.

Ollie Edwards had taken in his Third Brigade, and the First Brigade was coming up fast, ready to swing in on Ollie's flank. Russell intended to use those brigades to stabilize the line and grind back the Rebs. Then he'd unleash Upton and his Second Brigade.

Upton was an enigma, a hardened Christian, mean as a Turk. The boy-general's hostility to slavery was at least as fierce as that of a Knight Templar toward Mahomet. A brilliant, intolerant, merciless young man, Upton had seemed a madcap martinet, yet had outperformed every other officer in the entire army at Spotsylvania and Cold Harbor.

Russell meant to send in Upton the moment the Johnnies wavered.

Work to do in the meantime, though. He rode through the spatter kicked up by errant shells, ghosting through billows of smoke and passing knots of soldiers catching their wind after their flight. The stream of wounded only convinced him that everything hung on a few quick actions.

Half a soldier's torso hung from a tree.

After overtaking two regiments of his First Brigade, the 4th and 10th New Jersey, Russell personally led them forward until he was certain they were solidly on his line of attack. The men seemed game and grisly. Next, he rallied two orphaned regiments from Jim Ricketts' division, sending them up on the flank of the New Jersey men.

Russell could feel it, sense the momentum shifting. The Confederates had advanced too far, running themselves breathless and losing contact on their flanks. The balance was tipping again on this seesaw day.

He spotted Ollie Edwards from a distance, making out his profile through scarves of smoke. Ollie was in the thick of it, cap pulled down and sword thrust out, directing his brigade in the advance.

Russell gave his horse the spurs, warning himself to master his emotions: His impulse was to ignore his own resolve and call for Upton to go in immediately, to come up behind Edwards and add weight . . . but boldness was one thing, impetuosity another. Discipline, not passion, had to rule.

The world was alive with possibilities, though, with the prospect of victory, of the field redeemed. And Russell knew himself to be as ambitious as the next man.

Discipline, he warned himself. You ask it of your soldiers, show it yourself.

It was ever a thrill to command men going forward, to feel the power and thrust. There simply was nothing like it in the world. But it was a power that needed harnessing.

And he owed it to Little Phil to save this battle. After all, he had been Sheridan's captain back in the old Army, when their relationship had been reversed. Hadn't he trained Sheridan for his astonishing rise? Little Phil's victory—or loss—would be Russell's legacy, too.

As he neared the front line, men dropped on every side. The firing was quick and lethal, veterans killing veterans with resolve. Nor was he certain that either side wasn't firing on its own kind amid the confusion: There was no solid battlefront now, just a savage ebb and flow. Dueling batteries warred like the gods above the plains of Troy.

Amid the uproar, he caught up with Ollie Edwards.

"Charge them, Ollie. They'll fold like a poor hand at cards. Just charge and keep going."

12:55 p.m.
Dinkle farm, east fields

Colonel Oliver Edwards turned to explain that he planned to go forward *en echelon,* but as his mouth opened he heard a thud he recognized. Beside him, Russell jerked in the saddle, then stiffened.

"Good God, General . . . are you badly . . . how badly are you hurt?"

Clutching his side with one hand, Russell waved away his concerns with the other. "It makes no difference, Ollie. Not at a time like this." He gasped. "Go on and charge. Order your brigade to charge."

Russell appeared to be stuffing his shirt into his side, attempting to stop up a deep wound. Yet the general managed to draw his saber.

"Charge, Ollie! I'll go with you!"

A shell burst above the two officers, deafening, rending the air with gale force. Gashed at the neck, Edwards' horse reared and whinnied. As he struggled to control his mount, the brigade commander saw that fortune had favored him, but had finished Russell.

The division commander leaned oddly in his saddle, as if he meant to fall but was unable. Blood painted what was left of him. A third of his chest had been torn away.

Men rushed toward them. Russell's orderly reached the general first, but seemed afraid to touch him. Russell's cut-up horse meandered, wobbling. The general's body pitched about, but remained eerily in the saddle.

In a voice as fierce and heartless as battle demanded, Edwards told the orderly: "Leave him. Go find Upton. He's senior, he's got the division."

And God help us, Edwards thought.

1:00 p.m.
Center of the battlefield

And there was given unto him a great sword . . ."

Brigadier General Emory Upton had been chosen by the Lord for this day's purpose. The hand of Jehovah was at work, even in Russell's death. God's wisdom did not yield to the will of men, or to their sentiments.

He, Emory Upton, had been given a great sword.

"Maintain your ranks," he called to his hurrying soldiers.

The Lord had opened his eyes, as the Lord had seen fit to open them before, letting him spy the weakness of Satan's legions. How else explain the way he saw opportunities to which those who served beside him remained blind?

"Come *on*, men!" he called sharply. The double-quick pace was not quite quick enough, not for Emory Upton.

His men came on, and they had the force of a multitude. He had been mocked for his rigor at drill, his discipline. The unbelieving never understood. Now, in the storm of battle, on a field obscured, his brigade rushed forward with a precision unmatched and a bloodlust unrivaled. Men who had hated him cheered him. Reviled, he had redeemed himself in fire.

"And there was war in Heaven . . ."

He would shine again, upon this battlefield. His brigade—now it was his division, too—would gleam like the archangels. And *his* division would not take one step back.

"And out of his mouth goeth a sharp sword," he recited to himself, *"that with it he should smite the nations: and he shall rule them with a rod of iron; and he treadeth the winepress of the fierceness and wrath of Almighty God."*

The division's other brigades had staunched the slave-drivers' attack, and the Lord had revealed, as if divine light had cut through the clouds of smoke, that the enemies of God and man had an exposed flank as tasty as a cutlet.

He came up on Ranald Mackenzie, who had turned the 2nd Connecticut Heavy Artillery into an infantry regiment as good as any. Mackenzie was not a devout man. Upton even suspected him of unseemly lust toward women. But Mackenzie fought worthily, bravely, wonderfully. He, too, would be a tool of the Lord this day.

"Our day, Mackenzie, this is *our* day. Deploy when you reach those trees. The brigade pivots on you."

"Shame about Russell, sir."

"God's will be done."

Mackenzie rode to the head of the column, spirit immune to danger. His sword soon flashed, pointing the way, and the blue ranks began to unfold into battle formation, their actions crisp, nearly flawless. Bayonets shone like the fiery swords of angels.

The first rank disappeared into a grove between two batteries. Upton noted Tompkins, the corps' artillery chief, seated placidly on his horse, watching matters unfold as if he were viewing a sporting match of no particular interest. A man of suspect theology but courage, Tompkins, too, had done the Lord's work this day.

Upton rode southwest, until he found Oliver Edwards, whose brigade gnawed forward. The carnage was hideous to the eyes of men, but surely pleasing to the Lord as a sacrifice to the cause of Abolition.

Upton's first extended contact with Negroes had come at Oberlin College, to which he had walked, still a boy, from his family's farm on the hard soil of western New York. Striving beside them as he sought to prepare for a place at West Point—a place he prayed God would grant him, as God did—he had found those colored scholars reverent toward God, respectful toward men, and hungry for knowledge. They were no less human because of the hue of their flesh. No less, but more, by virtue of their suffering. Godly men, the lost tribe of Israel found, those sweet-souled Negroes had led him to fight slavery with every means in his power, standing—at first alone—against the Southern cadets at West Point, and now, on this day, on this field, for the sublime cause of freedom for all, a brigadier general, by the Lord's grace, at the age of twenty-five.

"Edwards, you've got to push *harder*. They're ready to break. Don't stop!"

He could read the other man's face, the face of a common sinner but fair soldier: temper, resentment.

Jealousy?

"Yes, *sir*." Edwards' eyes had narrowed, not from the smoke. The colonel added, "My boys have pushed them back a quarter mile, they're hardly shirking."

"A good start, Edwards. But no more than a start."

A roar rose on their right.

"Hamblin's got my brigade," Upton said. "Mackenzie's in the lead. They're splitting the Rebs open, the way they tried to split us. They'll break in your front, too. Run them down like dogs."

"I don't think my boys will have to be told."

"And don't fuss about prisoners," Upton added.

He next rode to Campbell, who led the division's First Brigade and its solid New Jersey regiments. Campbell's men had thrust past a farmyard encrusted with dead Rebels and crawling with wounded. It was a splendid sight, a righteous judgment.

After ensuring that Campbell understood he was to maintain his alignment with Edwards at all costs, Upton galloped back through the carnage and wasteland of smashed caissons and discarded weapons, avoiding the wounded as best he could but halting for no man, outrunning the staff inherited from Russell. He did not slow until he had caught up to his old brigade. With Mackenzie's defrocked cannoneers setting the pace, the brigade had burst from a grove a mere hundred yards from the flank of the Confederates.

The result had been devastating. The slave-drivers and whoremongers had barely resisted. Now they ran.

Upton rode to the fore of his advancing, unbroken ranks, careless of any Rebels who wished him harm. The Lord would take him when the Lord saw fit, and his soul would rise up as his body fell.

On his right flank, the Nineteenth Corps was under way again, punching forward, too.

Paring the air with his sword, Upton kept pace with the blue ranks striding westward. After their first contact with the enemy, the men of his old brigade had re-formed immediately, advancing shoulder to shoulder. These men had mocked his rigor, as another had been mocked. But not now, not today. In battle, they were as firm as Frederick's Prussians. He and the Lord had made them so.

"And there was war in Heaven . . . ," Upton whispered, *"and Satan which deceiveth the whole world: he was cast out . . . and his angels were cast out with him."*

The last Rebels quit their attempts at organized volleys and made for the rear, even as slave-master officers tried to rally them. Soon enough, Upton's ranks outpaced the smoke, emerging into a brilliant afternoon marred only by puffs from batteries resisting the Lord's judgment.

"And there was given unto him a great sword," Upton repeated.

2:00 p.m.
Gordon's Division

All chance of a victory was gone, bled out, and the best hope now was for a stalemate until dark, followed by another Yankee withdrawal. But Gordon had begun to doubt even that possibility. Sheridan would not quit; he felt it and feared it.

The shelling and rifle fire had grown so intense that he had dismounted, sending his horse back to lower ground. It was an action taken with great reluctance. The soldiers liked to see officers on horseback—especially him.

"Try again," he told Atkinson, wishing all the while Clem Evans were back. "Ed, I know the men are tired. But we have to silence that battery. Force them back, at least."

The Yankees opposite his division had finally brought their guns to bear effectively, disabling two of the precious cannon north of Red Bud Run and blunting every attempt at a fresh counterattack. His men had been driven back again and again to a rocky ledge, savages in gray confronting savages in blue and dying for a gain of a dozen yards, only to see it lost again.

The pounding of the artillery was terrific, the bass drums of battle beating a rhythm beneath the rifle volleys.

Atkinson's posture was that of an old man, a portrait of weariness, as if he had aged decades in a day. Traces of blood streaked the powder smudges on his forehead and cheeks.

"Yes, sir," he told Gordon. "Just need to fill their cartridge boxes."

"No. *Now.* You have to go now. I don't care if you have to use your bayonets."

"Sir . . ."

"Damn it, Ed. I feel for those men just as much as you do. I led them for most of this war. I know their names, I know their *wives'* names, I just about know each man's stink. But they have to do what they have to do."

Atkinson was willing, but barely able. Gone pale, despite the ravages of the sun.

"Come on," Gordon said. And he led the way himself, shouting at the Georgians, calling out the names of valiant men he knew, cajoling them to give their lives for the faintest of faint hopes.

He had discarded his sword and scabbard as too unwieldy, and he pointed the way with his pistol. His soldiers followed him again, some even cheering, despite their long-dry throats. They leapt from their cover of trees and lips of stone and broken walls, advancing raggedly but doggedly, their bravery scorned by Yankee volleys, a lottery of death.

"Don't stop, boys, don't stop!" But Gordon let the men pass him now, aware that he had to act as a major general, not a captain. Risk, yes. But not folly. Early needed him whole. The entire army needed him. As it needed Ramseur and Cull Battle, and Breckinridge, who had got caught up in a bad fight to the north. Rodes was dead, and Zeb York, of Gordon's Louisiana Brigade, had been carried off terribly wounded. And the toll down among the line officers was grim.

Returning to a scrap of trees, pursued by breathless aides, he turned only to see his men repelled again—not running, but retiring, their movements those of laborers exhausted by the hardest work of their lives, put to a task they just could not perform. As Gordon watched, a man threw wide his arms and fell.

For all that, the nearest Yankee battery appeared to be pulling back. Out of ammunition or out of nerve.

How many lives had that cost?

Don't try to count them now, Gordon told himself.

He wanted a drink of cool water, but there was none. Perhaps there'd be well water back at the house he'd picked as the centerpiece of his next position, should the Yankees force him back again.

Hold until night, just hold until night. Don't let them turn the flank.

A Yankee who had been too brave to survive, who had come

too far, sat bedazzled against the trunk of a tree, cramming intestines back into his belly. He didn't even move his lips, just clawed at his slopping innards. His hands worked like the paws of a frantic mouse.

That is war as it is, Gordon thought, not as men will remember it.

Had to give Early credit, that was a fact. After that pigheaded rush to Martinsburg and the break-a-man night march back, Early had shone on this battlefield, ornery but everywhere, full of bile, but equally full of fight. Gordon had to admit that for all the individual bravery he had witnessed, it was Early who had made the right decisions with promptitude, a man as gifted as he was unlikable.

The human species never failed to interest John Gordon.

"Here they come!" a soldier shouted.

And the Yankees took their turn at failure. Tiny gains were soon reduced to no gains. When this latest round of firing eased again on Gordon's front, the armies glared at each other over their guns, each unable to advance and unwilling to retreat.

They had come close, so close, to embarrassing Sheridan. Only to be driven back a mile and more. Now they stood behind barricades of hate. Waiting.

He would not, dare not, let on, but Gordon's spirit was not as firm as his posture. He sensed that if Sheridan managed to bring up more forces—if he had more troops available and used them with any art—Early could not hold on for very much longer. Valor might withstand numbers, but only to a point: After all, the Persians, not the Greeks, had won at Thermopylae.

Early understood. They all did. The jolly naïveté of this war's early days had been put to death. And every man in command knew that a retreat, if forced upon them now, would break not only morale, but perhaps the army. With Winchester at their backs, a debacle loomed.

The only hope was to hold on until night.

"I will encounter darkness as a bride, and hug it in mine arms . . ."
That was Shakespeare, Gordon knew, though he could not recall
which play. What good had his love of the classics done, after all?
War took men beyond words, exposed their uselessness. Strut an
hour upon the stage, indeed.

What if they couldn't hold, if they just could not? Fanny was
in Winchester, and she wouldn't be sensible. She'd wait for him,
or news of him, before leaving. And by then it might be too late.
She was such a hardheaded, irresistible woman.

A woman worth living for, that one.

In the lull that fell upon his weary soldiers, another encounter,
off to the north, grew audible. Were Breckinridge and Wharton
still up there, trying to stave off some unholy passel of Yankees?
Gordon knew that Early had sent repeated orders to Breckinridge
to come down to Winchester at once, but every battle had a mind
of its own. And if Breckinridge did obey, who would stand in the
way of a Yankee envelopment? Fitz Lee? Gordon had seen him in
passing that morning. Lee had been fit for a Chimborazo ward,
leading his tattered cavalry when he should have been in bed, taking quinine.

The cavalry weren't much these days, but Early was too dis-
missive of Fitz Lee.

Jubal Early. A man who might win battles, but never hearts.
And Bob Rodes dead, a thing still hard to believe. Zeb York carried off screaming.

Dear Christ, it was a bad day.

"They're coming again," a bloodied lieutenant warned.

2:00 p.m.
Eversole's Knoll

Plans change, Phil," Crook said. "Point is to win."

Sheridan nodded. "Grates on me, though. If you could've
swung south, cut off their retreat . . ."

"Have to get them to retreat first. Old Bricktop's right. I rode over there, had a look. If I extend his flank with one division and swing the other north of that creek bottom—"

"Red Bud Run," Sheridan said.

"—then clear out that artillery and recross, we can turn their flank and set them running like rabbits. I believe it'll do the trick, Phil, I really do."

Staff men kept their distance, sensing that the generals wanted privacy. Between the hill on which they stood and Winchester, volleys prickled on, but with less fury.

"Not just you, though," Sheridan said. "You flank them, George. And I'll resume the attack across the front. I'll be damned if a single man in this army won't do his part." His face was blotched and hard-set. "Whole day's been a piecemeal affair, I've made damned-fool mistakes. But I'm done making them." He snorted. "Would've liked to trap that bastard, though."

"Still might. We'll see."

"Cavalry were supposed to do it. Come in on their flank, not play at pony rides."

"Still might happen. Probably will," Crook reassured him. "Torbert's not one to take his ease on a battlefield. Nor are those boys of his. My bet's that we're going to give Early a whipping he won't forget. His quiver's about empty, way I figure."

"Hell, George, hasn't this been a wicked a day?"

"Isn't over."

"No." Sheridan sighed. "I'll miss Davey Russell, though. That sonofabitch."

Crook nodded, but just said, "I'll get my corps moving."

Sheridan broke off his foray into sentiment. "How long until you get up?"

Crook drew out his pocket watch. "Three. I can go in by three. My corps's well positioned for the movement." He neglected to add that he'd brought it up without orders.

"Do it, then," Sheridan said. "I'll have the Nineteenth Corps go in beside you." All of his decisiveness had returned. "Then the Sixth Corps, hit them with everything."

"Cavalry's going to show, you wait and see," Crook said, still bucking up his old comrade. "We'll make a pretty rout of this mess."

"Torbert had damned well *better* show. After I sang the cavalry's praises to Grant. Which division of yours makes the flanking move? North of the creek?"

"Duval's. Thoburn's division is leading my column, he'll break off and extend the Ninthteenth Corps' flank. Duval will keep on going across the creek, then wheel to the left."

"Duval's brigade commanders? Remind me."

"Hayes and Johnson. Only two brigades."

"That enough?"

"They're good men. The best."

"Hayes? The politician? The Ohio man?"

Crook smiled his old-Army smile, a phenomenon as thin as frontier rations. "He'll do. Waxes philosophical, then fights like a Comanche. Honest, for what that's worth nowadays."

"Honest? Politician?"

"No man I'd trust more."

Sheridan smiled, too. "Except for present company, you mean?"

Crook's smile, a mere cut between his lips, hinted at hidden teeth. "Excepting present company, of course."

Dropping his smile, Sheridan said, "Tear their guts out."

3:00 p.m.
Rutherford farm, north of Winchester

Fitz Lee beheld the most awe-inspiring spectacle he had witnessed in the war. It was not a welcome sight.

Across the open fields to the north of the grove to which he'd been driven, at least five thousand blue-clad troopers advanced stirrup to stirrup on a front that filled the horizon. Tidy as if on parade, the mounted men came on at a steady walk, flags and banners aloft, with brass bands urging them southward. It was a display of insolence, of arrogance, of shameless vanity, that filled Lee with raw hatred. And with envy.

Rare was the Confederate officer now who possessed a horse as sound as a Yankee private's.

One obstreperous band played "Rally 'Round the Flag," and another answered back with "Yankee Doodle." Above the thud of hooves on hardening soil, the tack and spurs, carbines and sabers, of all those thousands jangled.

"Dear, sweet Jesus," Billy Payne said, sitting his horse beside Lee under the trees. He swept his hand back over slicked-down hair.

"Sonsofbitches," Lee judged. His uncle would not have approved of his language, but his uncle wasn't there.

After receiving a final, peremptory order from Early, Breckinridge had slipped off with his infantry and guns, leaving Lee with his scattered, exhausted, wildly outnumbered horsemen to hold off what had to be the greatest concentration of cavalry since Ney led the French horse at Waterloo. The whooped-up charges of the Crimea, for all the singsong poesy they'd inspired, surely had been nothing compared to this.

And Lee had about six hundred riders on hand, commanded by Colonel Billy Payne, pure Virginia, a Warrenton lawyer and Black Horse hellion, still a young man and already sire of more children than a quartermaster could number. The rest of Lee's men had been spread wide to cover roads or regroup from encounters in which they'd been battered badly. He'd delayed Merritt and Averell—*two* of Torbert's divisions—since morning, but only a fool could believe the end wasn't near.

All around him, Virginians on hard-used horses cooed at the spectacle, some attempting jokes at which no one laughed. Payne looked as serious as a man about to be hanged and as murderous as a man who deserved the hanging.

Brave boys all, Lee knew, but the fear in the air was enough to choke a hog.

"You all right, sir?" Payne asked.

All right? And go to the devil. Lee felt sick as a failing consumptive and tired as a slut come Sunday morning. His left arm was bound high where a round had clipped him—the damned thing hurt—but the paw still served for the reins. He'd needed an aide to reload his revolver, though. No, he was not all right at all. Dizzy and puking sick. But that was not the sort of thing a man said to another man. Not at a time like this.

At the end of a man, when all else was used up—health and love and worth and even honor—duty remained.

"Wish they'd at least play a jig a man could cotton to," one trooper said.

Lee turned toward the voice. "Don't like the tunes they're playing, I reckon we'll have to register an objection." He looked at the grime-faced, hard-faced men about him. Then he turned to Payne.

"Got to buy time, only one thing to do," Lee said. "Order your men forward, Billy. Guide to the right of the Pike. You give the order."

Payne rose in his stirrups and barked the plain command. No time now for inspiration or flourishes.

They left the trees, a shabby gray line, solemn.

"Must admit, I'm not fond of the odds," Payne said to Lee. "Always fancy a pleasant gallop, though."

Lee nodded his assent. Payne rose again.

"Charge, Virginia!" the attorney-in-arms shouted. *"Charge!"*

Ants attacking a buffalo herd, Lee thought. Mean ants, though.

As they came to a gallop, the cavalrymen began screeching their Rebel yell. Some cursed ferociously, doing down the Devil himself and unleashing every shred of anger they'd ever known and held in. Lashing mounts that caught their desperation, the men drew carbines or revolvers, or unsheathed sabers, each turning to the weapon he had left.

The harvested field beneath their hooves had dried well enough, if not fully. It didn't much slow the horses, but caked mud flew everywhere, stinging faces and eyes.

They pounded into a depression, briefly losing sight of the advancing Yankees, and Lee had to slap down a dizzy fit before jumping the stream that meandered through the low ground.

They crested another field and, dear Lord, the Yankees spread before them in a multitude.

No man faltered, not one.

At first the Yankees hardly seemed to notice them. Or care. As if they were ants, indeed, or maybe nothing but a billow of black-flies. Belatedly, a Union regiment posted as skirmishers closed ranks.

Too late.

"Virginia! Virginia!" Payne cried, echoed by dozens of voices.

Remembering their pride, remembering that they had served under Stuart, the men charged as if not one cared for his life, devil-may-care as they had been in the early days of the war, when all things seemed a lark.

Lee just hoped he could stay in the saddle. He knew he couldn't wield a saber—his pistol would have to do. Above all, he did not intend to give the Yankees the pleasure of taking him prisoner.

The sickness that gripped him could not cloud his reason: He knew he should not have ridden forward himself. But the time for reason had passed.

As they closed on the Yankee skirmishers, Lee began to shout with the others, another madman in a hopeless world. His worn horse pounded to burst its heart.

They smashed into the Yankees, shooting and slashing, and tore through them, leaving empty saddles and bloodied blue-bellies in their wake.

"Don't stop!" Lee shouted. *"Charge, charge!"*

Payne was shouting, too.

Lee felt he might vomit over himself and his horse. The horizon wavered. But he shouted again and again between bouts of choking.

The Virginians swarmed forward, almost merry in their hatred now, their sullenness vanquished, their souls exhilarated. When more Yankee regiments spurred out to meet them, the collision cracked like doors slamming in Hell.

Reins tight in a left hand going numb, Lee shot a captain through the heart and swung his pistol across his horse's mane to fend off a sergeant. Nearby, two men skewered each other at the same moment, each man's blade propping up the other on their bewildered horses. It took but a minute for the Yankees to break.

Cheering, the Virginians—fewer now—followed after them. Billy Payne hallooed, as if riding to the family hounds back in Fauquier County.

"Virginia! Virginia!"

They pounded over another harvested field, hard on the tails of the Yankees. The bluecoats emptied their pistols toward them, firing wildly back over their saddles.

How many rounds had he fired? Lee tried to remember.

Near him, a horse collapsed, hurling its rider over its head.

"Come on, Nellie Gray," Lee urged his own horse. "There's oats on earth and plenty of corn in Heaven."

Who had said that? *His father.* The words had leapt out of him.

"Virginia!"

A jolly, deadly steeplechase ensued. They chased the shattered Yankees for a half mile, then more.

Lee knew it was time to stop, to re-form. They had become scattered, disordered. These men had done all that they could, it was time to call off the pursuit.

He also knew that it was already too late.

A band, all too near, struck up "Yankee Doodle."

The men they had chased re-formed behind a fresh blue wall of troopers. To the left, where that infernal music sounded, a full brigade, in perfect order, emerged from a swale in the earth.

Red scarves. Custer's men. The scum who killed Stuart.

Lee's dizziness left him. They were *not* going to kill him. Not those sonsofbitches.

He reined up. Fifty yards off, Payne drew back, too, calling for his Virginians to re-form. Too late, too late.

The Union cavalrymen to their front had divided, some dismounting with their carbines, while others rallied to countercharge. But the worst threat, Lee sensed, came from Custer's brigade. Who, unlike their brethren, did not draw pistols or carbines, but came on with their hundreds of sabers flashing.

In front, prancing before that brigade's flags, a black stallion bore a floppy-hatted officer with long locks.

Kill him myself, Lee swore.

But he knew he would not, could not. His purpose now had to be to rescue what remained of Payne's command.

"Yankee Doodle" was a hateful tune.

He heard a shout of "Wolverines!" And that minstrel-show officer, Custer, waved *l'arme blanche.*

Sabers leveled, Custer's brigade thundered at them from the flank. The Yankees to their front charged them as well.

Gathering back into a herd meant to serve as a formation, Payne's survivors didn't need orders to withdraw. They turned back south and gave their mounts the spurs.

They didn't get far before reining in again. A double line of blue horsemen blocked their retreat.

Custer's brigade wasted no time crashing down on them from the flank, men with sabers undeterred by men with empty revolvers. Lee fired his pistol until it clicked uselessly, then swung it at the troopers nearest him, hammering his way through. Sabers hacked flesh, and men died shouting obscenities. Fighting stirrup to stirrup, knee to knee, they splashed one another with sweat and blood, and faces foretold the hate and pain of damnation. Gray coats went under in a sea of blue.

Overwhelmed, Payne led his horsemen in a last charge back across the ground they had recently crossed with so much pride, riding headlong at the double line of Yankee cavalrymen in their path.

"Come on, you," Lee urged his horse. He spurred and lashed it, something he had not had to do in years: The beast was near quits.

Another crash of men, mounts, and metal, then a remainder of a remnant of Payne's troopers had, miraculously, broken through the lines blocking their retreat.

They rode hard. More horses collapsed. The Yankees pursued. Vengeful.

Asking the last of their horses, the Virginians made the woods from which they had charged. Fragments of other units awaited them there and did their best to halt the Yankees, but the bluecoats were unstoppable.

Lee tried to rally Payne's men for a final stand, but they were finished for now. He rode with them rearward, evading the Yankees, sick in body, sick in heart, hoping he might still gather enough men for one final stand.

Behind him, the Yankee bands struck up again.

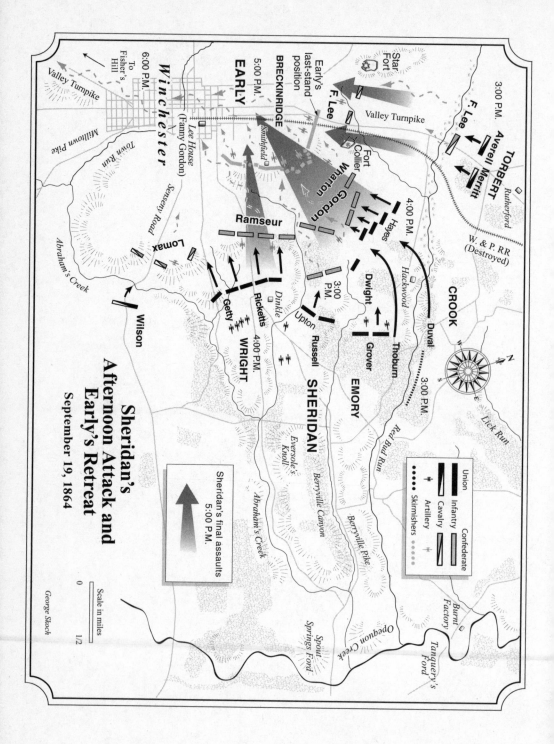

**Sheridan's
Afternoon Attack and
Early's Retreat**
September 19, 1864

Sheridan's final assaults
5:00 P.M.

Scale in miles

0   1/2

George Skoch

TWELVE

Rud Hayes halted his men and formed them in line of battle ten yards inside the tree line, out of sight. Then he waited.

"You didn't answer my question," his brother-in-law pestered. "You *still* think we can overcome the animus, put this country back together . . . as one nation? You really think that, Rud? After all this?"

"Yes," Hayes said, looking at his pocket watch.

"Well, then," Doc Joe said, "Lucy ought to make you wear a dunce cap." He stroked his horse's neck, soothing the beast. "This country won't be united in a hundred years. Too much killing, too much hate."

"Good men will repair it."

"The best men are dead."

"Thank you, Doctor, for that encouraging diagnosis. Joe, go on back to your surgery. You'll be busy enough before long, and I'm busy now."

Joe smiled. "All right. But no tomfoolery. My sister wouldn't make a kindly widow."

"Just git."

"Boils tolerable?"

"You just git."

After Doc Joe turned his horse, Russ Hastings sidled up. The adjutant's horse, Old Whitey, was admired throughout the brigade. "I thought we were going right in, sir?"

"General Crook doesn't want to go in headlong."

Neither man said anything about Kernstown, that hard-learned lesson.

And yes, the boils were tolerable. But sitting in a saddle was no delight.

The sounds of battle back across the creek were tired, grudging. But men were still dying. Hayes turned toward the soldiers he commanded, scanning the features of those who would lead the attack. Most faces were familiar to some degree. Not all, but most. What always struck him, once a man looked past the enforced uniformity, was that such men weren't uniform at all, not in the least. Each was complete unto himself. Distinct. Filled with yearnings, fears, and considerations as mundane as a fellow wishing he'd taken that last chance to drop his drawers and squat. *Human.*

He had begun to accept that his idol, Emerson, was far from a perfect guide to the human species. Introducing Swedenborg in *Representative Men,* Emerson had scorned the commoners "of the world of corn and money." But was any man truly common? Deserving of such condescension? The man who labored with his hands fed the man who worked with his mind. Wasn't one of the points of this war that all men should enjoy an equal right not only to freedom and justice, but to respect? Hayes would not dismiss the man who shouldered a rifled musket as lower in worth than one of greater intellect. These, his fellow citizens, the men he led in a fratricidal war . . . each possessed the same spark of life as Emerson, but these men had, the most of them, volunteered to risk that spark, that life, for a prospect greater than themselves, a vision few commanded the words to describe, but which they felt profoundly. Emerson and his ilk discussed ideas. These men would go forward and *die* for an idea, because they sensed instinctively it was right. Who was the worthier?

He took a drink from his canteen. His aide copied the action.

"Stay close to me, Russ," Hayes said. "When this thing starts."

The frail breeze could not pierce the grove. Flags hung limp. Men rustled and murmured. Waiting. That was somehow the worst of it, the waiting. Men wanted to *know*, that was the thing. The idled mind was the domain of devils.

Across the fields, a Rebel battery limbered up to leave. Were they aware of the impending attack? Had surprise already been lost?

His brigade would go forward, anyway.

He wondered what Lucy was doing at that moment. He hadn't had a letter from her in days. Had her pregnancy grown troubled? He always feared for her, not for himself. The slightness of his fate, amid all this, seemed a trivial matter.

"Sign me a leave to go home this minute, Colonel," a soldier called, "and I'll vote for you in every single election."

Before Hayes could reply, another soldier added, "Let *me* go, and I'll vote for you *twice* come election time."

Men laughed. That was good.

"Wouldn't mind going home myself," Hayes admitted. "But I'm told we have some pressing business hereabouts."

These good men.

Thrashing back in the trees. Riders. Colonel Duval, the division commander, and his party.

Time to go in?

Kicking thorns away from his trouser legs, Duval steered his horse through the briars.

"Rud," Duval said.

"Isaac." Hayes lifted his hat and settled it again. "Go in?"

Duval shook his head. "Don't know what's holding things up. Crook seemed ready. Then he sent McKinley back to find Sheridan."

"Well, we're fixed to go." Hayes canted his head toward his men.

"I know it's hard, the waiting," Duval said. "Makes my skin crawl."

More ride-through-the-canebrake racket rasped toward them. Hayes recognized Will McKinley. General Crook and a few aides followed after.

This was it, then.

Hayes kept his face impassive, the way a sound man waited out the vote count. He admired Crook. Sheridan had the effect of lightning on men who barely knew him, but Crook inspired loyalty in those who knew him well. He was a just man, George Crook, and fairness eluded the common run of generals, all of whom played favorites. Above all, when he made a mistake, Crook took responsibility. He lived by a code Hayes recognized.

Greetings all around, rendered quickly, by sweat-glazed officers striving not to betray their concerns to the soldiers.

"I see that battery turned tail," Crook said.

"Just pulled off, sir," Hayes told him.

Crook nodded. "Not sure that's a good thing, or a bad thing." He concentrated on Duval. "Your division ready, Isaac?"

"Yes, sir. Been ready."

Crook glanced at Hayes, then back at Duval. "Rud leads off?"

"Yes, sir."

"All right. Rud, as soon as you cross that field—get well across it, well onto their flank—you wheel left, recross the creek, and hit them hard. You understand?"

"Colonel Duval explained things, sir."

"When you charge the flank, the Nineteenth Corps will renew the attack on the enemy's front. Thoburn will come up on their right and your left, tie things together." Crook looked around at the tense, expectant faces. "You boys will have to set this brawl to rights."

Hayes saluted, triggering a flurry of raised hands. Turning their horses awkwardly in the underbrush, the others left Hayes, Hastings, and two couriers as the only men still mounted before the ranks.

Service in the wilds of West Virginia had convinced Hayes a sword was a bother. He left the blade in its scabbard and raised his hand.

"Brigade!"

"Regiment!"

"Regiment!"

"Regiment!"

"Regiment!"

"Atten*tion!*"

That command, too, was repeated down the line, first by regimental commanders, then by junior officers leading companies.

"For*ward!*"

Again, the word echoed.

"March!"

A grand, many-footed creature, the brigade broke through the last stretch of brush and ducked interfering branches, emerging into the westering light, with the sun still high enough to spare their eyes.

Clear of the trees, the veterans aligned themselves on the move. Color guards snapped out their flags. Officers afoot marched backward, facing their men, inspecting their lines before pivoting toward the foe again.

No one joshed now.

Sharpshooters opened from distant trees and thickets. A first man fell. A soldier from the second line scurried up to fill the gap.

These good men.

Hayes let the first rank pass him, but kept ahead of his second rank. Determined to see that all things were well done.

At least they did not have to assault that battery and face canister. Volleys were bad enough, but attacking guns across an open field was a downright terror.

Marching at quick-time, his soldiers devoured the high field, step by step. Where the Rebel guns had been, the earth was stained black and artillery waste lay about: a useless swab, split crates, a caisson overturned. If the Johnnies had lost any cannoneers, they had carted off their dead.

A shell burst to the front. Hayes tasted grit.

Men coughed.

How far across these fields was far enough? Before it came time to turn the brigade to the left and attack back across that creek? The ground looked different than it had from the tree line, more complex. Across the depression cut by the stream, the Confederates, in their thousands, were hard to spot, masked by trees and shrubbery, crouched behind walls. Wraiths of smoke blinked flames.

Hayes' brigade advanced through naked light.

The first shell had marked the range. Adjusted shells exploded in rapid succession. One struck near the first rank, downing several men.

The fire could not be returned. Their own batteries, du Pont's guns, trailed the advance. This ground just had to be crossed.

Sharpshooters felled more of his men. One of his couriers tumbled. The man's horse bolted.

Nothing to be done. Not now. Go forward. *Forward.*

"I love you, Lucy," he muttered. *"Know that. I loved you."*

He almost ordered the men to the double-quick, but feared losing control before they made their turn and crossed the streambed. They just had to face the shelling. *He* had to face it.

Such a terribly beautiful day. For *this.*

More shells. Men burst, scattering limbs. Bodies spewed innards. Other soldiers sprawled, uncannily still. As comrades stepped around them, the wounded writhed, clutching their changed flesh, bewildered. But every gap in the front rank filled again.

Straight ahead, Reb cavalrymen bolted from a copse like flushed game birds, racing off toward the Confederate rear.

Across the creek, to the south, the greater fight resumed, hungry for flesh and thirsty for blood again.

Hayes longed to walk Cincinnati's streets in peace. To live to do that, with Lucy on his arm.

Correcting his posture, he lifted his right hand. Holding it high. Letting all the regimental commanders see it. Letting all the sharpshooters see it, too.

He had never thought to bear such weight as this.

Russ Hastings twitched in the saddle and slammed to earth. One foot caught in a stirrup but broke free.

"Russ!"

The adjutant tried to get to his feet, but faltered. Blood marred his coat.

No time. No time to care for good men or for bad. *No time.*
Hayes turned his eyes to the front again.

Hoping he had gone far enough, that he was not just giving in
to fear, Hayes signaled for the brigade to wheel left, to face the
creek and the enemy beyond it.

Another battery loosed its guns upon them. Rifle fire spewed
from the far bank. A man shrieked—it always amazed Hayes that
so few of the wounded screamed.

Different men? Or differing pain? His own wound at South
Mountain had been excruciating. But he did not think he had
screamed.

Lucy had found him, nursed him. And Doc Joe.

"At the double-quick . . . forward!" he called to his men. He had
to get them out of these open fields. And across the creek.

He spurred his horse lightly, quickening its pace, though not
enough to outrace his forward rank: Wanton displays of valor were
an indulgence. The important thing was to keep control, not carry
on like a laird in Walter Scott.

Then came the great shock. Reaching the edge of the field,
where the earth dropped to the creek, his horse pulled up on its
own. Snorting, fearful. The ground dropped sharply through
brambles and scrub trees. But the worst of it was that the trickling stream they had splashed through a mile back had become a
swamp, a morass, a slough, a good twenty-five yards wide. And
the far bank required a steep climb to reach the enemy.

Bullets ripped past, an unwelcome bounty of them. The Johnnies had been waiting. It was all a horrible trap.

To right and left, men hesitated. Their officers shouted at them
to go on, while sergeants shoved the doubtful down the bank. The
attack was in danger of faltering before it had gotten properly under way.

Hayes spurred his horse. Harder this time. A better judge of
ground than its master, the beast choose its own course and carried him down. Hayes fought to remain in the saddle.

With the ranks collapsed, a number of soldiers beat him to the bottom. Hastily, they slung their cartridge boxes over their rifles, holding the weapons high as they plunged into shallows crusted with moss and scum.

Slapping it with the reins, Hayes drove his horse into the water. All around, men lost their footing and fell, gripped by the muck of the creekbed. His mount struggled to keep its footing and Hayes had to stab his spurs into its flanks.

A sergeant flopped in the water, sank, and did not reappear. Above the mad splashing and curses of struggling men, Hayes heard Southern catcalls. Concealed high on the far bank, the Johnnies were just shooting targets at a county fair.

His horse thrashed and whinnied, bucking and panicking, as it sank in the mud.

The stream—the morass that should have been a stream—was crowded with his soldiers now, companies and regiments a jumble. Some men tried to return fire, pausing foolishly in midslough, while others floated, facedown.

Hayes didn't see how he could go forward. His horse was stuck and terror-stricken. He waited for the bullet that would part him from Lucy forever.

Lucy.

He could save these men, some of them. The attack was a disaster. He could at least minimize the cost, preserve some lives, by ordering a withdrawal.

A soldier, halted in midstream, stared up at him. As if reading his thoughts. Waiting for his decision, the command to turn for the rear.

A bullet snapped back the soldier's head.

Go back. Take them back now. Spare them.

Hayes opened his mouth to give the order.

No.

There was no going back. If these men went back—these men, any men—the war would never end. And if he gave the order to withdraw, he would foul the memories of every man who'd fallen.

Hayes unholstered his pistol and dropped from his horse. Mud grabbed him. Tugging at him as if it were alive and starved for human flesh.

"Come on!" he shouted, battling the emulsion underfoot. His riding boots gulped water, demanding his surrender. Splashed by bullets peppering the surface, he plodded toward the far bank, unsure of each next step, as likely to drown as lead his brigade onward. Even where the bottom firmed, slime tricked a man's feet.

"Come on! Get through this slop. Come *on*, boys! We're going to give those Rebs a whipping, just get to the other side! Come on now!"

As soon as he called to the others, he felt a renewed strength. Drenched to his chest, he plunged ahead, dragging leaden weights instead of feet. He held up his pistol, keeping that one thing dry.

"Rally to me! Ohio! West Virginia! Rally to me!"

Mostly Ohio men, it looked like. No. West Virginia boys, too. All a muddle.

Wonderfully, miraculously, the trapped herd of men surged forward.

Still, when Hayes clawed up into the mud that passed for a bank, he was alone. With bullets hissing and hunting, sniffing close. Soaked and wrapped in slime, he got to his feet and stood with his back to the enemy. Waving on his men.

"Let's *go*, Ohio!" Hayes called. "Come *on*, West Virginia! *Come on!*"

Miracle after miracle. He had been alone. Now men—muck-covered, wonderful men—crowded around him. Some dropped down, exhausted, but the best of the veterans organized themselves without need of officers, hugging the slope and testing their weapons, drying their hands on the brush before handling their cartridges.

Beside Hayes, a man flopped backward. A wild hand slapped his shoulder and slipped away.

Lieutenant Reasoner, of the 36th Ohio, sat calmly on a rock, drawing off his boots to pour out the water. The action struck Hayes as eminently sensible: Hard to lead a charge hauling gallons of slime.

As quickly as he could, Hayes worked off his own boots, upended them—they gushed—and yanked them back on. Wet grit gripped his feet.

He stood up again, in the open, where the men could see him and he could see their officers. Jim Comly had drawn together some bucks from the 23rd Ohio, but the Rebs were still making sport of their predicament.

"Up that bank!" Hayes shouted. "Come on, boys. Pay them back!"

He scrambled ahead, thorns grazing hands and cheeks. Hoping the men would follow one more time.

They did. Hundreds of soaked and filthy men clawed their way up the south wall of the gulch, rushing to rob the Johnnies of time to reload.

Hayes surprised a big Reb working his ramrod. He pointed his pistol, giving the fellow one chance to surrender.

Deft as a gopher snake, the Johnny swung his weapon as a club. Hayes ducked the blow, reaimed, and pulled the trigger.

The revolver misfired.

Eyes met.

As soldiers in blue crowded up, the Rebel ran.

"Come on, boys!"

Their order may have been lost, but the men were furious. Shooting them down in that morass had been unfair, according to the odd views soldiers held. Of course, they would have done the same to the Johnnies, had the circumstances been reversed. But logic made no difference.

His men had taken the high ground, but the Rebs withdrew grudgingly, pausing to fire back at their tormentors.

Stubborn. Proud.

This whole war was about stubbornness and pride.

One Reb who had lost his rifle dropped his drawers and showed Hayes' men his ass.

"Officers! Take charge of the men around you," Hayes called. "Don't try to sort out your regiments. Soldiers! Rally to the nearest officer."

Never would have worked with green troops, Hayes knew. But these men had scrambled over mountains together, been bushwhacked, and fought countless, hard engagements that barely got a mention in the newspapers. They knew what to do.

As his men chased the retreating Rebs with a volley, it dawned on Hayes that his brigade was alone. The grand attack had not caught up on his left, nor did there seem to be anyone behind him.

Two hundred yards to the front, Reb cannoneers manhandled a section of guns, turning them to block the interlopers.

Hayes figured the militarily sensible thing to do would be to consolidate his position and wait for Thoburn's boys—or anyone—to come up. But he was angry, as much at himself as at the Rebs. That moment of weakness, of doubt, down in the creek had been unworthy.

Determined to do his duty, to be one of those "good colonels" among whom he liked to count himself, he wasted no time before leading his soldiers forward, toward the guns. After a brief, bloody interlude, the artillerymen scooted off, followed by the infantry supporting them.

Hayes read the Johnnies' predicament all too clearly: Those Rebs had been assigned an orphan position, forward of their main line, to protect the flank. Now they were hurrying back to their division to make a stand. Things weren't over, that was painfully certain.

But the prey had become the hunters. Grim and wary, his men forged on through a mist of smoke. Off to the left, the battle had gained such force, it shook the earth. A fight had flared up on the distant right as well. Hayes wondered what that signified.

He wished he could see more of the field, or that someone would tell him what was happening elsewhere. Colonel Duval owed him that much. He needed to *know*. He didn't want his brigade to be cut off, perhaps surrounded. . . .

But he just was not ready to stop. Nor were his men. Each yard gained had been earned with the blood of friends and comrades, of brothers.

His ragged line pressed on until the smoke thinned.

As they came within range of a fine-looking house, a volley flamed out, halting Hayes' men with its devastating power. This was it, the Rebs' next line of defense. Officers ordered their men to ground or drew them toward cover. They had gone as far as they could until support came up; each veteran sensed it.

Startling himself with his lust for blood, Hayes longed to go on, to shoot men down, to skewer them.

But he'd learned from the errors of others how alluring folly could be. Charging that position with the handful of men he had would have been an unforgivable sin, a collapse into passion worse than any carnal deed. The remnants of his brigade could not have been more disordered had they been stirred around in a witch's cauldron. His men had played their part well; now he had to play his own part wisely.

As he panted for breath and weighed the situation, stray Ohioans and mud-caked West Virginians gathered around, taking up positions behind a wall to trade shots with the Rebs. Listening to the ragged exchange, Hayes sensed something new: *The Rebs were only trying to hold on*. There was no hint of a counterattack, none of that feeling you got from the Johnnies when they were ready to pounce.

Off to the left—still too far to the left—the fighting had become a gale, a storm. Sheridan's entire army was on the attack.

No reinforcements here, though. Where was Johnson? Where was Thoburn?

Hayes sat down, struggling for clarity. Given that he didn't have the numbers to rush that house, what else might be done? Anything? Beyond waiting for reinforcement? Once ignited by action, he always found it hard to snuff the flame. He even feared that the day might come when he gave an insane order, maddened by the . . . the ecstasy.

For all the press of bodies, their stink and the raucous voices, he felt alone. And he *was* alone, in a very practical sense. Russ Hastings had gone down early—Hayes hoped the wound wasn't grave—and his last courier had disappeared. He had left his staff behind with orders to follow, but he saw none of them.

The men kept up their fire over the wall, pleased enough with what they'd done and telling the Johnnies—who couldn't hear one word—what a licking they were going to get, just wait. Hayes grew newly aware of his own breathing, of the sodden grip of his uniform, of the foul taste in his mouth, a gagging mix of blown powder and bad water.

It had been only moments since they halted.

It was time to sort out his regimental officers and to send a detail to bring up ammunition, in case the chain of supply had broken down. He needed runners. And skirmishers had to probe the flanks, to uncover who was out there. He had to identify the best point to strike when reinforcements came up and the advance resumed. . . .

When he tried to reload his pistol, his hand shook. He could barely open his soaked ammunition pouch.

With the suddenness of revelation, Will McKinley appeared. The young man looked sufficiently fresh to have found a wiser place to cross the creek. McKinley, bless him, had that sort of luck.

Kneeling beside Hayes, his former adjutant said, "Colonel Duval's been wounded, sir. Pretty bad. General Crook says you're to command the division."

4:00 p.m.
Gordon's front

Wasn't right, none of it. They'd whipped the Yankees fair and square, twice over. Then they'd caught the blue-belly fools trying to sneak around on them, just come right up on the flank, and by rights they should have whipped them a third time, catching them down in that swampy bottom, a true Slough of Despond, like in *Pilgrim's Progress*. But the Yankees seemed to have lost their senses this God-given day and they just kept on coming, plastered up and down with mud, a-saying, "Kill me, please, and thank you kindly," and even doing that—killing them—wasn't enough. One of their officers had near shot down Dan Frawley with a pistol, though Dan got away, and Nichols, unused to the new rifle he had taken up, had missed when he took a shot at the Yankee, who looked like a man from the town bank, the kind who prized ledgers and laws over the Lord. Then he had found himself going backward in anger and in shame, unwilling to be captured again by heathens, men apt and fitted to fornicate with niggers in broad daylight, men who would not be tolerated on the soil of Georgia, nor should have been anywheres else.

Tom Boyet was bleeding, but not quitting. None of them was anywheres close onto quitting. But it was like the Lord himself whispered to every man at the same time, saying not "Go down, Moses," but "Y'all git out of here now, too many Yankees."

How could the Lord allow this? To cause them to flee before Lucifer? When they were the Righteous, the Poor who would inherit?

He loaded and fired, loaded and fired, wishing he had his own fine rifle back, but glad of the yard wall by this rich man's house, a succor unto the people. The fellows had been as pleased to see him as pork chops when he came back, marveling at his tale of bold escape, maybe not believing every word of it—which was an injustice—but clapping him on the back and laughing and sharing their rations with him, even bottomless Dan Frawley, whose favorite miracle, surely, had to do with those loaves and fishes.

Elder Woodfin had called him "the Prodigal Son returned," which did not seem right, for Nichols did not believe he ever had behaved badly toward his father, not as the Prodigal Son had done, and he had never been a squandering, gambling, drinking fellow, displeasing to the Lord and rightly afflicted, but the chaplain was not a man to bear reply. Elder Woodfin was, after all, a Virginian and could not be reasoned with like the Georgia-born.

Firing at the blue hants in the smoke, Ive Summerlin said:

"I don't like this at all. I don't like this feeling."

None of them did, that was the gospel truth. With the Yankees whipped and whupped and whipped, and too ignorant to accept it, rumors of great wickedness had spread, luring men into the temptation of fear.

"More cartridges, boys," Sergeant Alderman called. "Come back one at a time and help yourselves."

A soldier clutched his face and collapsed backward.

General Gordon reappeared. A time back, things had been so ugly that even General Gordon, a man who feared naught but the wrath of the Lord, had dismounted and gone afoot. He was back up on his latest stallion, peerless.

There was shooting to do, but Nichols stole time to glimpse the true-Christian face, that Christian-soldier visage, of General Gordon passing. With that broken-cross scar on his cheek.

Nichols found no consolation there.

4:20 p.m.
Union Sixth Corps

Remarkable," Ricketts allowed. "Simply remarkable."

Rigid on his blood-streaked horse, George Getty snorted. "Can't say how the little runt brings it off." He spat.

"Sometimes, I don't think I know soldiers at all," Ricketts said.

"Volunteers. Different breed. The men we led would've laughed."

"I'm not sure," Ricketts said. "Remember how the Regulars cheered Zach Taylor?"

Around the two generals, litter bearers gathered up the wounded, deciding who would have a chance to live.

"Well, he got them going," Getty allowed.

To the astonishment of everyone on the field, Sheridan had

revitalized the attack by galloping the entire line of the Sixth
Corps, ten yards out in front of the men, grinning and waving his
hat, hallooing the Rebs with spectacular obscenities. He had continued on to the Nineteenth Corps, prolonging the stunt, all the
while in full view of the Confederates. The howls from the men
had smothered the noise of the guns.

"And here we are blathering," Getty said. Stalwart and taciturn,
George Getty was even more of an Old-Army man than Ricketts.
Sheridan's performance had excited him to what passed for ebul-
lience. "Got them untangled, time to get on."

Ricketts nodded. When the charge resumed, it had moved so
fast that their flank units had collided. It had required the division commanders themselves to sort things out.

To their front, another cheer resounded.

"Glad to get the worst of the ground behind me," Getty said,
lingering anyway. He turned up one side of his mouth. "You got
the easy dirt today."

"Not sure every one of my men would agree."

"Any more about Upton?"

"Just that he's wounded."

"Let his holy angels comfort him. Shame about Russell."

Their staffs, held at a distance, had grown restive. It was time
to rejoin the attack. Even generals had to be nudged along, in the
view of majors.

But generals were human, something that would not have occurred to Ricketts in the old days. They, too, needed their respites.

Getty tugged his riding gloves tighter. "All this ends, I look
forward to some quiet post in the Territories. Where all I have to
fuss about is corporals with the clap."

"They'll bust you down first. Both of us. Reversion to Regular
Army ranks."

Getty permitted himself what passed for a smile. "Hell, they
can make me a first lieutenant. Just give me an orderly life, wake-
ups at five a.m., and a good pair of boots."

Having been a lieutenant longer than Getty, Ricketts saw less appeal in such a demotion. He quite liked being a general, and Frances liked it, too. The orderly side of peace had its appeal, though: days refined by bugle calls and smoothed by regulations. There was something about the Army, the Army he had known, that was wonderfully pure.

"I don't think we'll revert to a grade below major," he said seriously.

That rekindled Getty's tiny smile. "See you in Winchester, Jim."

4:20 p.m.
Gordon's Division, Confederate left

As his soldiers carried Patton from the battlefield, the fury on the colonel's face struck Gordon. The wreckage of Patton's leg had to be painful, but it wasn't suffering that ruled poor George's features. It was rage, Homeric, unmatched in Gordon's experience.

"Bless you, George," Gordon said, riding beside the litter, rationing moments. "Splendid work, you held them."

Patton could not speak. He shook his head. Faintly. Glowering.

"Get you back in the fight before you know it," Gordon tried.

Patton closed his eyes. Bloody lips trembled.

He'll lose that leg, Gordon figured. If not his life. Patton's war was done.

Gordon's was not. But Patton's Brigade, Virginians from Breckinridge's Division, had arrived just in time to block another Yankee assault, granting Gordon a gift of time—precious minutes—to rally his shrinking division again, behind another web of stone walls, with the left refused and the line backed up against the Valley Pike, a hop from Winchester.

Leaving the wounded colonel, Gordon rode along his line again, encouraging his officers and men, cajoling them and promising a miracle. Hope remained, however slight, that they might hold the Yankees until dusk. On his right, Battle and Ramseur had rallied their men yet again, with Early crisscrossing the field, overflowing with threats and imprecations. But Gordon felt the noose closing.

His men *had* to hold on. He could not let them break, not before the men of the other divisions did. As the chances of the Confederacy winning the war declined from day to day, it was crucial not to be seen as one of those who invited defeat. Back in Georgia, men had to say, "We lost that war *despite* all Gordon did."

Gordon did not intend to be a failure, not in war, and not in peace. He had seen failure enough along his bloodline. His father had begun with a farm whose arcade of elms let it claim to be a plantation, bestowing upon the males the status of gentlemen, however threadbare. The elder Gordon then became a preacher, but pulpits and poverty ran too close a race. "Pap" had moved on through various enterprises, getting up a mineral springs retreat for the well-to-do and rhapsodizing over the prospect of imminent wealth, then moving—in veiled ignominy—to the mountains on the Alabama border, almost backing into Tennessee, where wheedled resources went into mining and timbering among hill folk who sold their land cheap, then worked it cheaper.

Along the way, Gordon acquired the manners of an aristocrat, but without the ducal purse. The curtain dropped in his senior year at the University of Georgia, where he had excelled in debates, the classics, and general *bonhomie*. Instead of standing up as valedictorian, he had outraced court orders and sheriffs' writs back to the mountains, where he worked a mine and falsified ledgers to save the family enterprise. Thereafter, he chose to read the law, already aware it was made of India rubber, and met his Fanny, whose family was as staid as his was irregular. Each of them longed to escape to the other's side.

But it had been in the mountains and mines where he first learned to lead men—indeed, to fool them, which was far from the least part of leadership. He had mastered that art amid desperation, shouldering creaking timbers underground, then tugging at numbers into the night by the glow of an oil lamp. Cornered by his father's truant ethics and plain lies, John Brown Gordon had vowed to armor himself in respectability, or its appearance.

Now he was here, on this awful field, determined not to be

blamed for the army's collapse. And that collapse was coming, all but certain. His men looked gaunt as ghouls, exhausted, approaching the point where resolve gave way to terror.

He dared not dispatch even one man to set Fanny on the road southward to safety. Every rifle counted, every visible body, each man the brick that, if removed, might cause the wall to crumble.

The Yankees had brought the weight of their guns to bear. A few hundred yards to the front, where Patton's Brigade still clung to its ground without its colonel, the pounding was incessant. Nor would the Federal infantry let up. Patton's boys held on, though. Running through their ammunition, but still brim-full of spite.

The cries and curses, smash of shot on stone, the awful splintering. Men bleeding, blinded, lost.

"Steady, boys," Gordon trumpeted. "Look at Patton's Virginians, aren't they fine?"

"They're fine with me," a soldier called, " 'long as they stay between us and the Yankees."

Hooting. The unstable merriment of soldiers facing death.

"Now, that's a fact," a powder-burned soldier agreed.

Hold until dusk. Until the Yankees had to quit. After that, an orderly withdrawal.

He just did not know how long he could master these men. Good men they were, the finest, fighting on with empty cartridge cases and empty bellies. But there came a point . . .

"I do believe," Gordon called as he rode the line, "that you boys have just about tuckered out the Yankees. You just hold on now. Night's coming. You hold on."

Fragile, the hearts of men. Immensely strong, and then abruptly fragile. War had less to do with rifles and guns, the external totems, than with the unmeasured depths within each breast.

Should've made Fanny go back South. Early had been right, that sour old man. But Gordon had found excuses to keep her near, blaming her own stubbornness.

The Yankees weren't barbarians, of course. She would not be mistreated. Quite the contrary, he expected. Knowing his Fanny, she'd soon be celebrated and waited on. But even the looming shame of her "capture" paled against the pain of separation.

The remnants of Patton's Brigade were caught in the fight of their lives. Gordon wished he could advance to support them. But he knew that the best he could hope for now was to keep his men steadied right here, behind these walls. Advance? He had all he could do to keep them from running.

His men. On this bad day.

Last until dusk.

Fanny.

All but deafened, he heard the growl of battle, the endless crack of rifles and thump of cannon, as if through water. There was bile in his empty belly and shit pressing his guts, but he didn't dare dismount even to piss. The men had to see him in the saddle now. He feared that simply getting down to water a tree would trigger a rumor that he had been wounded, even killed. And then they would run. Even the bravest longed for an excuse.

Their bodies were used up. All the folly of rushing off to Martinsburg, then that killing night march to get back. Shoulders bruised to a terrible tenderness by the kick of rifles, and forearms worn to cramping. Thirst. Spirit and temper were all that remained. Even loyalty, that loyalty on which he had relied for three grand years, would crack like sugar brittle.

"Good Lord! Look!"

Gordon turned, eyes following a captain's outstretched arm.

Hardly a rifle shot to the north, lines of blue-clad cavalry advanced at a trot, aimed at the flank and rear of Patton's Brigade. As Gordon watched, mortified, bugles sounded and the Yankees sped to a gallop, bending toward their horses' manes and leveling their sabers. The thunder of hooves pierced Gordon's deadened ears.

The scene robbed him of suitable commands, of any words.

His men had been positioned to spot the Yankees before Patton's boys could do so. The Virginians were fighting desperately, their flank refused and Yankees feeling beyond it. Each man out there had been occupied with his own immediate war.

Now the first of Patton's men grasped the danger. A few ran for the rear, toward the imagined safety of Gordon's line. Most stood, though. Brave men face-to-face with their executioners.

Nearing the Virginians, the Yankees raised a hurrah. Then came the crash, the human-animal-metal collision, the uproar. Horses leapt walls. Sabers flashed, hacking.

A few of Gordon's men fired at the Yankees, but the riders in blue jackets swarmed among the Virginians, making clean shots impossible.

There was not one thing to be done. Leaving the wall in a rescue attempt would only feed his men into the rout. For once, John Brown Gordon was at a loss.

More Virginians turned to run. The Yankees rode them down, slashing their blades into shoulders, at necks, across backs. Here and there, a soldier swung a rifle and unhorsed a rider, who could expect no mercy. But Patton's Brigade was being annihilated. As Gordon and his men watched.

"Goddamn them, god*damn* them," a soldier cried.

A fallow field away, hundreds of men in gray or shades of brown threw down their rifles. Well-drilled Yankee horsemen began to herd them. Like cattle.

"God*damn* them!"

Virginians who escaped leapt over the walls his men defended. Blind to anything but a vision of safety, they would not be stopped short of being shot down dead. And Gordon was not about to shoot down Confederates and risk destroying his future.

He was glad that poor George Patton had not remained to see his brigade end thus.

Then things got worse.

The Yankee cavalry parted, revealing advancing ranks of Federal infantry, rifles leveled at their waists, bayonets shimmering. The blue-backed horsemen wheeled to the north again, ready to sweep deep into Gordon's rear.

Where's *our* cavalry? Gordon demanded of no one. He knew the Confederate horse was weak, but, surely, Fitz Lee . . .

Where was the rest of Breckinridge's Division?

Confederate artillery began to shell the advancing Yankees. Some of the rounds landed amid the men just taken prisoner.

The sight further horrified Gordon's soldiers.

There was no one to dispatch to correct the guns. No time, anyway.

Some of his own men began to run, joining the fleeing Virginians. Then more broke. Gordon rode after them. Not far. Just far enough to turn on them.

"For God's sake, men! Stand! Stand! We'll beat them again, stand with me one more time!"

The fight was out of them, though. The trickle of those running became a flood.

Gordon tore off his hat and hurled it down.

"Don't shame your states! Georgia! Louisiana! Don't shame yourselves, boys!"

No one paused to reply.

Yankee artillery shells gave chase. Gordon pleaded, unwilling to show his rage. That was Early's foolish manner, not his.

A private grabbed his bridle and tried to turn Gordon's horse toward the rear.

"Save yourself, General! Save yourself!"

Tears flecked the boy's eyes.

Gordon looked down on him, burning. "Release my horse, son."

The private let go the leather strap, but didn't join those fleeing. Instead, he positioned himself in front of Gordon, back to the general and rifle across his chest, defying the entire Yankee army to try to get past him.

Gordon recognized the lad. Twelfth Georgia. If the boy was a day more than sixteen, it didn't tell.

The regiment's flag-bearer limped up and positioned himself by the private. He held up the banner, waving it.

More men joined them.

Nearby, another color-bearer paused, doubt on his face.

Gordon rode over to the man, grasped the pole from his hands, and said, "You'll let me borrow this?"

Lofting the tattered battle flag, Gordon rode through his men, making a miracle. Soldiers who had fled returned to the stone wall, took aim, and fired at the oncoming, hollering Yankees.

A Confederate battery found the correct range and pounded the Federals. For all Gordon knew, those were the same guns that had fired into the prisoners.

Fortunes of war.

His men applied themselves to the fight again. There were fewer of them now, far fewer. But those who remained meant to stand.

For Christmas—for that last, impoverished Christmas—Fanny had given him William Cowper's translation of the *Iliad*, an old copy with a leather cover burnished by many hands over the decades. She knew he loved that book above all others—although he favored the rendering by Pope.

Now he took his own stand, not on the plains of windy Troy, but on the fields before Winchester. Not an Achilles, but, perhaps, a Hector. With the doomed city at his back.

Lofting the flag and calling out encouragement, Gordon knew it was only a matter of time. But with his men rallied around him, it was a glorious time.

5:00 p.m.
Union center

Faster!" Emory Upton demanded. "Get up to the top of that rise, I need to see!"

The firing threatened to outdistance them.

His litter bearers picked up the pace, but not enough to satisfy him. The officers and orderlies accompanying the stretcher appeared doubtful, though they had given up on attempts at reason.

This was no time for reason. Not when he was winning.

He *knew* his wound was severe, didn't need to be told. He had tied off the thigh himself when the others hesitated. The pain blazed, not least when one of the bearers put a foot wrong. But pain could be endured. Jesus Christ had suffered worse than this, as had the Martyrs.

Think on the Oxford Martyrs. . . .

His men had broken through, that was what mattered, and now they raced the rest of the army to Winchester, brushing aside the last, enfeebled resistance. After a bloody afternoon's frustration, including a confrontation with a Nineteenth Corps colonel who proved a coward, Upton had driven his men on without mercy. And Mackenzie and the others had cracked the Rebel defense, bursting through their lines at last like a horde of avenging angels. His wounding amid that triumph had been a sign, a warning to shun mortal pride in an hour of glory. Perhaps it was even a riddle-wrapped sign of grace. . . .

He had kept faith. And the Lord had given him victory.

When he rose to his elbows, he saw the steeples of Winchester. The fighting was not done, the godless slavers harbored too much spite. Satan did not bow at the first blow. But Upton was determined that his men would be the first Union troops to reach the town. No matter the cost.

He prayed. Not for the Lord to ease the pain in his thigh, but for the strength to endure it and finish his work.

He had been granted a vision of how to smite them. All his reading in military science, his dedication to the art of war, was as naught before revelation. He had studied his trade until the last candle guttered, but Jomini shed little light beside the fiery sword of Jesus Christ.

"And there was given unto him a great sword . . . a great sword . . ."

Upton caught himself swooning. Much blood had been lost. He propped himself higher. Pain pierced him.

Nothing, he told himself, this is nothing.

"Tell Mackenzie he *must* press on." He wanted to add, but did not, "Show no mercy."

The true mercy would be to end this war, to break the chains of bondage forever and ever.

At an aide's command, the bearers lowered the stretcher to let a fresh team take it up. When they lifted him again, a bolt of pain made Upton want to shriek. He had forced himself to examine the wound at first, to confront this mortification of his flesh, but now he found it unsettling to view the ruptured meat.

We are but carrion, dross . . .

If the Lord wished to take his leg, even his life . . .

Not before *I* take Winchester, he blasphemed, surprising himself.

"Faster!" he snapped. "How can I command, if you can't keep up?"

Horsemen rushed out of the lengthening shadows. The first cool of evening preceded them, balm in Gilead.

"Put him down, for Christ's sake," a no-nonsense voice commanded.

Balancing care and haste, the bearers lowered Upton to the ground again.

"Damn it," the voice profaned. "I sent orders for you to go back to the surgeons."

Sheridan. Gazing down from that great black mount of his. The horse's mouth dripped slime.

"I can lead my division."

"The hell you can."

"Sir, I request . . ." Upton rallied against the pain. "I *demand* to remain in command of my division."

He could feel the air change around him, grasping that Sheridan would brook no man's defiance. He stiffened himself to withstand a blast of rage.

Instead, Sheridan slipped down from the saddle, instantly small when parted from his horse. He knelt over Upton.

Audible to the officers and men surrounding the litter, Sheridan announced, "General Upton, your performance has been heroic, selfless. No man has done more to turn the tide of battle. You have my personal thanks."

Then Sheridan leaned close, bitter of breath and flashing eyes as hard as the hardest gemstone. Lips almost kissing Upton's ear, he whispered, "Upton, you will go to the rear right now, or I will break you down to fucking private."

5:00 p.m.
The eastern edge of Winchester

Halt, you cowardly sonsofbitches," Jubal Early cried. "Stop, you cowards. God almighty, halt! Stop, I say, and fight like goddamned men."

5:00 p.m.
The northern approach to Winchester

What a jolly afternoon! Nothing like it in the great, wide world, Custer decided. Mankind had never devised a better sport. They'd run the Rebs mile after mile, the sorry devils.

Grinning, he returned to the head of his re-formed column of fours, facing the last scraps the enemy had mustered to guard his flank: a few bled-out troops of horse, a section of guns that could be enveloped easily, and a ruptured fort on a knoll. The fortification didn't interest Custer—an experienced cavalryman let fixed defenses rot—but he fancied taking those guns and finishing off the graybacks who'd dropped from the backs of their nags. Couldn't let Devin have all the fun, now, could he?

Turning to an orderly, Custer said, "Bring up the band."

He drew his saber.

5:15 p.m.
The northern edge of Winchester

Damnedest thing. Fitz Lee felt about the best he'd felt all day. He'd started out weaker than an old maid with the ague, got worse rushing about, sweating like a hog and worrying like a churchgoing gal on her wedding night, and then got whipped by Yankees more times than he could count, ending up here with his rump all but touching Winchester. His men had done their best, but they were scattered now, he'd lost contact with most of their commanders, and Breathed's guns appeared to have been put to another man's use. But, damnation, if he didn't feel almost peppery.

He didn't care to think that getting whipped might be good for a man. He didn't care to consider that at all.

Ask Breathed. What did his medical books say of such phenomena?

"Let 'em get close," Lee ordered, for the benefit of any man who could hear him over the racket. The horses weren't worth much now, and the party he had gathered fought dismounted. "Just wait, they'll come on sure. Just let them get close."

"Might care to slip down from the saddle yourself, sir," a captain suggested. "Air seems a trifle populated."

Lee pulled up a beard-spreader smile. "And let one of your bandits steal my horse? Rather chance it with those Yankee sharpshooters."

"Hoss?" a private asked in mock incredulity. His tone conjured the porch of a country store and genial times. Better times. "Genr'l, I took that critter you're settin' astride for a milk-cow. What have we come to, what has this army come to?"

Lee played along, waiting for the Federals to make their move. All he could do now was wait. "Cow? I'd cut myself a beefsteak right this minute!"

That was about true. Hadn't had so much as a cracker all day. Starved himself back to health, was that it? he wondered. Queerest thing: Even the dizziness had slipped away.

The dizziness was gone, but the Yankees weren't. Their pride, their haughty pride, had grown intolerable. They didn't even bother to wield their repeaters, just came on with sabers, as if mocking men who had beaten them steady for two years, then gave them a time for another year and a half. As if to say, "Yes, we have these fine new rifles that shoot jackrabbit fast, but we don't even need 'em for your sort." There was a cruelty in their condescension fiercer than the bite of blades on flesh.

"Get ready, boys."

The men tightened their grips on their weapons, coiling their innards. Across yet another inglorious field, Yankees trotted to and fro, up to some new deviltry.

Horse artillery rushed up on the flank. The cannoneers wore blue jackets, not gray.

Lee believed he heard fighting off behind him, down in the streets of Winchester, and hoped it was a fevered hallucination. Anyway, didn't do any good to ponder it. His place, his purpose, was here, and nowhere else. To hold until the rest of the army escaped.

Escape. A shameful, unaccustomed word. . . .

"They're coming!"

Bugles sounded. A band resumed its mockery. The Yankee gun section on the flank dropped its trails with handsome speed. In moments, the crews were ramming home their first shells.

"Let them get close," Lee called, speaking of the cavalry. There was nothing to be done about those guns, except bear the torment.

As the Union force advanced, increasing its pace to a canter with fine discipline, the horses first created a rumble that challenged the clamor of battle. But when they lowered their sabers and spurred to a gallop, their hoofbeats overwhelmed all other sounds.

A few of his men, the worst of them, didn't wait to fire, but ran for the town. Lee let them go, figuring they'd be cut down all the quicker.

The artillery on the flank opened up. One round fell short, but the next smashed into a tree that anchored Lee's line, hurling branches downward and men upward.

"Steady!" he called. He could make out the eyes of the horses. A few more yards, and he'd read the eyes of the men. *"Steady now!"*

Shells from some blessed, unseen Confederate battery struck

smack amidst the first wave of blue-clad horsemen. Mounts tripped and riders tumbled. Lee noticed that the men in the second rank had drawn their carbines, rather than sabers.

Yankees weren't taking chances, after all.

More bugles. But more artillery rounds shrieked overhead, plummeting toward the Yankees, flaying man and beast.

Lord Jesus, did he have a fighting chance?

His loss of consciousness was brief, if bewildering. He came to on the ground, grasping for the reins. Quicksilver pain raced over him, invading every part of his body at once. Lee fought for air. The wetness sheathing him wasn't sweat this time, he could tell that much.

"Get him out of here," a voice—raw with dread—commanded. "Carry him to the rear, we'll hold the bastards."

He tried to speak, but could not. The pain had crushing weight. Teeth, too. It bit with rabid fury, surpassing all previous wounds.

Pounding hooves. Men shouting. Clashing metal. Bring up your guns, Major Breathed. Where was Lomax? He needed to speak with Wickham, had to . . .

"Get him out of here," the voice repeated.

THIRTEEN

September 19, 6:00 p.m.
Winchester

Fanny Gordon stood in the street before the Lee house, all but choking on the dust and pleading with the soldiers to turn back. She never had imagined such a scene. To witness this army, and her husband's own men, running from the Yankees . . .

"Please," she begged, "go back and fight. Think of your honor!"

"Honor got kilt a ways back," a scarecrow told her.

But the soldiers were respectful, overall. Many knew her by sight. Those who did shied away, ashamed. Others plodded by, sullen. Even those who just plain ran were careful not to touch her. Dismayed officers tipped their caps in embarrassment. The passage of these hundreds retained no order, with flags and soldiers ajumble. Little united these men beyond their direction.

A cannonball smashed through a roof but didn't explode, content to cause a storm of splinters and dust. Glass chinked.

"Best go inside, ma'am," a grubby boy in a ravaged straw hat counseled.

She felt tears welling, but fought them down. John would not approve of a weeping wife at a time like this.

Was he all right? Might she . . . was it possible . . . that she might have cause for weeping?

Fanny Gordon whipped that thought away. Not her John. He'd be out there to the last, thrashing Yankees. Then he would ride off in an aura of glory. Alive and grinning.

"Please! Go back," she begged. "Think of your mothers and

wives!" Assailed by a swallow of dust, she coughed and struggled to ask, "Are there any Georgia men among you? Any Georgia men?"

A half dozen soldiers from her husband's old brigade made their way toward her.

"Ain't fitting for you to be out here, Mrs. Gordon," a sergeant warned her. His tone was of supplication, not command.

"And it isn't fitting for Georgia men to retreat."

Sunburned faces blushed. "We'll fight 'em again tomorrow," a private said. "Just not today, ma'am. Today just didn't go right."

Anxious to rejoin the flood, the once brave, emasculated men shuffled about until the sergeant asked, "Can we do something for you, ma'am?"

"Go back and fight."

The sergeant tipped his cap and the others nodded. Leaving her. But not to return to the battle.

"Wait! Is General Gordon all right?"

The Georgians were already submerged in the crowd, in the mob that had been a proud army.

Fanny glanced toward the porch, ensuring that young Frank remained indoors, where Laura Lee had promised to restrain him. A rambunctious boy, her second son was more like John than was his doe-eyed brother. She had broken her own rules by bringing Frank along on this visit, afraid—although she could not quite admit it—that the six-year-old might go through life with no memory of his father.

An ambulance fought through the crowd, so packed that bloodied limbs dangled over its drop-board. Behind it, more crimsoned men clung to a caisson. Rifle fire erupted, suddenly closer.

Why didn't any of these men turn and fight? There were so many of them. Surely they could make a stand, perhaps defeat the Yankees even now?

It was all she could do not to shriek at them.

She coughed up more dust.

Then she saw him, just as he spotted her and turned his horse.

Don't embarrass him, she warned herself. *Behave like the lady you know deep down you aren't. Don't you run and hug him, don't you start things.* After a decade of marriage, desire seized her still when she pressed against him, and in his arms her thoughts were not genteel.

As he forced his way through dejected men, with Yankee hurrahs hog-call close, she balled her fists and locked them on her hips. Ferocity was her only means to control herself.

John. Hat missing and locks awry. Filthy, his forehead gleamed as if smeared with lard. Even with that scar, he was still the handsomest man in the Confederacy.

When he drew a foot from a stirrup to dismount, she snapped, "John Gordon, you stay on that horse of yours. And you tell me the meaning of this spectacle."

Her sternness did the impossible, making him smile. Fleetingly.

Bending from the saddle, he asked, "Do I see before me my Penelope? Or is this Aphrodite descended to earth?"

"You hush."

"Fanny, go back in the house. You do no good out here."

"Well, you don't seem to be doing much good yourself, General Gordon. *Do* something with these men."

"Hasn't been our day. Don't blame these boys." He gestured toward the drop-shouldered stragglers avoiding the man on horseback and his queen. Those who glanced toward them did so warily.

She would not cry. She was determined not to let him see one tear.

"Go in the house now, Fanny. It's too late to leave. When the Yankees come, identify yourself to one of their field officers. They'll treat you with—"

She flared. "You see to your division, John Brown Gordon. The woman you married can manage fine by herself."

Gordon's eyebrows tightened. "Where's 'Neas? He should be seeing to you."

"Fool ran away. When they started shelling the town."

"I'll whip that nigger."

"You just whip those Yankees. I'll see to 'Neas."

"Yes, ma'am." He saluted, smiling again. "Reckon I'd best see to it, then. You go inside now, though, look after Frank. He'll be unsettled."

She wanted to scream, "I love you," to just shriek it. To grab his stirrup and never let go, to keep him.

When she raised her face to her husband, her features trembled.

"Go on," she said. "Go on now."

And he turned his horse—not in flight like the others, but toward the Yankees again, rallying a passel of soldiers who had remained with their flag. She watched as he charmed them, watching until they all disappeared behind a wall of buildings, her husband leading soldiers ragged as vagabonds.

I will *not* cry.

Aeneas had run off, probably north this time, but that was only part of the day's saga. She had risen early, setting off in the cool dark to join her husband at Martinsburg, meaning to surprise him, only to find herself in the midst of Rodes' Division as it hurried back to Winchester, trailed by Federal cavalry and rumors. One of Rodes' gallants had deployed his men to guard her as other soldiers hurried to mend an inopportune break of her buggy's tongue. She had returned to the Lee home just as the fuss became a battle.

That house would *not* be her refuge or her prison. She did *not* intend to be trapped inside with a bevy of silly women.

And she had her finest stroke of luck that day: The remnant of a Georgia company appeared, still led by its lieutenant. The men not only recognized her, but seemed bewildered at the sudden sight of her.

"You, Lieutenant! All of you!" she called. "If you men can't stand and fight, at least go out back and hitch the dapple-gray up to my buggy, the one with the green seat."

The men halted. Every one of them.

"Well, what are you waiting for?" she demanded. "Hoping to lay eggs?"

The lieutenant began to issue the order, but a few men were already moving. And though the others did not move one step back toward the Yankees, they did face about to defend her while she waited.

Quick as bugs in June, the soldiers brought her wagon around the house. Fanny didn't pause to fuss over private necessities, just ran inside to wrest Frank from Miss Laura Lee, a handsome 'fraidy-cat. After grabbing a mostly unpacked carpetbag—hoping for the best—she hastened back out to the street, as if the waiting buggy might evaporate.

A ragged sergeant stood holding the reins. Another soldier lifted Frank to his seat. She told the boy, "You sit still. And if you start to cry, I'll tan your backside." But the boy seemed more excited than afraid.

"*You*. And *you*," she called. "Those wounded men there, load them in back."

It sounded like the Yankees were atop them. Not all of the Georgia men had remained.

"Mrs. Gordon, you need to go fast now, you don't need to be encumbered—"

"You load those wounded men, or you'll feel this whip."

The soldiers did as told. One man she took aboard was a groaning young captain, a pretty thing hours before, who would not live to see his mother or sweetheart.

I will not cry. They will not *see me cry.*

She gee-upped the ancient horse, hoping the patched-up buggy tongue would hold.

As her vehicle joined the thinning stream of soldiers, she heard one of the Georgia voices announce, "That there woman's the toughest man in this army."

Fanny Gordon longed for night to fall. So she could burst out weeping.

6:15 p.m.
Winchester

As Hayes followed his 36th Ohio into the town, it was clear that the hard-fought day had ended in triumph. Pursuing the broken Rebs, his men had chased them with chants of "Kernstown! Kernstown!" And the Union sympathizers, a minority but an elated one, emerged from their homes before the fighting had fully passed, cheering on the dirty men in blue and holding up flags that had remained hidden for years, even when Union troops occupied the town.

It was different now, everyone sensed it. The Confederates—not Early, not anyone else—would never return again: Their might was broken. The seesaw swap of possessions in the Lower Valley was done.

And Rud Hayes just wanted water.

Surely thirsty too, his horse shied and nickered. Somehow, Will McKinley, smack in the midst of the battle and riding about to deliver orders from Crook, had found time to dispatch a man to retrieve Hayes' horse and lead it forward. The lad was a magnificent bundle of innocent, endless energy, bound for bigger things when this war was over.

Would it be over soon now? Might he even spend Christmas at home with Lucy and the boys? And, perhaps, with a new daughter?

"God bless you!" a man in high-waisted pants and suspenders called from a porch.

Hayes tipped his hat. His old brigade and, now, his division had even regained a rough appearance of order, the men sorting themselves out in the uncanny way they did once the shock of combat clicked into a rhythm. When they finally broke the last barricaded line at the edge of town, all serious resistance had collapsed—what there had been of it, at the end. They had advanced over fields strewn with dead and wounded, most of them in the rags the South counted as uniforms, past overturned wagons, an

ambulance broken in pieces by a shell, and the human affectations
discarded in war, playing cards, pipes, spilled haversacks, and folded
letters panting with the breeze. . . .

Emerson needed to see *that*.

A last few rifles crackled in the streets, but the only hint of organized resistance rose south of town—a Reb rear guard, no doubt.
Here, his men had only to round up prisoners, some of whom came
forward, hands raised, to surrender eagerly, while others sat dejected against a fence or stumbled about. Many a wounded man
who walked off the field had reached the end of his strength and
lay on a porch or sagged upon its steps. Few of the Johnnies were
arrogant now, although there were still some hard ones among the
wounded.

A boy with an arm the surgeons would take before morning
swore, "They'll be back. Our boys'll be back."

But Hayes did not believe they ever would.

With a cheer that became a roar, his Ohio soldiers reached the
shabby courthouse at the town's heart, laying claim to being first
in the city.

Hayes dismounted, handed off his horse, and walked forward
among his soldiers. Their joy seemed uncontainable. They cheered
him as he made his way, delighted with themselves and confident
enough to reach out and slap him on the back, praising him ful-
somely. He recalled reading, somewhere, the description "drunk
with victory."

A soldier with a magnificent red beard told him, "You'll end
up as governor after this."

6:30 p.m.
The Valley Pike, south of Winchester

Nichols hobbled a stretch beyond the clot of men from Ramseur's
Division that passed as a rear guard. Then he sat down by the roadside, just plain sat. His leg hurt like the horrors. It wasn't fair. None
of it was fair. Not one thing that had happened that day was fair.

The Yankees did seem to be tuckering out. That much might turn out decent. Maybe those boys lined up across the Pike could face them down. With dusk upon them and dark pressing in, maybe the blue-bellies had about had their fill.

Bad enough with the Yankees coming from every side, wily as Satan's legions, mighty as Gog and Magog. They'd fought them to the bottom of the well of what men had in them, and he'd done his part, standing when others ran high-tail. Only to be ordered back that last time, back to one final position, and while he was making his way as ordered—not running, not running, never running—some hot-metal wickedness had struck him in the back of the thigh, right in back of the same thigh where another piece of brimstone-made iron had struck him in the front back in July.

He had gone down with a yowl like a dog-bit girl. All confused. Captain Kennedy had paused to help him, bewildered himself, since once again there was no blood, no obvious break, just a great big heap of real sore hurt that kept him from standing up on his own two feet. The captain had helped him on back, telling him to use his rifle as a crutch from then on and just make his way to the rear, wherever that ended up. So he had gone on along, limping and huckle-bucking, moving with little leaps like in a hopscotch game, twinned in his dumbstruck misery by Jack Collins, a chawing man from Company K, who got all shot in the foot and was propping himself up with his rifle, too.

Times were, he feared to be overtaken, with all those hale and hearty men running past him through the streets, like boys racing for the prize of a bag of marbles. Most shameful thing ever witnessed, that reckless running. He had bumped along behind as best he could, calculating that getting himself captured once in a day was about enough.

A good woman had come out to her front gate, crying like Mammy and offering passing soldiers buns from a pan, and he had craved one as souls yearned for Salvation, but fleeter men grabbed them all before he could wiggle up through the crowd. And that woman just stood there with her empty pan, crying her eyes out, crying and crying, and the soldiers just went on past, ashamed, maybe, but not pausing to commiserate like Elder Woodfin said they should do with the poor.

Ive Summerlin had said, way back a piece, "Who's he got in mind any poorer than us?"

Moabites and Jebusites, the Yankees had set their artillery against the town. He passed a blasted, burning house, amid female lamentations.

Then all the fuss slackened up, with the shooting gone down to a pestering, and at one point, a posse of Yankee horsemen galloped across his path, ignoring his existence, a final insult.

He had never hated Yankees so much. And he did not think he'd known a worse day in his life, not even when nigh on dying in that Danville pesthouse pretending to be a hospital, with his insides pouring out of his sorriest part.

Unhorsed and limping in high boots, a lieutenant saw him sitting where he'd paused behind Ramseur's boys. The officer's face was pale in the near-dead light.

"Don't cry, son," the lieutenant said. "We'll whip them next time. You'll see."

"I ain't crying," Nichols said before realizing his face was doused with tears.

"Guess it's nothing but sweat, I wasn't looking right," the lieutenant said. "Why don't you come on along now. Come with us until you find your regiment. Don't want the Yankees catching up with you."

Nichols almost told him about his leg, how much it hurt, how he had only sat down because he did not think that any man, not David nor Goliath, could have taken one more step with that hurt upon him. But he didn't say it, would not be known for a complainer, which was hardly any better than a coward.

He fumbled back to his feet and said:

"Yes, sir, I reckon I'm coming."

7:00 p.m.
Winchester

Sheridan let Crook lead him through the streets. Apart from dejected bands of prisoners, everyone, soldiers and citizens, shared an air of jubilation. Of course, Sheridan realized, many a man and woman remained locked behind their doors and out of temper.

"This way, Phil," Crook said. He knew Winchester. And the right people, though hardly in the social sense.

Sheridan felt gay himself, immeasurably pleased. He had broken the curse of the Valley, winning the Union's first victory in its confines, the first real win in three and a half years, and a colossal victory it appeared. The satisfaction was so rich, he felt he must glow like a gas lamp.

The soldiers he passed cheered him. He loved it when men cheered him.

With the Johnnies on the run, he had ordered his corps commanders to assemble, their every delay, outburst, and blunder forgiven, erased by victory. Winning was the thing, the rest was wastage. If his plan had faltered, it didn't matter now. Victory purged every sin in the military decalogue.

"This way," Crook called again, straining to be heard above the ovation.

Old George had done splendidly by him, and Sheridan was delighted to have him near, forgiving, in this moment, Crook's annoying habit of being right. His "mountain-creepers" had done a marvelous job, fighting with the resolution of Regulars. Led well, volunteers sometimes worked wonders.

Triumphant, Sheridan banished all thoughts of his midday moment of doubt.

"Chased 'em like rabbits!" a soldier called out to him. "Run 'em like hares."

Sheridan tipped his hat. For a pained trance of seconds, he remembered Davey Russell. His army's losses had been severe on many counts.

But only victory mattered. War forbade sentiment. If a general wouldn't sacrifice his own mother to win a battle, he didn't deserve his stars.

Men lit makeshift torches. To celebrate, not to destroy. The destruction would come later, though not here.

He had ordered his cavalry to pursue Early's army, instructing Torbert not to ease the pressure. He knew the horses were blown, that any pursuit would peter out with nightfall. You had to press men, though. If his orders meant only an additional ten minutes of harassment of the enemy, that ten minutes made a difference. You determined just how much men could achieve, then demanded more.

Crook and the aide all but glued to him—McIntire? McGuinness?—halted their mounts before a two-story house, a better-kept affair than most of its like south of the Potomac. No frippery woodwork, though.

Quakers, Sheridan shook his head. Probably use 'em as provost guards in Heaven, make sure folks didn't take too much pleasure lounging on those clouds. He let himself down from Rienzi's back. It was a long way to the ground. It struck him, of a sudden, that he was exhausted. But this was no time for a man to indulge himself.

Crook and his aide waited on the porch. Sheridan strode up, saber banging the steps.

"Thought I'd let you have the honor," Crook told him.

Sheridan knocked on the door.

Prim but not without promise, a young woman opened the door. She held an oil lamp. Its light gilded her face, throwing shadows along a hallway.

After a swift appraisal of his uniform, she said, "Thee and thine are welcome in this house. Wouldst eat? Our fare is simple."

Sheridan smiled. Figuring that more than one of his soldiers had knocked on more than one door asking for food. If men couldn't have a woman after a battle, they'd settle for biscuits.

"Miss Wright? Rebecca Wright?" He saw by her eyes that she

was the girl and didn't wait for an answer. He removed his hat. "General Sheridan, ma'am. I believe you know the gentleman behind me."

Lifting the lantern, the lass peered over his shoulder.

"Miss Wright," Crook said, stepping forward.

Instead of appearing reassured, the girl looked almost frightened.

"Come in, come in. All are welcome."

After Sheridan and Crook entered, a few more officers thrust themselves in behind them. As quickly as she could, the lass shut the door, though. The house smelled of baking and lavender, of women living together without men.

Hat in hand, Sheridan said, "I've come to thank you, Miss Wright. Your Union has enjoyed a splendid victory, a triumph. Thanks to the information you sent by that slave."

The young woman stiffened. "He is no slave. Thou shouldst know we keep none."

"Of course, of course. Nonetheless, Miss Wright, you're the heroine of the day. I just wanted to pay my respects, to thank you."

The lass had gone from pale to paler. When she spoke again, her voice quavered. "I beg thee . . . thou must not speak so. Swear on thy sword thou willst not. I beg of thee."

Sheridan raised an eyebrow. Calling his thoughts to order. He had thought that Quakers didn't believe in oaths.

"If word were to spread," she explained, "my family's lives would be worthless. Thou knoweth not the hatred in these hearts."

Sheridan recalled that the young woman was a schoolteacher. He wondered if the children she taught had to endure her "thees" and "thous," or if she spoke plain English in her classroom.

He placed his hand on the grip of his sword. "Yes, of course. I swear that I will not compromise your family. None of us will. My apologies, Miss Wright."

The tension drained from the air.

"There is milk. And fresh bread," she told her guests. "And butter."

Sheridan smiled. "I don't doubt that my companions will partake, but I would be grateful if you led me to a desk or a table. I have messages to write."

McKinley. That was the name of Crook's new aide. The boy mooned over the Quaker girl the way a dog eyed a beef roast.

She led Sheridan through a hall and into a compact schoolroom. Lighting another lamp, she said, "I am glad our flag has returned."

"It's back to stay this time."

She set out pen, ink, and paper, aligning them neatly on her schoolmarm's desk.

"Willst have anything else?"

Sheridan shook his head. But then he said, "Water. Just water, please. And keep the rest of them occupied for ten minutes."

When she closed the door behind her, he began to write to Grant:

> *Winchester, September 19, 1864—7 p.m.*
> *I have the honor to report that I attacked the forces of General Early on the Berryville Pike at the crossing of Opequon Creek, and after a most stubborn and sanguinary engagement . . . completely defeated him.*

Midnight
The Valley Pike, Middletown

Early had kept his rage inside for hours, breaking out now and then in minor snarls, but letting his insides burn as hot as pitch. Didn't want anything to do with any man. Fools, all of them. Starting a war they were never going to win, then leaving him to fight it, because that was just the goddamned way men were, a damn-fool, worthless species, a blot on the earth.

He bore a great deal of blame for the day's debacle, he knew it plain, but he wasn't ready to face up to that yet. Low enough as it was. Would've had every last cavalryman whipped, though. Every last one of them. Starting with that highborn ass Fitz Lee, wounded or not. Nothing more convenient than a wound. Now was there?

Breckinridge had insisted on riding beside him. Making their way south, already fixed on Fisher's Hill, a position of refuge, a natural fortress that had never been taken. Rest up there, fit up. Bring in the stragglers. Then see what might be done.

Breckinridge. With those damned mustaches.

The night was clear, but dark. Whenever he spotted a campfire beyond the roadside, he dispatched a party to kick it dead. Men had to march on, not laze about and wait for the damned Yankee cavalry.

Breckinridge. Damned politician. *His* war. That's what this was. A war wrought by big talkers, pounding their desks and insisting that God almighty had established slavery at least as far back as the Garden of Eden, with darkies to polish the apples, and that "natural law" demanded that the institution be extended not just to Kansas, a worthless patch of prairie, but to all the Territories and, soon as they think of it, to the moon as well.

Served 'em right to take a whipping. If the white man had ever been the nigger's bane, the situation surely had reversed itself. All this, because rich men had been too tight of purse to pay their monkeys a few pennies for their labor.

Didn't mean no love lost for the Yankees, of course. He'd come to hate them more than a barrel could hold. Kill every one of them, every last one.

The only thing he had left was this war. A war that hadn't been his, but had become his dearest possession, his true home. And the sonsofbitches wanted to take that, too.

Breckinridge muttered something about a better day tomorrow.

Early turned on the former vice president, the famed Kentucky firebrand.

"Ha," he cackled. "Just you tell me, Breckinridge . . ." Early swung an arm at his retreating army. "Do tell me, *General* Breckinridge, what you think of the 'rights of the South in the Territories' now? Ain't that how you used to put it, back when you were bellowing in Washington?"

Breckinridge did not reply, disappointing Early, who had hoped to pick at least one fight he might win.

Beside them, their soldiers tramped southward.

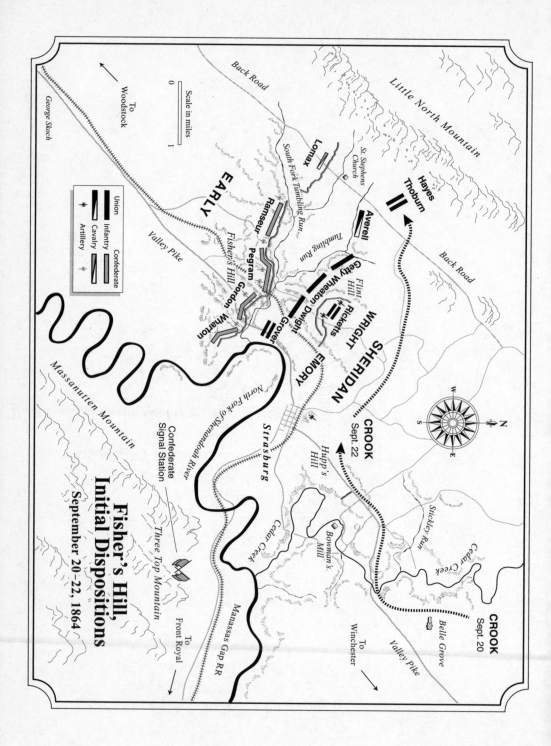

**Fisher's Hill,
Initial Dispositions**
September 20–22, 1864

George Skoch

To
Woodstock

Back Road

Little North Mountain

Scale in miles

0

1

Lomax

South Fork Tumbling Run

St. Stephens
Church

Hayes
Thoburn

EARLY

Ramseur

Averell

Pegram

Tumbling Run

Gordon

Getty

Wheaton

Flint
Hill

Dwight

Back Road

Fisher's Hill

Wharton

Grover

Ricketts

WRIGHT

Valley Pike

EMORY

SHERIDAN

Massanutten Mountain

North Fork of Shenandoah River

Strasburg

Hupp's
Hill

CROOK
Sept. 22

W

N

S

E

Confederate
Signal Station

Bowman's
Mill

Stickley Run

Cedar Creek

Three Top Mountain

To
Front Royal

Manassas Gap RR

Cedar Creek

To
Winchester

Belle Grove

CROOK
Sept. 20

Valley Pike

Union
Infantry
Cavalry
Artillery

Confederate

FOURTEEN

September 20, 1864, 3:30 p.m.
Fisher's Hill

"Glad you're back," Pendleton said as Hotchkiss dismounted. "Saul needs David to strum his cartographic harp."

The mapmaker passed his horse to the nearest orderly. The jest confounded him.

"Gordon," Pendleton explained. "That's what Gordon said. About you and the Old Man."

Hotchkiss rubbed his saddle-bothered legs. "Sounds like Gordon. How's Early?"

"About how you'd expect," the chief of staff told him. "Blaming the sun, the moon, and the stars." Normally fastidious, Pendleton was unkempt, dirty, and unshaven, with his collar undone and stained: He wore the look of a hard retreat, if not an outright disaster. "That's between us, of course. Need watering, Jed?"

"Horse does, I don't. Stopped at a farmhouse. He still on about the cavalry?"

"Hear him tell it, everything was their fault."

"How's Fitz Lee? Bad as the rumors?"

"Hit twice, maybe three times. Surgeons won't give out a firm opinion." Pendleton smirked. "Guess we've both seen enough of men protecting reputations they haven't got."

"Lee's tough, he might pull through. Despite the surgeons."

Around them, weary men purged old entrenchments of sediment. The weather was fine, if nothing else was.

"Touch of Jackson in Fitz Lee," Hotchkiss went on. "Not entirely likable, but nowhere a truer heart."

"I do miss Old Jack," Pendleton reminisced. "Still get sick to my stomach, recalling that night. . . ."

"Doesn't pay to think about it." But Hotchkiss often thought about Jackson himself, recalling the man's indomitable will and their shared Presbyterian prayers.

"Fitz Lee did all he could," Pendleton resumed. "The Old Man just won't see it. Yankees must be making cavalrymen up in those mills of theirs, never saw anything like it. Our boys tried. . . ."

The mapmaker nodded. "I passed the ambulance train."

"*One* of the ambulance trains," Pendleton corrected him.

"And the wagon with Rodes."

"Godwin's dead, too. Zeb York's hit bad, but we brought him off. Patton was dying, we had to leave him in Winchester." Pendleton sighed. "Not our best day."

"Other losses? The men?"

"Can't truly say, not yet. Strays still coming in."

"Hundreds, though?"

"Thousands."

"Bless us."

"And three guns. Old Man's angrier about the guns than anything."

"Except the cavalry?"

"Except the cavalry."

Hotchkiss glanced westward, scanning past a roadbed to the next height where men labored. He had been gone for hardly a week, back home in Loch Willow, then on to Staunton—where the Yankees had left a partisan force of bedbugs—but something way down deep had changed in the army. There was an odor of discontent to go with the routine stench.

"How are the men taking it?"

"Shocked," Pendleton admitted. "Oh, they're feisty again, talkwise. Going to lick Sheridan bare-handed, come next chance. But some of them have the jumps."

"Not used to being on the wrong side of the outcome."

The private truth was that Hotchkiss was sick of the war. Each time he went home, he found it harder to drag himself back to the army.

Pendleton stared northward, across the trickling run to the opposite ridge. Toward the enemy. "It's just . . ."

"Just?"

"The way Early blames the cavalry . . ."

"The men blame him?"

Pendleton nodded. "You can't help hearing things."

"They'll come around," Hotchkiss said. Hoping it was true. If he was weary of the war, he nonetheless did not want it to be lost.

Pendleton's eyes flashed anger. "He does his best, that's the thing they just can't see. He does his best, then cuts the ground out from under himself. He doesn't have one friend, he's pushed them away."

"He has you. And me, if I count."

"We *don't* count, that's the gist of it. It's the other generals. Oh, they follow his orders, more or less, and fight like riled-up wildcats. But they just don't *like* him." A frail thing this day, the chief of staff's temper collapsed, leaving Pendleton as glum as Hotchkiss ever had seen him. Once a font of humor—even with Jackson—the younger man had been subdued by marriage and sobered by war. Even the young were old now.

"Sheridan had the numbers," Pendleton went on in a voice that weakened from anger to resentment. "Must've had three times what we had in the field. If not four. Early put up the best darned fight he could, you should've seen him." He stared at the stubbled earth before his toe and kicked a clod. "I just wish he'd stop blaming everybody, talking them down. Doesn't do any good, just makes him more enemies." He grimaced. "Lord knows, I'm loyal to the man . . ."

"We both are," Hotchkiss said.

Pendleton's eyes were haunted. "You should have heard him an hour ago. Railing about Sheridan's incompetence, how Sheridan should've done this or that and how he outfoxed him by bringing off the army. Jed, we just took a licking, and a bad one. He doesn't help his cause, going on like that."

"He's never been a man to help his own cause." Hotchkiss pictured Early in his common stance, hat brim turned up and mouth turned down, stained beard and mistrustful eyes. A man who found little comfort in this world, or in thoughts of the next.

"And Breckinridge. *He's* off tomorrow," Pendleton said. "Wangled his way out, orders from Richmond. He's taking command down in southwestern Virginia."

"Not much of a command."

"He doesn't care."

"Always was some tension. Maybe it's better so."

Pendleton tried to smile. "How was your leave?"

Hotchkiss clicked his tongue, a childhood habit he never had managed to break. "Reckon I had a better week than you did. Oh, fine. Got Sara and the girls provisioned for winter. Folks are worried, though. Staunton's had as much experience with Yankees as any of the inhabitants desire." He began to parse his words, then decided on honesty. "Sandie, they're scared. They put up a good front, but they're scared to death, every one of them. They reckon that, if the Yankees come back again, it'll go a good sight worse than it did the last time."

"Chambersburg," Pendleton muttered.

Hotchkiss nodded. "Can't have a conversation, without the burning of Chambersburg coming into it. They fear the torch of vengeance. And they blame Early."

"I don't expect word about yesterday will provide a great deal of comfort." Pendleton struggled to shake off his cloak of gloom. "Oh, pshaw. We'll be all right. I'm just talking tired. Lee'll send Kershaw back, we'll be stronger than we were at Winchester."

Hotchkiss, in turn, looked northward. Many a mile distant, his New York birthplace still held his parents in thrall, but he had been won by the Shenandoah, this Eden. And if it was a hard-used paradise now, the end of the war would see it bloom again, of that he was certain. He knew the composition of the soil, the strata of rocks, the springs and watercourses, and he loved that earth as the Jews of old loved Israel.

"Yankees close?" he asked.

"Cavalry south of Strasburg, on the Pike. Throw a stone and hit them. And they're all over Hupp's Hill. Probably watching us through a spyglass."

For a second time, Hotchkiss surveyed the old position, covered again with men in gray and brown: Fisher's Hill, "the Gibraltar of the Valley." He wasn't a master of military art, not in its entirety. But he knew terrain. And if there was a natural fortress, a safe line of defense where a beaten army could nurse its wounds and recover, that ground was here. With the Shenandoah River a moat guarding the right flank, high bluffs rolled west for three miles before dropping down to the Back Road. Little North Mountain, rising sheer and running north to south, made a flanking movement on the left impossible. Fisher's Hill was the one exemplary bottleneck in the entire Valley, and the Yankees had never dared to assail it, no matter their numbers. You could move against it only from the front, and attacking that way was suicide.

"Well, we'll hold them here," Hotchkiss said. "Buy time for General Kershaw to come back. Reckon the Old Man has a mind to see me?"

Pendleton grinned, stretching gaunt cheeks. "Well, *I'm* so minded. Let him holler at somebody else for a while." The smiled curled. "You're going to catch it for being away, you certainly picked your time."

They walked toward a cluster of wall tents southward of the crest. Artillerymen unhitched half-lame teams and a cook got up a fire.

Pendleton said, "I had a letter from my wife. Newest Pendleton's set to arrive any time now." He peered across hilltops garlanded with regiments. "We're going to be very happy."

"Surely," Hotchkiss said.

We can't let up, can't give them time to recover," Sheridan said. A lantern lit the tent, turning faces orange. The gathered generals looked tired but sternly attentive. "I intend to finish this business, gentlemen."

Horatio Wright said, "I rode up to look at the ground in front of my corps. A direct assault would be madness."

Sheridan glared at the taller man. "Nobody said one word about a frontal assault. Now . . . any members of this august convocation have an idea? How to turn those bastards off that hill? I'm ready to listen." He pivoted to face Emory. "I heard you mumbling about a move on our left."

The Nineteenth Corps commander shook his head. "Took a good look. I'd have to cross the river twice, in full view of the Johnnies up on the bluffs. And the attacking force would lose contact with the main body, might be cut off."

Sheridan peered down at the map on his desk. The others crowded around. As if they might summon a sudden revelation.

"They've got us in a fix," Wright said.

Sheridan flared. "*No.* We've got *them* in a fix. And we're going to finish what we started at Winchester."

By preference last to speak, George Crook stood with crossed arms. "Only way to get around them, to envelop that position, is on our right."

Wright and Emory stared at him, incredulous.

"Over that mountain?" Wright asked.

"Work along the side of it. Say halfway up. Come down in their rear."

Wright all but sneered. "A scouting party might make it, not a corps."

"You couldn't keep a regiment in good order," Emory added. "The rocks, trees, brush . . . an attack would fall to pieces before one shot was fired."

Crook scratched beside his nose. "My men could do it. One division, maybe both."

Wright gave him a killing look that said Crook was just on the brag. There was jealousy aplenty in the air over credit for Winchester.

Sheridan said, "George . . . that's begging for failure."

Crook kept his tone as calm as if counting rations. "My men have spent this war scrambling over mountains, you should see the muscles in their legs. Little North Mountain's far from the worst climb they've faced." He briefly met Wright's eyes. "I believe such a movement offers us our best chance of success." His attention moved on to Emory, then to Averell, the only cavalryman present. "If anyone here has a better plan, I'll defer and shake his hand."

Sheridan's features mixed skepticism and hope. "You truly believe you could bring that off? And your corps wouldn't break down into a mob? Before you went three hundred yards? You think an entire division—not to say two—could negotiate that mountain and come down on the Rebels in fighting condition?"

Crook nodded. "I can swear we'd try. Look, Phil, all of you. The only weak spot in their entire position's on our right, out on their left. Smack at the foot of that mountain."

Sheridan turned to Averell. "What's Early got over there?"

"Cavalry. At least one battery of horse artillery. No sign of anything to their rear, though. Infantry are all up on that high ground."

"For now," Wright said.

Crook banished all emotion from his voice. "I've crossed Fisher's Hill on the march, more than once. It's a formidable position, nature's gift to a defense. But from the river to the foot of that mountain's nearly four miles. Takes a lot of men to man that line. And Early's got to be stretched thin, after yesterday. No, we don't know if we're seeing his final dispositions, but it looks like he's taking his risk at exactly the wrong place, figuring on the mountain to shield his flank. He should have an infantry division down there to anchor his line. But he doesn't *have* that division."

"Talked this over with your division commanders?" Sheridan asked.

"I wanted you to hear it first."

"Bring them in, I'd like to hear their views. George, you're playing for high stakes. I don't intend to undercut your authority, but I need a few more opinions. From those fabled 'mountain-creepers' of yours."

"I'll have them here in an hour. If they say I'm a fool, I'll shut my mouth."

8:45 p.m.
Sheridan's headquarters

Rud Hayes wished the baggage train had caught up with his division: He still wore mud stains and splashes of other men's blood. No one in the crowded tent was dressed for a ball, but neither did they look like they'd come from a hog wallow.

"Well, Hayes?" Sheridan asked in a voice that strained at camaraderie. "Division command suit you? I hear you took those boys of yours for a swim." Without allowing a response, he wheeled on Hayes' companion. "Come here, Thoburn. Look at this map. You too, Hayes."

The two colonels squeezed in beside the army commander. They towered over Sheridan.

"Look here. Little North Mountain. Know it?"

"Marched past it, sir," Thoburn told him with a shrug.

"What about you, Hayes?"

"Fields of boulders. Steep. Tangled undergrowth."

"Passable? I don't want a politician's answer now."

"Yes, sir. It's passable. With some difficulty."

"By a division?"

Surprised by the question, Hayes noted that Crook's eyes were fixed upon him. As was the attention of every man within the lantern's cast.

"Yes."

"Passable by an entire division? You're confident about that, Colonel?"

"It wouldn't go fast, but yes." He understood exactly what was afoot now: an effort to turn the Rebs out of their position. A throw of the dice, it nonetheless made sense.

"What about *two* divisions?"

Hayes glanced at Crook for guidance, but the corps commander's face was hewn of stone.

"Harder. Slower. More risk."

"But possible?"

Hayes had taken about as much as he felt he needed to take.

"Sir, I won't presume to speak for anyone else's men or anyone else's command. But my men have crawled over more boulders and worked their way through more mountainside thickets than any sensible fellow would have a mind to. My division can move along the side of that mountain or over it. With average luck, we can surprise the Johnnies, if that's the intent. But I won't make light of the effort."

Sheridan canted his head toward Thoburn. "What do *you* think? Is Colonel Hayes here a madman?"

"Rud's right. It can be done."

Peeved, Wright interrupted. "I can't believe we're contemplating this. The Confederates would spot the movement immediately. They can see everything we do from Three Top Mountain." He tucked in his chin, a ram about to charge. "I applaud the colonels' enthusiasm, but I don't believe they'd make it to Early's rear with more than a skirmish party."

"Well, you won't bear the responsibility, if they fail," Sheridan said. "I will."

Crook stepped closer to the table. The map's edges had curled. "Right now, they can't see a single man in my corps. We're still north of Cedar Creek, tucked out of sight."

"They'll see you when you move," Emory countered.

Crook looked at Sheridan. "I propose that the army move in close to keep Early occupied, hold his attention through tomorrow. Demonstrations, maybe a feint or two. Steal a little ground. Make it appear as though everybody's engaged, as though the whole army's up and we're positioning ourselves to hit him straight on. I'll move my corps tomorrow night, at dark. Get close enough to the base of the mountain, then give the men a rest, but keep them hidden all through the approach march. On the mountain itself, the foliage is still so thick they won't see us coming. And I'll make sure they don't hear us. We'll go in light, knapsacks grounded, canteens and scabbards secured." He stared down any last doubters. "We'll hit them well before dark, day after tomorrow."

"Give Early a full day?" Sheridan said sharply. "And most of another day?"

"We lose some time, granted. And Early keeps improving his defenses. But not on that flank. We'll turn Fisher's Hill into a trap. Catch him from behind in his own trenches, bury his army right there."

Sheridan reared up, a little bull. Everyone realized that the decision had been made.

"George, you'd damned well better keep your men out of sight. And if you can hide a corps from the Rebs, God bless you." He turned to Wright and Emory. "Push forward at first light tomorrow. Skirmish, keep the Rebs watching, parade around. Any local terrain we can use to advantage, drive the Rebs off it. But don't become decisively engaged. Just make Early drool in his beard, thinking we might be stupid enough to hit him from the front the following day."

He turned to Averell. "Push Lomax down the Back Road in the morning, make sure none of his scouts get near Crook's boys."

And to Wright: "What's your order of march? Who'll be closest to that mountain when you deploy?"

"Ricketts."

"Jim needs to show his mettle. Press the Rebs hard enough to keep them fixed and expecting a frontal assault over on their left. He'll have to chew forward a bit, accept some losses."

Sheridan considered the men gathered in the tent, the weary men who won the day at Winchester. The air under the canvas had grown humid and ripe from sweat. And sour with new rivalries.

Sheridan slapped the flat of his hand on the map. "When Crook's men begin rolling up Early's flank, I want everyone pressing forward, no matter how ugly it looks out there in front of you. Don't let Early shift troops to shore up that flank. Pound them. And when they break, by God, this time we'll finish them."

September 21, 5:00 p.m.
Gordon's Division

Gordon walked among his men on the high ground of Fisher's Hill, wielding a jovial mien to meet their complaints. The weather was a mercy, dry and clear, and Sheridan had been merciful as well. Beyond seizing the gun pits on Flint Hill, in between the armies, the Yankees hadn't made too much of a fuss. The soldiers around him had been spared this day.

"'Tain't fair, General," a thick-bearded corporal declared.

Per custom, Gordon played along. "And what, on this delectable afternoon, could trouble so fine a soldier?"

"We're way up here, up on this hill," the man explained.

Gordon reset the hat that Breckinridge had left him as a parting gift. It didn't fit nearly so well as the one he'd lost two days before.

"Well, it does seem to me," Gordon told his interlocutor, "that 'up here' isn't so bad a place to be. I'd rather be up here, with the Yankees down there, than the reverse."

"'Tain't the Yankees," the fellow said. His comrades had gathered around, sensing another of Gordon's famed exchanges. "No, General, it's that we're up here and those boys General Ramseur done took up are way over there, with another division between us."

"And why is 'over there' better than here? I confess my mystification."

"Well, lookee. They're right there above the cavalry, 'twixt them and that mountain. One of those nags drops down stone dead, all those boys have to do is trot on down and carve themselves out some dinner. All we get is crackers."

"Cavalry might have a say in the divvying up," Gordon observed. "Anyway, none of those nags have enough meat left on their bones to feed two Georgians." He smiled. Generously. A smile was about all he had left with which to be generous. "I reckon the point is that you boys are getting rambunctious for a good dinner. . . ."

"That's about right, sir."

An invisible hook raised a corner of Gordon's mouth. "Wouldn't mind a proper feed myself. Won't be tonight, though." His smile tightened. "Unless some noble Achilles were to intrude on General Sheridan's repast. . . ."

"That's the doggone thing, right there," a soldier declared. "Worst thing about losing a battle, you don't get to feed off the Yankees. Had my eye on a fellow looked like a great, big Dutchman, figured him for a haversack full of sausages. Then, 'fore you knowed it, I was headed the wrong way."

"And here we are," Gordon said. "I feel abused myself, boys. I've long been partial to letting our Northern *confrères* supplement our diet, only seems proper." He remembered, fondly, bags of coffee beans captured in the Wilderness. "We'll put things right, though. We're just taking a breathing spell."

"That's a fact," the first speaker said, contented to have fed on Gordon's attention, if not on salt pork.

"Boys, you'll have to excuse me. I daresay Colonel Pendleton's got his eye on me from yonder. I must not be truant."

"You tell General Early how to fix things," a bold man said. "He'll listen to you, General."

"As Agamemnon paid heed to Ulysses," Gordon said wryly, his private joke.

"Hope that ain't catching," a wag exclaimed to the common delight of the men.

Gordon gave them a soft salute, still studiedly genial, and strode off. In the distance, skirmishers crackled at each other, but the relative calmness of the day made Gordon wonder if Sheridan had been snake-bit bad enough to have grown wary. Or perhaps he was just flummoxed by Fisher's Hill. Either way, the respite was dearly welcome. The men needed time.

Pendleton met him in midfield, just below a battery tucked behind gabions.

"Any word on Clem Evans?" Gordon asked. Before the chief of staff could speak.

The younger man shook his head.

"Well, I know he was headed for Richmond," Gordon went on. "Could have used Clem back at Winchester, that's the truth." He repositioned the too-tight hat again. "Can't accuse John Breckinridge of having a swelled head." He removed the hat and held it in one hand. "Early calmed down?"

"Depends on when you walk in on him. Now he's on to how Sheridan's a coward for not attacking."

"Take a fool to attack us here."

"Well, that's the point, I'd say. The general *wants* Sheridan to attack. So he can redeem himself. He's convinced the Yankees will hit us tomorrow, come straight at us."

Gordon noted a slight alteration in Pendleton's tone, in his choice of words. The chief of staff was usually disinclined to criticize Early and eager to explain his worst behavior.

"I don't know," Gordon told him. "We've got Sheridan stuck, all right. But he's got us stuck every bit as bad. He can't attack, we can't retreat. Not without risking a whipping out in the open."

"He knows that. That's the heart of it, I think. He feels his hands are tied, he's not accustomed to it."

"Well, I'm all for resting this army a few more days. Morale's still a tad too flimsy for my comfort."

The two strolled down past the gun muzzles and back toward the cluster of headquarters tents. "Have something for me, Sandie?" Gordon asked. "Looked as though you were coming on with a purpose."

Gordon glimpsed reddening cheeks.

Pendleton confided, "I just needed to step away for a time. Told the general I was having a look to your front."

"Nothing new to see. You can report that in all honesty. Any word from home?"

"Yes, sir. Thanks for the asking. Just had a letter. In the middle of all this, isn't that some luck?"

"New addition to the family tree?"

"Not yet. Any day now."

Gordon donned a practiced smile. "You'll like being a father. Nothing like it."

"We're going to be very happy."

A lone cannon barked on the left. Pegram's front? Or Ramseur's? Early had rearranged the division commands, with Ramseur taking Bob Rodes' big division and Cull Battle sent back down to his brigade. Pegram now led Ramseur's old division, while Wharton remained in command of the men left behind by Breckinridge. And Lomax had the cavalry on the field, an uninspiring, inevitable choice.

Gordon understood the logic, but wasn't sure of the wisdom of the changes. When a fight was imminent, he preferred keeping officers above the men who knew them and with the men they knew. But what choice was there, after all? With Rodes gone? And Fitz Lee just hoping to live? Early was doing his best, Gordon had to grant, but something he couldn't quite nail down left him uneasy.

Then there was Sheridan, whose tenacity at Winchester had been fearsome. Clearly, the little fellow was in Grant's mold. It did not bode well.

"Any more word from Mrs. Gordon?" Pendleton asked, as if recalling that other men, too, had wives.

"Well on her way to Staunton, might even be there. Damn me down to the toenails, if she didn't get away cleaner than this army. Amazing woman, God's own blessing upon me."

Pendleton opened his mouth to speak, but he swallowed the words.

September 21, midnight
Gordon's position

More and more, he feared going to sleep. It wasn't a child's hants that troubled Nichols, nor was it the devil mind's sinful imaginings, but the things of the day that came rushing back at night. He didn't want to cry out in his sleep, the way Lem Davis did, waking men with his sudden shouts of "No, *no!*" But far too often the dead died again in his dreams, dead comrades and dead Yankees, crowding in on him. Sometimes they died exactly the same way he'd seen them perish, just doing the same thing over again. Other times their fates got twisted up, muddled and gruesome, beyond the power of any words to tell. Again and again, the dead tried to take him with them, beckoning with pale hands and horrid faces. He felt more dread, more terror, in the night than he ever had experienced in battle. In the night, in dreams, a man could not defend himself.

In the Good Book, dreams were either visions or warnings. What did *his* mean? Were they sent by the Lord, or by Satan?

He would have liked to talk to Elder Woodfin but was ashamed. A true man wasn't scared of things like nightmares. All he could do was to pray for the dreams to stop.

Lying awake on pebbled ground, on a blanket worn thin as muslin, he held his eyes open, watching the stars, on guard for his mortal soul.

What if a man shut his eyes and never returned? What if he couldn't wake up, couldn't escape? What if death—a sinner's death—left him eternally captive to his dreams? Nichols shuddered. The prospect seemed far worse than devils with pitchforks.

Someday, he promised himself, all this would end. He would go home and marry a woman as faithful and good as Ruth, and she would comfort him. He would close his mind against these things forever.

"Dear Jesus," he begged, "don't let none of my friends know I'm so afraid."

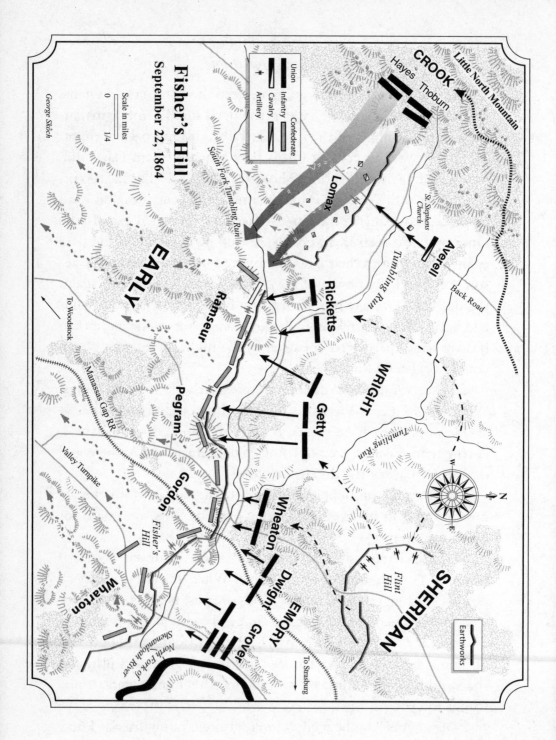

Fisher's Hill
September 22, 1864

Scale in miles
0   1/4

George Skoch

Union
Infantry
Cavalry
Artillery

Confederate

Little North Mountain

CROOK
Hayes Thoburn

Lomax

St. Stephens Church
Averell

South Fork Tumbling Run

Tumbling Run

Back Road

Ricketts

WRIGHT

Getty

Tumbling Run

EARLY

To Woodstock

Ramseur

Pegram

Manassas Gap RR

Gordon

Valley Turnpike

Fisher's Hill

Wharton

Wheaton

Dwight

Grover

EMORY

SHERIDAN

Flint Hill

N
W   E
S

To Strasburg

North Fork of Shenandoah River

Earthworks

FIFTEEN

September 22, 3:00 p.m.
Ricketts' division

Where was Crook? Ricketts had been swapping artillery rounds with the Rebs since morning and prodding them with his infantry, just hard enough to imply he might be serious. It hadn't been much of a fight, more a Punch and Judy show, though with real blood. And that was the problem: It irked him to squander men, even a few, on "demonstrations." Taking Flint Hill the day before had made good tactical sense, but this skirmishing struck him as frivolous.

By nature, he was given to doing things properly. Or not doing them. He understood the rationale for his orders, this need to keep the Johnnies mesmerized. Yet he felt he was frittering men away. The textbooks called such actions "amusing the enemy," but Jim Ricketts didn't find them entertaining.

The men were surprisingly game, though, whether playing cat and mouse with Confederate skirmishers or waging artillery duels. For all the losses at Winchester, victory had inspired his soldiers, opening new and promising possibilities, awakening bloodlust.

Up on the heights, the enemy lines bristled. Immobile. Confident.

Where was Crook?

Ricketts knew his men were running down. These mortal games made weary children of all. He wanted his division to remain strong enough to be in on the kill; his men had earned that.

Earned? He smiled at himself. Thinking of the evident jealousies

newly abroad in the army, resentments he once would have wal-
lowed in himself. The past five months, the carnage, had taught
him much—to the extent that a man learned anything of worth,
which was a separate issue. It just didn't pay to envy another's fame,
deserved or not: He had learned that painfully. You couldn't give
in to jealousy, or you poisoned yourself. And war was poison
enough.

Of course, praise made him preen, as it did any man, but the
approbation he wanted waited at home. He needed the respect of
his wife, Frances, a woman of immense courage and selflessness.
And he longed for the blessing of Harriet, the dead wife who
haunted him still. Had he ever praised either one of them enough?
His vanity, he saw, had been colossal. War was a mirror that rarely
flattered a man.

After Monocacy, *he* had been praised and Wallace, the effort's
architect, consigned to oblivion. Or to Baltimore, which was as
bad. At Winchester, though, it had been young Upton's turn to
gather laurels, with the sacrifices of Ricketts' division ignored.
Wright had been the savior of Washington. But Crook eclipsed him
easily at Winchester. Thus was glory allotted, almost as random
as cards dealt in a poker game.

Glory? Oh, he remembered that seductress, the murderous slut.
Hadn't the loins for her now. He was just a graying, begrimed man
in a bitter war, hoping to do his duty and evade shame.

Where the hell was Crook?

Hot and thirsty, all but irate, and sore from too many hours in
the saddle, Ricketts smiled. Had the fates already pivoted against
Crook? Had his movement along the side of the mountain failed?
The wheel of fortune turned, and a man had to be content not to
be crushed.

Where the devil *was* the fellow, though? Good men were dying.

Thanks to the intervening ridges and smoke, he couldn't see
much of the mountainside where Crook's men were supposed to
be sneaking along. All he could do was to wait. And continue sending men forward only to see fewer men return.

When Wright explained the plan to his subordinates, Ricketts had shared the general skepticism, but he certainly wanted Crook's fool trick to work. He feared the collapse of the flanking attempt would precipitate an order to launch a frontal attack. And his men had endured enough mindless assaults.

Spotsylvania. Good God. How much glory had its mud produced?

Up on the heights, Reb officers pranced on their horses, appearing to pay social calls. No soldierly eye would judge them much concerned.

Where was Crook?

Ricketts rode forward, through wisps of smoke, to order Keifer to bring up another regiment. To "amuse" the Johnnies. While waiting for deliverance.

3:15 p.m.
Early's headquarters

I don't like it," Early muttered. "I don't like this at all."

"Want me to draft the order, sir?" Sandie Pendleton asked.

"Write it up, write it up. Army's to withdraw, right after dark. Meantime, call up the wagons, just do it quiet. Come morning, I don't want that low-down cur to sniff one Confederate backside on this hill." Early drew a twist of tobacco from his pocket and bit off a chaw. "I'll see Sheridan in Hell, before this is over. Just not here, not here."

Early was correct, as far as tactics went. Pendleton saw that now. The position was fine, but the men were too thin on the ground and they had no reserve. Everyone had engaged in wishful thinking, declaring Fisher's Hill to be impregnable, desperate to believe it after Winchester. Defeat could be intoxicating, too, in a dreadful way, but as men sobered up they saw their weakness: The army lacked the numbers to hold this ground, if Sheridan applied brute force again. It was time to slip away before they were trapped, and Early was showing the fortitude to do the sensible thing, knowing the Richmond papers and even his own subordinates would condemn him. The Old Man was showing courage of a rare kind and could expect no thanks from any quarter.

Still, Pendleton feared for the army's morale if they retreated again without a fight.

He said nothing of that to Early. There simply were no good choices, and the Old Man had faced contention enough of late. His generals carped and quarreled, dissecting past events, when they needed to look the future in the eye. And Early sat up by a lantern's light, alone in his tent and muttering, until dawn.

Spitting amber juice, the general snapped, "I know what Sheridan's up to, I'm no fool. He's looking for the weak spot in our line. Planning to hit us first thing in the morning, come first light. Before we can be reinforced. Well, let him waste his powder, we'll be gone." He wiped wet from his beard. "Get that order in everybody's hands by five p.m. And no excuses."

"Yes, sir," Pendleton said. He never did make excuses, except for Early's behavior, but he knew not to take offense.

To the north, the *pock-pock* of skirmishing passed the time between battery squabbles. Despite the firing, it hadn't been much of a day. The Yankees seemed tuckered out, too, although it might well be that Early was right, that Sheridan was feeling their line and meant to attack in the morning. And another whipping like Winchester, Pendleton had to admit, would be a sight worse for morale than just marching off.

He dipped his best steel pen and began to write.

3:50 p.m.
Ramseur's position, left flank of Fisher's Hill

Stephen Dodson Ramseur had a headache. He sought shade when he could, only to feel guilty about leaving his soldiers out in their sun-punched trenches. Even the letter from his wife annoyed him. It was one of her playful "Dearest Doddie" missives, the kind he usually cherished, full of gossip, household details, and promises

that the child would arrive in October. Today, the curls of her pen-
manship made his head pound.

With the letter in his pocket, he walked the line again, watching the Yankees across the little valley. They swarmed like bees
without the heart to sting. His enemies had suffered, too. He had
made them suffer. He didn't believe they were eager to bleed again.

The only thing that worried him was their numbers. Only way
they'd won that fight: sheer numbers. Yanks hadn't shown a lick
of skill at Winchester, not one hint of tactical finesse.

Clouds off to the west, past Little North Mountain. Rain in
the night, Ramseur figured. Trenches would get muddy as pig-
pens in May. Nothing to be done about it.

He had to stop, to stand stone still, and close his eyes against
the throb in his head. Lord, the hordes of Yankees back at Winchester, those endless ranks of blue . . .

Winchester. He had expected praise from Jubal Early. His men
had been the first to fight in the morning and the last to leave the
battlefield at night. But all Early offered anyone was abuse. Ramseur
recalled, with a rueful smile, how he once had hoped to be Early's
favored subordinate. Early didn't like anyone.

Warm day. Not hot, but bright, painfully bright. The clouds
to the west moved so slowly, they seemed to hold still. Could have
used their shade that very minute. Head hurting like he'd been
kicked by Jenkins' mule.

Trailed by new aides in place of those lost at Winchester,
Ramseur strode toward the emplacements of the Fluvanna Artillery.

Bryan Grimes intercepted him. The brigadier was limping—
almost hopping—and clearly agitated.

"General Ramseur?"

"How may I serve you, Bryan?"

"Sir, we have to send a brigade, at least a brigade, down to
Lomax. Cavalry won't hold, not without support. There's Yankees
all over the mountain, they'll turn his flank."

What on earth?

Almost unwillingly, Ramseur turned to face Little North Mountain, shielding his eyes.

"What are you talking about?"

Grimes pointed. "That bald spot. Halfway up, or thereabouts. See that file of Yankees?"

Ramseur peered at the mountainside. "Only thing I see looks like a fence row. I don't see anything moving."

"Call for your field glasses, sir. There's Yankees up there. On my honor, one Tar Heel to another. They're going to come down behind Lomax, way they're moving."

Ramseur just wanted to close his eyes, but he forced an indulgent smile. He didn't want to get off to a bad start with a new subordinate. "Well, if you're right, it's probably just a scouting party. Even the Yankees aren't fools enough to attack that way, they'd fall to pieces."

Grimes opened his mouth to reply but seemed to think better of it.

"What's that limp of yours about?" Ramseur asked to soothe things.

The brigadier shrugged. "Damned-fool thing. Just plain walking along, not even running. And I gave my ankle a twist, craziest thing."

"Well, go sit down, rest up. You're apt to be needed over the next few days."

Grimes saluted, crestfallen. "Keep watch on that mountain, sir. I'd be beholden."

Alone again—but for his anxious aides—Ramseur continued on to the gun positions. He valued artillery and liked to display his knowledge. But as he walked in front of a piece drawn back for a repair, a sergeant said, "General, there's blue-bellies on that mountain yonder, a right bushel."

Ramseur took a breath to stay his temper.

"I know what's caught your eye. It's just a fence row."

"Well, sir, that there's a *moving* fence row, if it's a fence at all." The man's tone was all but insolent. Had Rodes allowed such back talk? Or was it yet another mark of defeat? Ramseur shook his head, just to himself, and it felt as though his brains banged around in his skull. Everybody had the jumps. And the cannoneers around him plainly put more stock in their comrade's words than in their general's.

Only one way to settle this, Ramseur decided. He turned to his nearest aide.

"Go back and fetch my field glasses."

But the battery commander had come up. He drew his own binoculars from their case. "Here. Use mine, sir."

With an outright sigh, Ramseur took the glasses, tilted up the front brim of his hat, and began to scan the mountain a mile or so off.

He saw nothing but jutting gray rocks. Trees. Green tresses and tangles.

Then he stopped and held the glasses steady.

"My God."

3:50 p.m.
Little North Mountain

Rud Hayes grabbed a branch in time to stop himself from tumbling down the mountainside.

"Careful, Rud," Crook told him. Crook was grinning, despite the day's exertions. "I need you to help me out of this fix I'm in."

But they weren't in a fix, at least not yet. The movement up the side of the mountain and then along its flank had required sweat and muscle-burning effort, as well as costing any number of busted ankles and one broken leg, but the men, coming along in Indian files, had suspended their common complaints, with every veteran grasping what they were doing and what it might mean. Quiet curses erupted now and then as men lost their footing or banged a knee, but the corps as a whole moved in remarkable quiet, eager and murderous.

Hayes' personal concern was the poison ivy, of which he had had quite enough across the summer.

Down where the armies faced one another, rifle fire annoyed the afternoon, inconsequential. These scrambling men would be Destiny's executors.

Destiny? Did such a thing exist? Or was there just an endless collision of human aspirations, governed by chance? Lucy believed in a good and gracious God shaping mortal affairs, and Hayes had never belittled her beliefs. Belief such as hers was a gift, a wonderful comfort, but one he lacked. If he were to fall this day, he expected to fade into nature, into the general immanence, nothing more. War made it hard to credit a merciful God.

"Rud, you're wheezing," Crook teased. The corps commander was a few years the younger, but looked to be the older of the two. Crook had lived rough in remote, hardscrabble garrisons, while Hayes had resided in pleasant homes and offices lined with law books.

"Just drinking deep of the fine Virginia air," Hayes told his superior. "Wouldn't be half-bad here, but for the war."

Correcting his footing, Crook said, "Ought to see the Northwest. Hard place, hard. But beautiful, the grandeur. You there, soldier! Tie up that canteen and stop making that racket."

Hayes and Crook moved a hundred yards behind the head of the column, with Hayes determined to lead and do his duty, and Crook as avid to maintain control. Joe Thoburn had walked along with them for a time before going back to hurry his men along.

Really, it was astonishing. They just might pull it off, Hayes told himself.

The trees broke for a dozen yards, offering a view of the armies below. Puffing smoke, irregular lines stretched toward the hidden river. Beyond, Three Top Mountain loomed. Early's army was a cork in a bottle.

And they were out to snap off the bottle's neck.

"By God, we're all but behind them," Crook said.

Shots cracked up ahead. Stray shots, then a flurry. No volleys, though.

Hayes felt Crook tense and understood: It wasn't the shots that worried him, Reb pickets had been inevitable. He just didn't want his men to start up a howl and warn Early of the size of the force about to descend on his flank.

Crook hurried forward, plowing through a tangle of poison ivy. Hayes went around the bushes and rushed to catch up.

He soon rejoined Crook, who was questioning a captain.

"Only pickets," the captain assured them both. "No more than a company, and a weak one. They skedaddled."

"Damn it, though," Crook said.

Panting, Hayes offered, "We've got them. It's all right."

Crook nodded. He told the captain, "Push on another two hundred yards, then hold up."

The Rebs knew something was doing, though. Artillery shells began crashing into the hillside, splintering trees. But the Johnnies were firing blind, guessing at targets.

"Hold up, *halt*!" Crook called.

"Division, halt!" Hayes echoed.

The order ran down the line. Hayes wondered how much the Rebs below them could hear. The Confederate artillery provided covering noise, a quirk of war, aiding an enemy.

"Left . . . *face*!"

That command ran down the column as well, converting the Indian files into two long ranks. Men pivoted as smartly as they could on the steep hillside. Hayes' division formed the southernmost wing of Crook's command, thrust beyond the Rebs' front line, and he figured the best formation was the simplest. Speed was of more value than finesse.

"Advance your men," Crook told him.

And off they went, gravity tugging them down the mountainside, with soldiers allowing themselves to hurry, barely maintaining a semblance of good order. Excitement sparked through the air.

Hayes soon caught the animal sense himself, the predator's fore-knowledge that this charge would be irresistible. In their haste, men tripped and plunged face-first. Rifles discharged accidentally. Struggling color-bearers trailed their flags, yanking them from the clutch of branches and briars. But every man's heart raced.

They were going to roll up the Rebs like a parlor carpet.

"Hold them back," Crook called as the bottom neared. "Hayes, keep your men together."

But the soldiers wouldn't wait. Sensing level, open ground ahead, the entire corps broke into a wild roar. Anticipating an order, men began charging.

Ignoring the pleas of their officers for discipline, dozens, then hundreds, then thousands, of men exploded from the tree line. Flags rose and unfurled. Soldiers hurrahed as if they'd already fought and won a victory. The savagery of it felt barbarous, as if his men were Huns from the pages of Gibbon.

"Come on, boys!" he shouted, unable to contain himself, encouraging men who needed no encouragement.

Ahead, a paltry line of Rebs fired from a barricade of fence rails. But they didn't fire long. Men in blue swept over the obstacle, knocking it to pieces, collaring prisoners whose faces still shone with amazement.

Hayes wasn't sure he commanded anything now. He was just one man among many, his rank stripped of its potency. He kept up as best he could.

The veterans didn't need his guidance, anyway. They stormed across the intervening low ground, brushing aside all resistance, to aim at the heights where the Reb infantry waited, up where the Johnnies were hurriedly countermarching and manhandling guns, shocked and caught unready.

The gray columns scrambling to refuse the flank were too few. Hayes saw that his division—his bellowing, beautiful mob—stretched well beyond the defenses. On his left, Thoburn's boys encountered resistance, blasted by artillery up on the hill, but they soon surged forward again.

The national colors, division and brigade flags, the torn regimental standards, all thrust onward, racing ahead, climbing the slope with their blue-coated clans about them. Few men fell. The handful of Johnnies opposing them couldn't reload fast enough to stop them.

On the right, the last Reb cavalry bolted, with Averell's troopers charging them in the wake of Crook's attack. To the left, Confederate infantry made a hopeless stand in Thoburn's path while cannoneers harnessed horses to save their guns. Straight ahead, a patchwork skirmish line faced Hayes' division.

"Straight for their rear!" Hayes called. "Go straight for their rear!"

Enraptured, he wasn't panting anymore. Pointing his pistol up the long slope, he shouted his throat raw.

On the distant left, the noise of battle swelled. Sheridan had advanced the rest of the army, Hayes figured, taking swift advantage of Crook's success.

Most of the Rebs on the heights turned tail and ran as their foes closed in, but a lone brigade stood its ground, ragged and fierce. They were giving Thoburn's lead regiments all they had.

Hayes had no idea who led those Johnnies, but he had to admire the man.

Colliding more than once with rushing men as he traversed the field, Hayes found Hiram Devol of his old brigade and ordered him to outflank the Rebs blocking Thoburn, to put an end to that lonely, desperate valor.

"Threaten their flank," Hayes said. "They'll break, they'll catch the panic."

The brigade's color-bearer staggered. Another man caught the flag.

Devol said, "They're already breaking, look."

Across the entire field, hurrahs rang out. Fleet with excitement, Hayes rushed back to his right, outpacing the younger officers on his staff. He couldn't recall such pure exhilaration, but he never had been part of so easy a victory.

When Hayes rejoined the vanguard of his division atop the heights, he saw an unrivaled spectacle of defeat. Men in gray and shades of mottled brown fled by the thousands, converging on the one road left to them all or just plain running through the countryside. Mounted batteries whipped their way southward and caissons overturned, crushing men and toppling the rear teams, tangling harness and panicking horses left upright. Waving their swords and evidently pleading, maddened officers rode through the mob that had been a proud army only minutes before. When an ambulance lost a wheel, its crazed team dragged it along until it splintered, flinging its cargo. In ruptured defenses, abandoned cannon waited, silent and prim, for a change of masters. A headquarters tent collapsed as men tripped over its ropes. Soldiers sprawled forward, shot in the back. A wagon laden with ammunition exploded.

It reminded Hayes of an illustration he'd seen of the Last Judgment.

5:00 p.m.
Confederate center

As Ramseur's worthless cowards ran, Early galloped for Pegram's leftmost regiment, a hundred honest men who had not budged. Closing on the trench line, he recognized the flag of the 13th Virginia.

Riding straight for Captain Sam Buck, Early shouted at the top of his voice, "You, Buck! You men, all of you! Stop those goddamned cowards down there. Shoot 'em like dogs, if they won't do their duty."

Buck's face showed incomprehension. What couldn't the lowborn simpleton understand?

"I said stop any coward who retreats," Early railed, hating the high-pitched sound of his own voice. "Any man who won't stop, shoot him dead!" Growing more furious by the moment, he shrieked, "What are you waiting for? Shoot those yellow bastards, shoot them now!"

Buck shook his head. Slowly. As if the damned fool couldn't do that much right. The Virginians closed around their captain, in evident support. Glaring at Early. Insubordinate. Traitorous.

Early pointed at the mob of fugitives again. "I said *shoot* them, damn you."

Sullen as a whipped buck nigger, a Virginian threw down his rifle, then just stood there. Eyes on Early. Another man cast down his weapon, too. Then another.

"I won't give that order, sir," Buck said at last.

"Then you be damned!"

5:00 p.m.
Union Sixth Corps

Sheridan wove in and out of the foremost skirmish line, waving his hat and shouting, "We've got 'em, boys, come on! Crook's in their rear, don't let him have all the glory! The cavalry's chasing them high-tail, come on, come on! Don't let up, go after them! Don't stop!"

Wherever he rode, men cheered as they rushed forward.

5:15 p.m.
Gordon's Division

Nobody could rightly tell what the devil was going on, only that something wasn't exactly right. Uproar aplenty, a ways over on the left, but the Yankees had been fussing around all day. Nichols couldn't see much, what with the turn of the ground and thickening smoke to westward. Just dark clouds high up, rolling over that mountain. But they all heard Yankee cheering and no Rebel yells.

It wasn't fear of the blue-bellies themselves that pestered Nichols. Wasn't scared of fighting them one bit, he didn't believe. But he'd sprouted a dread of being captured, and he wasn't apt to go handsome on his bad leg. It hurt, too, even when he kept his weight on the other foot. Not that there was much weight to him nowadays. All he could do was hobble, like Jackie Tate, the crippled fellow back home, the one who sat outside the livery barn, a butt of jokes. Clear as a vision from the Lord, Nichols foresaw Yankees overtaking him, pummeling him, mocking.

He stood in the trench beside his friends, growing uneasy but held in place by pride. Waiting for the Yankees to be fool enough to try to climb that bank right to their front. Steep as a wall, it made for the best position on Fisher's Hill, officers and men alike agreed. No Yankee was coming up that just-about cliff and living to brag on it.

And when the Yankees blundered forward at last, sure enough, they didn't get very far. They just fumbuddled around, as if they couldn't make up their minds to step up and do their duty. *They* weren't the problem, although they wanted watching. The worrisome doings were elsewhere, off in that westward ruckus, off where a man couldn't see.

Not knowing was a terrible thing.

General Gordon showed himself, though not for long. He rode off looking as though the Devil were at him, sour as pickles. In his wake, the officers got jittery, telling their men too often to stand tall.

"Gordon takes on that look of his, ain't nothing good ahead," Ive Summerlin noted.

And there wasn't nothing good. The battle marched nearer, still unseen. Scared fellows ran by, wailing that the Yankees were in the army's rear. All they got was hard jests for their yellowness. Then the artillerymen on the left dragged off their guns with ropes, hauling them back to be hitched up to their limbers.

It was the rarest thing for the guns to desert them. Without even waiting to learn what was afoot.

"Dear Jesus Lord," Tom Boyet cried.

And there they were, the Yankees. Over where that battery had been, one crest away.

"Going to be cut off, why don't we get orders?" Sergeant Alderman wondered. That itself was cause for worry, since Alderman was a steady man in a fight.

"Here they come!" Lem Davis shouted. It took a few seconds for the rest of them to realize he meant they were coming from the front, too.

Gog and Magog, Jebusites, Midianites . . . the Yankees who hadn't seemed to be doing no more than fussing around were advancing, in great numbers, heading straight for the hill, as if they couldn't see its awful steepness, its impossibility, or lacked the sense to care.

"They're in behind us, they're blocking the road!" a trash Jeremiah hollered.

Nichols didn't run at first. None of them did. They were John Gordon's soldiers, after all. They lit into the Yankees, firing down into the packets of skirmishers and then at the oncoming ranks with their insolent banners.

But catastrophe, like Judgment, could be evaded for only so long. Nichols wasn't the first to run, nor did he quite intend to run at all, but in a way he could not quite explain he found himself hopping rearward, doing his best to keep up, losing sight of his comrades before spotting them again and spying Colonel Atkinson, abandoned by all, attempting to free an artillery piece stuck in a ditch. Nichols' heart said go on down and help, but he reckoned his leg about robbed him of much use.

He did not want to be captured, that was the fact of it.

As he reached the rump of the hill and witnessed the awful spectacle of an army falling to pieces, an army dissolving like a mud cake splashed with a bucket of water, he muttered, "Sodom and Gomorrah," but he kept on going, unlikely to become a pillar of salt, but unwilling to be a captive of flesh and blood.

5:30 p.m.
Ricketts' advance

Ricketts spotted General Crook haranguing his men and rode over to the row of captured cannon. Crook sat astride a wretched-looking nag, which took Ricketts aback until he realized it, too, was a prize of war.

"What's the difficulty, sir?" Ricketts asked, approaching the breastworks.

"You tell me, Ricketts. You must have fifty men here, doing nothing. Why aren't they attacking?"

Surprised, Ricketts told him, "General Crook, they're hardly 'doing nothing.' They're taking off captured guns."

"No time for that. We need to press the attack."

"My entire division's attacking."

"Not these men. You've got them stealing guns my soldiers took."

"*My* men captured these guns."

"Really? Were you here? I didn't see you. And now you want to turn in these guns as your prizes." Crook snorted, frowned, growled. "My men went over this ground before a single soldier of yours advanced."

Ricketts felt compelled to point out that his men had been fighting for nearly two days, while Crook's corps dallied pleasantly in the rear. And if Crook hadn't seen him, he hadn't seen Crook. But it was no use. Crook was still angry about the gone-astray orders at Cool Springs; the man held a grudge. He also held higher rank.

Besides, Crook was the hero of the day again.

"Yes, sir," Ricketts said as dark clouds pressed. "I defer to your claim."

7:00 p.m.
The Valley Pike

As darkness deepened, rain spit. The Yankees were coming along, all right, Jed Hotchkiss had no doubt. Skirmishers still gnawed the retreating army, but it appeared that Sheridan had paused at last to reorganize his force south of the battlefield. They'd come on again, though, that was sure, in a multitude. Too fine an opportunity to be missed, with not just an army of thousands, but the hopes of millions ruined.

"Fine work, Jed," John Gordon told the mapmaker, loud enough to be heard by the cluster of officers. "You picked excellent ground."

"One thing I'm good for."

Beside the Pike, John Carpenter's two guns awaited the enemy, along with a cobbled-together force built on shreds of the 13th Virginia. When asked to stop and make a stand, Captain Buck, leading twenty men, had agreed immediately. Even more remarkable in that hour, his soldiers obeyed him. Strays from other regiments joined the rear guard thereafter, but those good souls were but a scrape and a scrap of the fleeing masses.

It made for a queer command, with two generals, Gordon and Pegram, and a covey of staff officers in charge of two hundred men. Their "reserve" was a huddle of colored servants, a stripped commissary wagon, and an ambulance drawn by a mule.

It wasn't much to face down Sheridan's army.

The rain picked up enough to sting their faces. If the day had been warm, the night promised to be cold.

"Where'd you last see Early?" Gordon asked.

"Back on the field," Hotchkiss answered. "Cursing the men to damnation. Sandie probably saw him after I did."

Sitting atop his dusky-white horse, Pendleton told them, "He came off, I'm fairly certain. Probably headed for Woodstock to rally the army."

"Let's hope," Gordon said wearily. "Ed Atkinson wasn't so lucky. Captured trying to bring off a gun, I swear it galls me. I'm getting sick to death of senseless valor."

Pegram rejoined the party. "Buck just told me about his run-in with Early."

"What happened?" Gordon asked him.

"Old Jube ordered the Thirteenth Virginia to fire on Ramseur's men. Of course, they refused."

"Early's like to charge them all with mutiny. If he remembers."

Pegram shook his head. "Couldn't make it stick, if he dared try. His stock's already low on the Richmond exchange. And now this." Annoyed, he lifted his hat, shook off the rain, and quickly resettled it. "Be ashamed of himself, when he comes to his senses."

"Shame," Gordon said, "is not among Early's salient characteristics."

Hotchkiss was surprised that Pendleton didn't leap to Early's defense. In the past, Sandie had taken such comments to heart.

Shots. Just to the north. Yankees hunting stragglers.

"Never thought I'd see a day like this," Pegram declared. "Never thought I'd live to see the day."

"At least you lived," Gordon said. Turning to Pendleton, the Georgian suggested, "Sandie, you ought to get along, find Early. He'll need you. Help him patch this army back together."

The younger man shook his head. His face seemed ghastly pale in the wet night. "I'm minded to stay here, sir. Make sure these boys don't bolt, give the Yanks free passage."

"Sam Buck won't run," Pegram said.

"Artillerymen might. Despite all Carpenter's efforts. Hasn't been their best day. Anyway, I have a mind to stay."

In lieu of further argument, Pegram grunted.

"Well, I suppose every man's his own commander now," Gordon allowed. "But one of you needs to go catch up with Early. Can't have his whole staff captured and hauled off like the Nervii chieftains. You've even got Hennie Douglas playing cannoneer."

"Jed, you go," Pendleton said. His voice was spectral in the darkness. "You organized this position, you did your part. I'll see it through."

"Just as soon stay myself," Hotchkiss countered. It wasn't that he truly wished to remain, but his sense of obligation went soul deep.

"Damn it, this isn't some ladies' sanitary committee," Gordon snapped. "One of you two, get on down the Pike. You, Jed. Get along. Sandie's right, you've done your part. Go find Early. Help the man, he needs you."

"Same might go for you and me," Pegram said. "Put the cob to chivalry, this ain't proper employment for men who ought to be rounding up their divisions."

"All of you go," Pendleton said. "This doesn't call for generals." Hotchkiss was startled by the tone the chief of staff took with men who outranked him by several grades. "If I can't handle this, I'm not worth a plug of tobacco. You go, I'll try to hold them for an hour. Maybe a tad longer, given the rain."

"Optimistic, young Leonidas," Gordon said. "But I'm for optimism, given the alternative. Sweep that road, when they come strutting down it. And thank the Almighty for this rain and darkness, they'll waste time calculating what all might be waiting for them. Trick is to keep them pondering."

"Gain what time you can," Pegram put in. "But don't be a damned fool, Pendleton. Come off this hill before you end up dead or on Johnson's Island."

The rain had skirmished. Now it attacked. Hotchkiss wished he had his oilcloth cape, but all of his belongings remained on the field, a threadbare feast for Yankee scavengers. None of those present had rain covers, for that matter. He wondered if they even had an army.

Sam Buck strode up to the clot of mounted officers, all of whom outranked him by a mile.

"Gentlemen," the Virginian said, "I do believe the Yankees are coming along."

8:00 p.m.
The Valley Pike

Captain Samuel Dawson Buck did all he could to fortify his men, but more and more rifles misfired in the rain. A few soldiers had already slipped away.

The Yankees seemed unbothered by the downpour. Gushing volleys, their lead regiments inched forward. Even if their fires were inaccurate in the darkness, the volume all but crushed a fellow's spirit. Why didn't the rain ruin their cartridges, too? All his men could bring to bear in return was the liquor of spite.

He heard neighing horses and dropping chains, followed by artillery commands. Canister, too, would have to be endured, as soon as they found the elevation and range. As for Carpenter's two guns, their ammunition was almost gone. It was only a matter of time before the Yankees had things their way.

Buck wasn't inclined to leave one moment sooner, though. He was newly embittered, driven to an irreconcilable fierceness, and Early's tantrum had been the least of its causes. The Yankees held Front Royal and Buckton again, if reports ran true. And if the Federals had dishonored his birthplace in the past, they had at least been driven off in turn. This time it was different, an addle-headed private could feel the change. This time the Yankees meant to stay for good. Winchester was lost, and the Lower Valley with it. His family had no wealth to display—before the war, he had gone to clerking a store—but the land they owned had been theirs for a hundred years.

He doubted he'd see his parents' home again.

"If you can't shoot, holler at them," Buck admonished a soldier. The men knelt or sprawled, wet through, struggling to keep the mud from their ramrods and bores, the rain from their cartridge pouches. For his part, Buck felt obliged to remain on his feet, roaming through the darkness, as much a dare to the Yankees as an example to his men.

And if he was a fool for strutting about, that lieutenant colonel, Pendleton, was the greater fool for riding high on that cream-white horse of his, another gentleman's son playing the gallant. Buck knew his men were not about to take orders from an unfamiliar staff officer, not this day, nor were the artillerymen likely to do so, either. They had stopped to fight because they were soldiers and that other fellow, gone now, had made a case for the ground and the necessity. They had stopped to fight because they were tired of running and not fighting, not hitting back. They had stopped because they were Valley men, most of them, ruing homes abandoned, and because they were all Virginians. And they'd stopped just because they'd stopped, because it just happened.

Yankee solid shot screamed overhead. Their gun crews were seeking the range.

"I cain't git this piece to fire," a kneeling soldier complained. Preparatory, Buck understood, to making for the rear.

"Go out and grab a new one from the Yankees, they've got plenty."

He moved on. Wasn't much more to be done. Hold one man by the ear? While a dozen others ran? If the Yankees came on in one big rush, they were finished.

Well, let them come on, Buck said to himself. I'll wait.

Walking close to Pendleton, Buck collided with the other staff man who'd stayed behind. After a clipped apology, Douglas stepped toward his comrade and called:

"For God's sake, Sandie, get down off that horse."

No sooner had the man spoken than Buck heard the slap-a-carcass sound of a bullet striking home.

A shadow, Pendleton toppled forward, groaning.

Douglas rushed to intercept his fall. Buck started to follow, then paused.

"*Kate,*" Pendleton called.

"Help me," Douglas pleaded, staggering under the weight as the wounded man slipped from the saddle into his arms.

Buck just would not do it. He knew that helping would reel him in, stealing him from the fight for precious minutes—a fight that was damned well more important than any man, no matter his rank or parentage or position.

"You, Grimshaw!" Buck said. "Help out there, jump to it."

Behind his back, the wounded man moaned piteously. Douglas cursed.

Resolute, Buck chose three other soldiers he judged apt to run anyway and sent them to help tote the wounded man to the rear. No more to be done.

Where are you hit?" Douglas begged. "Sandie, where are you hit?"

Pendleton moaned. Rain pounded.

"Keep him out of the mud," Douglas told the soldiers. "Hold him up until I see where he's hit."

He couldn't see much of anything by the muzzle flashes.

"It's his . . . it's lower down," a soldier told him. "I think he's hit down there."

The wounded man gasped, unable to form words.

"What do you mean, 'down there'?" Douglas demanded. Then he realized. "We have to get him out of here."

"Yes, sir. Sure now." The voice told Douglas that however brave these men had been an hour earlier, they were yard-dog happy at being left off the rope to take themselves rearward.

"He's soaking with blood, just soaking," another soldier announced. As if such things never happened in a war. "He's bleeding away."

"Hold him *up*, man." Forbidden a lantern by the enemy's presence, Douglas felt along the wounded man's body, reaching, of necessity, into private spots.

Pendleton screamed.

Douglas withdrew his hand. Pendleton's injury was unthinkable. For a helpless moment, the knowledge froze him. Then he just repeated, "Hold him up."

"Best carry him on back now," the soldier who seemed to have charge of the others told Douglas. "Best hurry along."

"Stop the Yankees . . . ," Pendleton moaned. "Have to stop them . . ."

"We're going to stop the Yankees," Douglas promised him.

Artillery rounds struck closer as the Yankees adjusted the range.

"You're going to be just fine, Sandie," Douglas added. His tone sounded false, even selfish, in his ears. As if he were the one who craved assurance.

There was no hope of a litter: The soldiers allotted Pendleton's limbs and weight between them.

"Kate," Pendleton muttered.

"You'll see Kate," Douglas told him as they stumbled back from the line. "You'll see her soon."

"Best bring his horse along, sir," a voice advised. " 'Case somebody stole that mule from the butcher's wagon."

Careless of the rounds streaking the air, Douglas slopped back through the mud toward the outline of Pendleton's horse. The animal waited calmly, uninjured and unconcerned. Leading it by the bridle, Douglas hastened to overtake the others.

When he rejoined the party, his friend was babbling: "Couldn't get the order out . . . no time . . . couldn't . . . no time . . ."

The Yankees fired a battery in sequence. Their final charge might come at any moment. Probably working around the flanks as well, Douglas decided. Was he glad to be leaving? Was he just the same as these four men, just armed with better manners and finer words? Was Pendleton's wound *his* excuse to run to the rear?

For all that, he knew that he would not leave the side of a man whom he counted just short of a brother.

As they lugged him along, Pendleton gasped again and again. Each suck of breath was as dreadful as a shriek.

Poor Sandie. He had to be in agony. How could a man live on with a wound like that? Would he want to?

"How bad is it, Hennie? How badly am I hit?" Pendleton asked, as if his mind had cleared, the pain abated.

"Bad enough for a pleasant leave back home. Let Kate nurse you up, impose on the family. Let them spoil you."

"Home," Pendleton mouthed. His mind strayed again, returning by another door. "*Must* hold them. Give the army time. Must . . ."

"Keep him up off the ground!" Douglas barked. He imagined Pendleton's mutilated parts dragging in the mud.

They stumbled about, half-lost, and Pendleton swooned, either from resurgent pain or loss of blood. Douglas wanted his friend to live but wasn't sure the sentiment was sound. Of all the wounds he had witnessed in the war, no other had shocked him so.

At last, they found the ambulance, tucked behind a shanty. The orderly and driver had disappeared, but a pair of darkies lurked, as if raising the courage to steal the mule.

Douglas stiffened his back and made the Negroes do what they did not want to do: help arrange the wounded man on one of the mounted litters and belt him down.

As they gentled Pendleton's limbs, he cried, *"They're running! Tell General Jackson!"*

"That man shot right through," a darkey commented.

"Shut your mouth," Douglas told him. "Either of you know how to drive a wagon, drive it right? Run reins on a mule?"

"Sho'. But I can't go. I belongs to Cap'n Carpenter, he'd take it harsh."

"How about you?"

"Yassuh. I can drive a mule jus' fine."

"Here. Start by tying this horse to the back of the wagon."

He turned to the soldier who had done most of the speaking. "What's your name?"

"Grimshaw."

"Rank?"

"Private. Nowadays. I been this and that."

"Where's your rifle?"

"Couldn't carry no rifle and him, too."

Reluctantly, Douglas drew out his revolver, a new Colt he had taken from a Yankee. "Here. That nigger tries to run away, you shoot him. Shoot anybody else who gets in your way. I'll catch up as soon as I fetch my horse. If I don't, you keep on straight to Woodstock or till you come up on a field surgery." He looked at the others in the hard-washed night. "Rest of you men can walk, and count your blessings."

September 23, 1:00 a.m.
Woodstock, the Murphy home

No need to lie to me, Dr. Maguire," Pendleton said. "I know I'm dying. It's God's will, I'm satisfied."

"Yes," Maguire said, "that's about the truth of it, I can't lie. I'll stay with you, though. I can do that, at least. We do go back."

"Old Jack," Pendleton murmured. After the nightmare journey in the ambulance, he had grown lucid in this soft, warm bed. And if he held perfectly still, the pain was bearable.

"Old Jack," the doctor echoed.

"I do believe I'll see him. Soon." Fighting down a spasm, he tried to joke. "I'll give him your compliments, tell him you'll be along. In your good time, of course."

"You do that."

"Doc?"

"Yes?"

"There's one thing you can do."

"Surely."

"Leave, go. The army needs you. I don't." He attempted a smile. "Not anymore."

He did not choose to think about his wound. But he thought about it.

"I'd prefer to stay," his old comrade said.

Pendleton groaned. He would have jackknifed up to clutch the pain, but lacked the strength to move.

"No. You go. Please. Do that for me."

"Sandie . . ."

"Don't want the Yankees capturing Old Jack's surgeon on my account. Probably parade you around in a medicine show."

"You rest now. I'll be right here."

"Tell me you'll go."

"Sure you won't take whiskey? Help the pain?"

Pendleton tried to shake his head. "Promised Kate."

"Anything I can tell her for you? Shall I take down a letter?"

Pendleton fought to master himself, to rally his spirit. The pain was so severe, it squeezed out tears. But his confusion was past, for that he was grateful.

"Tell her . . . tell her it's better so. I've been chosen early for that finer world, tell her we'll meet again—"

Abruptly, he lost consciousness and disorderly visions plagued him. He was back in the ambulance, jolted and suffering pain he had never imagined, wet as a babe in diapers, but with blood. The ambulance was taking him to Chancellorsville, but it wasn't Chancellorsville, it was Kate's family home, beautiful in the daylight, as she was beautiful beyond measure in the daylight.

It was still raining when next he woke, still night. Candles, no oil for the lamps. Yankees starving the South of every last thing. Someone was in the room, a woman. He tried to call out to his wife but faded again.

What was the name of that yellow dog the Salters kept tied in the yard? He always had yearned to untie it, let it loose. Was this Kate's bed, their bed? Would it ever be *their* bed? Someone had to bring up ammunition, Jackson was furious . . . that yellow dog . . .

He sensed, vaguely, that Dr. Maguire had honored his wish and gone back to the army, but the world had lost its sharpness, its boundaries, and he couldn't be certain. Only the pain was distinct.

Dawn found Sandie Pendleton still with the living. His last hour, far beyond suffering, was spent in the company of Yankee surgeons and officers.

"The pain . . . ," he muttered as he woke one last time.

"Shall I give him some more, do you think?" a Northern voice asked.

". . . pain's gone," Pendleton finished.

"More might kill him. Colonel Pendleton? Can you understand me? Is there anything at all that we can do for you?"

"My wife," he said.

"Yes, your wife. I understand. Is she nearby? Shall we bring her to you?"

"Child."

"Something about a child. I can't make it out."

He tried to lift his hand and could not.

"Colonel Pendleton, what do you want to say to this child? Or to your wife?"

"Love."

"What are you trying to say, son? We can't understand you."

"Better so."

PART
III

THE SHADOW

SIXTEEN

October 3, 1864, 9:00 p.m.
Petersburg, Virginia

Lieutenant Colonel Charles Marshall rose and extended the letter.

"From Governor Smith," the military secretary said.

"Again?"

"I'm afraid so, sir."

"The same matter?"

"Yes, sir."

Robert E. Lee paused short of Marshall's desk, exasperation poisoning his eyes. Six months back, the older man would have concealed his ire.

Lips tightened, Lee took the letter. He did not sit to read it, but steered to a table lamp and drew out his spectacles. The eyeglasses, too, had appeared only of late.

Masking his glances, Marshall considered the general. It had been yet another hard, bad day, with all of Grant's armies whittling away at the South, a wasting disease in blue. Lee's digestion and angina had improved since the awful spring and desolate summer, but his arthritis had worsened. Lee hid his discomfort from the men, maintaining a flawless posture in the saddle, but among his closest aides his crispness wilted.

Lee muttered to himself, another new habit.

The week before, Marshall had been struck by a revelation. Riding past soldiers gaunt as the victims of famine, Lee had been received not as a general, but as a wondrous father, even a savior. That was hardly new, but amid the cheers raised from jutting Adam's apples and starved throats, Marshall had realized that he himself no longer served out of loyalty to the Confederacy, but out of devotion to Lee. He suspected that Taylor and Venable, the other two members of the staff's triumvirate, felt just as he did.

It was not a matter gentlemen discussed. It smacked of treason.

Yet, it was true. Experiencing Richmond's haughty self-regard from nearby Petersburg was enough to dishearten any man. And were that squalid vanity insufficient, the way officials treated not only the hungry army but Lee himself was mortifying.

As he finished reading the letter, Lee's hand trembled. But the general composed himself and handed back the paper, revealing a frayed sleeve, a sight once unthinkable.

"Do you wish to reply, sir?"

Lee shook his head. "Not tonight, not tonight."

"Yes, sir."

The older man looked drained of all vitality.

"Any other matters, Colonel Marshall?"

"Nothing pressing, sir." There were, of course, countless matters that wanted attention, but Marshall preferred to handle them himself and let Lee rest.

The general nodded. Marshall expected Lee to leave the room, to retire to his bed in this once fine house, perhaps to ponder private woes in turn. His wife's condition had worsened again, and Custis, his son, remained ill. On top of that, his nephew had been severely wounded at Winchester. And after contemplating his private sorrows, Lee would pray, ravaged knees on bare planks. Marshall knew him better than Lee imagined, well enough to break a decent heart.

Instead of leaving the room, Lee took a chair. His flesh seemed to sigh.

"What does the man expect me to do? Who do I have to replace Early? Who could I send?"

Governor "Extra Billy" Smith's letter had been drafted with crimson claws.

"The governor's faction favors General Breckinridge," Marshall reminded him. "The soldiers are said to want Gordon."

"Not Gordon, not yet. Too soon. As for General Breckinridge . . ."

Marshall knew Lee well enough not to expect the completion of the sentence. Lee did not think Breckinridge had the gift of commanding armies, not even depleted ones.

"I feel . . . ," Lee went on, in one of his franker moods, "I feel that Governor Smith is behaving ignobly. Command appointments cannot be undone based on our antipathies. As for factions, Colonel Marshall, 'faction' will be the death of this Confederacy, should the Lord ever see fit to withdraw his favor."

"Hasn't come to that, sir," Marshall said. "Thanks be."

Not listening, Lee resumed speaking: "They don't understand Early, they refuse to see him entire. If my 'bad old man' is flawed, so are we all, Colonel Marshall, so are we all. Early's done his best, I cannot doubt that. Nor am I convinced that any of our generals would have proved abler. The newspaper people do him an injustice. And the Richmond papers . . ."

Marshall understood what went unsaid: The newssheets were despicable and none more so than Richmond's, accusing Early of everything from incompetence to drunkenness on the battlefield, charges against which even Breckinridge defended his sometime friend and erstwhile tormentor. Everyone assumed that Virginia's governor lurked behind the press as well. There was a torrent of bad blood between Old Jubilee and Extra Billy.

Lee had not finished. "What angers me, Colonel Marshall, what I find unacceptable—ungentlemanly—are these anonymous allegations, these unnamed sources of information Governor Smith proclaims he's sworn to protect. Think of it, think of it! What cowardice for a man to blacken another's reputation, yet lack the decency to sign his name. Anonymous attacks lack even the brute assassin's measure of courage. No man, Colonel . . . no man should ever malign another anonymously, the practice is contemptible."

Marshall knew that Lee also found Virginia's governor contemptible. And Marshall, who shared a Warrenton tie with Smith, agreed in full: Extra Billy had been a wretched officer and proved no better as an elected official. The governor was a man of endless schemes and few achievements. Lee, of course, would never voice such views, but Marshall could read his thoughts from a lifted eyebrow: Lee despised Smith. But Lee would never say as much to any man.

For his part, Marshall wished the general would confront Richmond's iniquities and handle President Davis with less deference. Lee's rigorous—almost ostentatious—subordination to civil authority, his unwillingness to chide even villains like Smith, threatened to lead the army into tragedy.

Lee was the last man trusted by all, yet he restricted himself to tactical questions. Marshall had begun to think it was possible to be too much of a gentleman.

"If I *had* another man, I *would* replace General Early," Lee said abruptly. "For his own sake, to spare him all this. But not because he was gainsaid a victory, not when I have fallen short myself." He pawed the air for invisible support. "This expectation of miracles, this pharisaic demand for impossible wonders, is as unjust as it is irreligious. General Early may be abrasive when out of temper—I grant you, I grant you—but no man has a higher sense of duty." Lee met his assistant's eyes. "Others talk, he fights."

Marshall agreed with much of what Lee had to say. But he also knew it wasn't only Smith who'd lost faith in Early. Accustomed as all were to victories in the Valley, two sharp defeats shocked soldiers and civilians, high and low. When misfortune struck, men didn't want explanations. They wanted someone to blame.

But Lee had chosen to send Early reinforcements, all the men possible, returning Kershaw's Division to the Valley, then dispatching Rosser and a cavalry brigade, stripping the Petersburg defenses to a dangerous degree. Even so, the reinforcements were paltry compared to Sheridan's newly reported strength.

Lee rose, not without effort. "I will *not* blame General Early.

But I do blame General Sheridan for this . . . this general alarm. His conduct, these . . . these atrocities . . . have no place in the affairs of civilized nations.”

Reports claimed that a man perched atop the Blue Ridge would see more fires blazing than he could count. Sheridan wasn’t making war on Early now, but on the entire Shenandoah Valley, on the people.

The bitterness graven on faces around the headquarters had grown fearsome, etched deep by concern that such might be the fate of the entire South. The one thing burning the Valley did not do was to incline men to surrender.

On the threshold of the parlor serving as Marshall’s office, Lee paused again.

“We must all have faith,” he said. “We must have faith.”

That seemed to end the evening’s exchange, but upon reaching the stairs, the older man turned and surprised Marshall with a smile.

“I forget myself, Colonel. You have a birthday today. My congratulations. I wish you many more.” The smile faltered. “In better times.”

October 3, 9:00 p.m.
Outside Harrisonburg

The darkness between the tents produced Doc Joe. Face bedeviled by shadows and the campfire’s orange light, he appeared to a mournful fiddle tune that rose from the depths of the camp.

“I come, dear brother-in-law, bearing good news.”

“Miracles do happen,” Hayes said. He moved to stir the fire, then chose to let the flames weaken. “Take a seat.”

“Little cold to be sitting out,” Joe said. “Fire or not.”

“Sit down, or tell your news standing.”

The surgeon took a camp chair. “It’s Russ Hastings. Sawbones’ telegraph tells me he’s likely to live.”

Hayes closed his eyes for a moment, thanking the Lord in whom he could not believe.

"That *is* good news. Wonderful news."

"Most of the pieces seemed to fit together. He may even look presentable again. To the extent that boy ever did."

"Get word to Will McKinley. He feels guilty."

Joe stirred up the fire Hayes had neglected. "Wait till morning, I expect."

"Still holding Russ at Winchester?"

The surgeon nodded. "Can't move him yet. May be some time."

"When we get back to Winchester, I need to see him."

"Sounds like it isn't only Will McKinley. Who's feeling guilty."

Hayes shook his head in denial, but he did feel a trace of guilt. He remembered telling Hastings, "Stay close to me." And the aide had stayed close and had paid for it.

"May not be that long," Joe said, "before you get to see him. I also hear, from a very different and generally dependable chain of informants—that would be the commissary sergeants—that we'll be moving north again right soon. To the Cedar Creek line, at least." He nodded at the southern horizon, the view that had kept Hayes mesmerized all evening. "Get away from all this."

"That's a military secret, Joe," Hayes noted.

"There aren't any secrets in the military," his brother-in-law said. "Might as well try to hide a dose of clap as a general's plans."

"Still . . ."

"I'm not pumping you. Just offering up what the sergeants are all saying. In case my cherished relative—who I hear has been recommended for brigadier general—in case that august gentleman has not been informed by the mighty powers about the latest change in the situation. Hate to see a hero look plain ignorant." Joe tossed the stick atop the reborn flames. "When were you going to tell me? About the promotion?"

"Hasn't happened yet."

"It will. And you know it. And next week, after the ballots are counted for the Ohio elections, you're going to be a congressman-elect. Yet, here you sit, moping like Hamlet in a traveling troupe." Casting a wild shadow on stained canvas, Joe stretched wide his arms, then slapped his hands together. "Papers back home are full of you, I hear. 'Hero of the Opequon.'" Joe chuckled. "Sounds a bit like 'The Song of Hiawatha.'"

"That about captures it, I'd say," Hayes told him. "Made-up stories."

"I will admit that the illustrations—'least, the one I saw—look somewhat more dashing than the somewhat unkempt reality. Lucy's going to be wondering who she married."

On the southern horizon, flames soared.

"You know," Hayes said, soft-voiced, "this is as close as I've ever come to taking your advice."

"About trimming that beard, if you want to keep the lice off?"

"About resigning my commission."

"Well, hallelujah! Let me shake your hand, Congressman Hayes. Boys are talking about you for governor, you know that? And it wouldn't hurt you to go home and stump for Lincoln ahead of November."

"I didn't say I was taking your advice. Only that I've never come so close."

"Well, come a little closer. You've done your part. Lucy and the boys need a husband and father."

"Nearing her time," Hayes said, changing the subject.

"Don't you worry about that, either. She'll be fine, that gal. Probably birth a twelve-pounder, in honor of du Pont's artillery."

"Her rheumatism worries me."

"Rheumatism doesn't affect childbirth. As a practitioner of the high science of medicine, I can attest to that with fair authority."

"But after."

"Worry about 'after' after. Lord almighty, Rud. You're about to be elected to Congress, you've been recommended for a general's star, you're a hero to the folks back home, and your wife is set to give birth to a healthy, strapping infant who, no doubt, will have the lungs of a company first sergeant. How about tossing some joy into the pot?"

Hayes gestured toward the countless glows that pinked the horizon in the direction of Staunton. "It's that, Joe. All that."

"Nothing you can do about it."

"No," Hayes agreed. "But I can be ashamed."

"Turn around and face north. Forget it. This damned war."

"These people won't forget it. Their great-great-grandchildren won't forget it."

Joe coughed up a laugh. "Two weeks ago, you were the apple-pie optimist. Telling me how good men would patch this country up."

"Not after this."

"They had it coming."

"No."

"Sounds insubordinate, Colonel Hayes. General Sheridan's orders—"

"I've followed my orders. But I don't have to *like* my orders."

"Seems to me, dear brother-in-law, you've gotten off light enough. 'Far as conscience goes. Our boys haven't had to do with the worst of it. Cavalry's been happy to do the chore."

"I've had over a dozen reports of unauthorized pillaging. Just today. Done by men in this division. Men in my old brigade, even our old regiment." He turned to face his relative, shunning the conflagration for a moment. "You might want to write a piece for that medical journal, that London one you read. About the epidemic breakdown of military discipline, how it spreads quicker than any plague known to man."

"I suspect," the physician said, voice half good-old-Joe and half sepulchral, "that the article has been written. By some unsavory Greek, if not a Babylonian in high dudgeon."

Hayes didn't answer but turned back to the horizon. He grasped the logic of the vast destruction, eliminating the Valley's ability to feed either an army or Virginia. Barns burned by the hundreds, haystacks by the thousands. Mills, forges, depots, granaries, even root cellars met the torch, while stock was driven off or simply slaughtered. Homes were to be spared, but some burned, too. Anyway, what good was shelter? After soldiers, whether under Pharaoh's standard or the flag of these dis-United States, robbed every ham from your smokehouse, the chickens from your yard, the last egg from your kitchen, and the final sack of flour from your pantry? When invaders made a science of denying you the food to feed yourself or nourish your children? Hayes understood the logic, and he hated it.

He imagined the same acts perpetrated against Lucy and the boys.

But he also knew that he would not resign. For the same reason as always: The men down in the ranks could not resign. And for a new reason now: It was more important than ever to end this war, to bring it to a conclusion, however baleful, before the torch and hunger made the breach truly irreparable.

For all that, for all the idealism that sounded more and more like a cheap tin bell, he hoped that he had seen his final battle, that Sheridan, Crook, and all the others were right, that Early was finished and the war's end near. And if the war had to last another winter, he hoped his men would draw an assignment guarding a railroad in some quiet corner.

Down in the tidy rows of tents, the fiddler played "Cumberland Gap."

"You know," Joe said, "you bewilder me, Rud. You and your darling Emerson. Or whichever other high-flown ink-dripper you're reading nowadays."

Hayes laughed, surprising his brother-in-law. "Hardly 'high-flown.' I just finished a novel Lucy sent me. *East Lynne,* by a Mrs. Wood." He shook his head. "I don't believe it was *meant* to be comical, but if a body could concoct a more impossible plot . . . well, I suppose I should stick to my practice of shunning novels. A man needs beefsteak, not just trimmings." He sighed. "I'm sure Lucy was trying to ease my mind, draw me away from all this." Again, he gestured toward the arson pinking the southward night.

"Now that," Joe said, "is what you and your literary friends back home might call a dichotomy, it's just what I was getting at.

Here we are, nearing—we hope—the end of a savage war. Hundreds of thousands dead, passel of whom shit themselves to death before hearing a shot. And you may not have liked it, but you didn't reject that war and all the killing on moral or ethical grounds. But now you're at your wits' end, brokenhearted, because inanimate objects, barns and corncribs, suffer the torch. Have you *thought* about that, Rud? That you're sitting here more outraged over a water mill or hay barn up in flames than you've ever been about the casualty lists? And by the way: I recall you devouring *Great Expectations* like a bowlful of fresh-picked cherries." He flashed uneven teeth by the fire's sear. "But, then, hypocrisy never disqualified a man from serving in Congress. Or the Army."

October 6, 5:00 p.m.
Harrisonburg

Well, Rosser," Early said, "I hear tell you're the 'Savior of the Valley,' sent to put us all to rights and show the rest of the cavalry how it's done. Wonder who spread that high-flown claim about? 'Savior of the Valley,' yes, sir! Wouldn't, by any chance, have been Brigadier General Thomas *Lafayette* Rosser himself now, would it?" Early cackled. "Best take care the Yankees don't crucify you, hah! I'm counting on you to perform your wonders first, turn this whole war around. God almighty, Rosser, I won't stand in your way, that I will not." Dripping spite, he added, "I'll expect you to demonstrate your supernatural proficiency by moving out tomorrow morning and teaching the Yankees a *proper* lesson, not the pissant skirmishing you did today."

"I assure you I'll do my best, sir," Rosser replied, "and the Laurel Brigade will consider it an honor to lead *your* cavalry to victory."

Early kicked a charred board and glared at the Texan who claimed a Virginia birth. "'Laurel Brigade,' hah! I want you on your warhorse, not your high horse, so get on down and don't you back-talk me, son." He knew all about Rosser's exploits at West Point and his departure to serve the Confederacy right before graduation. But the high jinks and gestures of 1861 didn't draw cards in 1864, and Early was unimpressed by Rosser's war record. On top of all, Rosser was just the sort of big, handsome, pomaded pet that Early detested.

Savior of the Valley, indeed. They'd soon see.

"Look around you, Rosser, look around you. Think 'gentlemen' burned that house and barn, that goddamned corncrib? And threw a cow down the well just to piss in the soup? Those were your West Point friends—Merritt, Custer, the pack of 'em." Early spit a brown gob and wiped his beard with the back of his hand. "You just forget about being a high-flown gentleman and give them a whipping like they've never had. And not just one whipping, either. Take those nag-kickers of yours and get revenge for . . . for all this." He waved an arm almost madly. "You go out there and forget what the Lord has to say about vengeance, Rosser, because it ain't his business this time. You take the Devil's vengeance on those bastards."

"I reckon we can handle Custer and Merritt," Rosser assured him.

October 8, 8:30 p.m.
Strasburg

Sheridan didn't just enter the house: He exploded through the door like a burst of canister. The gathered cavalry generals and colonels looked up from their plates in bewilderment followed by dread. No man among them had ever seen the army's commander in such a rage.

Taking in the bones of the turkey and the near-empty plates, Sheridan threw down his riding gloves and bellowed.

"Well, I'll be damned! If you ain't sitting here stuffing yourselves! You, Torbert—and you, Merritt—generals, staff, and all.

While the Rebs are riding right into our camp." He glared at Torbert. "Having a party, ain't we? While Rosser's carrying off your guns—next thing, he'll have Merritt's drawers off his dainty ass." Sheridan gave them a wordless growl and continued: "Oh, and you even got on your nice clothes and your clean shirts, ain't that a sweet picture! What is this, the king of Prussia throwing himself a ball? With all the fixings but Champagne and hoors?"

He lunged toward the table, as if barely restraining himself from striking out with his fists. "Torbert, mount quicker than Hell will scorch a feather. Follow me to headquarters." He growled again. "Leaving Custer out there to lose wagons and runaway darkies and his blacksmith train. Under *your* orders not to counterattack." He raised a hand as if to wipe the leavings from the table, then lowered it in disgust, eyeing Torbert again. "I should cashier you and have you horsewhipped besides." Heated past words, he glowered.

"Sir . . . ," Torbert stammered, "you . . . you said not to—"

"I don't give a *damn* what you think I said. I want you to go out there in the morning and *whip* that Rebel cavalry. Or get whipped yourself. Put every sonofabitch you can collar in the saddle. I'll be watching you—all of you—closer than a priest watching the poor box."

Sheridan turned and stamped out, leaving his gloves on the floor, unwilling to lower himself before any man.

Custer had been all but crying in his livid rage, harassed by Rosser for two days and restrained by orders not to turn on his antagonist and fight him. Sheridan had ordered a withdrawal, all right, but he hadn't expected his men to bend over for buggery.

What was Torbert thinking? Like a . . . what was the goddamned fancy word? A goddamned epicure. Gobbling a goddamned banquet when he should have been out taking scalps. The Rebs were whipped, finished. And here his cavalry, men he'd favored, were letting themselves be shamed by scarecrows on nags.

Sheridan galloped down the Valley Pike, trailing sparks from his horse's shoes and curses from his mouth.

October 9, 7:00 a.m.
Back Road, Tom's Brook

Custer was in such glorious spirits, he couldn't subdue his grin. The air was clean and crackling crisp, the sky was clear, and Pennington's boys, led by the 5th New York Cavalry, had just driven Tom Rosser's skirmishers all the way from Mt. Olive, down across the creek, and back against the main Rebel position.

As Peirce's guns rolled up to a forward position, Reb batteries tried to stop them, but the Regulars of the 2nd U.S. Artillery never faltered. Booms and blasts and splashing dirt soon quickened the morning, promising all the delicious splendors of battle.

This was it, his first real chance to show what he could do with his new division. And there was poor Tex Rosser across the creek, waiting to be played upon like the splintering piano at Benny Havens. Custer meant to hammer Rosser's keys, in fair return for the sport his West Point friend had enjoyed during the withdrawal.

God bless Sheridan, though! That little fellow showed more fight than a rally of rabid wildcats. Bless him, bless Little Phil!

With a breeze chill against his cheeks and autumn flaming, Custer trotted up to Pennington, who was assessing Rosser's position on the opposite ridge. Pennington's brigade had done its merry work since dawn, but Custer could feel the impetus weakening now, faced with a bristling defense and the naked glen before it. The stream at the bottom wasn't much, but any charge would plunge down one steep slope, then climb another. Rosser hadn't done badly when choosing his ground.

Custer rather wished he still had his Wolverines at hand, men whose qualities and quirks he knew. But taking over the Third Division had been too great a prize for him to resist.

"Isn't this grand?" Custer called to his subordinate. "Handsome day for a fight, it couldn't be better."

Pennington nodded toward the opposite ridge. "Rosser's no fool."

Delighted, Custer laughed. "Oh, but he *is*! Tom's a magnificent fool. Just wait and see!"

A fine Reb shot struck just in front of one of Peirce's twelve-pounders, splintering wheels and cutting down half the crew. The other cannoneers went about their business as if nothing at all had happened.

"Bully boys," Custer said. "Count on the Regulars."

Down a sharp slope to their front, blue-coated horsemen skirmished with dismounted Johnnies. The Rebs had stiffened and the lads from the 5th New York were no longer getting the best of it.

"Sound recall," Custer ordered, relishing the authority of his second star.

Pennington gaped, bewildered.

"Do it," Custer told him. "Now."

As the colonel turned to his bugler, Custer listened for battle noise off to the east, where Merritt's division and his old brigade were going at the rest of the Rebel cavalry on the Pike. It was vital to outdo Merritt, who had the advantage of numbers and Torbert's favor.

The bugler sounded the recall: sharp metal notes that fit the morning's snap.

Pennington eyed him, still showing surprise. "I give you that we appear to be outnumbered, sir. But we could hold here, keep the Johnnies busy, while General Merritt—"

"Nonsense," Custer told him. As the skirmishers filtered back, the firing quieted. "Watch this."

Spurring his mount down the forward slope, he tore off his hat and waved it, letting his hair flow and his grin expand. A few yards below the military crest, he reined in and made his stallion prance. Swinging his floppy hat like a tiny flag, he sought Tom Rosser's attention, offering up a display to all on the scene, in gray or blue.

"Let's have a fair fight!" he called cheerily to the Rebs. "No malice, boys!"

He made his horse dance a bit longer, letting the world admire him, convinced the Rebs would be too amused to shoot. All the while he inspected Rosser's lines, scouting the weak points.

When Custer had seen all he needed to see, he gave a last wave and spurred his horse back to the ridgetop.

Major Krom of the 5th New York had joined Pennington. Custer reined up and told him, "Neat work this morning, Krom. Well done!"

Krom nodded. Pennington said, "I make it three to two. Against us."

Custer's grin reappeared yet again. "But didn't I tell you, poor old Tom's a fool? Oh, the position's strong in itself, but he's dismounted all his men. That's all well and good against infantry, but not against us, gentlemen, not against us. He's given up his ability to maneuver."

Grasping that Custer meant to fight despite the odds, his subordinates hardened their faces. They, too, wanted revenge for their recent embarrassments. And with excellent timing, Colonel Wells, his other brigade commander, trotted up.

"Their left flank's dangling in thin air," Custer continued. "Just begging to be rolled up. Can't see it from here for that screen of trees, but I spotted it from down there." He looked at Wells and Krom, then back to Pennington. "Here's what we're going to do. . . ."

7:30 a.m.

Rosser said, "Yes, indeed, that was Old Curly. That's Custer through and through. He'll prance for Lucifer on the Day of Judgment, Georgie will." He smirked. "I intend to give him the best whipping today that he ever got. See if I don't."

7:45 a.m.

With his preparations nearly complete, Custer joined the 5th New York.

"Mind if I ride with your boys this morning, Krom?"

"Honored, sir." Abruptly, the major looked past him, eastward. Finding his hat's brim inadequate, Krom lifted a gloved hand to shield his eyes. "Who the devil . . . ?"

Custer turned.

A mile off, across rolling fields, blue-clad horsemen advanced in a column of fours, headed for Custer's position.

"Your glasses," Custer said. "Quick."

Krom unsnapped the case protecting his field glasses and tossed them over to Custer.

As soon as he found the focus, Custer blasphemed to himself. The riders were his Wolverines, instantly recognizable by their red scarves. Coming to his assistance. Or worse, *sent*. By Merritt.

He wouldn't have minded commanding them this day, but he damned well wouldn't *borrow* them from Merritt. As if Tex Rosser had thwarted him already, leaving him in need of his rival's help.

Worse, the column's approach suggested that Merritt had already dealt with his Rebs on the Pike. Wes had gotten a jump on him. It galled.

"Well, isn't that wonderful?" Custer declared for all around to hear. "Those are my old Wolverines, seems they can't stay away! Loyalty, boys, that's loyalty! Shall we show them how it's done, though?"

He didn't ride back to make certain that Pennington was ready. Nor did he pause to send orders to his band; the music could wait. He turned to his bugler and snapped, "Sound the advance!"

Wesley Merritt was not going to claim one shred of Custer's victory.

7:45 a.m.

Jim Breathed rode behind his guns in a barely contained rage. Rosser's overconfidence, his bravado, was a match and more for that devil Custer's theatrics. No wonder they were said to be fast friends.

His guns let loose in sequence, jarring the air around him, smoke thinning into a perfect October sky, gunners and officers adjusting elevations with cold precision. Beside and below the guns, the intermittent crackle of rifle fire seemed almost trivial.

As he reached the second battery, Breathed called encouragement to the cannoneers, determined to accomplish all that artillery could to stymie the Yankees this day. But experience told him two things. First, Rosser, a newcomer to this strain of Valley fighting, didn't grasp how the Federal horse had changed, what a formidable weapon their cavalry had become. Rosser had mistaken a few successful raids on wagon trains and inconsequential skirmishes over fords for telling victories. Now it looked like the Yankees had come out to fight.

Trouble a dog a time too many and he'd turn.

The second problem was the position Rosser had chosen. It looked just grand to a novice. High up on a ridge above a creek. And it might have done for an infantry division. But the guns could not be depressed enough to cover the low ground, not even for oblique fires. Worse, Rosser's flanks hung open, especially the left. And the Yankees had just demonstrated, twice, at Winchester and Fisher's Hill, that they had developed a taste for biting flanks.

What he wouldn't have given to have Fitz Lee back in command!

Peering across the little valley at Custer's force, Breathed didn't think the Yanks had the numbers to take the heights, at least not yet. But the one thing the Yankees did seem able to do was to prestidigitate a near-endless supply of timely reinforcements. No, time wasn't on Tom Rosser's side, nor was this dull-witted waiting, this queer chest-pounding passivity, that handed the initiative to that yellow-haired, primping dandy.

Waiting for the Federals to come on, all Breathed could do was to champion his batteries and be grateful that, this single time, the Yankees were the ones caught out with defective ammunition in their caissons, half of their shells just burrowing into the earth. Even so, he recognized the handiwork of the 2nd U.S. Artillery and Charlie Peirce, his old nemesis. Breathed had managed to knock out one of Peirce's guns early in the action, but—bad shells or not—the Yankee Regulars had done the same to one of his own pieces, tit for tat.

He'd tried to talk to Rosser, but there was no reasoning with the man, who seemed downright entranced by his opponent. Full of bluster, Rosser was empty of sense. Now all Breathed could do was to hope that Custer—the worst of the Yankee barn-burners and thieves—would be fool enough to mount a frontal attack.

Maybe it was just the disgruntlement that followed a string of defeats and devastation, Breathed figured, but for the first time in a war that long had pleased him he wondered if he should not have remained a physician.

With no further warning, a bugle rang out across the creek, soon seconded by others. And the Yankees came on, carbines and sabers glittering, headed straight for Breathed's horse artillery.

7:55 a.m.

Custer rode beside the 5th New York's color-bearer, pressing the nose of his horse ahead of the others. Pennington's men advanced in perfect measure: They crested the ridge at a walk and, dropping down toward the creek, answered the call to increase their pace to a trot with alert discipline, a thousand horsemen moving almost as one.

The ground was too steep for a textbook gallop, but this wasn't meant to be a classroom example. All he needed to do was to fix the Johnnies' attention, to keep them occupied with a pretty display.

"Sound the charge," he called back to his bugler.

Near instantly, the brigade and regimental buglers picked up the call. Hooves thundered and turf flew.

The Reb artillery concentrated their fires on the first rank, but the horsemen soon reached the bottom, where the guns could no longer find them. They leapt the creek and pounded up the far slope. Rifle volleys sought them now, unseating the first casualties.

"Keep blowing!" Custer bellowed over his shoulder. "Blow like Gabriel!"

But before the bugler could bring the mouthpiece back to his lips, other bugles sounded. High and off to the right.

Custer couldn't contain himself. He shouted, "Charge! Charge!" although his voice was lost in the thunder of hooves, the boom of guns, and the racket of rifles firing as fast as they could.

His men roared, a great blue beast. And their roar was answered by hurrahs from regiments still invisible. But Custer knew where they were.

So did the Rebs. Stalwart a moment before, they began to run. Racing for their horses, while the artillerymen hastened to withdraw their pieces.

"Go on! Go on!" Custer yelled, screamed.

Bugles, hooves, shouts, cries. But fewer and fewer shots.

Up on the ridge, Reb officers struggled on horseback, frantic in their efforts to hold their soldiers to the firing line.

Soon there was no firing line to save.

Custer was among the first to leap his horse over the shoddy, improvised breastworks, followed by dozens and then hundreds of other riders.

He saw them now, their sabers flashing, the regiments he had sent around the flank to turn Rosser's position. They advanced on a broad front, cutting down Rebs as they tried to reach their horses. For once, a plan had gone off perfectly, timed to the second by a sweet felicity, by that happenstance men referred to as "Custer's luck."

You were taught that you should never split your forces before the enemy, but he'd made the tactic his favorite. A man had to be bold and take his risks.

"New York!" he cried. "Vermont! Come on, boys. After 'em."

His men swept up prisoners, captured horses, and sabered men from caissons. Rebels brave enough to attempt to resist were swept away in clashes of steel or fell to flurries of carbine fire.

"Get their guns! Follow the guns!"

He reined in his stallion so sharply, its forelegs lifted. Briefly, he turned to look back over the field.

Yes. His own guns were following, quick as their wheels could turn, with Peirce riding at the fore as they jounced down the Back Road.

Elated and joyous, he turned his mount again and rejoined the pursuit.

8:20 a.m.

Breathed was so angry, he felt puking sick. "Physician, heal thyself!" he whispered wryly.

Through a miracle and grit, he'd brought off his guns. But the Yankees had snatched two caissons and some wagons. And after they'd chased him two miles, they were still coming on hot, delayed all too briefly by hasty defenses got up along the road by dispirited horsemen, defenses that melted quick as ice in summer.

Something had to be done.

And the choice, as Breathed saw things, was up to him. He could keep on going and save his guns, or take up a position and—maybe—save the damned cavalry from complete annihilation. It was a harder decision than any he had faced over a patient.

"Over there, Johnston," he shouted to his nearest battery commander. "Deploy up on that rise, in front of the tree line."

Spurring his horse back to his trailing battery, he called, "Thomson, take the other side of the road. Sweep the lower fields that Johnston can't cover."

His officers and soldiers didn't hesitate, but went into battery as smoothly as if drilling.

Clusters of blue-clad horsemen rushed into range, but Breathed's guns didn't open, letting the riders come on, aware of how wasteful long-range fires would be with half their ammunition lost and the Yankees dispersed by the speed of their success. Breathed raised his binoculars, only to see Yankees saber the drivers of a last few wagons careening southward.

Munford came up, though, with a good hundred men still under his command. Soon others joined them. A raw defense developed.

The Yankees had lost all order in their pursuit, galloping after prizes until the fields resembled a massive, madcap steeplechase.

Still gentleman enough to recall that profanity had to be stayed behind the lips, Breathed watched gray riders throw up their hands, some in surrender, others in the dependable reflex of men shot in the back.

But Munford gathered in more of his fleeing troopers. Then Payne came up with a company's worth of Virginians.

The men *wanted* to rally, that was the thing. They still had a dose of fight in them.

Where was Rosser? Not that Breathed missed him unto a heartache.

"Let them get close," Munford warned him. The colonel was sweating and panting, but hardly from fighting. Breathed had suffered about as many cavalrymen's prescriptions as he could abide in a single morning.

"I know my business," he said, voice sharpened past insult.

He was hot, he couldn't help it.

Munford looked at him hard, but let it go. The cavalryman rode back to the tree line and his much-diminished command.

When the leading Yankees spotted the guns, they weren't deterred in the least. Instead, they closed together again, into packs just short of military order, responding to animal instinct and training, neither factor weightier than the other. Some increased their pace and began to hurrah, swinging their sabers or extending their carbines.

Breathed trotted out into the roadway, where all of his artillerymen could see him. And he raised his hand.

Waiting. Listening to Yankee shots rip by, fired from the saddle and longing to hit him.

Closer. A little more.

As soon as the Yankees entered the effective fan of canister, he dropped his hand.

Horses and riders tumbled. But not enough, not nearly enough. The attack slowed, though, with riders milling about, as if they'd lost their bearings and needed orders.

His men reloaded, working swabs and ramrods with veteran speed.

Munford and Payne, the damned fools, didn't wait. With ragged cries, their horsemen burst from the trees, from swales, countercharging the Yankees.

And the Yankees turned all right, the few hundred of them who had neared the batteries. They took off like rabbits in their turn, pursued by hallooing Confederates. But Breathed's lips had tightened to a grimness. He knew every step of this cotillion and didn't care for the music the band would play next.

8:40 a.m.

Custer found his men in retreat, rallied them, and quickly repelled the Confederates who'd chase them. Had to admire the Johnnies' pluck, they kept up their end of the game as best they could. He had hoped to spot Tom Rosser—wouldn't it be lovely to capture old Tex?—but the big fellow hadn't showed since his lines collapsed.

Custer had called in his brigade commanders to issue new orders. Before his old brigade, advancing at a walk, could overtake them.

"Wells, you're on the right," he said. "Pennington, the left. Get your boys sorted out quickly. I want a division front, two ranks. And not a second to spare, you understand?"

He was not going to let Merritt in on this prize. Not even Merritt in the guise of his Wolverines.

Trailed by their pennants and flags, his brigade commanders

hurried off. After giving an aide instructions for Peirce and his artillery, he turned to scan the fields for his old brigade. Instead, he spotted damnable George Sanford, one of Torbert's pet captains and a creature who had always favored Merritt.

Sanford rode up and saluted. Custer returned the salute with a practiced smile.

"So glad I found you, sir," Sanford told him. "Given that you're lagging a bit, I thought you'd want to be apprised of developments. General Merritt has given Lomax a thrashing out on the Pike, it's a complete rout." Smirking like the cat that ate the prize goldfish, the captain added, "Merritt has taken five guns, it's been something of a spectacle."

"Sanford, you're just in time!" Custer said in the merriest voice he could scavenge. "Hold on a minute and I'll show you six."

Sanford raised an eyebrow under his kepi but said nothing.

"Sound the advance," Custer ordered. Hoping that Pennington and Wells had their men ready.

They were ready. The entire division moved forward, first at a walk, then at a trot. It was a glorious sight, almost rivaling Winchester, and Custer wished his darling girl could see it. Wouldn't she be proud of her boy today?

Rather to Custer's surprise, Sanford joined the advance. Custer called to him, less indulgently now, "Off you go, Sanford. If you see my old Wolverines, tell them they're welcome to follow and share in the spoils. Plenty for all, I'm not the jealous sort, you know." And he touched his horse's wet flanks with his spurs.

9:05 a.m.

Breathed saw the Yankees coming, with a few gray horsemen preceding them, heralds of disaster, men crying warnings of doom and dragging it with them.

He had tried to rally more troopers around his guns, but few had halted: Terror was the order of the day. Under such circumstances, the artillery officer's version of the Hippocratic oath said,

"First, save your guns." But Breathed had decided to risk everything. In the hope of buying a few more slivers of time, not for the cavalry to reorganize itself and put up a fight—that was beyond all hope now—but for the horsemen to escape to fight another day: They had been savaged, but not destroyed. Not yet. And Breathed saw clearly that only he stood between them and destruction.

He rode the lines of his two batteries in turn, giving an order he never had imagined would pass his lips.

"Fight the guns to the last. Then save yourselves. If we can bring them off, all right. But I want heroics *before* we're driven, not afterward. Fight the guns to the last, then leave them, if need be."

No man said a word. No japes, no gibes. Not even frowns. Just faces cast in mottled brass, as hard as any gunmetal.

Across the fields, a magnificent show materialized: blue lines, metal and leather gleaming, their front a half mile wide. Breathed guessed their number at two thousand horsemen. Maybe more.

In the distance, a band began to play a piece Breathed didn't recognize.

"Open at maximum range," he called. "No need to conserve ammunition now."

9:15 a.m.

New command, new music. Throughout his days leading a brigade, Custer had favored "Yankee Doodle" as the anthem for his attacks. Now, commanding a division, he'd decided he'd need something more distinctive, uniquely his own. And "Garryowen," an Irish jig, stuck in a fellow's ear and jollied the spirit.

The division's band, a hodgepodge affair not yet up to his standards, didn't render it perfectly, but could play it well enough to quicken a charge. He'd been saving it up all morning. For the *coup de grâce.*

And a lovely charge it was about to be, over perfect ground:

harvested fields with their fences long since removed by soldiers hunting firewood and copses of trees so slight they didn't figure. It was almost as he imagined the western plains.

A few quick clashes had brushed aside the ragged bits of resistance that turned up, and Custer was surprised to crest a low ridge and see, in the distance, guns in battery on each side of the road, apparently unsupported.

Those guns were *his,* he wouldn't let the Rebs bring them off a second time. He'd thought to bluff Sanford, but here the pieces were, after all, just begging to be captured. Six, at least.

Custer's luck.

The guns across the fields puffed smoke, and rounds whistled down their arcs. Explosive shells ruptured the earth before his ranks, hurling cascades of dirt and stone upward and outward.

"Sound the charge!" he called.

That clarion call. The rumble of hooves swelling into earthly thunder. And, behind them, the brass band striking up to give them "Garryowen."

Hurrahs. Lowered sabers. Flags snapping overhead.

The Johnnies reloaded quickly, but had trouble adjusting the range, given the speed of the attack. He'd issued the order to charge so quickly, the Rebs had been thrown off balance.

Along the Back Road, a lone lost wagon clattered between the forces, its teamster doubtless terrified.

The charge gobbled distance. Reb guns spit. Horses tumbled. Custer drew his own saber and leaned forward, torso paralleling his stallion's neck.

Men shouted, "New York!" or, "Pennsylvania!" or, "Vermont!" But the words were barely intelligible amid the uproar. The earth quivered.

He expected the Rebs to run up their limbers and try to haul off their guns. But they didn't. As the distance between the cannoneers and their attackers narrowed, the crews went about their work, as if unaware of the danger.

They got off last blasts of canister, the Rebs did. But too late to save them. And what damage Custer glimpsed was blessedly slight.

And the Rebs took off, abandoning their guns to leap on team horses cut free of harness, plunging back into the trees where a charge would slow and promptly lose order.

He had the guns, though. There were exactly six.

Noon

Custer's riders pursued the Rebs for a dozen miles and more, all the way to Woodstock and beyond the hard-used town. Their route had been scarred with the wreckage of an army, overturned wagons and caissons, lame horses left by their masters, dismounted men with terrified eyes, eager to surrender to the blue swarms covering the countryside or clearing the road ahead in a column of fours, sabers sheathed, so indisputably victorious that the pride-swollen riders rarely felt the need to draw a revolver.

Prisoners wept, cursed, asked for food, and stumbled northward in beggars' rags. Their wounded waited, disconsolate, by the roadside, objects of pity for the few, of satisfaction for others, but of disinterest to most.

Along the main street of Woodstock, Torbert and Merritt caught up, trailed by their staffs and—it seemed to Custer—ridiculously somber, under the circumstances.

"Why, gentlemen!" he called, doffing his hat. "Where have you been all morning?"

And yes, Merritt took only five guns.

The pursuit faded off. The horses were blown and there hardly seemed to be anything left worth chasing. The haul in booty was simply grand, given the awful poverty of the Johnnies. They'd taken Rosser's entire wagon train, his ambulances, a load of Enfield rifles still in their crates, a battalion's worth of caissons, strings of skeletal remounts, and, as Colonel Wells had ridden up in person to inform him, Rosser's headquarters equipage, complete with the general's personal effects.

Wouldn't Tex have a fit, though? He'd have to send him a thank-you note for the gifts. He pictured the color rising in Rosser's face through choler to blue.

Custer already had decided that the day's events would be christened "the Woodstock Races," canceling the embarrassment of the previous year's "Buckland Races," a decidedly lesser affair across the Blue Ridge. That time, the Johnnies had printed captured love letters from Libbie in their papers, a despicable act, and Tom Rosser was going to get a taste of it now.

Poor Tex!

Oh, it was all grand, bully, splendid, though! The smell of a hot horse on a cool day, a drink of sweet water, and a proper shit to crown the victory. He wished the band had been able to keep up, but he reckoned he'd worn their lungs out.

Followed by a staff drunk on elation, Custer rode back through the ramshackle town whistling his newly chosen musical signature and enjoying the sullen looks of the Rebel gals who dared to come out on their porches.

A little tornado of red leaves danced around him.

On such days, Custer wished the war could last. Certainly, he wanted to see his darling—needed to see her, to caress her and the rest, to hear her whisper, "Oh, Autie!" in the darkness. But what else would be left when this was over? And, he feared, it would be over soon. He meant to stay in the Army, of course, could imagine no other life, no other calling. But what would it be like when the Army returned to its duties on the Plains, with its dusty, dreary garrisons and uneventful days, the rare, one-sided clashes and plodding chases that ended in frustration more often than not, or, at best, in the capture of a few starved and stinking wretches? The frontier was a place, Custer foresaw, where a man might soon be forgotten by the world.

All right, Torbert, all right," Sheridan said, all but laughing with pleasure at the reports of captives and booty, of the vaunted Confederate horsemen scattered with unprecedented ease. "It's the greatest overthrow of their cavalry in this war, I can hardly believe it myself. Almost pity the hopeless, hapless bastards." He shook his head. "Early's finished, this proves it beyond a doubt."

The officers in the crowded headquarters tent murmured their agreement. More than a few of them wished to get on to a celebratory round or two of whiskey, Sheridan knew. But he wasn't quite finished.

"Casualties to the Cavalry Corps?" he asked Torbert. "What was the butcher's bill?"

"Nine killed, forty-eight wounded," Torbert said. "And some horses, of course."

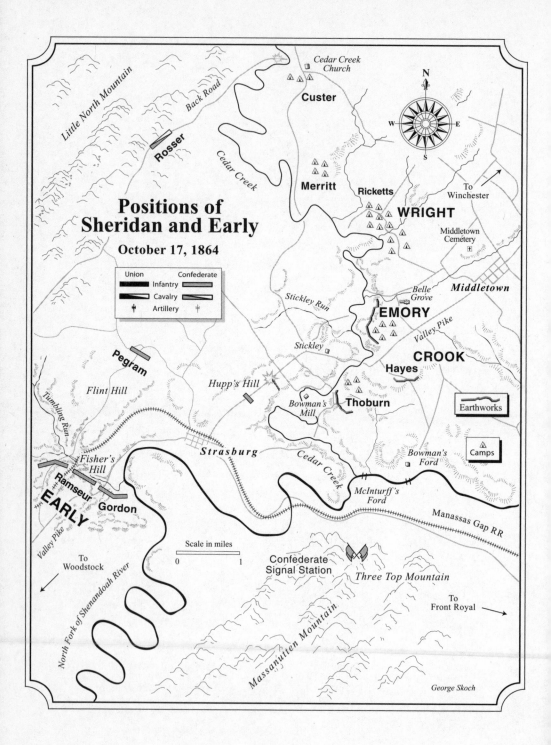

Little North Mountain

Back Road

Rosser

Cedar Creek

Cedar Creek Church

Custer

Merritt

Ricketts

WRIGHT

To Winchester

Middletown Cemetery

Positions of Sheridan and Early

October 17, 1864

Union	Confederate
Infantry	
Cavalry	
⚐ Artillery	⚐

Stickley Run

Belle Grove

Middletown

EMORY

Stickley

CROOK

Hayes

Pegram

Flint Hill

Hupp's Hill

Bowman's Mill

Thoburn

Valley Pike

Earthworks

Tumbling Run

Strasburg

Cedar Creek

Bowman's Ford

⚐ Camps

Fisher's Hill

Ramseur

EARLY

Gordon

McInturff's Ford

Manassas Gap R.R.

Valley Pike

To Woodstock

North Fork of Shenandoah River

Scale in miles

0   1

Confederate Signal Station

Three Top Mountain

To Front Royal

Massanutten Mountain

George Skoch

SEVENTEEN

October 17, noon
Fisher's Hill

"Congratulations!" Clem Evans said as the farmhouse emptied. "Child's a wonderful thing, a perfect blessing."

"I *do* feel blessed," Ramseur told him. His expression was milder than Evans ever had seen it. "More blessed than any man has a right to feel. And Grimes got his own good news right after mine." His eyes traveled far. "Whip Phil Sheridan . . . maybe I can go home. See Nellie, the baby."

"Boy or girl?"

Ramseur ran a palm over his gone-bald-too-young scalp. "Signal didn't say. Just that everything went fine, the crisis passed."

"Well, that's blessing enough." Evans paused, revisiting his own happiness. "Will say, though, a little girl's less trouble. My boy, my Doodie now . . . he's a trial to his mama, mischief he gets up to." A proud, indulgent smile warmed his face. "Love the little devil, man can't help himself. You'll see."

It was a wonderful thing, a thing worth pondering, Evans decided, an outright mercy. The way news of the birth of another man's child could lift so many hearts amid a war. Friends and comrades did not content themselves with the standard felicities, but showed an honest pleasure, almost delight, in another man's news—even if the event rekindled their own longing for home, for their own loved ones. Perhaps, Evans thought, it was just the affirmation of life between all the deaths, the promise that a man's blood would go on, a swaddled, mewling hint of resurrection.

After Early abruptly ended the meeting, Evans had waited to

be the last to shake Dod Ramseur's hand, allowing his fellow generals and their attendant colonels pride of place. He reckoned that humility was as becoming in an officer as in a preacher. Rare, though.

As the last of their fellow commanders escaped the headquarters, leaving the mice and wrecked furniture to hurry back to their empty-bellied troops, the two men lingered, each unwilling to let go of the moment. Sparked with happiness, Ramseur added:

"Speaking of devils, Clem . . . I hear you gave the boys a blaze of a sermon, downright fiery. Glad to have our 'fighting parson' back."

Evans refreshed his smile, the way a man sometimes had to in the pulpit, when worldly tremors shook the hope of Heaven. Ramseur was a good and sturdy Christian, if no Methodist, but the youthful general's faith had a darkling tinge. Evans hoped that his Sunday sermon had, indeed, been heartening, but it hadn't been "fiery," not in the hellfire sense. As the war turned ever grimmer, his faith shone kindlier. Never had been a hard-gospel man, for that matter.

Evans moved the wrong way and a spear pierced his right side. *Those pins.* He still suffered breathtaking pains when he stirred himself heedlessly: The surgeons had not been able to extract all the fragments left by the packet of pins that got in that bullet's way on the Monocacy. But a man could live with pain, he could learn how.

Wistfully, Evans remembered his train trip home, barely able to stand and his stitches oozing—sometimes bleeding—and there on a platform he'd spotted his wife by blessed chance as she waited to board a train headed north to find him. Their encounter amid Georgia's suffering and confusion had been a little miracle of the Lord's. He had hugged her tight right there, in front of all, gripping her fiercely, almost wantonly, with his wound shocking him with bolt after bolt of pain. His flesh shrieked, "Let her go!" insistent and heartless, but he would not, could not, do it, utterly unable to release her, clutching her warm and living and loved against him, and Allie clinging in return, making the pain ever worse until hot tears fled from his eyes, and as she felt the wet on her pressed-close cheek, she had said, sweetly bewildered, "Clem! You're weeping."

"Best be off, I reckon," Ramseur said. "Plenty to do before morning."

"Surely."

Neither man moved.

"Like to hear a *real* plan," Ramseur added, glancing around to be certain Early was gone. "Old Jube's keeping things close."

"I suspect we'll hear this evening."

"Doesn't leave much time."

"Not much."

Both men had lost their smiles.

"I do miss Sandie Pendleton, that's the truth," Ramseur admitted. "Kept the old man as close to even-keeled as anyone could."

"I've prayed for his soul," Evans said.

General Gordon, on whom Evans had been waiting, broke off a discussion with Jed Hotchkiss. The Georgian left the mapmaker hunting through papers.

"Well, Dod," Gordon said, voice rich, "you're shining like the polished shield of Perseus, like the bright helm of Achilles." When Gordon grinned, the left side of his mouth lagged behind the right, constricted by an old scar. His Antietam wound, Evans knew. "Fatherhood will do that to a man."

"Feel like I could run barefoot to North Carolina," Ramseur said, reminded that there was happiness in the world. "I want to see Nellie and the baby so bad."

"Well, don't run off just yet," Gordon told him. "We're going to need you. Way I've been in terrible need of Clem here, while he was home luxuriating." He settled a hand, briefly, on Ramseur's shoulder. "And when you do go, Dod, I suggest the train."

"Do *you* have any sense of what Early's thinking?" Ramseur

asked. "He called us all in here, then told us round about nothing. Just 'prepare to attack in the morning.' That's hardly . . ."

"Hardly like to build confidence," Gordon completed the
thought. "Fact is I don't believe he's made up his mind. About
this attack, how to do it. He's looking at hitting them on their
right, over where the ground gentles out. But that's too obvious,
and he knows it." He gestured toward the landscape beyond the
walls. "And Fisher's Hill doesn't bring back the best of memories."
He turned to Evans. "Be glad you weren't there, Clem."

"Strength's back up, though," Ramseur countered. "With Kershaw back. We've got almost as many men as we did before Winchester."

Gordon nodded and folded his arms, a favorite stance. "Numbers are fine, but I'm not sure about morale. These men need to
win. And as for reinforcements, Kershaw's it. No more men in Lee's
pocket, we have to get this one right. Or the Valley's gone forever."

Deprived of his cheer again, Ramseur stared at the floor.

Laying a hand on the younger man's shoulder, Gordon told
him, "Go on back to your men, Dod. Do what you have to do.
Then think about your good news, let yourself savor it. Hotchkiss
and I are going to have a look at things, see if we can't devise some
martial astonishment." He turned. "Clem, you're welcome to come
along, I'm minded toward your company. If you feel ready to drag
that carcass along."

"Where?"

"Signal station. Up on Three Top. Tough climb, I'm told. Fair
warning."

Evans caught Gordon glancing at his side.

"Hotchkiss was up there in August," Gordon continued, "makes
it sound like Mount Olympus, only prettier. Claims a man can see
the entire world." He produced a smaller, fiercer smile. "Figure
we'll have a look at Sheridan's bunch, see if those boys are still sitting on their backsides, gobbling salt pork." The smile died. "Find
out what's waiting for us, if nothing else."

October 17, noon
The War Department, Washington, D.C.

No," Sheridan said.

He looked in turn at the two men arrayed against him, meeting their glowers with an assurance he had not felt on his last visit to this office. Two months and a string of victories made the difference.

The room smelled of wax and cigar smoke.

"No," he repeated. "I just don't see it."

First, he addressed Halleck, a bug-eyed, blustering man who had saved him from obscurity three years before, a man who'd possessed the skill to organize armies, but not the gift for leading them in battle. Now his hour was past, eclipsed by Grant.

"Such extensive fortifications would only tie down my army. And a fortress built to protect Manassas Gap and the railroad line wouldn't even stop that horse thief Mosby. We *must* remain mobile, mobility's the key."

"Grant's not mobile," Halleck said. "He hasn't moved from Petersburg since June." Halleck was a man who could not keep spite from his voice on the best of days. And this was not his best day.

"*He* doesn't have to be," Sheridan answered. "That's my point. Lee's made a fortress of Petersburg and Richmond. And he's sacrificed his freedom to maneuver. Lee's trapped himself, now it's only a matter of time."

A far greater menace than Halleck, Secretary Stanton reentered the fray from behind his desk: "There can be no more advances on Washington, Sheridan. Not so much as a feint. Not a one-horse raid." He sat back, locking his fingers together as if grinding a tiny creature between his palms. Frozen behind spectacles, Stanton's eyes never faltered in a staring match. "That, I believe, is what General Halleck seeks to communicate, the point of his recommendations. With the election but weeks away"—he freed the invisible animal, waving it off—"I won't have any embarrassments. Do I speak with sufficient clarity, General Sheridan?"

Gesturing toward a table covered with plans he found ridiculous,

Sheridan replied, "Those fortifications couldn't be finished before the election, anyway."

He was instantly sorry he'd said it. The observation was so obvious, so embarrassing to the scheme's proponents, it smacked of insolence.

"We must . . . we have to consider the period *after* the election, too," Halleck spluttered. "The war's not over, nothing's guaranteed. The security of Washington . . ." The man wet the air when he spoke, misting the faces of anyone sitting too near.

"Of course," Sheridan said as a gesture of appeasement, "your design *is* the classic solution, General Halleck, classic Vauban. No West Point man could miss it. But with the South nearing collapse . . . there's a stronger case for leaving a limited maneuver force in the Valley, just enough men to keep an eye on things, while the Sixth Corps moves to reinforce Grant and bring all this to an end. We have to move against Lee with all we have. We have to *move*."

"But you don't deny the inherent merit of fortifications," Halleck tried. "History instructs us in their value, you know."

"Of course not. Fortresses . . . have their place. It's only a matter of using our resources as effectively as possible. At *this* stage in the war." To soothe his old master further, he added, without a grain of sincerity, "It's a shame your plan, this fortified line, wasn't put in place years ago. It would . . . have made a difference. Earlier."

He glanced at Stanton and met reptile's eyes behind glinting spectacles. Stanton understood what he had just done, of course. But the secretary of war was no longer concerned with Halleck, an ally who had failed him.

"Grant," Stanton said, "believes you should move your army across the Blue Ridge. And take Charlottesville. Then go on to Lynchburg, close the noose around Lee."

Sheridan saw the trap, but not an easy way out of it. Grant was his protector, the man who had forced his appointment past these two men when they questioned his ability. But Grant didn't see the difficulties such a move would face with the Valley ruined—if they'd cut off food and fodder for the Rebels, they'd done the same to themselves, and a long supply line over the Blue Ridge or even switched to the east merely invited partisan attacks. He'd need as many men to guard his rear as he had at the front. That wasn't the mobility he had in mind.

But he wouldn't criticize Grant before these men. Stanton and Halleck practiced divide-and-conquer. And Sheridan had no intention of being conquered.

"General Grant sees the thing entire, of course. I defer to him," he lied.

He had no intention of marching across the Blue Ridge in the winter, emulating Napoleon's retreat from Moscow in reverse. Grant could be persuaded, given time. Sheridan had already determined that when the game reached its final moves, he would be fighting at Grant's side, not licking his wounds after a march to nowhere or sitting in some useless fortress, waiting for an attack by a phantom army.

"General Halleck?" Stanton said coolly. "My apologies for keeping you from your labors. I'll see off General Sheridan."

Dismissed, humiliated, and, apparently, growing accustomed to such treatment, Halleck mumbled farewell.

When the door shut behind the chief of staff, Stanton permitted silence to fill the room, to gather force. Sheridan's ears fell prey to the suddenly audible noise from the teeming avenue—a thoroughfare even busier and more prosperous than it had been mere months before. Riches bloomed from corpses, at least in the North. Willard's Hotel, where he'd breakfasted in haste, harbored as many men of business and favor seekers as it did do-nothing officers.

The secretary of war sat unnervingly still, a judge before whom no felon would choose to stand.

Sheridan had to remind himself that he was no felon. On the contrary, he had given Stanton victories.

The secretary introduced a tiny sound, that of fingertips tapping a closed fist.

Sheridan met his stare, refusing to waver.

At last, Stanton spoke: "It's a splendid thing, I suppose, to see oneself celebrated in all the newspapers." He separated his hands. "No doubt, it's a heady feeling, intoxicating." His viper's eyes fixed Sheridan. "Of course, you're too sound a man to succumb to all that. You're wise enough to know . . . that today's hero often proves tomorrow's fool."

The slit of Stanton's mouth shifted in what might have been a smile. "Poor George McClellan, for example. I recall how beloved the fellow was, adored by the men and women of the North. By children, too, for that matter." He laid a white hand on his desk. "Who worships McClellan now? A handful of traitorous Copperheads, and even they have doubts." The faint realignment of the lips recurred. "And he dreamed of becoming president? After the press had moved on to more promising men, after ridicule had begun to coil around him? Military men . . . lose themselves in the labyrinth of politics, a netherworld they find inscrutably foreign. McClellan never had a chance, he hadn't the subtle mind such matters require. And now? He's become a horse's ass, a ruined man. The election hasn't taken place and he's already half-forgotten."

This time, Stanton's smile was unmistakable. "And what of the soldiers, I ask you? The men on whom he counted, whose hearts he believed he'd won for all eternity? Fickle as spoiled girls. Now that we're winning the war, they'll go for Lincoln. Little Mac never understood human nature." The secretary tilted his head slightly to one side, just as Sheridan had seen rattlesnakes do. "He assumed that adulation doesn't expire. But the affections of the herd are merely the froth on a pail of milk. The bubbles fade as you watch."

Peering over his spectacles, Stanton's eyes glowed from the shadows of his brow. "But you, Sheridan? I look at you . . . and I see a man of high talent, of eminent suitability for your profession. And, I hope, of commensurate sense." The not-quite-smile flickered. "The esteem of the public can be destroyed overnight, you understand."

Stanton sat up straight, changing his posture as he changed the subject. "You're absolutely convinced that Early's finished? What about that encounter a few days back?"

"Hardly more than a skirmish."

"Our forces withdrew, though."

"Hupp's Hill has no value to us. Not now. Early was just trying to salvage his pride. What little remains of it."

Stanton nodded. "I'm also told that your signalmen intercepted a curious message. To the effect that General Longstreet had arrived."

The secretary's knowledge startled Sheridan.

"I don't believe it for an instant," he told Stanton. "The Rebs would never let the cat out of the bag by waving signal flags in our faces. They'd throw away any chance they had of surprise." He leaned toward Stanton. "And surprise would be their *only* chance. No, that signal was nothing but a ruse. Longstreet never came."

"But to what purpose? This ruse?"

"Early's afraid, that's my guess. He's trying to spook me, deter us from attacking him. He can't afford another debacle."

"He followed you down the Valley, though."

"Matter of pride, all of it's about their endless pride. Trying to show he's active, doing something. He won't last long. There's not a crumb to eat between my army and Lexington, and I took most of his wagons. He can't keep his men supplied right now, let alone as the weather worsens." He met Stanton's relentless stare again. "Early's played out."

"One hopes," Stanton said. He rose. Again, he almost smiled. "My congratulations once more on your torrent of victories." He made no move to come from behind the desk and offer a handshake. "I hope I shall never hear the usual calumnies leveled at you—journalists are unforgiving, mind you. Look at George Meade. It's almost as if someone poisoned the press against him. Of course, you'll always count *me* among your supporters, Sheridan." He canted his head again. "But there's only so much a single man can do."

When Sheridan didn't answer, Stanton added, "I believe you have a special train? Don't let me keep you, General."

Sheridan nodded. "I want to get back to my army."

"You have concerns?"

"No. I've just never cared for the Cedar Creek line. I intend to fall back on Winchester. Better ground." He gave Stanton hard eye for hard eye. "I was summoned to Washington before I could start my movement."

"Ah, yes. Conflicting demands, the vicissitudes of generalship." The secretary took up a paper from his desk, as if it suddenly needed his attention.

Sheridan saluted. Stanton chose not to notice.

His ordeal in the city he hated wasn't over. Halleck lurked mid-hallway. He had two colonels with him, one detestably fat and the other skeletal.

"Sheridan!" the chief of staff called in a mighty whisper. "Unfinished business, if you please."

Christ, what now? Sheridan wondered.

"These men . . . my engineers . . . they worked on the fortress plan. Splendid work, you saw the drawings yourself. I thought they might go with you to the Valley. Men of such caliber might be a help in siting your lines for the winter. You can show them the ground around Winchester yourself, *en route* to your army."

When Sheridan hesitated, Halleck added almost pathetically, "It's the least you might do."

"Of course," Sheridan said instantly. "They'll be a great help."

"Good, good. That's all. *Bonne chance.* Splendid work. Proud of you, Philip. I always could spot ability, you know. You, Grant. Had to protect you both from the wrathful powers. . . ."

"My gratitude," Sheridan said, "can't be put into words."

October 17, 3:30 p.m.
Three Top Mountain, Signal Knob

Words failed Gordon. Of all the opportunities he had witnessed—and seen squandered—nothing approached this, not even that dangling Union flank in the Wilderness.

"My, oh, my!" Clem Evans said. It was the third time in as many minutes that Evans had used the expression.

"Indeed," Gordon commented. On a rock above them, a signalman waved his flags.

"I told you," Hotchkiss said.

Far below, arranged like toys on a tabletop, Sheridan's army revealed itself. The unaided eye could detect not only division encampments, but brigade allotments and regimental tent lines. With field glasses a man could spy the different uniform facings, the red of the artillery, cavalry yellow, and the pale blue that condemned a man to the infantry. Gordon could count every gun and every wagon. He could even confirm the report that the army was headquartered in the Belle Grove plantation house, busy now with the comings and goings of couriers and staff men.

Done right, a surprise attack might capture Sheridan.

"Beautiful, too," Clem said. "Fair as the rose of Sharon." And he was right. The Valley and its guardian mountains flamed, but with autumn reds and oranges, copper and gold, and not because of Sheridan's pyromania. The air was bracing and clear as a maiden's conscience, and down below—at a bruising climb's remove—the Shenandoah gleamed as it ran northward, clinging snugly to the mountain's base.

But Gordon had a poor eye for nature this day. His interest lay in Sheridan's lax dispositions.

"I make it two to one against us," Hotchkiss said.

"I like that better than three to one," Gordon told him. Still a tad short of breath, he sighed. "Well, we know where he expects us to attack. To the extent he's worried about an attack at all."

"Cavalry massed on the left," Hotchkiss agreed. "Just where General Early's minded to go."

"Not sure we'd even get across the creek, not over there. Not without paying a price we can't afford."

"I make that the Sixth Corps back toward Middletown, to the rear," Evans put in.

"Army of the Potomac arrangement, unmistakable," Hotchkiss said.

"Makes sense, putting them there," Gordon told his companions. "Their best corps behind the cavalry, positioned to move to the south or west." He passed the glasses back to Hotchkiss. "What I *do* find interesting is the rest of that army. Why on earth place a lone division off by itself, a mile to the south of its nearest support?"

"Looks flat from up here, I know, but they're on high ground. Overlooking the creek bend," Hotchkiss explained.

"I understand that," Gordon told him. "What I *don't* understand is why they're all but abandoned out there. Just begging to be snapped up."

"Bait?" Hotchkiss asked.

Gordon shook his head. "Can't see how they'd spring the trap, the way the camps are disposed. And look behind them, up at the middle encampments. They've dug their earthworks, piled up their share of dirt." He turned to Evans. "But what do you see? What do *you* see, Clem?"

"They all face south, every one of them. And the Sixth Corps hasn't really entrenched at all."

"Exactly. I don't see a single stretch of fieldworks facing east. Not even southeast. Not one."

"Problem," Hotchkiss said, "would be getting there. Take the Front Royal road out of Strasburg to get up on that flank and they'd spot us, day or night."

Gordon ignored the caution. "Any fords up there?"

"On the creek? Or the river?"

"The river. East of the mouth of the creek. A ford where we could get ourselves on their flank."

"Find a farm by a river, find a ford. Wouldn't solve the problem of getting there, though."

"We'll have to move along the side of the mountain. In the trees."

Gordon saw Clem Evans lift a hand to his side, his wound. Clem had been game, but the climb, for which their riding boots had not been suited, clearly had pained him. Hellfire, it had been the Devil's own ordeal for all of them, scrambling over rocks on all fours and forcing their way through thickets for hours, then tracing the ridgeback, thirsty and exhausted. Gordon had felt the strain of his own wounds, healed years before.

Worth it, though.

"Don't see how," Hotchkiss said. "River hugs the mountain tight as a corset."

"Crook's boys did it to us at Fisher's Hill."

"Smaller mountain," Hotchkiss said. "And there wasn't a river to be crossed twice, once when we set out, then right under Sheridan's nose."

Burning with visions of how a splendid battle could be won, Gordon let impatience rule his voice. "For God's sake, Jed! *You're* the one who wanted me to climb up here. *You* knew Early's scheme wouldn't work, before we saw all this. And here before us, welcome as revelation, is a potential Marathon, a Plataea. And you're a naysayer?"

"Not a naysayer, General. Just raising a few details. Details do have a way of troubling plans, seen enough of that." He kicked a disguise of leaves away from a rock. "I agree this has a beckoning look. I just don't see how to get where we need to go."

"Got to be a way," Clem Evans said. Fire had kindled in his voice, too.

"We'll *find* a way," Gordon insisted. "Jed, we'll find a way, you know we can. But you need to be with me, locking arms, when we put this to Early. If it's me alone . . ."

Hotchkiss nodded. "I'm with you. That's not the question."

"What we need," Gordon told them, "is one more day. Early's impatient, we all know rations are short. But we need a good stretch of daylight to find a trail, a back road, anything. Find a way to pass Strasburg without being seen. Then find a ford that can cross, say, half the army."

A fusillade of yellow leaves crackled toward them.

"I'll pray on it," Evans said.

October 17, 8:00 p.m.
Belle Grove plantation

It's the right thing to do," Emory insisted. "Early's no threat, he's finished."

Horatio Wright was doubtful. Sheridan had left him in command for the duration of his hasty excursion to Washington. The responsibility weighed more heavily than Wright had expected.

"What do you think, George?" he asked Crook.

Crook lowered a near-empty glass. Taking their ease at the day's end, the generals were sharing a dose of whiskey. None drank heavily, and Wright only sipped his ration.

"Well," Crook said, "I suppose I have no objection. The men are tired. Lord knows, they've done good service."

"If I saw the least danger, I'd be the first to oppose it," Emory argued. The firelight glinted orange in his red hair.

The fire was welcome: The nights were growing cold.

And yes, the men were tired.

"I'll have the order published in the morning," Wright told them. "Too late tonight, we'd just make a hash of things."

"They'll be grateful, the boys," Emory assured him. "Standing to their weapons at two a.m. was the sensible thing a month ago. Not now, though. Campaign's over."

Crook had another taste of Virginia whiskey, the last wealth of the plantation's looted cellar. "I suppose we can let the men sleep," he said with only a slight hesitation.

October 17, 8:00 p.m.
Fisher's Hill

God almighty, Gordon," Early said. "If I offered you angel's wings, you'd cuss the feathers."

Lit by a pair of candles, the cold room reeked. An orderly had tried to build a fire, but the chimney refused the smoke, driving out the staff. Cackling at the weakness of his subordinates, Early had declined to move his headquarters.

"I wish you could have seen it for yourself." Speaking, Gordon studied the big, bent-over man, whose rheumatism had forbidden the climb. "If Jed and I find a route for the approach march, we could hit them just before dawn day after tomorrow, run right over them. Half their divisions aren't in supporting distance of one another. And every last one is facing the wrong way, the way they expect us to come. They'd go down like dominoes."

"You say." Early spit tobacco juice into the blackened fireplace. "Haven't seen them go down like dominoes yet."

"Be it on my head, if this attack fails."

"Damn you, Gordon, don't be asinine. We get ourselves whipped, it won't fall on your head. And you damned well know it."

Hotchkiss stepped in. "General Early, Sheridan's got his entire cavalry corps massed on his right. If we attack the way . . . the way we considered . . . we'd run right into them. Then the Sixth Corps would come right down on top of us."

Slowly, bitterly, Early shook his head. "Sucking at the same teat as Gordon, are you?" He grunted. "Sandie Pendleton came back from the grave, I'd take a strap to his back for getting killed."

"General Gordon's asking for one day, sir. And I believe—"

"Oh, surely. 'One day.' And let the men eat shoe leather for dinner. Except they haven't got any goddamned shoes."

"It's not as bad as that," Gordon said.

"Not *yet*." Early turned and stared at the fouled hearth. "God almighty, God almighty . . ." He wheeled again, ignoring Hotchkiss to shoot his scorn for all straight-backed, pomaded, woman-pleasing men in Gordon's direction. "All right. All right, then, *General* Gordon. You take your day. Let it never be said I was unreasonable, let that never be said." His spite overflowed toward Hotchkiss as well. "You take your goddamned day."

He clomped out of his headquarters.

Gordon and Hotchkiss looked at each other.

"I'd almost describe that as pleasant," Gordon said.

October 18, 6:30 a.m.
Fisher's Hill

Dan Frawley fried up the rancid bacon, trying to burn the stink off it. The other men took turns tossing hardtack into the spitting grease. Nichols reckoned that none of them had figured when they signed up that the day would come when they'd be pleased to eat filth.

"Give my favorite hound for a cup of coffee," Ive Summerlin said. "For half a cup." In the unfixed light, he looked more like a Cherokee than ever.

"Doubt you own a hound worth a cup of coffee," Corporal Holloway told him.

"Tell you, that's how the Yankees been whipping us lately," Tom Boyet offered. "They're all rallied up on coffee. We got none."

"Well, now," Sergeant Alderman said, "maybe you should stroll over there for a visit, bring us some back."

"I reckon that's about what Old Jube's thinking," Dan Frawley put in. "Rations need to come from somewheres, men do have to eat. And Richmond ain't no help." He shuffled the bacon in the pan. It really did stink, no matter the frying inflicted. Still, it gave off enough bacon smell to madden a man.

Nichols knew he'd eat it, even if he puked it right back up.

Returned from a visit to the trees, Lem Davis said, "Surprised we haven't gone over there already. Shows you what rumors are worth. Expected we'd take us a few Yankee haversacks, have a right full dinner."

"I don't mind staying put," Ive admitted. "Not one little bit. I'm tired of getting whupped. Early's played out."

"Too late for Early." Tom Boyet repeated the popular joke.

"Oh, we'll attack," Sergeant Alderman cautioned them all.

"Only reason we're sitting on Fisher's Hill again. Early won't try to defend it, not after last time. He means to attack, don't you worry."

"Place just makes my skin crawl," Ive said.

"That's your lice," Holloway told him.

"I wager on chiggers," Tom Boyet added. "Never had 'em worse than I did around here."

"Hand over your plates," Dan said. "Before this cooks to nothing."

Careful not to nudge a comrade aside, the men accepted their portions, a mouthful apiece.

Being a town man, Tom Boyet gagged. "I can't eat this," he said.

But he ate it, after all.

The greased-over hardtack was fouler than the bacon, but every man chawed his to a pulp and swallowed it.

"Slick a man's guts right through," Lem Davis said.

"Know who I dreamed on last night?" Holloway asked. "Zib Collins. Poor Zib."

"I dreamed about one of those big Pennsylvania gals," Ive snapped. He and Zib had been close. "Man wouldn't never sleep cold wrapped in that lard."

They all had slept cold the night before. October had grown traitorous.

A leaf floated into the frying pan that Dan had laid aside.

"Quick, fry that up!" Ive told him. "Better than this ptomaine fatback, I bet."

Dan picked the leaf from the pan and considered it. As if he really might take a bite.

Dreams. Nichols did not want to think about dreams, not about Zib and not about big, fat Dutch girls. He'd rather eat slops.

His night-world had grown violent and grisly, haunting him into the light near every day. That night, he had dreamed that his home was burning down with his ma inside. Chained by the unholy laws of sleep, he had only been able to watch, immobile and helpless. Other dreams of late had been much worse.

In his dreams the dead were not angels. And twice he had met a living woman in sleep, an unclothed woman, whose body was riddled with snakes like a cheese with worms. He dreamed of being hunted, never of hunting. Even his fondest night thoughts brought him shame.

Despite sharing blankets with Ive, he had lain awake shivering after that dream of fire. With his ma burning in a Hell made by men with torches. He did not think he'd cried out, though. That was something. In the depths of the night, sleepers shouted as they struggled with their dreams. At times, you heard whimpers in voices that surprised you. Strong by day, men shrank in the dark, and outbursts that once would've made for a morning of ribbing passed without comment. At dawn, men met each other's eyes less often and hands trembled over tin plates.

Rising, Tom Boyet declared, "'Fraid I'm coming down with the trots again."

Seemed like just about everyone had the bloody runs on and off. Nichols had been fortunate so far. He ascribed his good luck to nearly dying back in that Danville hospital: Maybe once you had it really bad, it didn't come back. Kind of like the measles.

"Lord, for a cup of coffee," Ive lamented. "Wouldn't care how fast it scoured my guts."

Elder Woodfin appeared, lugging the big Bible he favored in camp. The chaplain had grown a touch softer of late, just on the rough side of pleasant. Lem believed he was jealous of General Evans, whose sermons raised a man's spirits instead of whipping him into a corner and keeping him there. Elder Woodfin's homilies were ferocious, hard enough to kill any Yankee in earshot, but they weren't always a comfort.

The chaplain squatted close enough to the fire to borrow some warmth.

"I want you boys to recall Psalm One Forty-four today. I'll speak it out, and you're welcome to recite with me." He looked sternly at Nichols, demanding allegiance.

Leaves charged over the knoll.

"*Blessed be the Lord my strength*," the chaplain began, "*which teacheth my hands to war,* and *my fingers to fight . . .*"

Nichols recited along. He had his psalms near perfect.

Fueled by the Word, Elder Woodfin's voice gained power. "*Bow thy heavens, O Lord, and come down; touch the mountains, and they shall smoke . . .*"

Eager, Nichols plunged ahead: "*Cast forth lightning, and scatter them: shoot out thine arrows, and destroy them.*"

Elder Woodfin smiled with big brown teeth. Dan and Lem kept up fair, forgetting bits but then rejoining the psalm as it rolled past the "hurtful sword" and on to the plea: "*Deliver me from the hand of strange children, whose mouth speaketh vanity . . .*"

That stretch baffled Nichols every time: Weren't children supposed to be innocent? Up to no good sometimes, even downright nasty, but why did children trouble David enough to nag his psalm? How could a warrior-king be frightened of brats? Couldn't folks back then just take a strap to them?

Had "strange children" haunted David's dreams?

Sun tore the haze. It would be another fine, God-given day. They would not fight.

Nichols decided to fix his mind on the last line of the psalm: "*Happy* is that *people whose God* is *the Lord.*"

He and his brethren were the Lord's people, weren't they? Surely they would be happy when God was ready.

October 18, 10:00 a.m.
Bowman's Ford

Yankees are like to shoot us, they catch us in these duds," Hotchkiss said cheerily.

Pausing to scrape the soil with his hoe, Gordon grinned and told him, "Not me, Jed. Generals only get shot on the battlefield. Otherwise, we're protected by the gods and a certain etiquette." He cleared his throat portentously. "But a lesser fellow now, one who might not possess such august rank . . . were such a one caught in civilian clothes, he'd have some explaining to do. I'd put in a word for you, though."

"I'd take that kindly."

Shifting his stance, Gordon caught a mighty whiff of the rags he wore. Vermin were a given. Surely this day would count among the sacrifices he'd offered up to the Cause.

"Let's go on a ways," he told the mapmaker.

Careful not to appear in a hurry, they puttered down the harvested field, stopping now and again to prod the soil, as if its condition demanded close inspection. Glimpsed through gaps down in the trees, the sun glinted off the Shenandoah's brown waters.

Gordon halted sharply—more abruptly than he meant to.

Feigning interest in the earth again, he asked, "See them?"

"Two. Midstream."

"Right. Water's at least a foot below their stirrups."

"Farmer wasn't lying."

"In my experience," Gordon said, "the sons of Ceres don't lie. But they do prevaricate upon occasion."

"Don't waste soap and water on their clothes, either," Hotchkiss noted. "Won't mind parting with this fancy dress."

"Go on back up. Get your uniform on and head back to camp, catch up with Ramseur. But start off slow, they're watching us."

"What about you?"

"Just visiting that fork over by the tree line. Tug a branch across the far trail, block it. So we don't stray off tonight. Things do get confusing in the darkness, and I can't risk posting a guide this close to the ford."

"I could do it for you," Hotchkiss told him.

"You go on. I need to have another look at things."

"Be careful, sir."

Gordon smiled. "I don't intend to frequent a Yankee prison, I assure you. Fanny's reaction, I fear, would be intemperate." He became very much the general again. "Go on back, I'll catch up. And if I don't, tell Early about the trail and about this ford. Ramseur will back you now, he saw enough. Convince him, Jed." He gave his scalp a respite from the borrowed straw hat. "We can beat Sheridan bloody, smash his army. Early just has to have faith."

October 18, 10:15 a.m.
Bowman's Ford

You're a farmer," the cavalry corporal told his companion.

The river streamed around their horses' legs.

"Yup," the cavalry private agreed.

"And I'm a farmer," the corporal said.

"Yup."

"Ever see farmers act like those two fellers?"

"Nope."

"Can't figure out what they're doing."

"Ain't farming." The private spit into the stream. "And them two ain't no farmers."

"That's what I been trying to tell you, Amos."

"Didn't need telling."

"Captain Heurich might need telling. Rebs might be up to something."

"No good telling that bullheaded Dutchman anything," the private said.

"We're down here to 'observe.' And I'm observing."

"That man won't listen, though. He don't listen no more than a widow's mule. Afraid to stir things up."

"Well, I reckon we'll report and see what happens."

The private shook his head, watching the pair in the high field go their separate ways.

"Them two ain't no farmers," he repeated.

October 18, 2:00 p.m.
Near Winchester

Sheridan cursed Halleck. The two engineers imposed on him, the fat colonel and the lean, may have been wonders at planning fortifications for Halleck's fantasies, but neither man could ride a horse worth a damn. He watched them bounce in their saddles as he and his retinue waited for them to catch up.

Wary of any men on horseback, a string of darkies paused in their search for bodies. After a month, the battlefield still held secrets. And it stank.

"You boys!" Sheridan yelled. He pointed. "Get down in that ditch there and look. That's where soldiers would be."

The crew had collected a wheelbarrow-load of leathers, brass, and weapons. A decayed corpse in blue rags topped the load. Sheridan wondered briefly whether the coloreds put to such labor felt all that a white man would. He decided it didn't matter.

The fatter engineer beat the lean one to Sheridan.

"This is simply marvelous!" he declared. "Seeing the battlefield like this, right at your side, sir! It's all so complex, the defiant geometries . . . so different from the newspapers."

"I expect so," Sheridan said through gritted teeth. "How about my winter lines? Any recommendations?"

Joining them, the lean colonel struggled to master his horse. He had no idea how to manage the reins except by yanking them. Sheridan decided not to offer advice.

"Oh, we'll have to consult the maps for that. Make calculations."

"You could've consulted maps in Washington."

"General Halleck thought—"

"I know what General Halleck thought." Sheridan cut him off.

Sweating grandly, the portly colonel said, "These manly pursuits do tire one, do they not, sir? After a time, the eye doesn't see so acutely. . . ."

You'll see your dinner sharp enough, Sheridan figured. Recalling the old debt he owed Henry Halleck, though, he refrained from calling the engineers "worthless bastards."

"You've got my attention," Sheridan snapped. "I suggest you two make use of it. Tired or not. I can't spare any more time after today, there's an army to lead."

Without further comment, he spurred Rienzi off across the fields, letting the others follow as best they could. The previous afternoon had been squandered on a slow ride from Martinsburg as the two engineers fought to stay in their saddles and pestered him with questions. Now this precious day had been wasted, too: By the time all this nonsense was done, it would be too late to ride down to Belle Grove and rejoin the army.

First thing after breakfast, though, he intended to be in the saddle.

October 18, 2:00 p.m.
Fisher's Hill

No time to waste," Early told the assembled generals. "You've got the details, so let's review this quick and get the men ready." He glanced toward Gordon with less than his normal distaste. "Gordon commands the right wing. Until we all join back up. Right wing consists of Ramseur's Division and Pegram's, along with Gordon's mongrels under Evans." He grimaced, unable to help himself. "For this goddamned plan to work, Gordon has to move half this army across the river at dark and pass the woods Indian file. *Then* cross again east of Sheridan before dawn. Tall order. But I expect everybody to make this work." He looked around the room and repeated, "Everybody."

He curled toward Kershaw and Wharton, the two division commanders he'd oversee personally. "Kershaw, you're going to sweep right over that division they got dangling, catch 'em snoring and farting. Keep the rest of the Federals looking south. While Gordon comes down on their heads like bats in the shitter."

He grunted, clearing his throat of phlegm and grudges. "On Kershaw's left, Wharton advances along the Valley Pike, followed by the artillery when ordered—everything's got to be boneyard quiet, so no wagons, not even ambulances. Not until the attack's begun to grip." He nodded, as if weighing a small matter, then returned to the plan. "Wharton seizes the Cedar Creek bridge, takes the high ground, then he keeps on moving."

With a smirk, he turned to Rosser. "Who knew the Laurel was a running vine, hah? If they don't take off again, Rosser's jockeys will fix the Yankee cavalry on our left, keep the bastards occupied. I want the Yankees looking every which way. All understand?"

The assembled generals murmured what passed for agreement. Early turned to Gordon. "Anything else?"

"Bears repeating," Gordon said, "that soldiers are to leave behind their canteens, cups, bedrolls, and any bayonets without full scabbards, anything that could make the least noise or slow a man. And no talking, to include officers. As far as the right wing goes, Jed Hotchkiss is out setting in guides at every point where the column could make a wrong turn, up to the Front Royal road, above the river. I'll lead myself after that, I've walked the ground."

He caught himself in an oversight: "And no horses for officers, not even generals. Not until we're all across that river. Horses can follow the last of the infantry. One obstreperous horse could ruin everything, we need silence." He judged the gathered faces, finding bloodlust, impatience, and at least a few traces of doubt. "Any matters not resolved to your satisfaction, gentlemen?"

"Boys are going to come out of that water cold," Pegram said. "Nights have gone chill. And you have them crossing twice."

Gordon shrugged. "No choice. Don't worry, they'll move faster to warm up." He scratched his head, still purging refugees from the farmer's clothes. His answer hadn't satisfied Pegram, but all he could add was, "Speed will be everything, catch them in their tents. Keep moving, head for Belle Grove, take their headquarters. Tear their army apart before they're even awake." And pray to the Lord it works, he told himself. "Other questions?"

"John," Ramseur spoke up, "earlier, you said Payne's cavalry would meet us up along the Front Royal road. To clear the vedettes at the river and cover our flank. I'm assuming they'll have their horses? Which means there'll be noise, no matter what we do."

"Payne's taking a roundabout route, something of a feint. I've warned him to keep things quiet near the river." Gordon forced a smile. "Not sure those nags of his have the grit left to make much fuss."

There were no more questions. With orders to step off the moment darkness fell, every general wished to rejoin his troops, to set things in motion, and not to be the delinquent blamed for disaster. If disaster there was to be. And several men doubted the plan, that much was evident.

Plenty of fight in them, though. Gordon could feel it. They only needed a taste of winning again.

October 18, 9:30 p.m.
Belle Grove

Only a few more, sir," the aide commiserated.

Horatio Wright yawned. He had expected Sheridan back, but word had just come that the army commander would remain in Winchester overnight.

Unlike Sheridan. Had something gone wrong in Washington?

Well, there was always something wrong in Washington. And Sheridan was welcome to this job, he couldn't come back soon enough for Wright. For all his experience as a corps commander, he hadn't realized the full extent of an army commander's less inspiring duties. The paperwork never ended, nor did the irksome demands on a fellow's time.

Fighting a corps was a far better proposition.

He caressed his tired eyes with thumb and forefinger. "All right," he told the aide, "go on. I'll stop you if I want to read anything through."

The aide bent close to the candles sheathed in glass. "Cavalry vedettes report a pair of men dressed as farmers acting queer. Across the river, near the Front Royal road."

"Never knew a farmer who wasn't odd," Wright said. "Go on to the next report."

Ripping leaves from a screen of trees, the wind needled wet soldiers. After a maddening scare stirred up by Pegram, the right wing had made its first crossing of the river and thousands of men filed along the mountainside trail in careful silence. As if each of them grasped what was at stake.

This was a last chance, the last good chance.

Gordon tried to pay attention to each step and every crushed leaf, but he found his thoughts returning to Jubal Early. The old man had not resisted his final plan, not for a moment. It was as if Early had run out of spleen. And Gordon had truly seen Early, really seen him, for the first time in weeks, if not months. He had found a sharply aged man, with beleaguered eyes retreating under the barricades of his eyebrows. The skin around those eyes was tense and ruined, and Early's hair had grayed markedly. Only his beard remained unchanged, as crusted and foul as ever.

Seeing the man so clearly had startled Gordon. It was as if he saw not flesh and blood, but a specter, a shade, of the nemesis with whom he had quarreled so bitterly. He'd never seen a being so worn through. Not with the mundane weariness of men marched or fought to exhaustion, but with a depletion of the very soul.

Gordon stumbled over a root. And as he regained his balance he came to his senses: Pity was an emotion for women and fools.

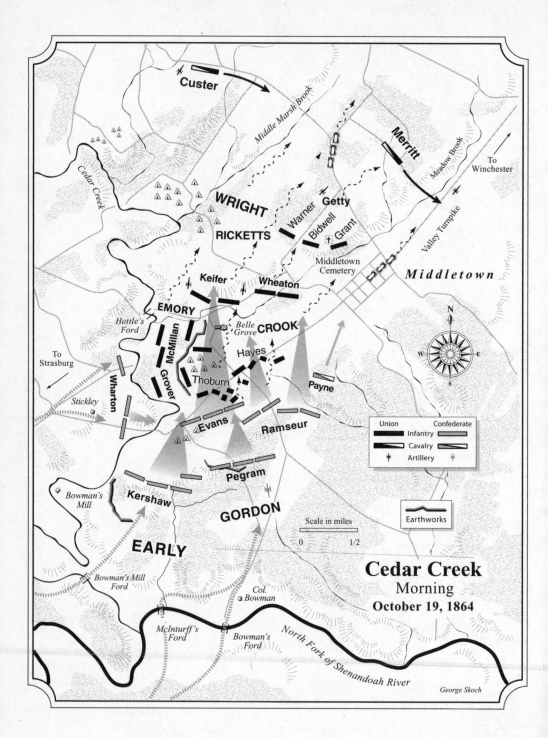

Custer

Merritt

To
Winchester

Middle Marsh Brook

Meadow Brook

WRIGHT

Warner   Getty

RICKETTS

Bidwell   Grant

Valley Turnpike

Cedar Creek

Middletown
Cemetery

Middletown

Keifer

Wheaton

EMORY

Hottle's
Ford

McMillan

Belle
Grove   CROOK

To
Strasburg

Grover

Hayes

Thoburn

Payne

Wharton

Stickley

Evans

Ramseur

N
W   E
S

Bowman's
Mill

Pegram

Union   Confederate
            Infantry
            Cavalry
        Artillery

Kershaw

GORDON

Scale in miles

0   1/2

Earthworks

EARLY

Cedar Creek

Bowman's Mill
Ford

Col.
Bowman

Morning
October 19, 1864

McInturff's
Ford

Bowman's
Ford

North Fork of Shenandoah River

George Skoch

EIGHTEEN

Gordon stopped. It just looked wrong. He was certain he'd drawn that branch across the right fork, not the left.

Behind him, three divisions lurched to a halt. Cold air prickled.

He looked again, rubbed his eyes, tried to remember. He had slept little for days and used his body hard. He feared his mind had slipped.

Mist spooked up from the river and gathered into a fog, evoking that desperate morning at Spotsylvania. No spitting rain this day, though, only stillness. He remembered, too, his mammy's tales of bottomland hants in the haze, her nigger belief in the mischievousness of the dead. Well, if the Lord granted, *this* mist would be a friend to living men, concealing them from murderous Yankee eyes.

He shuddered nonetheless. The cold, he told himself. Although he was not wet through like the men, at least not yet. He had ridden across the first ford as they set out, only thereafter surrendering his horse. He had permitted himself that indulgence.

He thought of the six thousand men and more shivering behind him, gripped by the mist.

Major Jones of his staff eased up beside him. "Something wrong, sir?" he whispered.

"Maybe. Go on back up to that cabin, last one we passed. Roust the farmer. Ask him whether the left fork here leads down to the ford, or if it's the right one. I swear that branch moved."

The imprecision of weariness marked Gordon's mouthing. He consoled himself that it would be all right, once they went forward. The excitement would revive him. It always did.

The wind had fled, but its rear guard troubled the leaves. He was glad of that: The autumnal rasp covered the sound of the men, their rustling and sharp breathing.

Gordon waited. No point explaining the halt. Just make a fuss, spark worries. They'd go forward when they went forward.

Still, time pressed. He longed to strike a match, to check his watch, but dared not do so. His wing of the army had to be across the river and up on the high ground, a mile past the ford, and ready to advance at five a.m.

Around him, officers waited in silence, unasked questions heavy in the air.

Mist wet Gordon's cheeks, his brow.

A shadow approached, pushed along by a gust. Ramseur, recognizable by his shoulders. That old familiarity.

"Yankees?" Ramseur whispered. His division would cross here, led on by Gordon, with Pegram trailing. Clem Evans would take another ford a few hundred yards upstream, guided by a soldier of local blood.

"No Yankees yet," Gordon assured him. He smiled, wryly, in the haunted darkness. There had been an embarrassing incident back a stretch, when scouts reported two Yankee pickets just ahead, far from where the Federals should have been. The column had halted and Jones had led a party forward to capture them, only to surround two cedar bushes.

They were all tired. Worn. Seeing things.

And hungry, the men were hungry. He knew that, too.

But they would fight.

Gordon tapped the ground with the toe of his boot. What was delaying Jones? Had he managed to get himself lost? Were things already awry?

"This fork here," Gordon explained to Ramseur, his voice a conspirator's whisper. "Seems I've confounded myself. Thought I'd laid that branch the other way." He yawned, sighed, shivered. "I sent Jones back to inquire."

"John?"

"Yes?"

Ramseur stepped breath-smell close. "I've got an ugly feeling. I know it's foolish . . ."

"About the attack?"

Gordon felt more than saw the morbid shake of Ramseur's head. "I have never given credence to presentiments," the new father said. "They're un-Christian. Unless a man's a prophet, a claim I'd stay shy of. I have this feeling, though . . ."

"Come on, Dod. We're all tired."

"I believe I'm going to die today."

Gordon almost raised his voice, but hushed himself severely. "That's nonsense. And you know it." He wished he could deploy his jovial laugh, the studied tone that warmed men. "Tonight, we'll be drinking up Phil Sheridan's brandy, reclining like Roman dandies at Belle Grove. Toasting our victory. *And* the newest member of the Ramseur clan."

The young division commander was not to be jollied. "Lord have mercy on me, I hope you're right."

"Don't doubt it." He gripped Ramseur's shoulder. "Hardly like you to be melancholy, Dod. But, then, I've been standing here wondering if I'm in my right mind myself." He let go of the wool cloaking muscle and bone. "Been a long night. With a long day ahead."

"Surely."

"I'm going to tease you unmercifully tonight." Gordon smiled, though it would not be seen. "All this gloom and glumness . . . while our dear, embattled Confederacy, *couchant*, demands the cool perspicacity and martial gifts of Stephen Dodson Ramseur."

A better tone colored Ramseur's soft reply: "Remember when Beauregard called your bluff and spoke to you in French?"

"I recall the laughter. But that Creole patter is hardly the tongue of Napoleon. Hugo himself would have begged for a translation."

"John, were you ever properly spanked as a child?"

Jones returned, almost colliding with Gordon. The fog had grown heavy, wetting the leaves underfoot.

"It's the left fork, sir. It's the left one, all right. Farmer moved that branch himself, fetching a load of firewood."

Gordon dragged the branch clear with his own hands.

"On such twists of fortune," he whispered to his companions, "the fate of kingdoms turns. Dod, get your boys moving."

He began to feel a refreshing thrill of energy, a rekindled alertness.

Passing back the reminder to maintain silence, he led the column downward, pushing through the wet gauze of the air, feeling his way along wagon ruts, next thing to blind.

Somehow, the men brought it off. They were veterans, soldiers who had survived this long because of an extra sense they had developed, a wordless awareness of what must be done just when. The Indian files had become double files back up at the Front Royal road. Now the men eased into columns of fours and regiments sidled into fields, letting full divisions edge up to the river.

They were so close they could hear the jingle of tack when a Yankee sentinel's horse stirred in midstream. Now and then a voice cracked the silence as one Federal hailed another, pretending to joke but wanting a comrade's assurance in the fog.

Gordon sent Jones and another officer back to make certain the farm track was clear of soldiers for Payne's horsemen. When they returned, Billy Payne himself was with them, though on foot.

After whispered greetings, Gordon asked, "Ready?"

"I reckon," Payne said. "Go in?"

"Have a watch? That works?"

"My pappy's. Right here in this pocket."

"Your men? They're up on the road?"

"On the road, sir."

"When you get back up there, get under what cover you can and check the time. I need you to hit that water at four thirty, on the minute. So I can get these boys here up on that high ground by five."

"Going to be some cold soldiers. That there water."

"They'll forget it when the shooting starts. Speaking of shooting, this has to go quickly, Billy. As little firing as possible. I need this to pass for a blow-over of nothing, pickets with the jumps. And quiet again."

"Do what I can, General."

"Virginia won't let this army down, I know it."

"I'd best git."

"Glad your boys are with us," Gordon told him. "You go on."

And they waited. Quailing cold in a fog that clung like syrup. Starting at the occasional neigh of a mount out in the ford, at a Yankee complaint of *"Verdammt noch mal."*

Jones sidled up and asked, "Want me to have your horse brought up, sir? Right behind Payne's boys? Won't make any extra fuss."

It was tempting. Gordon felt no particular desire to feel cold water gush into his riding boots. But he answered, "No. Not until we get across the river."

The soldiers had to see him beside them, bearing the same cross. Even if hardly a dozen men would spot him in the fog, that dozen would pass along the word that "Gordon was right there with us, right there in that river. I'm telling you, boys, he wasn't high and mighty up on no horse. Got wet as a private."

Part of leadership was the naked lie that you were like them. The other part was the lie that you were a god.

At last, he heard muffled hooves descending, Billy Payne's Virginians. The cavalry colonel paused for a clip off a moment, telling Gordon, "Best git on with it, I expect." His voice smiled: Payne was a scrapper. "Then see if we can't set off and bag Sheridan, stuff that little feller in a sack."

The colonel mounted and, behind him, his men eased up into

their saddles. Gordon barely heard the tiny spur clinks, the slap of cloth-bound man-meat on worn leather. Faint snaps told of opening holsters as pistols slithered out.

For one last instant, the world held its equilibrium.

Payne spurred his horse.

4:40 a.m.
McInturff's Ford

That water. Hard as iron, devil-cold. A greedy river, tugging you on in as you plunged ahead, grabbing your wicked parts. And you still shaking and chattering from your half-dunking hours before, never quite dried out, rags gripping you like they wanted to squeeze out all your juice, maybe your blood. Smack into that water you went, pressed on by hundreds of others, the water cold as a dead-of-winter creek back in dear Georgia and this only October, damn Virginia, damn every place but home.

Trying not to slip and get full wet, the soles of your shoes worn thin as those wet leaves back along the trail, holes inviting the water to bite flesh, begging stones to bruise and the mud to fool your footing. Splashing through that unpardonable cold, that heathen-heart chill, jostled and driven by men back of men, all of them rampaging forward, gasping at the first shock of that water, then breathing fiercely as they strove to cross, and you trying to keep upright, with Sergeant Alderman hush-voiced, but maybe not hushed enough, telling every man to keep on moving, to get on through, just get on through it, and you didn't need no encouragement, but you did want to thrust the butt of your rifle into whoever was shoving you from behind, even if it was a good man, even a friend. Your soul grew wicked.

Fog burdened the river, clotted cotton.

Shooting was done, though. Over quick. Cavalry had gone in, thrashing the water without their usual *yip-yip-yip*ping, just a flurry of oaths and pistol shots, then it was done, the Yankee sentinels vanquished, but every man facing that river punished nonetheless, simply for being alive in the not-quite-morning, for violating some unknown commandment, descending into the make-a-tired-man-weep embrace of that river, every last soldier afoot envying, hating, despising the cavalry up on their rude nags, those lucky men who might get splashed—perhaps even annoyed—but not wet through like the brave and mortified infantry, the only consolation being that General Evans submitted himself to the same misery as the aggrieved rest of them, a Christian martyr, a Peter, pushing on through that water all raw and heedless, through a gurgling flow that surely was as far from the Jordan as a man could get, unless he reached the Potomac, that hell-water. Who among them then could be a Judas and turn back, when General Evans himself displayed such fortitude, and him bedeviled, as all men knew, by his wound from the Monocacy?

You gripped, slipped, climbed up from the water, mud-sheathed from thigh to wretched shoes, lucky to be among the first regiments across—Dear Jesus, thank you—because that bank was going to churn into a pigsty, its earth hewn by a thousand feet, by thousands. And yet, how silent! As the officers guided you—everyone shivering, body-sorrowed, running now—along a track that followed the river for some hundreds of yards, and that earth dissolving foot-pressed, too, there was no yelling, no bold hollering, just a great, queer rustle, a threshery, as an army of ghosts swarmed through the fog.

As you pant along, you see nothing much, just those closest now, all got into a regular column of fours, as if by the spell of a wisewoman from the swamps, like Widow Kirby, a crone embowered in some back, black shack every nigger avoided, her eyes of strange milk, her flesh indecent, her spells unholy (although unhappy womenfolk sought her out), and maybe that was war, the work of some monstrous sorceress contending with the Lord, for surely war was not *His* work, not this war, so far from sanctity, no matter what men said, and you knew that, you knew it now, in the cold, black morning you had to admit it, maybe the Lord wasn't on nobody's side, it was all just men doing unto others this terrible

way, and black, black, black—let morning come—with General
Gordon suddenly there, beside the misbegotten, wayward course
that led uphill now, General Gordon saying, softly, softly, firmly,
"Up that hill, boys, up that road! Going to have us a portion of
Yankees for breakfast!"

John Gordon, a Joshua.

And not a shot, not a whimper, from the Yankees? Where were
they, where were they? Couldn't find a hog with a lantern in this
burying fog, so you just followed the man in front of you, Dan
Frawley this time, and your wet woolens gripped you viciously,
shrinking you all up, but, by God, you had had the wits to keep
your rifle, your cartridges, the things that mattered, dry, and you
were glad of that much because you were mean, made mean, chilled
to meanness, and after all this let the Yankees look out, for there
was a wildness, a contagion, a heart-swell of hatred in the air, in
this cold, enshrouded air, and you and your kind made not the
sound of a herd, but only the slap-patter of an unnatural rain
tapping the earth, a muted deluge of footfalls, where were the
Yankees?

So darned cold.

You ran forever, maybe twenty minutes. The ground leveled
somewhat and you sensed—didn't see—that you were no longer
among trees, but advancing between fields, high fields, and the
regiment puckered, forming up, a smaller thing than it had been
in gay springtime, but still willing. Sergeants hissed like cotton-
mouths with stripes, and the order went down the line to load and
you did, keeping the ramrod's tinkle as quiet as haste allowed, but,
still, with thousands and thousands of ramrods in play, surely the
Yankees heard them?

"I'd shoot the man dead who thought up this adventure," Tom
Boyet, town-learned, whispered, but every man knew that he would
not, that he was just gnawed on by misery, like the rest of them.

Captain Kennedy walked by, another ghost, a ghost among
thousands of ghosts, saying, "Shoulder to shoulder men, maintain
your order, stay together now."

And you were off, rifle ready, strutting through distempered fields, through a wanton world ungleaned, *shish-shish-shish*ing along, all those feet beyond yours, wet feet, attached to the lowest extremities of sharp-faced, hard-eyed men, blinded by fog thick as any battle smoke, but ready to kill and yearning.

Trees broke your ranks, a shallow windbreak of trees. Black trunks loomed, branches stabbed. Sodden leaves, dawdling on low limbs like ticks, fixed to your cheek, your hands, until you freed yourself. You and your brethren formed up again, the action instinctive, protective. And you felt the pulse of the great gray beast of which you were one small part, and you knew a hint of light was overdue, the solace of morning, but the world was bandaged by this soggy mist.

Shots. Distant shots. A fuss of them. Off to the left, front and left. *That* would wake the Yankees, get them ready.

Officers and sergeants chided men onward.

The distant riflery faded. And resumed. You imagined you heard voices, Rebel yells.

Then you really did hear them. Close. Perhaps a brigade away. You were running, howling yourself, plunging into the fog, ripping open its belly.

Firefly-brevity rifle flame. Glimpsed once, thrice, a dozen times, the blinking chased by loud cracks. A pathetic volley faded into more yelling than shots and quick metal clashes. Bewildered voices pleaded. You stumbled over a root.

Not a root, but a stand of Yankee rifles. They crashed down. Yankees, up close, weaponless, ape-dumb in their unmentionables. Astonished in the glow of smoldering campfires.

Tents. Men kicked the pegs and slashed ropes as they ran past, trapping grunting occupants and firing merrily into the squirming canvas, damning the doomed to Hell. Yankees appeared with their hands up high, but some got belly-shot anyway—the cold, the anger—and one fellow dropped to his knees, praying to the Lord, his reward a rifle stock swung into his mouth.

You just went on, funneled through scrupulous tent lines,

guided by the glow of more fires, some tamped, some blazing for breakfast.

Screaming. Joyous. Lewd with death inflicted.

Those cackling around you ordered Yankees caught barefoot to walk rearward. You joined in, mocking, almost unknown to yourself in your spirit's cruelty: Let *them* learn what it was like to suffer.

Transformed into sheep, the blue-bellies obeyed, every last living one of them. A few of your own kind broke off to rummage through the tents.

You ran on, raw of throat but yowling and yiking like a dog at full moon, a mad dog. And you came upon one perfect rank of Yankees, ready and disciplined, waiting to fire. Except that they were facing just the wrong way and you and your war-kin swarmed over them, soon colliding with some of Ramseur's misdirected men, touchy, snarling, possessive of this earth, though no one knew where they were, not really.

A sergeant lined the broken Yankees back up and set them to marching, weaponless, deep into Dixie.

Let *them* feel hunger, let *them* feel cold.

No end of Yankee camps, but no real fight. Fog thick as frosting on a holiday cake. One cannon boomed, then another, their reports pay-attention close. You couldn't spot the muzzle-flames.

Ive Summerlin, charging ahead, rifle shifted to his left hand now, a Yankee coffeepot waving in his right. He drank from it as he ran, surely scalding himself and caring no whit, sloshing the precious brown liquid down through his beard and over his uniform, a man in ecstasy.

A volley. Near. A soldier toppled face-first into a campfire and did not move until a comrade dragged him off by the ankles, disbelieving his death until he turned his friend over and read the seared flesh and baked eyes. But the Yankee volley had done more harm to a herd of disarmed blue-bellies.

At last, the gray-flannel light softened to rich pearl.

You shot a man as he turned his rifle on you. Chest-shot, eyes startled, thick brows and beard, falling. His rifle clattered.

Howling, you clamored back into your clan and Dan Frawley said, "Georgie, get yourself a cup. Be quick."

And soon you were running forward again, slopping glorious, wondrous coffee all over yourself as you glugged it down, rendered as mindless as Ive, scorching your throat, your tongue, and not caring at all, the pain magnificent, quickening.

And then the cup was empty and discarded. You joined a line and added to a volley, aiming loosely at shadows a curse away. Dead and wounded Yankees lay underfoot, while others, unmanned, pleaded not to be shot. Chased by exultant demons, their comrades ran.

Officers sought to guide you, to maintain some hint of order, but the most effective means to keep things going was just to let you and your kind stick to yourselves.

You shot at a mounted officer, a full-bearded man in a dark frock coat who was pointing out positions to his men, struggling to rally them. You hit the horse, not the man, but the beast bucked and threw him.

It sounded like a proper battle now, with packs of Yankees here and there attempting to fight back and cannon firing blindly into the fog, contributing smoke.

"Great Jehovah!" Corporal Holloway called, just as you smelled something glorious in the war-stink. Ignoring a pair of befuddled Yankee cooks, Holloway flaunted a skillet of thick-cut pork—not bacon, but salt pork, maybe even fresh—that had been fried up for some officers' mess. Or maybe Yankee privates ate like that.

Men burned their fingers—you burned yours—grabbing meat from a pan black as Uncle Joe, stuffing your mouth, burning lips and tongue again, exciting blisters and swallowing unchawed clumps of fire-hot meat, the worst of your wet-cold hatefulness forgot.

In a camp as tidy as a Methodist chapel, a delighted rooster of a man had rounded up a passel of Yankee bandsmen. As you and your burned-belly brethren rushed through the luminous mist, he made the Yanks play "Dixie" on their tooters, drawing Rebel yells from across the field.

You were mighty, an ancient Israelite victorious. Leaping over flattened tents, over bodies and past captives, proud at the sight of captured flags and cannon, yelling your head off.

Saved.

6:00 a.m.
Camp of Hayes' Division

Rud Hayes watched his division dissolve. What little he could see of it, anyway. He had just assured Kitching, an insolent young colonel newly attached, that his men would hold against any Reb assault, when thousands of screaming Johnnies burst from the fog behind his left flank. Stunned, the one brigade he had managed to get into line buckled, then broke and disintegrated. Now he rode among swirls of air made visible, alternately ordering and begging his men to rally. Of all the brave soldiers he had led through three years of battles, few heeded him now.

Those who did not run walked crisply rearward, avoiding his eyes. With those Rebel wails of damned souls resounding from every side, the successes he had in halting men were brief. Even his favorite horse became unmanageable.

Guided by echoes in the murk, Hayes rode toward the grumble of a battery, chiding any soldiers he encountered, but warned by a half-crazed captain with a pistol belt over his nightshirt that all was hopeless and he should save himself.

The busy guns belonged to Henry du Pont, his Ohio Lights. Firing blindly into the opacity, doing what little they could.

Reb howls erupted behind him.

How had they done it? Where had they all come from?

His horse shied from a private's shoeless body. The Johnnies hadn't wasted time with that one.

"Henry!" Hayes shouted.

The captain couldn't hear him. Du Pont was spun of pure gold, though. Seen through a rip in the fog, the artilleryman sat his horse calmly amid the storm, mouthing orders Hayes could not hear, steady as if merely drilling his men.

The guns topped a low ridge that dropped off sharply behind.

Hayes reached du Pont's side and called over the din: "Henry, hold as long as you can." Hayes caught himself and corrected his words. "I don't need to tell you that, I didn't mean that. But you're all that's left. I've been trying to rally the men, but I can't stop them."

"Lost my Pennsylvanians," du Pont shouted back.

"And the Regulars?"

Du Pont shrugged. "Don't know. Been busy here."

Although his manners were flawless, the captain was transparently impatient. Hayes grasped that he was only interfering: Du Pont knew exactly what he needed to do. And how to do it. His efforts were better spent on his unnerved men.

"All right," Hayes yelled over another cannon blast. The air moved and the gun recoiled toward them. "I'll do what I can to support you."

He rode back into the veil of fog and smoke, guessing at his direction, riding past strays in ones and twos, then, to his shocked alarm, right through a pack of Johnnies. As soon as he found himself among his own kind again, he tugged his horse about and shouted orders, but all flares of courage were fragile. The men no longer seemed to be madly panicked, but they stubbornly refused to defend this ground. As if to punish their officers for having let them down, for permitting this to happen.

To his delight, Hayes found, at last, a rough line of his men—West Virginians—waiting for the enemy.

"Just stay where you are," Hayes told their lieutenant. "Hold your position. Gather in stragglers."

That too-familiar *thwack* struck horribly close. His horse reared, then dropped on its forelegs. It all went too fast and Hayes flew off, going black the moment he thumped the earth.

Perhaps the racket woke him. He sensed that he had not been

unconscious long. He tried to gain his feet, only to collapse, hands grabbing his ankle before his brain had classified the pain.

Broken? Please, no. He tested the lower shinbone, down to the working bones and ligaments, that hard knuckle. He could have used Doc Joe, but had not seen him since the fighting began.

Quickly, Hayes fought his way to his feet, growling down his pain. His soldiers were gone. Had they thought him dead? He made an agonized effort to follow after them.

"You halt right there and surrender, you sonofabitch," a Southern voice called.

Killing close?

Hayes ran. Hobbled and ablaze with pain, he cast himself into a gnarl of trees, ignoring the penny-nail thorns. Every other step sent a shock through his body.

Bullets sought him.

In another of the morning's maddened turns, he found himself in a throng of milling soldiers, his own men.

"Boys! Come on, boys! We'll stand, we'll hold them here," he shouted, limping and hoping.

Something slammed into the back of his head, knocking him to the ground and leaving him dizzied but conscious. He understood that he had been shot and urgently thrust a paw back over his skull.

No blood. Wonderfully, amazingly. Only a stunned feeling that his head was ten times its size, plus a wild ringing and a terrible moment's loss of vision. Either the bullet had been utterly spent or its velocity had been slowed by a passage through other flesh.

During the moments required to make sense of his situation, his soldiers had fled again: A fallen commander hardly inspired courage.

An aide appeared, miraculously, from the mist, clomping forward on a roan as bullets wasped the air. He spotted Hayes and dismounted.

"You all right, sir?"

"That . . . would be an exaggeration. Good enough, though."

"They told me you were dead. I thought I should—"

"I'm not. No thanks to the Johnnies."

The aide helped him to his feet. Hayes winced and buckled. "Ankle."

"Take my horse, sir. You're more of a prize than I am."

Briefly, Hayes considered turning him down: the old notions of honor, of Walter Scott gallantry. But he saw quickly enough that rallying what remained of his division and buying time for the army to deploy—playing his assigned part—mattered far more than storybook chivalry.

"Help me up."

Hayes rode rearward, leaving the aide behind. With his head throbbing, the ankle pain sharp as a toothache when he pressed the stirrup, and visibility still a matter of yards, he did his best to gain the Valley Pike, certain that would be the line where the resolute men rallied, a marker on the landscape that made sense and promised order. And that was where the generals would be, organizing the defense and bringing up the Sixth Corps. That was where the Rebels could be stopped.

As he reckoned his way northwestward—wishing that he'd pocketed his compass—he managed to gather a few small clusters of men from his division, captains leading companies the size of water details and sergeants too ill-tempered to give up, all of them ready to follow him as long as he was heading away from the Rebels. By the time his new mount's hooves struck the hardened Pike, Hayes had rallied sixty of the fourteen hundred men who had been present for duty an hour before.

His head throbbed, leaving his vision blurred at the edges.

He worked his way up the grade of the Pike between overturned wagons and inexplicable wreckage, calling to the hundreds of soldiers drifting rearward, attempting to graft strays from other divisions to his command, to build a useful force, but the plodding soldiers ignored him.

At least he seemed to have gained some ground on the Rebs: Their racket lagged back a ways.

He found Generals Crook and Wright by the lane to Belle Grove. Crook appeared grim, and Wright's lower face was crusted with blood and dripping. They hadn't much to tell him: only that Ricketts was bringing up the Sixth Corps and that Hayes' fellow division commander Joe Thoburn was dead.

The Rebel yell crested waves of rifle fire. His head pulsed monstrously.

Appraising the shameful shred of Hayes' Division left by the roadside, Crook said, "Form your men, Rud. This fight isn't over."

7:30 a.m.
The fields of Belle Grove

Jim Ricketts coughed, spit, and said, "That goddamned Wheaton."

He knew he was being unfair. New to division command, Frank Wheaton was doing his best. They all were. Himself, he was struggling to direct a corps for the first time. But battle allowed no excuses, and in the little time Ricketts had been seeing to his own division—fighting under Warren Keifer this day—Wheaton had fed his brigades into the butcher's grinder piecemeal.

The damned Johnnies seemed to be everywhere. It was worse, far worse, than Monocacy. There you could at least see what was coming toward you.

Wright had ordered him to align the corps on the Pike, facing east and southeast, while staff officers and hangers-on hastened to pack up the headquarters at Belle Grove. At first, the danger had seemed to come from the left. Then Wheaton had his right turned, driving him back across a ravine and costing him a brigade. That tore a gap in the center of the corps. Keifer, too, was barely holding on and worried about being flanked himself.

Ricketts rode carelessly through pale fog, letting his horse sense the ground as best it could. It was not an hour for caution. Behind him, aides and orderlies, flag-bearers and a bugler, strove to keep up while avoiding the retreating men dashing here and there.

He had half a mind to ride a few down on purpose. It was the most shameful debacle since Bull Run. Of which he did not have the best of memories: Left for dead was not a pleasant condition, and thank God for Frances.

No, let the provost marshal see to cowards. Holding the Sixth Corps together amid this onslaught of chaos trumped all else.

Where had Early gotten so many men? His strength seemed to have doubled, at the very least. Had Longstreet really come, had that signal been true?

In the past, he had longed for a corps command, but granted it temporarily while encamped, he had not expected to lead it into battle. They all had agreed that Early was finished off.

Now here they were.

He yanked back on the reins so hard, his horse reared. Johnnies. Straight ahead. He'd almost galloped straight into their flank, headed directly toward that ragged red flag.

His escort cascaded to a stop around him. One man exclaimed, "Jesus Christ!"

If the Rebs were here, where the devil was Wheaton?

Correcting his course westward, he topped a crest and let his mount judge its way down a slope he half recognized. Infernal mess, all of it. Lucky if he wasn't shot down by his own men in this confusion. A guesswork battle.

Rebs had guessed better.

He jumped a narrow streambed, reading the battle by sound. He hoped Keifer had the sense to refuse his left flank now. Did he even know Wheaton had pulled back? Where the devil was he?

The only man on whom he truly could count was old George Getty. Two of a kind they were, old Regulars, unfit for parlors but steady in a fight. Getty held the high ground on the Pike just this side of Middletown, holding open the army's line of retreat.

Retreat. A damned disgrace. Conquered by scarecrows.

Too weak now to grip a hillside, the fog thinned up ahead. Ricketts saw uneven blue lines top a crest.

"There!" he shouted, pointing.

But if he could see his own men now—those had to be Wheaton's boys—he couldn't see the Johnnies, only hear their keening howls, hair-raising in the fog.

As his horse climbed the slope, the men in blue decided they shouldn't shoot him, but it looked a near thing. Even veterans kept fingers taut on their triggers. Earlier, he'd mentally chastised Wright for leading two regiments into a breach himself. The situation had been desperate—and still was—but an army's commander, temporary or not, shouldn't gad about leading tactical charges. Now here *he* was, blundering into Rebs as he searched for his lines, hardly a clever turn for a corps commander.

A drift of fog enshrouded the ridge anew.

"Where's General Wheaton? Damn it, where's General Wheaton?"

Nobody knew. But the men looked at him expectantly: He was a general, a father in uniform, supposed to be wiser than his powder-blotched sons, expected to wield secrets.

"Here they come!" somebody cried. The fellow had sharper eyes than Ricketts possessed.

Sure enough, that *kee-yip* wail rose from the streambed below, sepulchral and horrible.

Frank Wheaton materialized. "General Ricketts?"

"Frank, do you know where you are?"

"I think so."

"Smarter man than me, then. Look, you have to hold. Until Wright can rally the army." He paused. "Or bring it off."

"That bad?" Wheaton asked.

"What do you think?"

"I've lost a brigade. They broke, I'm sorry."

"I know. Don't lose another."

"It's goddamned contagious. The fear."

"So is courage."

A friendly volley punished their ears. The Rebel shrieking collapsed, but soon renewed itself. Closer now. A soldier turned to run and Wheaton shot him.

"No man runs," the Rhode Islander barked.

Ricketts grimaced but nodded. It was that bad.

"All right, Frank," he said. "Do all you can. The army's count-ing on us."

An uproar arose on Wheaton's right. As if, God forbid, the Rebs had flanked them again.

"I'd best see to that," Wheaton said.

"Get your flanks tied in. I'm heading back to Keifer." Before turning his horse, Ricketts added, "This is when we earn our pit-tance, Frank."

Scanning his shrunken escort, Ricketts called, "Owens, can you lead us back to Belle Grove?"

A former Regular with service on the Plains, the cavalryman rode up, saluted, and said, "Right to the house, sir. *If* the Rebs ain't already visiting."

"Keifer should hold them."

"Like you say, sir." The old scout led them off.

How long could the fog persist? It thinned only to thicken again, tore open to reseal itself as tight as a cholera coffin. Rick-etts had never seen anything quite like it, not on a battlefield. Even at Spotsylvania the mists had cleared as the morning grew, leav-ing men face-to-face, clubbing each other's brains out in the rain.

More cannon now. Rebs must have brought up theirs. The roar of battle menaced from three sides.

This was soldiering: not leading dashing charges on sunny days and gathering brevets, but clinging to worthless ground with un-steady men who shit in their drawers, unable to leave the firing line. Stubbornness was aces, valor a jack of diamonds.

And "stubbornness" described George Washington Getty. Getty would hold. No need to worry over his division.

Balls hissed by. It was hard to tell which side was shooting at the mounted party. Or if men were firing blindly into the mist.

In a hollow, Owens, the horn-hard old trooper, halted them.

"Ain't right, sir," he told Ricketts. "Don't feel right." As he spoke, soldiers in blue uniforms burst from the mist and streamed past them. Sixth Corps men. From Ricketts' own division. Far from where their regiments should have been.

"Turn around, damn you!" Ricketts roared. "The Rebs are tired out! Turn back, boys, and we'll whip them. . . ."

"Them Johnnies ain't tired a lick," a scurrying soldier corrected him.

But they had to be weary, didn't they? They must have been marching all night to bring this off. There *had* to be hope. If only his line could hold.

Did he still have a line?

He turned his horse in the direction from whence the soldiers had come.

The old scout called, "Sir, I wouldn't—"

A blow to the chest knocked Ricketts from the saddle. Pain grabbed his shoulder before he smacked the ground. Shock piled on shock.

"Son of a goddamn bitch," Ricketts muttered, or thought he did.

Cold earth. Warm blood.

Aides dismounted and swarmed him.

"Let me breathe . . . Christ's sake . . ."

"Get his coat open, open his coat."

"I can do it," Ricketts said. But he couldn't. Hands tore at him.

"Hold on, sir." Familiar voice. Whose voice? He couldn't see. Pillows of fog pressed down upon his eyes.

"Frances," he muttered. Then he straightened his spirit, if not his body. "Tell Getty . . . find General Getty . . . tell him he has the corps."

He had his senses again, though. The sardonic thought pierced him that he had gotten his corps command at last—and made a bloody mess of it. Well, you played the cards that fell to you and only novices at the game complained. You played your cards as well as you could and then fortune decided.

Men lifted him up amid a riot of sounds.

He wondered, as he had back on the Monocacy, what would

happen if he died. Would his spirit ascend to rejoin his first wife, Harriet? How unfair that would be to poor, dear Frances—what would become of her?

"He's gushing blood," a fearful voice exclaimed. "Put him down, we have to staunch it . . ."

He wanted to tell the lad to go to Hell. Instead he said, in a voice so calm it surprised him, "Just get me to the rear, boys. I don't have a mind to be captured again."

"Yes, sir. Sure enough, sir."

Oh, it hurt, though. He'd been shot enough times to qualify as a connoisseur of wounds, and this variety seemed uniquely painful.

"Don't worry," he said, but his voice was weaker now. "I won't die."

And he *had* resolved to live. Never liked to fold a hand too soon. He just plain resolved to live. He owed Frances that much, after all she'd done for him. But Jim Ricketts also knew the worth of mortal resolutions.

8:30 a.m.
Lost Brook

Riding his prancing black, Custer exploded from the haze, displaying himself to Merritt and his staff. Doffing his hat, the better to fling back his locks, the intruder called, "Say, Merritt! What news, old fellow?"

Not entirely pleased by Custer's advent, Brigadier General Wesley Merritt said, "Damned mess. That's evident. You should be back with your men, George."

Merritt understood exactly what Custer was about: George's division held the westernmost ground, farthest from the battlefield. George was worried that he'd be left behind to watch the flank, stranded out there, while others got into the fight and—a bane to George—gathered the laurels.

"Oh, my boys are fine." Custer winked at Devin. "How-do,

Tom? Got your Irish up?" Without waiting for a reply, he turned again to Merritt and said, "Rosser's spooked, he won't be any trouble. He's had enough for one morning. I know him inside out."

"Orders still apply, George."

Custer smiled. He had the innocent-yet-mischievous grin of a child, complete with one twisted tooth. But for all his clowning and flamboyance, Custer was a bloody-handed instrument, Merritt knew. George didn't just love to fight, he loved to kill.

"Just thought I'd see what was going on. Bit dull out where I'm stuck." Custer waved his hand toward the cacophony off to the east. In the high fields, well away from the river and creekbed, the mist was retreating. Soldiers in blue could be seen in the middle distance, fleeing as individuals or in clusters. "Ought to give them a sharp taste of the saber," Custer added. "Damned cowards."

"I've got men out there rounding them up," Merritt told him.

Merritt, too, was impatient to join the fight and couldn't understand why Torbert or even Wright hadn't sent down an order to stem what seemed a shameful defeat. Had Wright lost control entirely? Or plain forgotten the cavalry? Sheridan wouldn't have.

Merritt had concerns and ambitions aplenty, but unlike his fellow division commander, he believed in discipline and sobriety. Some of the troopers, amused by the contrast, had nicknamed the two of them "Poker-face and Joker-face." Merritt didn't mind—as long as he had the poker-face.

For his part, Custer imposed draconian discipline on subordinates, but took a long list of liberties himself. Starting with his costume, that velveteen sailor's blouse festooned with stars of ludicrous size, the red silk scarf, and the floppy hat with its coiled snakes of braid. And the hair, of course, gleaming with Macassar oil. As far as literal sobriety went, Custer wasn't a drunkard—he had that to his credit—but the joke ran that he needn't bother with whiskey, since George was drunk on himself.

"What if old Torbert's been captured? Could be why we haven't gotten orders."

"Don't be an ass, George." But Merritt felt his own impatience welling.

"What do *you* think, Tom?" Custer asked Devin. "Wouldn't *you* like to ride over and join the revels?"

Devin bristled, shrugged. Tom Devin shared his view of Custer, Merritt knew, admiring George's pluck on the battlefield, but otherwise annoyed at his shenanigans. And there was a bit of jealousy, Merritt had to concede. Not least on Devin's part. Given Tom's service record, he should have had a division long before George got one of his own. But Sheridan treated Custer as a son, if an improbable one.

For all the temptation to quarrel, they fought well together, Merritt had to admit. Rivalries had their virtues as well as their dangers.

"Halloo!" Custer called, although there was no need for shouting. The battle's noise, while troubling, was off in its box. But Custer had spotted the galloping rider first through the mist's rear guard and couldn't restrain himself. The man's exuberance was uncontrollable.

Merritt was certain the rider would carry the order to join the fight. Or at least to cover the army's withdrawal. Of a sudden, he longed, even ached, to give his men the order to remount and ride eastward at a trot. Tom Devin, too, had quickened. But Merritt maintained his outward rigor, "straight of spine and straight of deed," as his father liked to describe a worthy man.

Flinging sweat despite the morning's coolness, the courier made straight for Merritt, drawing a folded scrap of paper from his pouch and extending it before his horse had steadied.

Yes. It was an order to move north of Middletown, to establish a line, halt the rearward flow of soldiers, and block the Rebel advance.

He couldn't resist tormenting Custer, though, and kept the order to himself for a few delicious moments. He even made his face show disappointment.

George squirmed in the saddle, a child with worms.

"Anything in there for me?" Custer begged.

Merritt tightened his brow, affecting to squint at the hand-writing.

"What does it say, Wes? What does it say, are we in it?"

At last, Merritt passed the note over to Custer. "You're to leave a detachment to keep an eye on Rosser. But we're in it, George."

8:45 a.m.
The Valley Pike, south of Middletown

Brigadier General George Washington Getty still couldn't see a damned thing beyond pistol range. But he had his division in hand. He always did.

With their line crossing the Pike at a slight diagonal, his men had thrown back a flurry of Rebel assaults. But even as Getty held his ground, the army crumbled around him. He hadn't seen Jim Ricketts for an hour and guessed that he'd gone to do what he could for Wheaton.

Lew Grant, commanding his Vermont Brigade, found Getty in the white air acrid with gunsmoke.

"Sir, my flank's dangling like bait on a hook. I've sent out flankers to reestablish contact, but Wheaton's boys are plain gone."

"Gone to Hell," Getty grumped. "Bugger this whole goddamned day." Dressed with the meticulous care of a Regular, he stiffened his spine to match his starched high collar. "Going to pull back, Lew. Nothing for it. But I want no running, no disorder."

"Vermont men don't run."

"We'll see."

"Position in mind?"

"I always have a position in mind." Getty was instantly sorry he'd said that, it sounded too much like a brag. But it was true. He'd learned early on, in fighting the Seminoles, that an officer had to pay attention to every slight variation in the terrain. He'd carried that habit with him through peace and war, never occupying so much as a temporary camp without inspecting the ground for fighting positions, as if he might be attacked at any moment.

As the army had been attacked this cursed morning.

"Sounds like they're getting ready to hit us again," Grant said. "Bringing up artillery. Listen."

Getty snorted. "Probably our own guns they've captured. Sonsofbitches." He turned back to business. "Keep your alignment. We'll pull straight back, west by northwest. Get through that creek gully quick and up the other side. We'll make a stand on that ridge with the cemetery."

"Yes, sir. I know it. Good ground."

"It's the *only* ground, goddamn it. Steep slopes, clean fields of fire. I've sent orders to McKnight to shift his guns. If the earth hasn't swallowed him whole." The forty-five-year-old former artilleryman added, "Guns or no guns, we're going to hold on to those heights like a whore grips a gold piece."

"Johnnies may ignore us. Head straight north through the town and cut us off."

"They won't. Flies to honey. They'll swarm on us, wait and see." The nearest Rebs sounded truculent, ready to try them again. "Too much damned talk. Get your boys back on that ridge. In good order. I'll get the rest of this division moving." He almost smiled, but even on the best of days Getty had little capacity for mirth. "I'll be watching, Lew. To see whether Vermonters run or not."

Truth was, Getty would not have traded the Vermont Brigade for any other in the army. But it didn't hurt to give Lew Grant something to prove.

As they withdrew through the fields that dropped from the Pike, the Rebs did hit them. Twice. But the assaults were hasty and disorganized. Noisy, but not strong enough to break his division's ranks.

Lonely damned place, though. He couldn't tell if a single other division remained engaged. Ricketts' boys under Keifer had just vanished, and it didn't sound as though Wheaton was doing much. Mostly, it felt like Rebs out there in the fog—which was weakening, but still not thinned enough for aimed shots and accurate gunnery.

That was a blessing at the moment, though. The ground his men had to cover lay wide open, and the drop to the streambed waited. If the Rebs caught them down in that gully . . .

The Johnnies missed their chance. His division crossed the trickling run and made the high ground intact, as close to a miracle as the morning offered. Hard training paid in gold. Soldiers didn't like it—hell, they hated Lew Grant for trying to outdo the Regulars—but in hours such as these fierce training saved Heaven and earth: Even frightful commands were obeyed instantly.

All through his career, George Washington Getty had prided himself on executing orders promptly and fully, no matter how they grated. He expected no less of his men.

Atop the ridge, a grove stretched northward to a balding cemetery. Getty rode back and forth, without a thought for his safety, testing the ground and firming up his lines, but unable to resist supervising the positioning of McKnight's battery—which hadn't disappeared, after all.

In ten minutes, his new line was as ready as it was going to be, with Bidwell's brigade stretching northward beyond the gravestones and facing the town, Lew Grant and his Vermonters in the center where the hardest blows would land, and Warner's brigade bending back to the right, overlooking a still-invisible Belle Grove. He even had the unexpected luck of finding a brigade of cavalry dismounting to guard his right flank.

And luck mattered. Study all the books about war you wanted, but luck mattered.

He heard the Rebs before he saw them, what must have been a full division, tramping toward them, roostering their war cry in poor-white voices. Cannon fired blindly over their heads, hunting Getty's position.

"Steady, boys," he snapped. "Those sonsofbitches don't know

what they're in for. Officers, have your men lie down. No need to give the Johnnies easy targets."

He also knew that men lying down were far less apt to run, simply because of the extra effort required. Law of inertia, taught to you at West Point, though not for this purpose.

West Point. So long ago.

Just had to get the men back on their feet at the last moment. Inertia was the science, judgment the art.

What the devil had happened to Jim Ricketts? Jim was another old artilleryman, a fellow veteran of Mexico and of many a lonesome, under-rationed garrison. Getty had always felt he could count on Ricketts, despite the fuss over Fitz John Porter's court-martial—he didn't know one officer with nothing on his conscience, so he wasn't going to shun Ricketts over that business. But Jim seemed to have let the corps break up.

No point in blaming Ricketts, Getty corrected himself. Not Jim or anyone else. Blaming others was the resort of the lowest kind of officer. Just do your duty, Getty thought, and let other men see to their own concerns.

Jesus Christ, though, how had the Rebs pulled it off?

He heard them coming closer, thrashing dew-heavy grass, with their officers calling orders to straighten ranks and their intervals, shouting in accents he knew so well from the old Army they'd shared.

This war was madness.

"Steady, steady!" he called out. "Nobody rises or fires until they're within thirty yards. Just stay down, boys, and listen for your commands." He gulped breath. "Officers, do your duty. Thirty yards, thirty yards."

He'd already spoken more than his wont. His preference was to issue orders and let his subordinates see to their tasks unbothered. But this day was an exception, reeking of disaster and desperation.

And Getty didn't mean to be part of the failure.

He saw man-shadows down below, in the fog that clutched the

brook. And he listened, again, to those ever-familiar voices. They echoed from bygone garrison parades, from late night poker rounds fueled by poor cigars and poorer whiskey, handsome voices ordering men to kill him.

McKnight let them have canister. Getty felt, could not quite see, the gashes torn through the lines and the bloodied air.

"Steady!"

He knew what the men were feeling, their worry that their officers would tell them to rise too late, that the Rebs would be atop them. Training and discipline couldn't banish fear. They just helped a man resist his natural impulses.

And there they were, bursting through curls of mist, a dozen, a hundred, hundreds, banners waving, a horde of screaming men rushing up the thigh-tormenting slope, lines melting into a swarm.

He saw beards. Faces. Eyes.

"Now!"

With not a second of hesitation, his officers got the men to their feet, raced through the briefest commands, and unleashed a volley that stopped the Rebs a third of the way up the slope.

He watched, merciless and pitying at once, as gray-clad officers— brave men—lashed their soldiers with words and wielded the flat of their sabers, demanding a more-than-human effort. But their orders grew confused. Some demanded that their soldiers charge on and break Getty's lines, while others halted their men to return fire.

His own men discharged a second, disciplined volley, dropping Rebs by the score, some within ten paces.

One of McKnight's guns wheeled about to clear the slope with more canister. A round swept the Reb line diagonally. Blood cascaded, blink-quick.

A third volley from his men repulsed the attack.

His soldiers cheered. It was the first Union cheer he'd heard that day.

"Officers, see to your men. Get the stretcher-monkeys up. Prepare your lines to receive another attack. They'll come back up."

"And we'll send 'em back down again," a soldier responded, his voice Northern, flinty, formed by woodlands and mountains, an accent more foreign to an old Regular than the cawing and drawls of the enemy.

Getty rode his line northward, pausing at the highest point of the cemetery, straining to see. He did believe the mist was thinning to haze, but he'd thought the same thing earlier. *Did* seem to be patchier. He would have liked to get a look at the battlefield. But if the fog lifted and he could see the Johnnies, the Rebs would see his men, too. Exposed to their artillery.

Off in the murk, his enemies sent up a whoop. Signaling another triumph? Over whom? Or was the ruckus a greeting for some general?

He heard a voice call out his rank and name, but couldn't spot the man.

"Up here," Getty shouted. "Top of this damned boneyard." Hoping he wasn't summoning Rebel sharpshooters as well. Even in this muck of haze and smoke, he dreaded sharpshooters. Remembering Uncle John Sedgwick.

The courier, a major, found him. Getty recognized him as one of Wright's staff boys.

"General Getty? General Wright's compliments. General Ricketts has been wounded, sir. You're to take command of the corps."

"How bad's Jim hit?"

"Bad, sir. In the chest."

Getty felt an unaccustomed pang. Of course, Jim hadn't let him down. Couldn't do much with a bullet deep in your meat.

"He's a tough bugger," Getty said. "As for the goddamned corps, I don't know where it is. Just this division."

"Other side of Middletown, sir. The officers are rallying the men. General Wright wants you to—"

"Emerson's bunch? Crook's lot?"

Wary, as staff officers often were, the major hesitated. "The Nineteenth Corps is . . . there are signs that order *may* be reestablished. Given time, sir."

Well, I've goddamned well been giving you time, Getty thought. "Crook's pack?"

"Very much reduced. Not presently effective."

"Any sign of Sheridan?"

The staff man shook his head. "Not that I know of."

"Christ. Where will I find General Wright?"

"North of town, sir. Rallying the troops. He wants you to—"

"I *know* what he wants, Major. But, near as I can tell, *this* division's the only thing keeping the Johnnies from finishing what they've started."

"Yes, sir."

"Oh, bugger it. All right." Reminding himself of his boast that he never disobeyed orders, he realized that he had to leave his division. As senior brigade commander, Lew Grant would have to see this business through. Well, the men could do worse than that hardheaded bastard. Tell him to hold, and Grant would be stubborn as stones.

"All right, Major. You come along with me. Let me transfer command and we'll get going."

He spotted Grant as the Rebs swept forward again. Surprising Getty, the second assault, instead of having been reinforced, felt weaker than the first.

As he and the staff major rode up behind Grant, the brigadier cut a fine figure on his mount, hewn from cold blue granite. Getty let him fight his action, which proved blessedly brief, with the Rebs hurled back again.

Still unaware of Getty's presence, Grant rose in his stirrups, shaking his fist at the retreating Johnnies and calling, *"Vermonters don't run, damn you! Vermont doesn't run!"*

He'll do, Getty thought.

Brusquely, he told Grant, "I've got the corps, you've got the division. Hold this ground. Until I send further orders."

As he turned his horse northward, a red sun burned through the mist.

10:00 a.m.
Southern edge of Middletown

Gordon found Early just where he'd left him half an hour back. As the army reunited along the Pike, Early had resumed overall command, sending Gordon down to his division. When last seen, Early had been raving about "the sun of Middletown," as if he'd rivaled Napoleon at Austerlitz, as if that fierce red ball's abrupt appearance had been a tribute to Jubal Early from God.

Since then, the attack had withered and lost direction, and no orders had come down. Except for clumsy assaults on the Union Sixth Corps—identified on the ridge cradling that cemetery—there seemed to be no movement, no push, of significance.

That alarmed Gordon.

When he reached the army commander, Early was still grinning like a lunatic. Very much alive, "doomed" Dod Ramseur sat his horse beside him. Dod had found a white flower for his buttonhole, despite the turn of the seasons. Wharton had come up, too. It looked as though all were enjoying a pleasant chat.

"General Early," Gordon began, reining in his mount, "everybody's stopped."

"Hah! Let me get a good look at you, now that a man can see." Early turned to Ramseur. "Ain't that something! John Gordon, *Gentleman* John Gordon, with mud up over his ass and a dirty face. Ever seen the like?"

"We did get a tad muddy down by the river," Ramseur told him. Eager to keep the peace.

Gordon spared no time on banter. "General Early, we have to push on, to finish them."

"Gordon, you'd shit at a wedding. Just to call attention to yourself." But Early was in unconquerable spirits. He rebuilt his smile and said, "Glory enough for one day. Even for you." He slapped a hand down on his thigh, positively gleeful. "You know what day this is, Gordon? October nineteenth, that's what day it is. One month ago, precisely one month ago today, we were going in the opposite direction."

"All the more reason to keep going northward now. General Early, it's all very well, but we have to strike one more blow and finish this. Hit them one more time, with everything. Start by sweeping that ridge clean of those Sixth Corps boys. Strike them one more blow, and there won't be one infantry company left standing in Sheridan's army."

"Want me to shoot the wounded, too? And the prisoners? Then keep on going to Washington again? Damn you, Gordon. Don't you know a victory when you see one?"

Gordon looked to Ramseur and Wharton, but both men were determined to stay out of it. Given Dod's premonition of the night before and how such imaginings rattled even a strong man, Gordon figured Ramseur was glad the fighting was over. He'd done his part that morning, though. No holding back.

"Sir," Gordon tried again, "just one more effort. My division's ready. Ready enough. But we *all* have to go, destroy the Sixth Corps forever. Do that, and Sheridan won't have any army."

"God almighty, can't you see that your men are blown, that they're plain tuckered out? We've worn them to a nub, can't ask for more. That night march of yours. Everything else. They're plain worn out, used up." Early sharpened his features. Gone mean. "And *you* want to grind them to nothing. For one last sliver of glory." He snorted. "Half *your* men have fallen out, picking those Yankee camps clean. *More* than half of them." He delivered a second, grander snort. With effluvia. "Seems to me that your men are a damned mob. Worse than back in Martinsburg. I doubt you've got enough soldiers in ranks to fight through a Mex bordello."

That was a foul exaggeration. Some men had fallen out, indeed, but only to scoop up rations. But Gordon did not intend to be diverted by that argument. The air had cleared of haze and most of the smoke, and he pointed to the ridge not a mile to the west, still bristling with Yankees, the last shred of resistance.

"Give me Ramseur's Division. To cooperate with my own. Just let me clear that ridge. Just that."

Early took off his hat, scratched his head, and inspected his paw, as if he'd collected a louse under a fingernail. "No use in that. Dod's boys already had a go at that hill, you know it yourself. Wharton here went, too. Waste of lives, at this point. Yankees are finished. That bunch will go off directly, they'll all go directly."

"That's the Sixth Corps, General. It won't go, unless we drive it from the field."

"Gordon, sometimes you don't know your butt from a stump. Listen to me. They'll go, too. Directly." Early's grin widened, growing enormous, sharing his black-gummed, tobacco-stained teeth with the world. "Now just you look over there. Just have yourself a good look, *General* Gordon."

Gordon looked. And his heart sank. The Union troops were, indeed, evacuating the ridge. Before they could be erased from the Union rolls.

"Hit them now."

"No use. They're quitting. It's over."

"They're moving with good discipline. They've been ordered off, not beaten."

"They were only covering the retreat. Sheridan's finished. Hah! Captured half his guns. Likely three-quarters. Nothing but a sham, reputation built on tinder-sticks. I told you he was no general."

Gordon felt sick. Heart right down in his boots. He remembered Early halting before, at Gettysburg. And his unwillingness to attack that flank in the Wilderness.

This was a victory, certainly. But it wasn't victory enough.

The artillery renewed their harassment of the withdrawing Union troops. Shells burst amid half-stripped trees and distant gravestones. It wasn't enough, wasn't enough.

Hennie Douglas emerged from Middletown, coming on at a broken trot. His horse seemed reluctant to run. Yes, every living thing, each man and beast, was weary to falling down. But one more effort . . .

As the aide closed toward them, Early called, "Bring me the news, son. They still running? Or they slowed to a walk now? Hah!"

There was trouble in Hennie's eyes. The young man was no fool.

"They've got their cavalry lined up. On the Pike and to the east. Say, a mile north of town. Infantry's regrouping to the west."

A few seconds tardy in his reply, Early said, "Rear guard. Covering the retreat. Picket line of cavalry, you say?"

Douglas shook his head. "Not just pickets. Looks like most all of them, at least five thousand up there. Pickets out front, all right, but the rest behind them."

"Just covering the retreat," Early repeated. But he had grown agitated, less assured. He turned on Gordon:

"About time you got back to your men. We'll hold right where we are. Let the Yankees take their tails to Winchester at their leisure."

"At least," Gordon tried, "withdraw the army to better ground. We've won the day, I grant you. But we can't hold this terrain any more than the Yankees could. Our flanks are open, and their cavalry—"

"God almighty," Early snapped. "A minute ago, you wanted us all to attack. Now you want to retreat. As if we'd got our tails whipped." Early's face expressed limitless disgust. And anger. And—just perhaps—a first glimmer of fear.

"I didn't say 'retreat.' Just take up better—"

"Go back to your damned division," Early told him.

11:00 a.m.
Belle Grove grounds

Nichols was mud happy. Hadn't they whupped the Yankees, though? Hadn't they just done it? Live to be a hundred, even two hundred, a man would never forget the sight of those blue-bellies running like deer and grunting like pigs, or dumb-face Dutchmen with their hands up and their drawers down, the streams of prisoners. And all of it done before dinner.

"I reckon these will do," Tom Boyet said, trying on a pair of shoes left in a half-down tent. The Yankee camps were realms of treasure, and once it was clear that the fighting was over, Nichols had followed the lead of his brethren and drifted back to the nearest Yankee tentage. Even picked over by many an earlier scavenger, the abandoned Yankee lines held such wealth that it was a trial to choose what to carry off.

And as they searched through tents and rucksacks and commissary chests, every man ate his fill. Nichols had gobbled a can of sardines in oil, unsure if he liked the taste but unable to stop stuffing them in his mouth. He drank the oil.

The Yankees were so rich. Why couldn't they just leave the South alone? Did they love niggers that much? Or were they just wicked?

Perhaps, as Elder Woodfin put it, they were Moabites and Jebusites, sent as a trial for Israel, God's handiwork, God's test.

Well, the Lord had been good that morning: Not one of his war-kin had been killed or even muchly scratched. Just chilled by that river, a baptism Nichols did not wish to repeat.

As his friends and many a stranger from other divisions harvested the crop of Yankee abundance, a lieutenant rode up wearing trouble on his face. Nichols didn't recognize the man, but took him for a staff officer, since only staff lieutenants rode these days. The real lieutenants walked, just like the men.

The lieutenant halted before Lem Davis and Dan Frawley. Dan was wrestling with a pair of trousers too small for his bulk, even with Dan starved down.

"You men!" the lieutenant called. Seen close, he had that my-kin-got-money-and-land-and-yours-ain't look Nichols never cottoned to. The sneering boy drew his revolver. "You're no better than deserters, you're endangering the army. Rejoin your regiments. Immediately."

When no one seemed willing to turn from all the abundance, the lieutenant repeated, "This is no better than desertion, what you're doing. And desertion's a capital offense. Return to your ranks, every one of you."

To Nichols' surprise, Sergeant Alderman stepped forward. Alderman was a good man, decent and brave, and a capable sergeant. But he never had been one to contest authority.

"Lieutenant," Alderman said, "these boys just fought, they took all this. Knocked those Yankees back a goodly sight, and not a man here broke ranks till ordered to halt. Now they're just trying to feed themselves up and gather some winter duds."

"There's no excuse for disorder. If you all remained in your ranks, rations would be delivered."

The nearby soldiers guffawed.

"Why, I guess Bobby Lee'll drive 'em up in a wagon hisself," a soldier mocked. "Beefsteak and fried 'taters, coffee and pie."

The lieutenant whipped around in the saddle, set to point his pistol.

"Don't *any* of you, don't any man, say a word against General Lee."

"No man said a word against General Lee," Alderman assured him.

"Well, all of you get back to your regiments now. Before I have to take action." He hefted the revolver, a captured Yankee Colt, but didn't lower the barrel toward the men.

Again, the soldiers laughed. But the laughter this time had a meaner edge.

"Just what action you going to take now, sonny?" the jokester asked.

"This is mutiny!" the lieutenant declared.

Alderman stepped closer to him and his horse. The lieutenant recoiled slightly.

In a voice kept low, but barely controlled, Sergeant Alderman said, "Lieutenant, that's a fine horse. And that's a mighty fine uniform you're wearing. I'm sure you're a mighty fine officer. But these men are hungry, and they're going to eat. They're barefoot, and, by God, they're leaving here shod. Courtesy of General Philip Sheridan. And when they're fed and shod, they'll rejoin their regiments. And they'll do service as good as they've ever done." Alderman glared up at the boy, face as hard as Nichols had ever seen it. "Now, you can put that iron back in its holster and ride on, or if you mean to shoot down your own kind, you can start with me."

"Who's your commanding officer?"

"Captain Kennedy. Sixty-first Georgia. Evans' Brigade, Gordon's Division. And, though you haven't bothered to ask, my name's Alderman. Sergeant J. W. Alderman, CSA."

Stymied to quivering, the lieutenant showed white spittle at his mouth's edges, like an old man nodding away on a store's front porch.

"You won't be a sergeant for long," the boy declared. He gee-upped his mount and rode off.

"I did like that horse of his'n," a stranger commented.

But as the men rallied to congratulate Alderman, he repelled them, barking, "The lieutenant's right, you all just hurry up. Ten more minutes, and you're back in ranks. Y'all get moving."

When Private George W. Nichols rejoined his company, he was laden with two unsullied tent flies, two good blankets, a rubber ground cloth, two handsome overshirts, and, best of all, two hardly worn pairs of shoes that cuddled his feet like a softhearted gal might apply herself to a man.

It was, by far, his best day of the war.

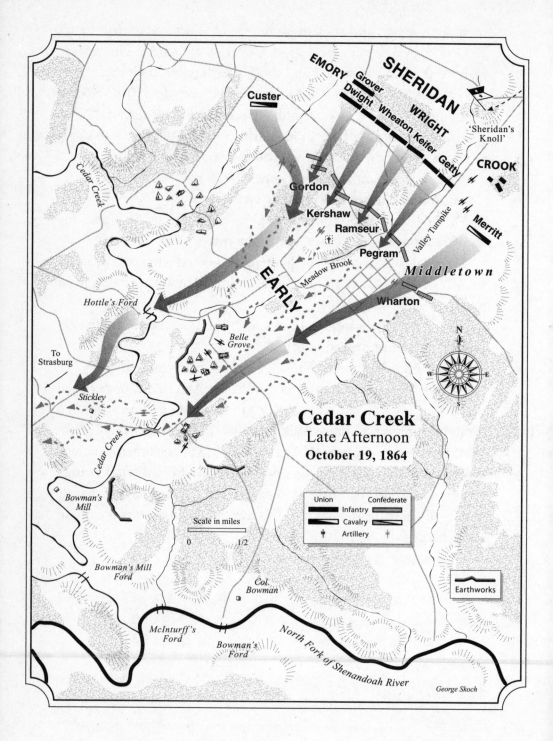

EMORY · SHERIDAN

Grover

Dwight Wheaton Keifer Getty

WRIGHT

Custer

'Sheridan's Knoll'

CROOK

Gordon

Kershaw

Ramseur

Merritt

Pegram

Valley Turnpike

Middletown

EARLY

Meadow Brook

Wharton

Cedar Creek

Hottle's Ford

Belle Grove

To Strasburg

N

W — E

S

Stickley

Cedar Creek

Cedar Creek
Late Afternoon
October 19, 1864

Bowman's Mill

Scale in miles

0   1/2

Union	Confederate	
Infantry		
Cavalry		
Artillery		

Earthworks

Bowman's Mill Ford

Col. Bowman

McInturff's Ford

Bowman's Ford

North Fork of Shenandoah River

George Skoch

NINETEEN

October 19, 9:15 a.m.
Valley Pike, south of Winchester

Sheridan reached the crest and beheld disaster. Another train of supply wagons had stopped in confusion, blocking the Pike. This time it wasn't rumors that had brought them to a halt. Nor was it the sound of cannon echoing from the south. Hundreds of soldiers fled northward, choking the roadway and spilling into the fields. In the clearing day, some appeared to be wounded. Most did not.

"Good God," Sheridan muttered.

Pierced by the scene, he reminded himself that even great armies looked rotten in the rear, that realm of skulkers and clerks. But less welcome thoughts flooded over him: He remembered that peculiar signal about Longstreet's arrival and Stanton's threats couched as praise; he rued his dismissal of the first reports of firing from the officer of the day and drowsing on at Winchester; and it sickened him that he'd bothered with breakfast at all, even if eaten standing and in gulps.

Yes, he had heard it, sensed it, known it, before he saw it. The sound of the guns had been moving northward as he and his escort rode southward: a fighting withdrawal, if not an outright defeat.

Now this. As he spurred Rienzi forward, maintaining a moderate pace to show no fear, the number of men running from the fight increased, clotting the fields and overwhelming the wagons pointed south. At the head of the train, an ambulance contested the right-of-way. Teamsters waved their arms and shouted, their words smothered by the din.

If it *was* a defeat . . . if Longstreet . . . if . . .

He'd have to establish a new defensive line closer to Winchester. Along Mill Creek? And try to hold.

Miserably, he grasped how much he'd enjoyed his newfound fame, his mantle of glory. He always loved the fighting itself, but had found the applause far sweeter than expected.

Would Grant relieve him?

Grim and glowering, he led his aides and escort through the first knots of frightened men. He felt the unease of the officers riding behind him, sensed Forsyth forming a question, choosing his words.

Don't show fear, Sheridan cautioned himself again.

And he *wasn't* afraid. Not of wounds or death.

But shame was another matter. Failure and shame.

Poisonous Stanton, a viper behind a desk. Halleck, blustering and unforgiving. Then the way newspapermen turned on a man . . .

A horseman galloping northward abandoned the Pike to skirt the wagon train. As the fellow raced through a field, dodging broken soldiers, Sheridan recognized his chief of commissary.

The colonel waved to Sheridan, coming on hard, horse shimmering with sweat.

Sheridan reined up. "What the devil, Brown?"

Panting as though he might burst out of his uniform, the colonel declared, "It's all lost, General. All gone. They've captured your headquarters, the army's broken, dispersed . . ."

Looking at the man, listening to him, witnessing the fear disgracing another, changed Sheridan utterly. In the time it took to flick away a fly, he brushed off his worries: He would *not* retreat to Winchester.

Damn it, he wasn't going to retreat at all.

Leaning toward the commissary officer, he said, hard-voiced but low, "Brown, get a grip on yourself. Don't let the men see you like this."

He turned to Forsyth, his favorite aide. "You and O'Keefe will

come with me. Cut out fifty of the best riders from the escort."
He gave the rest of his staff a get-ready look. "The rest of you,
stop these men. Turn them around. Alexander, ride back to Winchester, have the garrison deploy across the Pike. No man retreats
from here. Have the rest of the escort set up a cordon." He glared.
"*Do* it, goddamn it!"

He turned Rienzi southward again, followed only by his flag-
bearer and O'Keefe, confident that Forsyth would overtake them.
The Pike was clogged and useless, so he leapt a ditch and a stone
wall to ride through the fields, increasing his pace to a canter.

His army would *not* be defeated.

What the buggering hell had Wright let happen?

As he rode along, men stopped. Dumbfounded. A few cheered.

He waved his cap. Even that had gone wrong: In his belated
haste to get out of Winchester, he'd been unable to find his favorite hat and had to settle for a kepi an orderly produced. He needed
the men to recognize him from a distance this blasted day. And
they knew that old hat of his.

Hat or no hat, there was work to be done.

Far more of the men shambling northward were unwounded
than were casualties. Some had run bare-handed and only half-
dressed, but most carried their rifles. When more of them cheered
him from the dust of the Pike, he turned and bellowed:

"I'm with you now, boys! If I'd been with you this morning,
we wouldn't be in the shit. Face the other way now, turn around!
We're going back to our camps. . . ."

The men howled. But not all heeded his call.

Some did, though. Some did.

He passed hundreds of soldiers, then met thousands. At times,
he could ride the Pike for a stretch only to be forced to take to the
fields again. But he made damned sure that every officer he encountered understood that he was to rally his men and rejoin the
army.

If army there still was. . . .

Deeming the distance between themselves and the Rebs sufficient for safety, gaggles of soldiers had paused by the side of the Pike to brew up coffee.

"Drink up and follow me," Sheridan hollered, a grin masking his fury. "We're going back to whip those sonsofbitches. We'll make our coffee from Cedar Creek water tonight!"

The cheers grew in conviction.

By the time he reached the outskirts of Newtown, though, the demoralization facing him was appalling. Hard to believe that this was the army he'd led, his victorious army. Intact batteries inched northward amid throngs of disorderly soldiers. Wagons, sutlers' carts, officers lacking troops, and sheeplike troops without officers all had bottled themselves in the little town, struggling to get through the streets, like a fat woman wiggling into a young girl's corset.

And Newtown was a Reb nest, body and soul. The inhabitants were surely in their glory.

When he'd ridden out of Winchester that morning, Confederate-minded women had stepped out onto their porches to shake their aprons and skirts as he passed by, an insult peculiar to their stubborn world. Somehow, they'd known . . . it was the strangest thing. . . .

"You're headed the wrong way, boys," he called, forcing a smile. "I'm heading south myself, you come along now. We're going to smash those no-good sonsofbitches."

Again the men cheered. And more of them turned to follow.

Avoiding the stoppered-up streets, he veered back into the fields and met Captain McKinley, one of Crook's aides. To his credit, the boy was rounding up troops with a passion, although with mixed success.

Sheridan pulled up. McKinley saluted. Red-faced. And grinning like a moron. McKinley was one of those eternal smilers.

"General, sir, I sure am—"

"Glad to see me. McKinley, you ride through this traveling circus and tell every bastard you see that Sheridan's back. I'm going to drive those Rebs till they shit blood."

Blood was the truth of war. Just south of Newtown, by the side of the Pike, a field hospital might as well have been a slaughterhouse. Every man passing saw the mounds of limbs, heard the groans and occasional screams, registered the bodies laid in a row. The surgeons' aprons were red as a harlot's dress.

Sam Grant had it right: You couldn't fix on the casualties, you could not let yourself do that. You had to think about winning and nothing else.

He rode on, galloping hard now, pushing Rienzi over the last miles. Stabbing his boots into the stirrup hoods hiding his tiny feet, he let the great black horse have its head and charge. All he could do was to shout a few raw words and stay in the saddle as the marvelous beast pounded over harvested fields, leaping any fences that had not already done their duty as firewood. His escort trailed by hundreds of yards, and only his flag-bearer kept up, maintaining the perfect distance behind his spur, a small man, hardly more in size than a boy, on a horse that seemed but a pony beside Rienzi.

Well, Sheridan knew what little men could do.

Emerging from a creekbed, he sought the Pike again, impatient to close the distance to what might be left of his lines. But the roadway remained obstructed, albeit with the normal business of an army's rear now. Gaining another low crest, he spotted troops assembling off to the west. The blue mass was fixed in one place, if not well-ordered. A passing courier identified the remnants of Ricketts' and Wheaton's divisions.

Good Lord, the Sixth Corps driven, too?

At least those men weren't running. Not anymore.

He didn't turn toward the re-forming divisions, but galloped straight for the firing, which had grown sporadic, almost desultory. For whatever reason, the Rebs had eased their pressure.

Regrouping for the final blow?

He saw a line of battle ahead, a frail one.

Torbert met him in the fields. He looked as tense as Sheridan ever had seen the man.

"My God!" the cavalry chief called. "I *am* glad you've come, it's good to see you, Phil."

"What the buggering Jesus happened, Torbert?"

They rode toward the last blue line.

"Not sure anybody really knows. They just burst over the infantry. From the south and east, I think. Just burst over them. Wrecked George Crook's bunch first, then tore up Emory's. Couldn't see a blessed thing for hours, fog thick as wool. The Rebs just came out of nowhere."

"What about the Sixth Corps?" Sheridan demanded. "*They* couldn't hold?"

"Wright did what he could. Ricketts had the corps, but he was hit."

"Bad? Will he live?"

Torbert nodded. "Chest and shoulder. Toss a coin."

"Damn it."

"I brought up my boys, they're on the line now. Holding. Put a scare into the Rebs. With those repeaters. But if any man saved the army, it was Getty. And that stick-up-the-ass Vermonter of his, the one who looks like an undertaker."

They reached Getty's division north of Middletown. Three miles from their old camps. The men had thrown up barricades along a rail fence and Torbert had deployed cavalry on both flanks.

The line was thin as watered whiskey, though. Why hadn't the Rebs pressed on?

Sheridan spurred Rienzi hard and the animal gave its all, sailing over the rail fence, putting him between his own men and the Rebs fussing in the distance.

Showing himself to the men, he waved his cap.

Recognizing him, the soldiers rose. Cheering wildly and wonderfully this time. An officer rode out to greet him: Lew Grant, a

New Englander of the soberest, solemnest sort. Who really did look like an undertaker, Sheridan had to admit.

"The acting division commander reports, sir," Grant said, saluting.

"Where's Getty?"

"General Getty has the corps, sir."

"I know he has the damned corps. Where *is* the man?"

"Rallying the other divisions, sir. He means to fight, if the Johnnies have a mind to."

"Fuck the Johnnies. *I've* got a mind to fight." Sheridan softened. "I hear you did splendidly, Grant. Bully for you."

The Vermonter refused to smile. Christ, they were cold porridge, Sheridan told himself.

He meant to ride back to find Getty and look for Wright, but as soon as he passed to the rear of Getty's division he was startled by a line of flags shooting up from the earth, as if rising out of graves. The men gathered about the banners cheered: George Crook's men. Sheridan saw Rud Hayes.

A politician unlike any other he'd met, Hayes always struck him as thoughtful and honest. Brave, too. Traits Sheridan didn't associate with the run of elected officials.

He rode closer.

"Devil of a morning, I hear."

"That's putting it gently, sir. We were surprised, we—"

"No matter, we'll see things right. Just got our knuckles bruised." Sheridan looked more closely at the colonel—a man awaiting a promised star—and added, "You all right, Hayes? You look like the convict's last breakfast."

"I'll do, sir. A minor discomfiture. I'll do fine. As will my men."

His men. Barely a handful. But there would be more, in time, Sheridan believed. And Hayes? Dear Jesus. What kind of officer—or politician—used a word like "discomfiture"? Unless he was describing a case of clap?

For all that, Hayes had done well enough at Opequon and

Fisher's Hill. Damned well. Probably too good a man to go far in politics.

Before he rode off, Sheridan bellowed down the line of flags—a line with as many officers as men: "You boys just wait. Those sonsofbitches might think they've wrung the chicken's neck this morning, but they'll be the ones cooked in the soup tonight. You're going to sleep in your own damned camps, we're going back."

Robust cheers, from too few throats. And cheers were not bullets.

Not yet.

As they continued rearward, searching for Wright and Getty, Torbert asked, "You really do mean to attack, sir? After—"

"I'm going to shit all over them."

Found at last, Horatio Wright shocked Sheridan with his appearance. Blood all over the man. Face swollen up like a monkey's. Yet Wright seemed alert enough. Beside him, Getty's own mug was set in stone. Except for eyes that betrayed the strain of the day.

"You look like a whore cracked you over the snout with a bottle."

"Would've preferred that," Wright told him, struggling to pronounce his words with clarity. "Grazed my chin. Looks worse than it is."

"I hear Ricketts is down."

Wright grimaced. "Did what he could, Jim did. Chance he'll live, but no more than a chance. Thoburn's dead."

"Done's done," Sheridan said. "The living have work to do. Where's George Crook? And Emory?"

"Rounding up their men."

"Well, gather the rest of yours. I mean to attack."

That raised eyebrows. Even Getty's.

Sheridan drew his watch from his vest: It wasn't even noon.

He turned to Torbert. "I need to know whether Longstreet's on the field. Or anyone else we weren't expecting to call. Have your men take prisoners, find out." He faced Wright and Getty again. "As soon as you can, get all of your divisions back in the line, free up Torbert's Comanches for flanking movements. Emory's pack will go back in, as well. What's left of Crook's divisions can form the reserve."

Wright stammered, "Sir . . . we need time. It's going to take—"

"We've got the time," Sheridan told him. "The Rebs don't."

11:30 a.m.
Middletown

Early thought: *What the hell did those Yankees have to cheer about?*

1:15 p.m.
Northwest of Middletown

Gordon watched his men slump back.

"Couldn't do it," Clem Evans told him. "Yanks have thickened up, would've cut us to pieces."

Gordon nodded. Ruefully. "'Ripeness is all.'"

"Try again, though? Slip left, get around their flank?"

"No. They've got cavalry over there, I'm sure of it. Don't want you cut off."

Evans took off his hat, scrubbed the sweat from his brow with his sleeve, and said, "We should've kept going. This morning."

It wasn't an accusation, just a statement of fact, like a man saying "It's hot" in a Georgia August. Gordon didn't reply.

Early had, at last, ordered a renewal of the attack, but couched in such cautious and qualified language that it seemed too kind to describe it as halfhearted. It was clear that the army commander's desire to hold what he'd gained still outweighed the hope of achieving more. It wasn't like Jubal Early—not the Early who'd fought, fiery and foulmouthed, for three hard years—and this unexpected collapse into timidity, on this day of all days, made Gordon sick and furious at once.

He had advanced his men and they stepped off dutifully. But

the weather deep down in their souls had changed. Exhaustion had caught up with them in that pair of do-nothing hours. Worse, they'd had time to think themselves into a scare. The attack hadn't failed so much as petered out, the only saving grace the low count of casualties.

They'd been deserted by the gods, like those obstreperous Greeks on the plains of Troy. And no sacrificial libations were going to help.

The waste, the waste . . .

Between Early's order to halt and his tardy directive to nudge forward again, something had happened to the Yankees, too. A clamor of cheers had arisen from those blue blots on the horizon. Gordon could not fix the cause—not after the Federals had suffered so great an embarrassment—but he was certain the reason for that new and boisterous confidence would prove unwelcome.

Reinforcements? Had less of Sheridan's army been on the field than they had reckoned? Had they done less damage than every man in a gray uniform believed? That made no sense. They'd taken prisoners from every Yankee division known to be in the Valley.

Reinforcements from Grant, then, their arrival fatefully timed? What else could those whipped wastrels have to cheer about?

Gordon felt exhausted himself, head clouded all around the edges of thought. Every man from Middletown south needed sleep.

For their part, the Yankees appeared to have caught their wind. Well enough to deliver confident volleys and stand their ground. By the time his men had worked their way forward through the copses and swales, it also had become evident that the Yankees had gathered in many of their runaways. The lines encountered were skeletal no more.

As the gun smoke quit, the earth gleamed between the armies. The beauty of the day seemed unjust and cruel, almost dizzying. A man just wanted to nap under a tree.

His last, bloodied men passed Gordon. Their eyes reproached him, an unusual thing.

Surely they didn't blame *him* for the morning's halt? When, dudgeoned nigh unto mutiny, he'd pushed Early to continue, even begged?

Probably just plain angry at the world, those threadbare devils. The men had common sense, that was the thing. Those who had survived this long in the ranks were little generals, one and all, keen as to what made sense and what did not. They knew the army should have kept going, back when the going was all peaches and plums. And they'd grasped that this late, enfeebled attack was a waste. The hour of triumph had passed, and his soldiers knew it.

On the far right, the advance by Ramseur's Division had been paltry, with even less action between the army's wings. Was Dod still spooked by that premonition of his? For Dod, of all people, to let his fire go out, and on *this* day . . . Gordon remembered him sitting on his horse, mouth sealed, as Early stopped them short of destroying Sheridan. Any other day, Dod would have spoken up, as hungry for glory as a preacher for beefsteak. But in that crucial moment he'd held his peace.

And now the spark was out of the men, leaving them surly and restive. They knew as well as he did that their position was a wretched one, inviting the Yankees to come and take revenge. Cavalry country lay beyond their left, conjuring memories of the debacle at Winchester. They knew, those veterans did, that the sensible thing, the wise thing now, would be to withdraw to ground that could be defended, even if it meant giving up the field.

But Gordon also knew that Early was resolute. Jubal Early wasn't hard to figure, not on this marred, upside-down of a day. He'd scared himself with victory, unable to quite believe it. Aching to put his row of defeats behind him, he'd longed for a win so terribly that the ease and speed of the morning's success unnerved him. Now the old man hoped to claim this ground through sunset, to prevent the Yankees from pronouncing all this a mere raid. The traditions of warfare—pernicious things—held that the army occupying the field at the close of the day had won the battle. Jubal Early just wanted to keep what he had.

Gordon feared losing everything.

2:00 p.m.
Sheridan's knoll

Lying on his side on the grass, with his head propped on one hand, Sheridan watched young Forsyth dismount and approach. The captain looked as though he meant to chaw nails and spit out bullets.

"Got an itch there, Forsyth?"

The captain all but tore into him. "The Rebs couldn't make their advance stick anywhere. They've peaked, sir, they've used themselves up."

"So I hear," Sheridan noted.

The aide could not contain himself. "It seems to me, General, that we ought to advance. I came to you hoping for orders."

Sheridan sat up. He was not one to take advice, let alone a scolding, from a junior officer. But before he could speak, he caught the sudden look of terror on Forsyth's face: The younger man had realized in an instant just how far he'd overstepped.

Sheridan laughed out loud. Stray officers nearby chuckled along on cue.

"Sir, I . . ."

Sheridan waved away the captain's alarm. Better to have officers who longed to fight than the sort who always saw reasons for doing nothing.

"Not yet, Forsyth, not yet. Go back and wait."

And Sheridan left it at that.

Of course, it had been tempting, the impulse to order a broad counterattack when the Rebs sought to resume their advance and crumbled before they'd come to serious blows. But Sheridan was still waiting for the cavalry to confirm that Longstreet was merely a spook and not a presence. While presenting a front of unconcern—

all but lolling atop the knoll where he'd fixed his headquarters flag—he kept an eye on the constant stream of men returning to seek out their regiments. He could read their hearts, the way the shame of the morning's defeat was transforming itself into anger. They needed to stew a little longer, though. Meanwhile, the damned quartermasters and ordnance officers, the supply sergeants, and each last corporal had to do their work and put cartridges in pouches, pouches on men, and men back under arms.

As for Jubal Early, his brazenness was admirable. He'd almost pulled off the great *coup de main* of the war. But "almost" wasn't cash money. And soon he was going to pay.

When Forsyth reappeared an hour later, agitated as only the young can be, Sheridan didn't give him a chance to speak, but grinned and repeated, "Not yet, Captain, not yet."

3:30 p.m.
North of Middletown

*L*ucy.

Lucy and the boys.

It seemed to Hayes that nothing else mattered at all. War? This madness? He'd had his fill of it, wanted nothing more to do with the carnage.

And yet . . .

His borrowed horse stirred mildly. Hayes took off his hat and tilted back his head. Sniffing up the last blood.

His skull throbbed. Worst headache of his life. Cracked skull? Couldn't tell. And many another feature of his body pained him, too. Not least, that ankle. He would've liked Doc Joe to look him over, but that was not going to happen for some time. His brother-in-law was busy just to rearward, sawing and sewing and sweating amid the gore of a field hospital missing all the tools left in Rebel hands.

The queer thing was that he had not really bled from all the thumping. Not until midafternoon, when a sudden gush from his nose crimsoned his shirtfront. Even that seemed to have stopped, for the most part. But his head felt the size of a mountain.

He longed to leave it all and return to Lucy, to life, to a pretense, at least, that men could live in harmony and accord, to go back to his law books, to Shakespeare, to lamplit evenings in a familiar chair.

But he knew that, even now, he wouldn't go. He would keep his promise to these men around him, would not leave their ranks until, together, they were paroled into peace.

Correcting his posture for the hundredth time that afternoon, he looked about himself, at the faces. Faces with names he knew. A motley bunch, they were, these men of Ohio and West Virginia, weathered and withered by war. Some had trousers but no shirt or jacket. A few wore only undergarments. Others were as barefoot as the Rebs now, though not as toughened against the claws of the earth. Hats were rare.

But they had returned. To him. He had thought his division gone. And yes, it had suffered. But *these* men had come back to rally around their uncaptured flags, most returning of their own free will, but some driven by the provost marshal's horsemen and others cajoled by the likes of Will McKinley.

Lucy. He closed his eyes and let himself ache with longing for a last moment. Then he forced himself back to his unwanted duty.

Crook had told him that his division and poor Joe Thoburn's—under Harris now—would not join the coming counterattack, but would be held in reserve. He should have welcomed the news, he knew. And in one sense he had. Yet these men around him, who had endured so much through years of war, must not be left with the sense that they had failed. They had fought too hard, won too often, and seen too many comrades fall away to finish what might be their last great battle like this, as defeated men left standing in their undergarments, stripped of their possessions and their pride. These men deserved better.

Crook understood, of course. Hayes had not needed to speak up on the matter. He'd read Crook's voice, his expression, even the way his fingers clutched the reins.

These men did not deserve to be left behind when the others went forward. They did not deserve to be shamed. No, it was not the division it had been one day before. But it did not deserve shame.

It struck Hayes, again, how much he loved these men. Not with the odd, perfunctory love many officers professed, but in a bared and honest sense that was almost familial. He saw the paradox, of course, in his desire to lead them back into battle against his own dear wishes, against all reason, merely to save that intangible thing called "pride." What an odd thing it was, that almost embarrassing tenderness you came to feel toward your brothers in arms. Was it possible to love so broadly? Was "love" even the right word? Was the human heart, so often sordid, capable of emotion so enormous?

Nearby, a sergeant returning to his troops from a personal errand hitched up his trousers and announced, "Boys, I've just taken the grandest shit of my life. 'Twas pure magnificence. I wish it had gone right down Early's gullet."

Wiping a drop of blood from his nose, Hayes smiled. Love had to take a number of things in stride.

3:40 p.m.
Sheridan's knoll

All right, Forsyth," Sheridan said. "Issue the order. The army will advance at four o'clock."

The confirmation had come at last that all the Longstreet rumors were pure nonsense. And the men were ready now, angry as wasps whose nest had been poked with a stick.

Forsyth rushed off. All around, officers and orderlies stirred into action. The air sparked. Even before the order could be transmitted, the blue lines beyond the knoll seemed to quicken and stiffen.

It was not a time for refinement. His plan was straightforward. Attack head-on with the infantry to knock the Rebs out of position, then envelop them with cavalry on both flanks. Early's dispositions were idiotic, his flanks petered out in thin air, a display of overconfidence that hearkened back to the earliest months of the war. Jubal Early's arrogance would be Jubal Early's destruction.

Unexpected, unwanted, and, as usual, uncontrollable, Custer galloped up, fair hurled himself from his snorting, prancing mount, rushed over to Sheridan, wrapped him in his arms, and picked him up, dancing him around.

"Put me down, damn it!"

Custer cried, "Phil, it's grand to see you! Now we'll give them a licking!"

"Put me *down*!"

Grinning like a boundless fool, Custer set him back upon the earth.

Although the gaudy young cavalryman was oblivious, every two-legged being near them had tensed. Hushed. Waiting for a burst of outraged temper.

Instead, Sheridan smiled, shaking his head as at a naughty boy. "George, I've sent down the order to attack. You should be with your men, they'll go in late."

Custer's delight collapsed. He looked like a lad who'd been told he might miss out on the cherry pie.

"I've been shifted about all day," Custer said apologetically. "I just wanted to—"

"George, go back to your men and see to the enemy," Sheridan said more firmly. Cannily and cruelly, he added, "Wesley Merritt's already got the jump on you."

A quarter mile to the south, the Sixth Corps received the order to attack. The army that had broken that morning roared.

4:40 p.m.

Middletown

Ramseur's holding," Early snapped. "God almighty, he's got infantry *and* cavalry on him. He's holding, you can hold."

Gordon peered toward Ramseur's end of the line, but could

see little for the smoke. "Whether he holds or not, I can't. Not out there, not without being reinforced."

"Damn you, Gordon, you know there's no reinforcements."

They sat on their horses on a patch of high ground outside of Middletown, careless of the lead thickening the air.

"Well, then," Gordon said. "Pull back. Before it's too late. If it isn't too late already."

"Just go back out there and hold your position."

Gordon reached to grasp Early by the arm, but the ferocious, almost crazed expression worn by the other man stopped him.

"General Early, I'm struggling to hold back their infantry. Their cavalry's on the way. I don't know why they've waited, but the cavalry's going to hit my flank and rear, I'd bet my life on it." A deathly smile possessed his mouth. "I *am* betting my life on it."

"Refuse your left, then."

"I already have. It opened up my right. We need to—"

"*Damn you,* don't you tell me what we need. I command this army, not you. Now go on back to your division. And be a man. Like Ramseur."

The world howled, barked, shrieked: the men, the guns, the banshee shells in flight.

Ignoring the insult, Gordon tried a last ploy: "General, you've won a great victory. Don't throw it away. Order a withdrawal."

Early snorted, spit. "Why don't you just go, if you're so yellow. I'm not leaving this field."

Gordon saluted, a gesture of sarcasm now. He turned his horse.

Barely halfway back to the tumult engulfing his division, he saw thousands of sabers flash as Sheridan's truant cavalrymen exploded over a ridge, aiming for his flank and the army's rear.

4:50 p.m.
Confederate right flank

He'd held them. Threw back their cavalry, then threw back their infantry. Then his division held against simultaneous attacks. But

Stephen Dodson Ramseur understood—hated it, but understood—that his line was near to breaking.

A well-aimed Yankee shell struck a caisson, playing havoc with his last sound battery. Half-butchered horses shrieked, while those less injured struggled against their harnesses. A cannoneer circled madly, like a spring-loaded toy, spraying blood from a shoulder missing its arm.

The first few shirkers had begun to slink rearward, but the guards he'd posted turned them back to the fight. On threat of death.

If they could hold until dark . . .

Ramseur smirked. Remembering another day and the very same thought. They would not hold until dark. They would fight on, but would not hold. Their plight was as unforgiving as mathematics.

He saw the futility, yet he felt no fear. All that silliness about dying today. He regretted—would ever regret—sharing his melancholy with John Gordon. Gordon would remember it as weakness and there it would be, forever, a quietly mocking glint in Gordon's eye.

Dying? His interest was in killing. In killing Yankees. In killing every damned Yankee that crossed those fields. He meant to kill Yankees and keep on killing Yankees. He'd kill them for months, for years, if they kept coming. And then, when the last smoke cleared, when the last filthy Yankee was dead, he'd go home to his wife and take their child in his arms.

John Pegram rode up. Face stained black as a coon's. Eyes huge. Horse skittish.

Shells chased him.

"Sir, they're set to flank us."

"Bloody 'em up," Ramseur told him. "They'll think better of it."

"It's their cavalry. They're massing. All but behind us."

But what was to be done, what choice was left? It was too late for an orderly withdrawal, damn Jubal Early. Leaving them stranded on this useless ground.

"Just fight," Ramseur told him.

5:00 p.m.
Hayes' division

General Crook rode up, trailing flags and orderlies. Behind Crook, the Rebs were losing their grip on the field. At first, the Johnnies had put up a bitter fight, almost a daunting one. But they were breaking now. For all the smoke, it was easy enough to tell.

Hayes saluted. Crook smiled.

"Take your division in," his superior told him. Then, in a louder voice, "Your men are needed."

No, they weren't needed. Crook even gave him a wink. Sheridan had understood. These men needed to be in on the kill. It was as if Little Phil had been right there beside him when, shortly after the counterattack began, a soldier had presumed to ask Hayes, "Sir, we being punished? 'Cause of this morning?"

How strange, how endlessly strange! That men who knew war so well should want more of it.

Excitement pulsed through his reduced, half-clad ranks; the fervor was unmistakable. It was all he and his officers could do to restrain the men, to keep them in formation as they advanced, flags lofted high and two rescued drums beating cadence, all of them marching square-shouldered into the smoke. They wanted, needed, to get at the Rebs, while there were still Rebs to be gotten at.

And as they neared the half-managed chaos of battle, Hayes, too, shrugged off reason and decency, surrendering to pride and the urge to kill.

5:00 p.m.
Gordon's Division

Nichols gave up and ran. Wasn't right, none of it. Yankees everywhere. After they'd whipped them fair that very morning.

He'd stopped his rearward trot twice, once when General Gordon, that scar carved into his left cheek like a broken cross and standing out in a face hot as pink sow meat, that time, that moment, when John Brown Gordon, a Joshua but a false prophet, swept in among them, crying, "Rally, boys, rally! We can whip 'em, if we just stand our ground." That one time John Gordon proved a liar. For the Yankees were on them like the Plagues of Egypt, like sickness upon those firstborns, and they pulled the ground right out from under their feet, that was how it felt, the Yankees thieving the very earth they'd earned.

The other time was when General Evans, a saint among men, fooled him and half the others just as bad, calling to them, "Stand, men! We can hold!" General Evans, a Methodist, lying like a no-good Irish drunkard. Worse.

Yankees everywhere. First, their infantry, that whipped and whupped-on blue-belly infantry, came crashing down upon them, rushing into the breaks in their line like floodwater, splashing bluecoats every which way and drowning all hope.

That was *before* their cavalry came on. The cavalry just finished them, adding more scare to the big scoot back to the rear. The men on horseback were cruel, showing no mercy.

Without quite deciding, Nichols stopped and turned. He raised the rifle he somehow had loaded and fired at a Yankee horseman, one as good as another, but missed for shaking. And he was not given to shaking, never that kind of scared, but tired, Lord, he was tired enough to lie down and just give up, though he would not.

A file of cantering Yankees cut off Sergeant Alderman, who had tarried.

He wouldn't have run, not one step, had it been up to him. No, he did not believe he would have run. But all the others sure did. And when that happened, a fellow just went along and couldn't help it. Some of them, Nichols included, had re-formed back a ways by the regiment's flag, encouraged by Gordon. That hadn't lasted. Then they rallied, briefly, by broken-up companies, herded by General Evans, that good shepherd. Finally, the survivors only paused in flame-spitting huddles or by themselves. Then they just ran.

All the treasure was lost, left behind, discarded, the tent halves and blankets finer than store-bought town ones. All encumbrances were discharged so a man could run deer-fleet, until, some terrible how, Nichols lost the spare pair of foraged shoes, the finer pair of the two, saved up, reducing him to the possessions he had ferried across the river before dawn, all else gone except for the one good pair of Yankee brogues he'd had the presence of mind to tie onto his feet back when things were quiet.

Lem Davis all but crashed into him, only to veer away, mad-eyed, glancing back as though he recognized no man. At least Lem was alive. Couldn't see anyone else. Just the pillaged Yankee camps receding underfoot, one after another, prizes hard-won, even if by guile, and around him blue-jacketed troopers slashing blades down upon not armor but thin wool and cotton worn to a see-through, steel biting into flesh and muscle and bone, hard men atop beasts.

Let the dark come quick. Oh, let the dark come quick. . . .

Surely, I come quickly. Saith the Lord.

No time to pray.

Behind him, beside him, Yankees cheered, cursed, catcalled. Wasn't much artillery now, the attack had outrun its guns, but the Yankees had themselves a time blazing away from their saddles with those devil repeaters, making a game of death, maybe even betting on which man could hit what and keeping score.

He reached the Pike and found there was no army left, just a mob forcing wagons into ditches to make way for the terrified and cannoneers whipping men away from their limbers, only to be pulled off and beaten themselves. Yankee horsemen, maybe an entire regiment, dismounted on the high ground and shot into the mass.

Nichols believed his heart was bound to fail him, set to burst, and his lungs felt like a barn-burner got at them. Only his feet, blessed by those splendid shoes, a provenance of the Lord, went along untroubled.

Leaving the Pike, he thrashed through brush and scrub trees, trying to work away from the feast of killing, only to find himself drawn back to higher ground and another plundered Yankee camp, where dead men lay in shameless states of undress, not yet swelled up but a first few stiffened in rictus.

Two soldiers, his own kind, sat before a dead campfire and spooned beans from a pot that had not been emptied.

"Yankees are coming!" Nichols warned them.

"Set a spell," one soldier encouraged him placidly. "Them's good beans, and plenty."

"Yankees—"

"Oh, let him go, Ezra," the other soldier said. "He ain't figured out this here war's over."

Ezra nodded. "I reckon." He looked up at Nichols, kindly enough. "You take yourself a paw-full of them beans, boy. There's to spare, and beans won't slow you down."

Nichols ran back into the brush, away from the all-but-encircling shots and shouts, seeking the low ground, the creek or the river, safety.

How had it happened? When they'd whipped the Yankees so complete? How had it happened? Briars clawed him. Imagining Yankees all around and closing in, he had to fight the urge to drop his rifle.

How had it come to this? How had they sinned?

He emerged from the woods not in a quiet corner, but just east of the bridge over the creek. In the fading light, it offered a scene from Hell. On the southern bank, on the heights, some good men had put their cannon in battery and were firing back at the Yankees, brave as David, fending off a Federal Goliath, doing what they could to punish the blue-belly hordes closing on the bridge below.

The bridge itself was all wickedness. Men swung their rifles at their own kind to clear a path, and soldiers toppled shrieking into the water. Some tried to wade or swim across. Bodies floated downstream. On the narrow span, an ambulance was no more welcome than any other box set up on four wheels.

He *would've* stopped to fight, he told himself. But it wouldn't do no good. Even before he turned away, determined to save at least one Confederate soldier and that one himself, he heard bugles pierce the thunderous racket and saw, in the half-light, Yankee cavalry sweep into view on the heights held by the battery, long blades catching the last rays of the sun.

In moments, that golden light was gone and the battery taken.

Trapped on the bridge, men hollered like women with snake-fright, brave men screaming. Soldiers tossed their rifles in the creek and raised their hands, so many of them that the Yankee horses couldn't make any headway on the Pike, either side of the creek.

Nichols ran, stumbled, and crashed through brush and brambles, one of a few men nosing down the bank, trying to get out of sight of the swarming Yankees, out of any possible lines of fire, just trying to git.

The autumn dark fell fast, suggesting mercy. Nichols heard his own breathing, the gasps of a hunted animal. He heard other men, too, but could not see them. The world seemed newly vast, his day-scorched eyes reluctant to make sense of darkened spaces. Searching along the bank of the creek, he could not find one ford, though he reckoned there had to be several. Nor had he reached the river, he could tell that much.

He fell in with two of his own sort, South-talking men and notable for their smell, the three of them bumbling into each other and Nichols cry-whispering, "Don't shoot, I'm of your'n." And they went along together, which only made sense, as the war grated on in the distance and a wicked Yankee band far off played an Irish jig of a tune, its merriment like pissing on the dead.

That tune, or some other deviltry, worked on his new companions—one of them, anyway—for when they came upon a can't-get-up Yankee, a shot-through man who must've lain there since morning, and he greeted their brush-thrashing footfalls with a plea of, "Water . . . for Mother's sake . . . ," that soured new comrade hefted the stock of his rifle and beat the Yankee's skull in, no reason to it, just spite, the way Nichols once had seen a boy smash in a turtle's shell with a rock, just to feel bigger and better than something else, to kill something weaker, like he was saying, "I'm alive, goddamn you, and you're not."

Then they found what seemed to be, what had to be, a ford,

for it wore an apron of mud and a trail led from it, climbing back up the hill, or so it seemed in that darkness unpricked by camp-fires or torches, and they waded in, Nichols last, just in case, for he was not much of a swimmer, not much at all, but, Lord, they did want to get away from the Yankees, all three of them did, you could smell it on them like stink, and when the creek proved their judgment wrong and the opposite of the sea parting for Moses, the two dark shapes before him fell waterward at the exact same moment, their splashes small but terrible, and only one emerged again to flail his arms and make wildly for the southern bank, while the other disappeared into that water and never resurfaced, not even to cry out in lamentation like the children of Israel. Perhaps he had been punished by the Lord for the sin of Cain, for pulping that Yankee's brains—surely the Lord had selected the right man—and there in that creek, that creek that had swallowed a man as surely as the great whale swallowed Jonah, Nichols scared up and turned back.

As he struggled, unnerved and shivering, toward the Yankee bank, the mud stole one of his fine, new shoes, just sucked it off, though he'd laced it on real tight, and the creek wouldn't let his bared foot find it again.

Returned to dry land—or to the bank mud, anyway—he tried to go on with one foot shod and the other as good as naked, but that was no use at all. In a sorrow immeasurable he kicked off, tore off, the left-behind shoe, a grand shoe of stout leather, a sad-as-a-family-burying, useless shoe, and he picked it up, adoring it with his fingers one last time, then he pitched it into the creek to rejoin its mate.

7:30 p.m.
Cedar Creek

None of it had the dignity of a retreat: It was a rout from start to finish. If, indeed, it was anywhere near finished. Which hardly seemed the case, with the Yanks giving chase.

Gordon had tried to rally them—his own men and the rest—to make a stand first on one bank of the creek, then on the other. Each time, it was no good. The Yankees were everywhere, and that "everywhere" was usually right behind any line he formed.

He'd heard early on in the collapse that Ramseur had been wounded, perhaps fatally. Perhaps Dod's premonition had been real. More to Heaven and earth than any philosophy could contain, he recalled a line in *Hamlet* to that effect. More likely, though, Dod meeting a bullet had been one of war's coincidences. War found infinite ways to tease a man, sometimes to death.

Later, in the flame-streaked dark, amid the report of rifles and clang of sabers, John Pegram, tearful, had told him that the ambulance carrying Dod had been taken by Yankees. He wouldn't even die among his kind.

Never did get to see his infant, Dod did not. But Gordon intended to live.

He was trying to halt the two guns left to a battery, to snatch a few more minutes from the Yankees and allow another shred of the army to flee, when yet another throng of blood-glutton horsemen swept down upon them.

So fast, it all went so fast.

In the grave-dark night, with moonrise hours off, he all but gutted his horse with his spurs, guiding the beast toward what seemed the least-Yankee-bothered corner of the field.

After dashing along for a few dozen yards, his horse shied and reared up.

Gordon stayed in the saddle. And somehow he saw, grasped, understood, that horse and rider had come to the edge of a precipice.

"There's one of those bastards. Over there," a Northern voice called.

Gordon didn't know if the man meant him or some other unfortunate, but he did not intend to become a guest of the Yankees.

He said, aloud, "Fanny, I love you." And he drove his horse over into the unknown.

He couldn't bear the interior any longer. A chaotic mix of head-quarters, surgery, and refuge for the dying, the old mansion reeked of the dark side of the war, of the place beyond glory. He went outdoors, sidling down the steps, careful of his spurs, and posi-tioned himself before the fire in the yard. He'd borne enough in the hours past and did not need to witness any more misery. Or listen to any more excuses from staff men who'd found their way back only after the battle. He just wanted to stand there alone and unbothered.

Of course, he couldn't—and wouldn't—avoid the couriers re-porting the ever-increasing count of cannon and flags taken, of guns and wagons recovered, of prisoners captured. He reveled in those numbers; he'd just had too large a ration of human beings. His usual mood of celebration in the wake of a victory, the urge to be surrounded by good men sharing a bottle, of that he was inexplicably bereaved.

Arms folded across his chest, he lingered before the bonfire, its crackle and flare fueled by empty ammunition crates and the scraps of a wagon splintered by a shell. The fire's warmth was a fine thing, wonderfully inhuman, and welcome in the stiffening autumn night.

Within the house, a man screamed. Sheridan damned the soft-hearted fool who'd allowed the surgeons to set themselves up in his headquarters. How on earth was a fellow supposed to think? You had to be hard, harder than the man on the other side.

Had he been damned lucky, though? Was that the truth of the matter? Blessed not to have been present for the debacle in the morning? Would his presence have made a difference, or would he have faltered as the others had? Had he been better placed by fate at Winchester, so he could ride, untainted, to rescue the army after others failed? The newspapermen who'd stayed with the army, the few who hadn't fled, had already pawed him up, thrilled at the

story they had to tell and equally pleased that their absent colleagues
had missed it.

They would not merely report his feat, they'd exaggerate it beyond the bounds of the plausible. Not because they admired him,
not really, but because they wanted to top each other's versions.

Just in case, he had treated them to whiskey while he regaled
them. Not all of his staff's papers and maps had been rescued in
the morning's evacuation, but some intelligent orderly saved the
liquor. And there, on the field he had reclaimed, he had poured
the ginger-colored broth into the scribblers' cups with his own
hand, letting them laud him with praise of his achievement.

Now they were gone, those creatures of ink, in a race to the
nearest military telegraph office, with his signed authorization to
transmit their stories and grant them priority over routine messages. And his generals, too, had heaped on the congratulations,
as if he were Napoleon and Frederick made one, and he had praised
his generals in turn, and no more was said about the mistakes of
the morning or about flawed dispositions and poor vigilance.

He considered taking a dose of whiskey himself, but preferred
not to go inside the house to get it. He could not explain his mood,
but felt that any movement from his spot would be for the worse.
Flames snapped and the tower of wood fell inward. Sparks leapt
into the night like fleeing men, as if the fire had suddenly grown
too hot for them. In the distance, far to the south, flurries of shots
marked the continuing pursuit.

Cruel, to run men to ground like that. But there was no other
way to make an end of things. And the Johnnies had asked for it.

Early was broken this time, broken for good. He had misjudged
the man's resilience, true enough, but this day had a finality none
could mistake. Early was finished, and soon enough the Confederacy would be finished, probably after tormenting itself through
one last hungry winter.

The fire was mesmerizing, inexplicably pleasing, but the paper
assault that followed a battle could be held off no longer. He remained by the fire but reviewed reports, gave authorizations, and

signed a dispatch he'd dictated—wouldn't Grant be pleased? Riders came and went. Forsyth brought him scalding coffee in his bone china mug—Sheridan did not tolerate tin cups—and he cradled it in his hands, taking in the aroma, suddenly aware that he'd wanted just this thing: to be alive on this cold night with a mug of fresh-made coffee. To be *alive*. And victorious.

"Something to eat, sir?" Forsyth asked.

"This'll do fine. Not hungry."

But he knew Forsyth well enough to calculate, almost to the minute, when the aide would reappear with a slice of ham or the like between two cuts of bread.

A cavalcade approached. It didn't take a bonfire's light to recognize George Custer.

George dismounted theatrically, with acrobatics worthy of a circus show. Grinning like a damned fool all the while.

"Ain't it splendid?" Custer called, pulling off his gloves, striding, shaking off the saddle stiffness the way a dog sheds water. "It's the most complete victory of the entire war! Ain't it glorious?"

"Yes, George," Sheridan agreed. "Good work."

"I feel like dancing and howling at the moon."

For a moment, Sheridan feared that the younger man would pick him up again. He tensed at the thought.

But Custer just slapped one glove against the other. "Don't think I lost more than a few dozen men, you should've seen it."

"I saw enough. By the way, Charlie Lowell's dying. Or dead by now."

"Oh, bad luck." Custer sounded as though he'd missed the soup course.

"And Ramseur. Isn't he a friend of yours?"

"Old Dod? We were at West Point at the same time. What about him?"

"You don't know?"

Still half grinning, Custer said, "Old Doddie get himself captured? He'll be hot. . . ."

"For God's sake, George. Your own men captured the ambulance he was in. They brought him here, he's inside."

"Wounded?"

"Dying."

Custer considered that. "Hard luck. I'm sorry to hear it."

They stood before the fire, each waiting for the other to speak first. At last, Sheridan asked, "Don't you think you should see him? He's still conscious. At least, he was when I looked in on him. Not feeling much pain, I don't think. But the surgeons agree he won't live through the night. Don't you want to say good-bye to him, George?"

Fidgeting like a child during a sermon, Custer said, "I suppose I should. I mean, I don't want to crowd in on him, add to his burden."

"Merritt sat with him. As long as he could."

"Wesley's good at that sort of business. Ain't he?"

"George . . ."

"Oh, well. Poor Dod. Better have a look, I suppose. Buck him up."

"Christ, George. Don't try to 'buck him up.' I understand his wife's just had a baby. He's never seen it, doesn't know if it's a son or daughter. And, for God's sake, don't go bragging about your victory."

Wounded, Custer said, "I don't think I brag." He looked up dolefully. "Do you, Phil?"

Good Christ. "I think he'll be glad to see you, George. You're the very breath of life. Now go on in."

Reluctant but obedient, Custer jingled up the stairs to the busy house. Sheridan thought: After the war, we'll have to keep the bugger in the Army. Wouldn't be fair to turn him loose on the citizenry.

Alone and staring into the fire again, into the blaze that celebrated his triumph, Sheridan felt possessed by a wordless sorrow.

That ended when Forsyth brought him some beef on a biscuit.

11:00 p.m.
Cedar Creek

Gordon could not judge how long he'd lain unconscious or how far he'd fallen. He tested each limb, each finger, and explored his throbbing skull. Hardly felt ready to lead off the cotillion, but he seemed to be intact within his skin.

Ached like the devil, though. When he rose, his head swam through muddied-up air. His eyes struggled. Leaving him a touch dizzy.

Tore hell out of his uniform. New one, too. Still, just standing up whole counted as a miracle.

The second miracle was that his horse stood nearby, nosing in the grass, another unlikely survivor.

Gordon listened. The firing, what there was of it, had moved off. Nearby, though, up on the high ground, hooves pounded. And there were shouts. Cavalry. Searching.

He petted his mount, making low and soothing sounds, cooing to a baby. Carefully, gently, he traced the animal's limbs.

The horse seemed fine, a wonder. But even if they could have climbed back up that bank, riding off across Yankee-owned ground seemed a tad ill-considered.

Where there was such a drop, though, there had to be a streambed. And streams led to creeks, and creeks led on to rivers. Gordon figured he'd best walk the horse along the ravine until he found a trail far enough removed from the fray and fuss to give him a chance. Failing in that, he could work along to a ford down on the river.

He was glad to be in one piece after that leap, but couldn't say he'd had the finest luck, not overall. After the glorious morning, Fortuna had turned her wheel, leaving him a victor robbed of his victory and a general without a division. Or even a hat.

Well, hats could be purchased, divisions reassembled. Irate though he was, he knew he should count his blessings. He would bear no blame.

He stumbled along, hushing the horse, determined.

And not just determined to rejoin the army—or what bits and pieces remained of it. He intended to find a way to have himself recalled from the Valley. Early's reputation was played out, beyond repair. Any man who remained with him would see his own reputation tarnished as well. Early was finished, the Valley was finished. But John Gordon wasn't done.

Come what might of the war, advantage waited at Robert E. Lee's side. Lee was the one who'd escape vilification, no matter what happened, and those seen as close to Lee would be judged the stalwarts. The trick now was to become Lee's man, not Early's.

With a dried-up streambed's stones annoying his feet through the soles of his boots—fine boots, but worn thin as slippers—Gordon swore he'd get back to the Petersburg lines, even if it required the Labors of Hercules.

As for Jubal Early, he owed the man nothing.

October 20, 2:00 a.m.
The Valley of the Shenandoah

His feet were in a sorrow. And the scrap of sleep hadn't helped none. Nor did the sight he saw when he woke up.

The moon had run high. Reckoning that he and the passel of fugitives he'd joined must be near the base of Three Top Mountain, Nichols stepped from the trees into a clearing to fix his bearings. He let the moon tug his eyes on south, and the outline of Three Top—unmistakable even seen from an unexpected slant—just hit him like a fist aimed low in the belly.

Three Top was there, all right. But they weren't nowheres near the foot of that refuge, nor did they just need to find a ford to scoot through. The mountain had slipped a goodly distance south. Which meant they'd blundered in the earlier dark, men who hadn't slept for two days and who'd just got a licking, and, fool him, he'd let that lieutenant gather him up and lead him along, since that was what officers were supposed to do.

Gripping himself, just straightening right up, Nichols dashed back into the scrub trees and kicked apart the fire the others were raising.

"What the hell, you crazy sumbitch?"

"*Yankees.* We got all turned around. We're in their rear, talk quiet."

The lieutenant—name of Baskett, how it sounded—said, "That can't be."

"Lieutenant, we need to get on. *Now.* Come daylight, we'll be taken up."

Befuddled, the lieutenant just repeated, "That can't be."

"Come look out here," Nichols invited him, heading back to that field of revelation, but cautious this time.

"Can't be," the lieutenant said again, brushing off the last grip of his sleep.

"Where y'all from, Lieutenant?" Nichols had begun to add things up and he wasn't fond of the sum.

"Miss'ippi. Kershaw's Division."

Yes, that explained it some. This officer and his maybe eight men all lost as children got into a blackwater swamp, and a hard stroke on him for joining up with them.

"You and your men just been here a speck of days. I hoofed this ground till I'm tired even thinking on it. You look down there, Lieutenant. That outline, that there mountain, right of the moon."

"I see it."

"Sir, that's Three Top. Looks different from up here, but you look close. Remember looking east from Fisher's Hill? That mountain across the river?"

"Can't be. That one there's six miles away."

"Look close."

"I'm looking."

"You *seeing*?"

"I'm seeing. Oh, Lord Jesus."

Nichols let it all burn deep. The lieutenant shook his head in the silver light. Getting his first good look at the man, at this officer who had held out a promise of rescue hours back, Nichols realized that if there was a year's age between them, it wasn't more than that. Just made him feel sicker, pondering that. As if he'd been fooled by a city feller come out on the train.

"What are we going to do?" the lieutenant asked.

"Reckon we ought to get going, sir. Cover what ground we can. Before the light comes up."

"I just don't know how we got so turned around," the lieutenant said, dropped in a pot of wonder, with embarrassment stirred in. He edged closer to Nichols and lowered his voice again. "Figure you could lead us out of here? I'll appoint you as our scout, like it's official."

"Do the best I can, sir. But we got to go soon, and we got to go on quiet."

"I'll see to that." But he didn't move. "You think we can make it?" he asked, all of the officer gone out of him now. Church-earnest. Maybe afraid. Afraid, surely.

Nichols was spooked, too. He'd heard the stories about those Yankee prisons. Elmira, worst of all. He knew, heart-deep, that his own kind would never treat prisoners like that.

He also knew—understood in the queer way men did—that *he* was the leader now, that the lieutenant would inhabit his rank again only when they were safe. If safe they ever were.

"Best get on," Nichols said. Firmly.

And they went, the men grumbling for a stretch, then too tired to whisper. Nichols' bare feet had lost some of their toughness, and more than just some, across a summer and autumn of shod going. He winced at the hurt, even felt girl tears come up.

Ain't going to cry, he told himself, *ain't nothing on this earth can make me cry.* But he did not turn around, would not let those trailing him see his face, as he led that little chain of Mississippians, men even farther from their homes than he was. He clutched his rifle, his last possession, in a strangler's grip, meaning to brace his manhood and steady his innards. But in that cold-handed, Yankee-haunted dark, the tears came anyway.

Walking into the moon, walking south into that white, revealing moon, Nichols gave his word to the Lord above and to all men below that he wasn't wet of cheek because they'd been whipped again, maybe for good this time, nor because he couldn't know just what had become of Sergeant Alderman, whether those saber-swinging Yankees had killed or spared him. He didn't know the come-outs of his other war-kin, either, whether Lem Davis and Dan Frawley, Tom Boyet or Ive Summerlin, or even Elder Wood-fin, all righteous men, had escaped the tribulation.

He wasn't even crying because, for the first time, for the first true can't-fool-yourself time, he had to ask what would become of them all, of their whole world, if they lost the war. He wasn't dripping from the tip of his nose and tasting salt because he was scared or homesick, either. Not even because he'd had his fill of fighting and wanted to wake up in a bed and not rise till he was ready. He wasn't weeping over unmet girls or from dreaming of his still-nameless bride, unsullied and inevitable, nor even because his heart was broken like a buttermilk jug hurled down, no reason to it. Wasn't even the hurtsome way of the world. It was another, bitter loss entirely:

Them shoes.

EPILOGUE

Sleet bit the faces of the twelve hundred men who remained in Early's Army of the Valley. Arrayed on a ridge just west of the town of Waynesboro, with the Shenandoah curving at their backs, the sick and starving remnants of a once great force stared out through an ugly sky as thousands of Union cavalrymen—not blue, but brown from mud—arrived on the road from Staunton. Men flinched, and not just from the ice-needles hunting their eyes.

Their general was determined to make a stand. Long enough to evacuate five guns stranded without limbers or teams and a few last supplies. Perhaps even long enough to discourage Sheridan from crossing the Blue Ridge here, at Rockfish Gap.

Old Jube knew he was outnumbered ten to one, that his own force was barely a fifteenth the size of the columns he had led into Maryland in July. But he held high ground, and for once, the weather seemed helpful. The fields rising to his lines had become mires, promising to stunt a cavalry charge. His numbers might not reach far enough to anchor his flanks on the river, but a man fought with the tools he had at hand. On this day, those tools were not quite a thousand infantrymen, a bare hundred horsemen still riding under Rosser, and one good battery of six ice-sheathed guns.

Fingers froze as shivering men clutched weapons. Too cold and weary to dig entrenchments and brace them in the slop, they waited behind piled fence rails. And they waited.

Against all reason, Early believed he could hold. Because he *had* to hold. And because he was Jubal Early. Who could not let Sheridan pass by unmolested.

Midafternoon. No rations, hot or cold. Men wet through, rifles slick with water that turned to ice.

More Federal horsemen, grim on the horizon.

Peering at his enemies, fired with the passion of an exemplary hater, and stubborn to death even now, Early could not identify Custer's division, or Merritt's trailing behind. Their flags were rolled and sheathed against the sleet, and mud-clotted rubber ponchos hid identities. It didn't matter. He and his men would fight whoever came at them.

Even as Early received reports of dismounted troopers working around his left, even as he heard the *tap-pop* of their Spencers, he believed that he could hold that last position.

Even as two thousand horsemen advanced toward his line, with two thousand more behind them, four thousand pairs of shoulders bent by the weather, even then, as he watched their mounts plod forward, smacking up mud and more mud, even then Early believed that he could hold.

The Yankees to his front came on relentlessly, some mounted, others on foot now. Their well-fed mounts spurned the mire and, answering buglers, increased their pace to a canter. Knees tight against wet saddles, men drew sabers. On the flank, the firing, the cheers, grew louder, closer, wilder.

One bugler after another sounded the charge. The Yankees' horses kicked up a screen of mud, hiding all behind them. On they came, all the riders shouting now.

And Early *still* believed his men might hold, that they would stand.

They didn't. Couldn't. They ran.

With Yankees swarming his shattered line by the hundreds, Early, too, rode for the rear.

Accompanied by a small contingent of generals without commands and staff men with no purpose, he pounded across a river bridge just in time. Fewer than two dozen riders escaped.

Turning to look back from atop a hill, still hoping he might somehow rally his soldiers, hoping that they, too, might cross that river and join him for another fight somewhere else, Jubal Early watched, mortified, as his shrunken, starving army surrendered en masse.

It was the old soldier's last battle.

JUBAL EARLY

After the debacle at Waynesboro, Early made his way east to rejoin Lee, hoping, in those final weeks of the war, to be granted another command. Lee could not oblige him. Hostility toward Early was too general. Anyway, there were no commands to be had. Lee sent his "bad old man" home to Rocky Mount to "await orders." News of the surrender at Appomattox found Early drinking whiskey and cursing madly, his inner fire undimmed.

He would not make peace. This man who had stood bravely and vociferously against secession in 1861 had come to hate the blue-clad enemy and many a former friend with a fury even decades would not weaken. He went to Mexico, hoping for employment under Maximilian, but the emperor's regime was nearing collapse. Old Jube went next to Canada, where he lived in poverty, surviving—barely—on handouts from relations and old friends back in the South, many of them impoverished themselves amid the upheavals of Reconstruction. He was often ill.

At last, grinding stained teeth, he returned to Virginia, where his law practice would have left him as hungry as the soldiers he once had led had he not been persuaded to lend his good name to the bad cause of the Louisiana Lottery, which thickened his purse while thinning the fortunes of others.

He became the leading apostle of the Lost Cause myth and the one man most responsible for the beatification of Robert E. Lee. *And* for the vilification of his personal rival, Confederate Lieutenant General James Longstreet. To the very end of his Yankee-hating life, Early reviled all things Northern; espoused the justice of the Confederate Cause; and elevated Lee above flesh and blood.

He died in 1894, bitter as tobacco juice.

JOHN BROWN GORDON

Recalled to Petersburg, Gordon became Lee's favorite subordinate. During the last, tumultuous retreat, he commanded half of the Army of Northern Virginia. When Lee and Longstreet declined to lead their threadbare thousands of soldiers to surrender their arms at Appomattox, Gordon, in one of his finest hours, accepted the responsibility. As always, he rode at the front of his men.

After the war, he hurled himself into Reconstruction politics, fighting for a restoration of Georgia's legal rights. He may have become the first Grand Dragon of Georgia's Ku Klux Klan, but, canny as ever, he left no evidence either way. By 1873, he was in Washington as a senator from Georgia (and would return to that office again). In 1886, he became his state's governor.

Unlike his comrade and nemesis, Jubal Early, the convivial Gordon made himself beloved, first in Georgia and then throughout the South, while managing to become a popular figure in the North as well, and much in demand for high-society dinners. In private matters, he prospered, although not all of his business partners fared well.

He and Fanny continued to share one of the greatest love stories of their age.

When Gordon died at Miami in 1904, thousands wept, although not all of them could have explained why.

CLEMENT ANSELM EVANS

Clem Evans formally joined the ministry of the Methodist Episcopal Church. Thereafter, this truest of Southern gentlemen refused many an offer to climb high, preferring to serve his neighbors and preach the Word, while caring for his ever-growing family.

Eschewing the treasures of this world, he gained a wealth of admirers. Upon his retirement from the active ministry, and still suffering the effects of his five war wounds, he served the United Confederate Veterans and edited the massive *Confederate Military History*.

His wartime letters to his beloved Allie offer incomparable insights into the emotions, logic, and daily concerns of the finest breed of Confederate officer.

GEORGE W. NICHOLS

Private Nichols survived the war, although illness spared him the pain of Appomattox. In the following years, he read far beyond the Bible, educating himself in a homespun fashion, until, in the waning years of his century, he produced the classic memoir *A Soldier's Story of His Regiment (61st Georgia); and Incidentally of the Lawton-Gordon-Evans Brigade, Army of Northern Virginia*. A wonderful, if occasionally inaccurate, reminiscence, it included vignettes of his repeated bruising from shell fragments—lightning did strike twice—and of his brief captivity at Third Winchester (Opequon Creek), as well as of his close-run escape from the wreckage of Cedar Creek.

The memoir praised General Gordon in heroic, almost superhuman, terms. Gordon approved.

LEW WALLACE

The general who saved Washington never received another combat command. Yet those who grasped what he had done did not forget him. In 1878, he received a presidential appointment as governor of the New Mexico Territory, where he dealt with Billy the Kid, the Lincoln County range war, and Indian uprisings. Working at night in the decaying Palace of the Governors in Santa Fe, he completed a novel he'd labored over for years, *Ben-Hur*.

Captivated by the book, fellow Civil War veteran President

James Garfield appointed Wallace to head the American mission to the Sublime Porte of the Ottoman Empire, which ruled the Holy Land from Constantinople. Garfield hoped the sojourn would inspire further novels of faith; instead, his emissary delivered potent diplomacy. Wallace upended protocol and approached the "unapproachable" sultan, caliph to all Muslims, with midwestern openness. To the shock and chagrin of Europe's overstuffed envoys, the sultan, after a moment's surprise and confusion, took Wallace's extended hand. Soon, Wallace was the sultan's trusted adviser.

When administrations changed and Wallace made way for a new president's appointee, the sultan, too, broke protocol in turn and wrote to Washington, expressing his befuddlement that a mere change of presidents would rob him of his treasured American friend.

From Constantinople, Wallace retired to Crawfordsville, Indiana, his cherished home. He continued writing, while encouraging young authors and fathering an "Indiana renaissance." At his death in 1905, he had just completed describing the Battle of Monocacy for his memoirs. The old ache of being scapegoated for Shiloh never quit him, but he left a greater legacy in *Ben-Hur,* one of the greatest best sellers in the history of the book and a tale destined to captivate the great creative medium of the new century, the movies.

His persecutor, Henry Halleck, is forgotten by most and mocked by the remainder.

JAMES B. RICKETTS

Jim Ricketts survived his final wounding, but never recovered full health. Forced by his disabilities to shed his uniform after the war, he retired with the rank of major general. He found happiness with his wife, Frances, and his family.

GEORGE ARMSTRONG CUSTER

Custer's fear of being forgotten on the frontier proved un-founded: In one of fate's endless pranks, he is remembered—or misremembered—not for his brilliance and courage during the War of the Rebellion, but for that day above the Little Big Horn when his favorite tactic of dividing his force to envelop the enemy didn't quite work out.

PHILIP HENRY SHERIDAN

After destroying the pitiful remnants of Early's army at Waynes-boro, Sheridan turned east. He joined Grant for the final weeks of the war, when his aggressive soldiering reached its zenith. The men under his command crushed Lee's reeling army in one battle after another before rushing ahead to block the Army of Northern Virginia's last hope of escape at Appomattox.

To his great annoyance, he missed his army's grand review in Washington (where Custer, of course, made a spectacle of himself). As soon as the guns of North and South fell silent, Grant dispatched him to demonstrate our country's newfound military strength on the Mexican border and pressure France to withdraw its support for Emperor Maximilian. Too much the hardheaded soldier to suit Reconstruction duties, he was given command of the military department responsible for suppressing the Indian tribes. President Grant promoted his old subordinate to lieutenant general.

But as the years passed, Sheridan's vanity increased along with his girth. He fell out with his old friend George Crook over Indian policy, then, in a pompous memoir, took credit for Crook's tactical devices at Third Winchester and Fisher's Hill. To the surprise of all who knew him, he married a minor society girl, reduced his drinking, and subdued (most of) his profanity. In 1884, he followed retiring William Tecumseh Sherman to wear a fourth star as commanding general of the Army, our country's highest military office at the time.

Rotund, vindictive, and vain, he died at fifty-seven of fine living.

WILLIAM MCKINLEY

In 1897, Major William McKinley took his oath as the twenty-fifth president of the United States, the last of the Civil War veterans to hold that office. His military experience helped him shape wise strategic decisions during our war with Spain, and the United States inherited an empire. At home, McKinley presided over a dramatic expansion of American wealth. He was assassinated by an anarchist in the early months of his second term. Fresh from martial exploits of his own, his vice president, Theodore Roosevelt, succeeded him.

RUTHERFORD B. "RUD" HAYES

Rud Hayes became president in the wake of the disputed election of 1876. Overcoming the electoral shenanigans and backroom deals that allowed his inauguration after months of stalemate, Hayes proved a fair-minded, skillful, and honest president. He began his term in office by outraging his own party when he insisted on appointing the best-qualified men to cabinet posts, regardless of their past affiliations.

Obliged to end Reconstruction in the South, Hayes concentrated on education and fair treatment for former slaves and their descendants. His monetary policy protected the common man. Faced with the Great Railroad Strike of 1877, he refused to let the government take sides, intervening only when strikers turned to the widespread destruction of property. Not least, this man of conscience and integrity was the first president to fight to professionalize the civil service and end the spoils system. In the face of resistance from both political parties, his initial success was limited, but Hayes had begun a process that could never be fully reversed by the backroom boys.

The gravest complaint about his administration came from Washington's corps of foreign diplomats: Out of respect for the Temperance scruples of his adored Lucy, Hayes banned wine and liquor from state dinners. Europe has never forgiven us.

All but forgotten now, Hayes grew broadly popular while in office and could have won reelection without effort. But he had campaigned on the promise that if elected, he would limit himself to one term. Despite calls to renege on his position, Hayes remained, as always, a man of his word. He went back to Ohio.

For the rest of his life, Hayes devoted himself to education reform and social improvement. But his favorite activity was to host regular reunions of the soldiers he had led through four years of war. It is a military custom for senior officers to claim they love their soldiers, but the statement all too often sounds perfunctory. Hayes truly did love his men, though. And in the greatest tribute soldiers can pay to their commander, they loved him back.

Memorial Day 2014

Author's Note

When first I mustered the nerve to write about our Civil War, a scarred veteran of the genre offered advice. He told me that the secret to selling books on the subject, fiction or nonfiction, was to stick to the same five generals (Lee, Jackson, Stuart, Longstreet, and, as a token Yankee, Grant) and the same five battles (First Bull Run, Shiloh, Fredericksburg, Chancellorsville, and Gettysburg). He did not believe that readers would tolerate anyone who disturbed the idealized narrative.

I disagreed.

For me, what appealed was the chance to share untold tales, to reincarnate on the page men who did not deserve to be forgotten, and to strive, as a former soldier, to communicate the complexity of our most tragic war—to go behind the gallant charges to honor the midnight doubts. Since bards and historians (once the same thing) began recounting wars, there has been a universal impulse to elevate one great hero, a Joshua or Alexander, or at most a small circle of heroes, such as those who contended on the plains of Troy. But armies, whether of the Bronze Age or our own, are complicated assemblies of human beings, requiring a range of efforts from the many. Even Homer's heroes had to eat, be re-equipped, and have their gashes treated. The conquering armies of Assyria could not have marched without their logisticians. And even when a general made a wise decision, it always has been up to the men whom Rutherford B. Hayes called "the good colonels" to lead the fighting.

I wanted to better understand the men obscured by their own famous names, but also to credit the heroes cast aside, such as Lew Wallace, and to recognize dependable officers, such as Clem Evans or Jim Ricketts, who may have lacked genius and flare, but whose sense of duty and courage often made the difference on the battlefield.

I also was counseled to avoid writing about the latter half of the war—anything after Gettysburg was forbidden—since accounts of Southern defeats "don't sell." Yet it was in 1864 that Lee's tactical genius survived its greatest tests, while the remarkable courage of Early's ever-outnumbered Army of the Valley seems to me a greater proof of the quality, guts, and tenacity of the Confederate infantry than earlier campaigns against milder odds and less capable Federal commanders. The shrunken number of characters who survive into this novel's final pages tells us a great deal about the desperate nature of the fighting between the first days of July and October 19, 1864. This was naked war, stripped of all fancies.

North or South, rivalries, ambitions, and bouts of selfishness made these figures human and left them, for me, more worthy still when they overcame their flaws. And, of course, a marvelous rogue and natural soldier such as John Brown Gordon is a treat for any writer to engage (Gordon seems the kind of man who captivates everyone at the restaurant table, but never picks up the check).

I hope the reader will learn a bit from this book and from the others in the cycle (the next installment, *The Damned of Petersburg,* returns to eastern Virginia and July 1864). But no reader will learn as much as I have learned and continue to learn by grappling with these men, by trying to grip them with adjectives and clauses, 150 years after their deeds. Though a Yankee from Pennsylvania, I'm ever more deeply awed by the infantry of the Army of Northern Virginia (from whence most of Early's men came) for its skill, resilience, and spirit. I search the annals of history to find other soldiers their equals, but see none. I hope that this novel provides some sense of how tough those Johnnies were, of how much they endured. It's an easy thing to be faithful and bold in victory, but their determination to fight on as defeats piled atop one another is an indelible testament to the *American* character.

I owe thanks to far more people than I can list, from historians who have shared their research and knowledge to the enlisted men and NCOs in "my" Army, who showed me, as their comrade, how men in uniform actually behave (I hope that by now they have forgiven me for becoming an officer). Everyone beside whom I served taught me something (not all of it enjoyable, I confess), and without those decades in the field, on scouts, and on various staffs, I never could have written with such authenticity. On a basic human level, soldiers have always been soldiers, whether armed with spears, rifled muskets, or assault rifles. Thank you all for teaching me that—and so much more.

To my benefit and the reader's, George Skoch agreed to create the maps for this novel, too. George is a master of precision and balance, of the art of providing essential information without overwhelming the eye. His contribution is indispensable.

And my thanks to the wonderful team at Forge. It's almost obligatory for authors to complain about their publisher, but I simply can't. In a thirty-five-year career of trying to capture life in words, I've been lucky, overall, but I've never before worked with a team so dedicated to producing a quality "package." I appreciate the patience and skill of the design and production team, whose artists have created beautiful dust jackets and identified ideal typefaces, while taking extraordinary pains with the internal layout of these novels. Such care and attention to detail gives the reader something extra, even if unrecognized by most.

My editor, Bob Gleason, has been almost bewilderingly supportive; the copy editor for these books, Sona Vogel, has humiliated me wonderfully by discovering errors in manuscripts I thought had been purged of all flaws; Whitney Ross, Bob's "chief of staff," has been gracious and effective in treating the madness that infects all authors; and the publicity and marketing team has managed to persuade enough readers to take a chance on these novels to enable me to keep writing (it turns out that readers *didn't* just want the same five generals and same five battles, after all). Tom Doherty, publisher and strategist, makes it all go.

Writing a novel is a solitary, obsessive endeavor. But getting a handsome book into a reader's hands takes an "army."

In *Cain at Gettysburg* and *Hell or Richmond,* I used the author's notes to recommend additional books to readers hungry to learn more about the people and events I'd tried to revive. I was tempted to skip it this time: Some authors were miffed that their books weren't featured, while readers versed in the Civil War took me to task for ignoring their favorite works. But these selections aren't meant to be definitive or exhaustive, or to serve as a bibliography. And I do not mean to slight any fellow authors (as in the military, I prefer mutual support to fratricide). I just want to help readers *begin* to sort through the daunting array of titles now available.

So here we go:

Original sources. As always, there is no substitute for reading the words of the men who served on those fields—while recognizing that they, too, could be mistaken or bluntly dishonest. The *Official Records* are indispensable, but beyond that great compilation, I love the letter collections and the diaries, the immediacy of their reportage. Next best are the memoirs written after the war, even allowing that many a passage was sharpened to settle a score. For further reading about the battles in this book, seek out the splendid, voluminous, warmhearted letters of Clement Anselm Evans, compiled and edited in *Intrepid Warrior* by Robert Grier Stephens, Jr. This is my favorite letter collection from the entire war. *Make Me a Map of the Valley,* culled from the diaries of Jedediah Hotchkiss by Archie P. McDonald, offers insights from a very well-placed observer, but be forewarned: While Hotchkiss thought like an engineer, he also wrote like an engineer.

Among the many memoirs of this campaign, my favorite is John Brown Gordon's *Reminiscences of the Civil War*—despite Gordon's calculated efforts to win over readers North as well as South. Gordon was a master of airbrushing history long before the airbrush was invented. (Yet compared with Jubal Early, he was a paragon of integrity. These things, too, are relative.) Then there's the wonderful *A Soldier's Story of His Regiment (61st Georgia),* by "Private G. W. Nichols." This little book provides a great, soldier's-eye view of events, from murderous hospital wards to the battlefield's front lines. Accurate overall, the memoir, written long after the war, also illumines how memory betrays us. Nichols recalls General Evans as present at Third Winchester, while Evans' carefully dated letters home show that, returning from his convalescence, he had not passed north of Staunton by the time Fisher's Hill was lost. This adds to the confusion created by the Confederate habit of calling brigades after their commanders—even when under the temporary command of another officer. But let us be generous: Nichols made honest errors, while higher-ranking contemporaries doctored history until they killed the patient.

The Personal Memoirs of P. H. Sheridan, for example, must be taken with several quarries' worth of salt. By the time he wrote, Sheridan had changed from the often generous commander he had been to what later generations would call a "glory hog." He was a great soldier, but not a great man. Still, there's no avoiding the book—you have to read it. *An Autobiography,* by Lew Wallace, is rich in detail and honest overall, but written in a florid late-Victorian style that makes it difficult going for modern readers. For those who want easier marching, *The Sword & the Pen: A Life of Lew Wallace,* by Ray E. Boomhower, provides a brief but first-rate overview of this neglected hero's life. If any Civil War figure and nineteenth-century American deserves a full-length, scholarly biography, it's Lew Wallace (my nominee for patron saint of soldier-authors).

I also recommend *With the Old Confeds,* by Captain Samuel D. Buck; *Under Custer's Command: The Civil War Journal of James Henry Avery,* compiled by Karla Jean Husby and edited by Eric J.

Wittenberg; and the unique eyewitness account, buttressed by research, of Monocacy, *Fighting for Time*, by Glenn H. Worthington, who experienced the battle swirling around him when he and his family were trapped in his childhood home.

Biographies. Sometimes you fall in love with both a book and its subject. For me, that was the case with *Rutherford B. Hayes: Warrior & President*, a magnificent biography by Ari Hoogenboom. It's worth reading not only for the detailed, fair-minded, and inspiring portrait of Hayes as soldier and president, but for the panorama it provides of our country in the middle decades of the nineteenth century. As for William McKinley, he's due for a fresh, full-scale biography. Meanwhile, *Major McKinley: William McKinley & the Civil War*, by William H. Armstrong, provides a solid overview of McKinley's military service.

I must interject: During my research, I found that a few historians quibbled about the extent of Hayes' heroism at Third Winchester and whether he made a difference. One suspects they might feel differently had they been a brigade commander trapped in a swamp under enemy fire with the responsibility not only for his dying men, but for his army's flank amid a battle not going as planned. As a soldier, I admire Hayes enormously—a great *and* a good man who made the right decision when others wavered.

Jubal: The Life and Times of General Jubal A. Early, CSA, by Charles C. Osborne, will remain the definitive biography of this uncompromising, brave, difficult, hard to admire, yet somehow admirable man. Just as Early did the best he could with what he had, his biographer has done the best with what *he* had. I found Early the most challenging character to capture in this novel: Even when he behaved awfully, I kept rooting for him, remembering the wretched odds he faced. I fear I have not done him justice. *John Brown Gordon: Soldier, Southerner, American*, by Ralph Lowell Eckert, is a well-executed, balanced account of the life of this unique, magnetic, thoroughly American character. *Terrible Swift Sword*, by Joseph Wheelan, is a much more trustworthy account of Sheridan's life than the man's own memoir; it's handsomely written, too. Not least, *Fighting with Jeb Stuart: Major James Breathed and the Confederate Horse Artillery,* by David P. Bridges, got—and kept—my attention.

Campaign and battle histories. On Monocacy, it's worth tracking down Edwin Bearss's reprinted monograph *The Battle of Monocacy,* which not only contains excellent maps, but was instrumental in saving the battlefield (just one more of Ed's innumerable contributions to preserving and exploring our Civil War history). For full-blown accounts of the battle, two books run neck and neck: *Desperate Engagement,* by Marc Leepson, and *Last Chance for Victory,* by Brett W. Spaulding. These two worthy books disagree on a number of points. My approach when authors or eyewitnesses quarrel is always the same: I ask myself what would have made military sense, or how a soldier would have responded. I find it noteworthy how often first-rate historians are at odds with one another—but, then, a dozen participants can take away a dozen different perceptions of what happened on the same battlefield.

For an overview of the autumn of 1864 campaign in the Valley, it's impossible to do better than Jeffry D. Wert's superb *From Winchester to Cedar Creek.* Yet I'm still fond of *Sheridan in the Shenandoah,* by Edward J. Stackpole, which is highly readable, if a bit dated. Specifically for Third Winchester (Opequon Creek), *The Last Battle of Winchester,* by Scott C. Patchan, is one of the best, most-detailed battle studies I've encountered. I found myself turning to it with embarrassing frequency (although I differed on a very few conclusions).

Fisher's Hill is often treated as a sideshow (while Tom's Brook goes ignored), so it's good to have *The Battle of Fisher's Hill,* by Jonathan A. Noyalas, in print. It's a short book about a battle that cast a long shadow. I recommend it.

For cavalry operations, there are a number of good titles, but I'll just list *Custer Victorious,* by Gregory J. W. Urwin, which is well researched and very readable, and *Sheridan's Lieutenants,* by David Coffey, an excellent summary study.

Last in this too-short list comes *The Guns of Cedar Creek,* by

Thomas A. Lewis, another extremely impressive battle study. It provides a well-balanced, enthralling account of this unique and tragic fight, cutting through the myths to reach the men.

In closing, let me beg readers who've been drawn in by this novel to visit the battlefields I've struggled to describe. Monocacy, Third Winchester, Fisher's Hill, and Cedar Creek all have been bayoneted by interstate highways—because so many Civil War battles were fought along major roads, and the same routes, slightly offset, remain in use. Nonetheless, each battlefield has a great deal to offer.

Except for that highway cut—near where McCausland first blundered into Ricketts—Monocacy is remarkably well preserved. To the sorrow of those of us who regard these battlefields as sacred, much of the terrain on which Third Winchester was fought has been encrusted with housing developments, shopping malls, gas stations, a school, and vast expanses of macadam. Even so, a late but determined effort saved as much land as possible, and we can still walk the fields where Breathed's artillery went into action and Rud Hayes led his men through a deadly creek bottom. The walking trails are well signposted and thoughtfully laid out.

Fisher's Hill, by contrast, is almost perfectly preserved. Except for that highway cut and a few new homes on the opposing ridge, this is the field on which those armies contended much as it was. Additional preservation efforts are under way, but we all can do more, and must.

Tom's Brook, the Confederate cavalry's worst rout of the war, was fought in two parts. Wesley Merritt's battlefield by the town has suffered development, but Custer's action along Back Road took place on land still largely unchanged. Its preservation, though, has been incidental, and it isn't even marked by a roadside sign.

Then there is Cedar Creek, where a coalition of organizations has been doing worthy work to preserve as much of the battlefield as possible—and a remarkable portion of it remains intact, despite the nearby junction of two interstates. This great, decisive battle not only deserves to be better known to Americans, but would benefit from a network of walking trails. Let's hope that happens.

On the northern edge of Middletown, near Jubal Early's limit of advance, there's a small National Park Service museum tucked into a strip mall. The bare-bones staff is enthusiastic and knowledgeable, and for those of us who fondly recall the "Electric Map" at Gettysburg, there's a smaller LED-dotted map that gives the visitor a clear, clean overview of a battle that was hardly clean or clear. Most cars simply rush past on the Valley Pike (now widened and smoothly paved). Thanks to history's fickleness, this great battle has been forgotten by the average American, as have the other battles in this book. For *young* Americans—taught to despise history as useless—even the cartoon version of Custer has faded, while Rutherford B. Hayes and Stephen Dodson Ramseur, Philip Sheridan and Jubal Early, aren't even names in a schoolbook. I find it heartbreaking.

This book is a call to remember.